Content

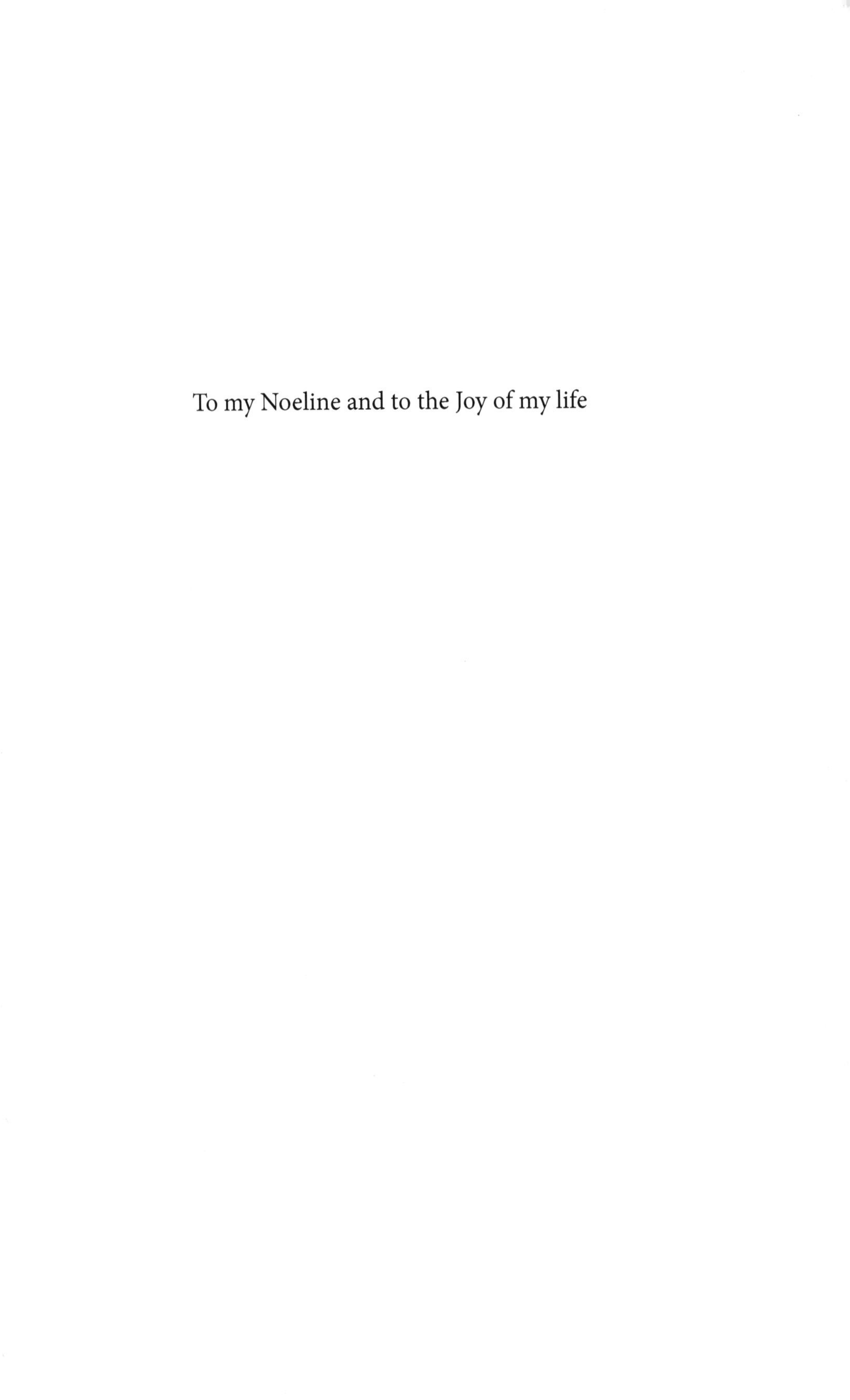

To my Noeline and to the Joy of my life

Thank you to my editor Sharon Umbaugh,
for turning my words into a book worth reading.

My thanks to Rachel at Entrada
for all her hard work and encouragement.

The Wood Hunt

"Come on Stumpy, hop to it!" Laughter followed and Billi sighed because by now they really shouldn't find it funny. Unfortunately, the mothers had used the same words since being at school with Billi and their littluns picked it up. No point in him complaining since that 'joke' would still be funny to someone when Billi was old and grey. He gripped the chair arms and rose smoothly, about the only smooth movement Billi could manage. Billi tucked the crutches with the big wads of soft fur under his arms and Rabbit roused in the corner, tail thumping.

"Come on Rabbit, let's go chase sticks." The song in Billi's head, the connection between Hunter and Hound, answered eagerly, happily, and Rabbit came to his feet just as smoothly. Then he hopped forward on three legs towards the door. Despite his missing leg, Rabbit still moved much faster than Billi, or any man for that matter. A yellow eye opened in the corner by the fire, then slowly closed because One-shut wouldn't be going out in the cold until after dark.

At night the big tomcat, One-shut, dozed in the chicken coop and collected his supper from the rodents that never could resist the spilled feed. One leg, three legs and one eye, the three of them were one big joke really but it all worked. Billi reached for the bow and quiver and smiled a little. Crippled he might be, but the other Hunters were pleased to give him a share of their catch because Villagers needed a Hunter and Hound along if they ventured into the Forest.

Each Hunter gave Billi a very small share to escort their kin to gather wood or herbs, but a small share from many added up to several good meals. Add that to the meagre amount of prey Billi could take and carry with one leg along with any foolish deer that strayed too near the hut, and Billi ended up with enough meat. In addition, he gave the nearby farmer a tenth of the take in return for running traplines in the fields for rabbits in summer and pelts in winter. With the chickens and three goats and the vegetables from his little patch of land Billi and Rabbit ate well enough, and sometimes had meat as well as pelts to trade.

Billi's little patch didn't even come close to a full landshare, and he couldn't blame Da for that since Billi would never be able to farm. He didn't need to when, during his sixteenth summer, Rabbit turned up on the doorstep. A Hound, even three-legged, meant Billi could hunt, and even if he couldn't bring in much he could support himself. Only those with a Hound could venture beneath the Forest trees with impunity, which meant the Village relied on the Hunters to bring in meat. Extra meat that the Farm couldn't produce, meat to feed the villagers in winter. Even if he couldn't bring in extra, Billi could escort villagers while collecting firewood or Forest fruit and berries so the other Hunters didn't have to.

Billi's landshare had been split between his two Bro's landshares and his Sis's brideshare. In return they raised this hut for him and split the posts and rails for the fencing. They would occasionally drop off cabbages, roots such as carrots, or a sack of taters, and in return Billi sometimes looked after their littluns. The door rattled again and youths shouted. "Brr, 'tis cold out here. Hippety-hop, Rabbit."

As soon as the door opened far enough, Billi lunged outside, and as Rabbit followed, he slammed the thick timber closed behind him to keep the heat in. "Since 'tis cold, I needed to be wrapped up."

Nobody answered directly. The five older lasses were too polite, and it hadn't been them complaining. The comments came from the six youths though they wouldn't be cheeky to Billi's face. The seven unbonded girls, the maids, were why the youths were acting up and showing off. "No littluns today?" Usually there would be half a dozen youngsters running about underfoot, enjoying the outing.

"No Billi. The snow is too deep today and would chill and tire them. We want to make good time because we must go further." Mandy looked at Billi's crutches. "We wondered if it is too deep for you?"

Billi weighed up the depth of the drifts, and some were deep enough to be hard work but he would avoid those. "We may have to walk even slower, but I can manage thank ye Mandy." The crutches sank deeper into the snow than his foot, so Billi knew he would have to take care even where the snow wasn't deep.

Billi could hear the first quiet grumbles from the youths as he set off. "This will take forever."

"We could guard everyone."

"I'm good enough with a bow."

"Nothing will bother a party this big." Though they, and everyone in the party, knew that the party needed a Hunter and Hound or none might come back. At least one grumble had some truth; without littluns the party would have pushed on faster than Billi could. Billi braced his shoulders and set off at a steady pace that he could keep up for hours, if need be, ignoring the mutters. They couldn't go without him because the Law of the Wild and the Forest forbade it. Any human stepping off the carefully tended acres and under the spreading branches without a Hound and a bow or spear became prey.

Billi had his bow, strung and across his shoulder, and other Hunters reckoned Billi one of the best archers if he had the chance to set himself properly first. He also had a spear of course, slung across his back along with the ropes and hatchet for firewood. Billi hoped the situation never got that serious because using the spear on unwounded animals required some agility. Billi carried a spear solely for finishing wounded prey.

Billi kept going along the track at his steady pace and eventually the trees reached across the sky, and the party halted before entering the Forest. The stark contrast between Forest and Farm made sure nobody made a mistake, as not even the smallest shrub survived on the tilled fields and pastures. The title, Farm, covered all the farms surrounding the Village of Trail's End. In contrast the Forest included all land not classed as Farm with only the trails made by the animals breaking the untamed riot of growth. Most of the branches were bare and gaunt against the grey winter sky, but not all and Billi kept a close eye on the evergreens. The Wild, the creatures of the Forest, would be hungry in this weather and one of the hunting beasts might take a chance.

"Since there seems to be some doubt, perhaps we had better make sure everyone remembers the Laws." Mandy raised a hand to still the muttering and complaints, and glared at the youths. "From a few of the comments, some have forgotten why we have a Hunter and Hound with us. Edan, you seemed to be having most trouble, so you can start us off."

Edan, a tall thin youth of nearly seventeen summers, glanced around as some of the maids sniggered, but Mandy kept glaring at him. Normally the youngest would recite the Laws before entering the Forest, because the maids and youths should already know them. "But everyone here knows the Laws, Mandy. We are all grown up, not littluns."

"Some aren't grown up yet." Hektor's words were quiet but Edan rounded on him, then scowled at the big smiles on the faces of the maids.

"That might take another five or six summers for some," said Bliss, the Tanner's maid, who tried not to giggle.

Though she did, as did several other maids, a quieter voice from the back said "a score of summers for some."

"Enough!" Mandy cut into the banter. "Unless you all like standing in the cold, I want to hear the Laws, and sharpish. Edan?"

Edan straightened his face before turning back to Mandy, then sighed dramatically. "The Law of the Wild is what we call the laws that keep us all safe. The Law of the Wild is the agreement between Man and the Wild, the Forest and the Farm." He delivered the words in a monotone voice and then stopped and turned towards the Forest.

"That isn't the Laws." He'd really annoyed Mandy now, since 'twas Edan that claimed the wood gatherers didn't need a Hunter and Hound, in direct conflict with the Laws. "Now recite them."

Edan went to sigh, thought better of it when he caught the gleam in Mandy's eye, and recited the Laws just as he had at school. "There are six main Laws that all villagers must heed.

Only hunt for meat, not sport. If you hunt it, eat it, or take the meat back to the Farm to be eaten there.

No hunting without a Hound, as all wounded Prey must be tracked and finished.

All Prey will be gutted where it falls, and the offal left as a tithe to the Wild.

No pits, traps, or snares may be dug or set in the Forest. All can be used in the fields and farmyard, where the Law of the Farm rules, but must be checked regularly so the prey does not suffer overlong.

No live Forest tree may be felled. Only dead wood can be taken from the Forest. The trees on the Farm, the orchards and hedgerows, are not Forest and may be felled or pruned.

All people or stock venturing into the Forest are Prey unless there is a Hound and a Hunter with his bow. With a Hunter and Hound, everything else is Prey." As he finished Edan glanced at Billi's bow, sticking up from behind his shoulder.

"Good. Now since we have a Hunter and a Hound we can go and find wood. Will you lead the way Edan, since you've said your piece? Break the drifts as you go to make the path easier for my old bones." Mandy glanced at Billi as she said it and smiled, since that would also make life easier for a one-legged man.

Edan stomped off, which did a good job of clearing the path, and Billi followed because he had to be near the front so his bow and Rabbit kept the Wild hunters away. Behind him Billi could hear Mandy, who had apparently decided that the youths and maids needed something to occupy themselves. "Hektor, since you seem to think you are much more grown up, explain the other times that either farm animals or the villagers can become Prey."

A definite edge of humour sounded in Hektor's answer, since he and the rest had also had this drummed into them at school and home. "All the land that is not in the Forest belongs to the Farm, but the creatures of the Wild do not always respect boundaries. Any flocks and herds without a guardian can become Prey though anyone can kill the creatures of the Wild if they venture out to take them. There is no need for a Hunter. The greatest hunting beasts may be killed by a Farmer's or a youth's arrow." Hektor paused. "Though my Da says that 'tis best to have a Hound and Hunter nearby if the flocks and herds are close to the Forest edge."

Mandy sounded a bit happier now. "True, though even that won't stop a few of them risking it if they are hungry enough. Nor does it stop the deer from raiding the crops at night when most folk are abed."

"My Da doesn't mind the deer getting a mouthful of greenery from the fields now and then." Laughter rippled around the group, since Bliss was the Tanner's daughter. The deer didn't eat his greenery, but Viktor would get a share of the meat from any that were caught, for curing the hide.

"Since you've enough breath for chatter you can remind us how the Farm grows, how we can wrest more land from the Forest." Mandy had cheered up and so did the rest as they heard the smile in her voice. All except Edan, who still stomped and muttered just ahead of Billi.

"The Farm grows slowly because we cannot take land straight from the Forest. We can only take land that has been cleared by fire or flood." Bliss stopped reciting for a moment. "Have we ever had a flood, Mandy?"

"Not in Trail's End, but when the Laws were agreed there must have been places where there were floods." Mandy paused and from her tone of voice Billi knew her brow would be furrowed as she thought about that. "After all, if the trees are drowned, they will be just as dead as if they burned."

"More firewood though, once they dried out. Then there'd be no need to go wood gathering."

"You'll be back in the warm soon enough, Seifort. If you want to go faster, you can give Edan a break?" Mandy chuckled. "Since you volunteered, how is land claimed after a fire or flood?"

Seifort recited his part in the same sing-song fashion the teachers used. "Man can claim the burned Forest if it is cleared and has stock or a crop on it before the following midsummer. The land is claimed by the farmer whose landclaim borders the new section, or by the one who found it, or sometimes by a partnership. The Hunters guard them as they claim it, for yearly shares or a single, larger payment. The fields become part of the family landclaim, and part of the Farm."

"Perfectly recited." A crashing and excited shouts interrupted Mandy.

"Yes! Go on Billi. Hurry up with the bow." The youths were pointing at a bounding shape heading off through the trees as they urged the Hunter to take the chance at getting some meat.

"Moving at that speed and away? It would not be a clean kill, and Rabbit would have to track so we could finish it. You know the Law, that no wounded animal can be left." Billi kept stumping along and glanced at the nearest youths. "Rabbit might not be able to turn it quickly, and by the time I'd caught up there'd be no time for wood collection."

If Billi had raised his bow, he would have heard a firm rejection in his mind, a clear signal in that continual little tune in his head that connected Billi to Rabbit. Rabbit would be reminding Billi that chasing a wounded animal in the snow was a bad idea for one-legged Hunters and three-legged Hounds. Right now Rabbit sang a happy, lilting tune, as he always did when he first stepped among the trees. Billi sometimes thought that happiness might be the only reason he still struggled out here to hunt with his one leg.

Edan sneered. "I could have hit it. I've spent hours on the practice targets and my Da and Bro brought me out on their last two hunts."

"When's the last time you tried to hit something going that fast? Or even something moving at all?" Seifort taunted Edan because everyone knew that even though others could come into the Forest if they were guarded, only a Hunter could loosen an arrow there. That meant a youth rarely, if ever, aimed a bow at a moving animal until he already had a Hound.

"Not just that, but you seem to have recited the Laws without listening to them, Edan." Mandy had her next victim. "Perhaps you could try with some more. How can the Forest claim land back from the Farm?"

Stomping as Edan broke through a drift was her only answer for a few moments, but Edan had his voice under control by the time he spoke and stayed polite. "The Forest cannot claim land back from the Farm. If a Farmer neglects their land and allows bushes and young trees to grow, it becomes Forest again. This will never happen in a well-run Village because the Eldest will step in to arrange for the land to be maintained. Then the landclaim becomes common land for all to use."

"But that's not quite right, is it Mandy? The Wild can come and claim land back and then the trees grow and it becomes Forest." The maid's voice sounded unsure. "That's what the Winter Tales tell us." Those stories were usually aired in the winter. They formed the Histories of Man and the Wild, to be repeated when everyone huddled around the big fire in the alehouse or the hall. The shorter tales were retold when a family gathered around the hearth and the littluns needed amusing, and all the tales had a moral. They were at least partly to teach the littluns that the Laws must be kept, though that didn't stop them from being entertaining, or popular.

"You are right Eweyna, but only after Man broke the Laws. The Tinkerers and the Traders travel the trails to trade with us, and they know of whole villages that have gone back to Forest betwixt one visit and the next." Mandy raised her voice. "That's enough Edan. Seifort will take over for a while and then we'll see who else has spare breath."

Eweyna hadn't finished. "But it can be just one cottage or farmhouse, especially one belonging to a careless or arrogant Hunter. Then noises in the night, and in the morning there are marks of great paws and hooves and the stock and crops are gone." Despite her lowered, sombre tones, Eweyna obviously enjoyed those parts. "The tales speak of broken doors and shattered shutters, smashed fences and even the bodies of the family gone for ever. Then the buildings are left for the Wild to reclaim as the price Man must pay if the Law is broken."

"I think we should get you to tell a few winter tales, with a voice like that."

"Ooh, Mandy, are you saying that Eweyna is an elder?" Edan had recovered enough to tease Eweyna, and elders did usually recite the tales.

"I don't mind telling a tale or two." Hektor laughed as several others mentioned that at sixteen summers he didn't look old enough. "I'll tell the ones about big beautiful pelts taken when the Wild has broken the Law of Man and hunted in the farmland or even farmyards."

"There's a Winter Tale about the Great-Wolf's head in the alehouse. I've never seen it because a maid can't go in the alehouse, but I've been told the fangs are this long." Bliss really sounded interested in seeing that head. Billi smiled because the giant wolf's head was old and threadbare, and stories of the size of its teeth were probably exaggerated. The real size of the massive canines still in the head were a valuable warning of what might lurk behind the green wall of the Forest. Though not valuable enough to stop the occasional youth from risking the Forest to gather the extravagant, brightly coloured blooms for a maid he wanted to impress, or in response to a dare from his mates after an ale or two.

Billi lost interest in the talking because something hid in the Forest ahead. Rabbit's song sharpened, then held a hint of resignation because they weren't hunting today. Billi knew why when a small wild pig burst out of some low evergreen bushes and raced away. A pig small enough for Billi to carry home and so worth an arrow if he'd been on his own. With Rabbit's warning Billi would have been ready with his bow, and the pig wouldn't have run far if he hit it.

"Come on Billi. Da tells me you are one of the best with a bow on the targets." Seifort still stamped along in front and had a good view of the pork dinner that had just escaped.

"He's too slow getting that bow because of the crutches." Edan reverted to having another go at Billi.

"I already knew what hid and where because Rabbit told me, so if I'd wanted to try I would have been ready." Billi cursed silently because he shouldn't let the youths get to him. "No Hunter can be sure of a clean kill every time, and I'm responsible for keeping you safe."

Mandy had heard enough. "Mind your manners Edan. Any more trouble and I'll be asking someone's Da to make sure a certain youth gets some extra teaching. You are all old enough to know the Law, and showing ignorance won't impress any maids." The youths turned to berating the red-faced Edan and the maids joined in.

Mandy had moved up just behind Billi and ignored the banter behind. "Edan is old enough for a Hound now Billi. When did you get Rabbit?"

"Just past sixteen summers, Mandy. I'm told he limped right through the Village, door to door, and then out along the lane to Da's farm. He scratched and whined until Ma opened the door." Billi sniggered. "That was some shock for Ma, a Hound on the doorstep. He limped over to my chair, the one with wheels, and sat next to it." Billi sighed. "I came into the room and there he sat, and I heard the song."

"That's always the way." Billi heard Mandy sigh as well. "The Hound comes from the Forest, and looks all over the Farm until he finds his Hunter. They only come for one youth, and once they're together, only death will part them." She shook her head. "All the Hunters speak of something, a connection, though only you call it a song."

Billi didn't answer because he was lost in memory, lost in that wonderful moment eight summers ago when Rabbit's song had burst into his head, full of joy and welcome. The wordless song had been there ever since, and there it would stay while they both lived. A Hound, the giant oversized Forest version of a dog, lived as long as his Hunter and then pined and died of grief.

Occasionally Hounds died when prey fought back. The Hunters who didn't stay by the body until the Wild took them both were few and far between, sad old men with the grief stark on their faces. Most of those went out to meet the Wild one day with just a spear, knowing that they would never come home. Among the lines of skulls upon the great rock those of Hunters were clear, as a Hound skull lay alongside each one. Billi knew that if that gentle song humming in the back of his mind ever silenced he would also take his spear to meet the Wild. Then someone would place a small token on Skull Rock, to show where his skull and Rabbit's should have rested.

* * *

The way ahead became less clear as the animal trails became fainter. "Far enough Seifort, and thank ye. I'll stay out front now." Billi turned to Mandy as Seifort joined the rest and began to add his own teasing. Mandy had come with the wood gathering party today for a special purpose, as a guide. "How much further, Mandy? I've never taken wood gatherers past here, and usually hunt along the river." Billi didn't go deeper into the Forest because he couldn't carry the meat from larger prey, or carry anything much through the thicker undergrowth.

"I'm not sure now we're past the usual trails, Billi, only the general direction. I've been gathering wood plenty of times, but only came this way once before today." She sighed. "This winter is a long one, and all the decent windfall branches have been gathered from the usual places. It was the same back then."

One of the maids stopped teasing the youths for a moment. "When was that Mandy?"

"Before ye were born, Bliss. That was a bad winter and so Da and Unk brought the whole family, even us littluns. We brought back a huge load even if it took much longer. I've kept the memory against the day 'twas needed and there should be plenty of big branches fallen since then." She looked around and pointed confidently. "There, Billi. The two tall evergreens and the path up the little valley betwixt them. I'd hoped they'd still be here."

"Trees like that will be here when your littluns are bringing their own littluns this way, Mandy. They grow slow and 'twould take something terrible to knock one down." Billi went ahead up the dip between the trees so that he and Rabbit could check the undergrowth and especially those trees. "All safe everyone, you can come through now."

"That's why I'm pleased it's you, Billi. One of the other Hunters would be complaining about the extra time and distance, but you just keep going."

"No trouble at all, Mandy." Billi had a soft spot for anyone who treated him decently and Mandy always did, though most of the Village and farmers ignored him if possible. Billi was an oddity, and some resented a cripple getting a Hound when many healthy men never did. In return Billi kept out of the way in his little hut. He knew he didn't really pull his weight, that he rarely brought back extra meat to help feed the Village.

The party pushed on and Billi, and especially Rabbit, were warier now. They had come well past the usual areas travelled by escorted parties and the Wild would be stronger, a little more bolder. Behind him the youths grumbled and teased the maids and the maids mocked the youths, while Mandy stopped them getting out of hand.

Billi thought they would do well to look around at the Forest and remember it, especially the youths since they might never come this far again. Youths who were not chosen by a Hound before their eighteenth summer knew they were destined to be wheelwrights, farmers, leather workers, carpenters, merchants or blacksmiths. They could specialise, learn or improve upon a skill, and if skilful enough could prosper. Others worked for tradesfolk earning extra food or silver, or helped out with the farming or in the business that would be partly theirs someday. Either way the youths would stay in the Village, working, and their littluns and lasses would collect wood.

Many were pleased to work in the Village instead of risking the creatures of the Wild. Hunting was a dangerous occupation, though the rewards could be great if a man and Hound were lucky. Hunters roamed all over the nearby Forest, though not much further since few risked staying out overnight. The Hunters would look in streams for the occasional stones and nuggets that were prized by the Traders or Tinkerers, and for any signs of ironstone or blackstone for the blacksmith. Only Hunters could find the fallen trees, and be paid finder's fee and guard fee when the Villagers came with ponies to drag the trunks home to supply timber. Even a one-legged Hunter always had some income because all those who ventured into the Forest, even for firewood, needed a Hunter and Hound nearby.

* * *

Billi had been keeping an eye out, but he relied on Rabbit's much keener senses to warn him of any real threat because wood gathering wasn't hunting. Scaring animals away rather than sneaking up meant Billi could relax, or he could until the song gave him a wake-up note. Rabbit crouched down a little, but not all the way because he only had three legs. After the sharp warning note, Billi felt a trickle of excitement and anticipation in his head that might mean prey they could take. He also stopped, with a hand raised. "Hush."

"Why, what's…?"

Edan stopped because Mandy had a hand on his mouth and as the rest stared at her she said, very quietly, "Hunter said hush." Billi saw the shock on the faces of youngsters who really had never processed it despite parroting the Laws. To them he was Stumpy Billi who lived in the little hut with Hoppity, a three-legged Hound and a one-eyed cat, but now it hit home. Only a real Hunter could escort them and even three-legged, hoppity Rabbit really was a Hound. If the Wild had allowed them to guard the Villagers, the Wild considered Stumpy Billi a true Hunter and now all the older lasses were glaring at the youngsters and nodding. Well in that case Billi thought he had better act like a Hunter. He beckoned Mandy close.

"Rabbit says prey, maybe. Upwind and so far not alarmed." Billi shrugged. "It's not small. I'm minded to make a noise and scare it away because of the maids. If the first arrow doesn't drop it, it might charge."

"It might be worth taking a chance, Billi, because the Village is running short of meat, really short. This cold has gone on too long and the Hunters are coming back empty-handed. If ye can take anything, there'll be those who will be grateful." Mandy smiled. "Only you wouldn't know how bad it is."

"As long as there's enough for us, I don't really bother anyone." Billi listened to the song in his head. Prey, real prey, and still not moving away judging by Rabbit's interest. "I'll try. Now who is steady enough to carry my spear?" Her eyes widened. "I'm going to be using my bow and will be just ahead, in sight, but I want my spear back here."

Billi indicated the group behind them. "If anything in the Wild is feeling hungry and comes looking, everyone must yell at it. If someone waves a spear it'll hesitate and I'll stick an arrow in whatever it is." Mandy looked hard at him, weighing it up. Then she nodded, satisfied that Billi thought the villagers would be safe. "Keep me in sight, quiet and not too close and please make sure they all know. If I stop they must freeze." He grinned at Mandy. "I'm the slow careful type." Mandy smiled back, fully aware Billi couldn't be anything else. "Now who is steady, and will stay at the back and alert?"

She thought a moment and beckoned to Hektor, a strapping youth who could be getting a Hound any time if the Wild favoured him. "Billi has a job for you. Keep very quiet."

Hektor looked at Billi, who took his pack off slowly and carefully. "Have you practiced with a spear?" Billi held out the hunting spear with its wide, sharp blade and Hektor stared at it.

Then he nodded. "I have, just in case." Hektor glanced at Rabbit. "In case the Forest sends me a Hound." Every youth Hektor's age hoped for a Hound.

"Then you are guarding the rear. Take the spear." Hektor took the proffered spear and held it with easy assurance and Billi felt relieved; the youth really had practiced.

Though Hektor's eyes were wide as he looked from the weapon to Billi. "But." His voice stayed very quiet, but strained. "In the Forest?"

"You aren't trying to be a Hunter or using a bow. You must stay at the rear and watch for anything unusual. If any animal appears, everyone must shout and you get set with that." Billi put as much confidence as possible into his voice. "It'll stop to weigh you up and I will get whatever it is with my bow, but sometimes it takes them a few moments to die. You will slow the beast up, make it cautious enough for me to get a second arrow in it."

Hektor relaxed. "All right Billi, er, Hunter. Da says you are better than him with a bow." Hektor stood up very straight. "I'll not let you down."

"Good, now go to the back while I find out if this is all for nothing." Behind Hektor, Billi could see Mandy and the older lasses talking to the rest. As Hektor went past the group to take up position at the back, Ethan started to speak, but Mandy hushed him. The youth subsided but shot a glare at Billi. Hektor took station at the rear with a very determined look about him and Billi began to move cautiously forward.

Billi soon knew why the prey hadn't heard the villagers. He could hear the animal grunting and splashing up ahead, making too much noise to hear anything else. Nor would it scent the party, because the wind blew Billi's scent back, away from the sounds. Billi kept checking that everyone kept up, moving slowly forward until a note of urgency came into Rabbit's song. Billi put his hand up and glanced back. Everyone stopped and some even crouched a little. He pointed at the bushes ahead and mimed opening them and then loosening an arrow, then made a 'stay there' gesture. A round of nods came back, mostly accompanied by wide smiles and shining eyes.

Billi should have realised that none of them had been on a hunt before, except a couple of the older youths who had accompanied a parent. Maids never ever went on a hunt, and here they were in the Forest creeping up on prey! This could be the most exciting moment of their lives, even if they still might not see a hunt. Despite what Mandy said, if whatever Billi saw through the bushes looked too big and dangerous then Billi would snap a twig to spook it and let it go.

He wouldn't risk a wounded animal getting to the others even though the youths would be scathing in their mockery if food got away. These were villagers who had come to collect firewood, not Hunters. Billi concentrated on moving quietly up the gentle slope and into the bushes, keeping a thick tree trunk betwixt him and the beast. He could do this almost silently, even on crutches, because Billi had practised for years. At least the creature ahead still grunted and snorted and splashed loudly enough to cover any small rustle of leaf or grass.

Rabbit crouched as low as possibly while still moving quietly. The Hound disappeared into the bushes and Billi could feel Rabbit's interest spike and settle into real intent. The hunt was on! Billi finally reached the tree and eased an eye far enough round the trunk to see the prey, a boar. Not a yearling, but a big old lad in his prime. Even if his flanks were a bit gaunt, the great hump of muscle on the boar's shoulders would feed half the Village.

Billi's shoulder's slumped because a boar would definitely charge if wounded but not crippled. Then if the beast made it past Billi, villagers would die. Worse, if the boar killed or even crippled Billi, the Villagers would be defenceless when the Wild moved in. He even reached out to snap a small branch but hesitated, since Mandy had made it clear the Village really needed meat. Sideways on, the boar stood just like the target at home, the target Billi had spent long hours aiming at to hit the perfect killing spot.

The song in his head sounded eager, expectant, so Rabbit thought that Billi could do this, should do this. Billi took one quick glance back and the wood gatherers were all keeping low and still. Though he could see the youths straining forward, wanting to be here, wanting to see. Except for Hektor, still looking back the way they had come with the spear held firm and ready.

Billi carefully propped his crutches against the tree, leaned his back against the wood, fitted the shaft and half-drew his bow. Then he swivelled his foot and with a practised movement rolled his back slowly around the trunk. The boar still rooted in the marshy bank for succulent roots, up to his hocks in the sand of the stream bed. The animal looked hungry and probably felt over-confident; only a Great Hunter would tackle such a big boar, or a Hunter with a bow. The bow came up inch by slow inch, no jerking to catch the boar's eye, and Billi could feel Rabbit's anticipation. He blessed the arm muscles built by years of heaving himself about as the feathers tickled his lips for a moment and Billi loosed.

Perfect shot! And Billi knew it from the moment he loosened his fingers, that special feeling that meant a perfect Bullseye. He reached for a second shaft, while Rabbit bounced forward through the stream well behind the stricken beast. The Hound bayed as he did, drowning all other sound and attracting the boar's attention. The beast tried to turn to challenge what threatened from behind and screamed in rage and pain, but the challenge faltered as bright arterial blood gushed around those great tusks.

The boar tried to turn back again as Rabbit went up onto the far bank. The animal thrashed frantically because the soft sand and mud were giving him no purchase and the bank directly in front of him was too slippery to climb, and then Rabbit crouched in front of his snout. The Hound snarled and threatened, keeping the boar's attention on him and that steep slippery bank in front. The boar tried to heave himself up the bank by sheer brute force, and Billi froze momentarily when its chest came clear of the water and mud and he saw the true size of the beast.

But the feathers of the second shaft tickled Billi's lips as years of practice kept him moving and the bow moved a little as Billi concentrated on the red splash and short exclamation mark of the first shaft. His aim dropped from the marker to drive his second shaft lower, deep into that big barrel of a chest. Panic joined the pain and rage when the shaft struck and the boar lunged up the slippery bank again. But already the blood filling the beast's lungs sapped the power of his frantic lunges, every breath spraying crimson into the water and the mud. Even though he still fought to live, the dying prey, definitely prey now, wouldn't run far or mount a real charge. Billi put his bow over his shoulder, picked up his crutches and looked back.

"Come up into the bushes to see, but don't go near yet." There the rest came forward in a stampede but Hektor came slow and steady, still looking back down the trail. Billi made a quick decision. That really was a tremendous application of willpower in a youth and deserved a reward. "Hektor." The youth's head came round. "How much training have you had with the spear?"

"I killed the pig a moon ago but it was held. Da showed me exactly how to strike." That meant Hektor would have used the same killing thrust through the throat the Hunters used to finish downed prey, exactly what the Laws demanded right now.

"Well if you don't mind getting cold and wet you can kill another, and it will save time since I'm a bit slow with getting my boot off." The lad's eyes were eager and sparkling with excitement but Hektor glanced at Mandy, who looked in turn at Billi. He answered the question in her eyes. "He earned it. I kept an eye on everyone and Hektor always had his eyes back there, even when the boar squealed. He guarded the rear as well as any Hunter."

"Boar?" With a big smile Mandy turned to Hektor and her voice became very serious. "The Hunter says you earned it, but you be careful since it's a big chance. Don't mess this up and cause the Hunter any trouble." Hektor answered with a quick head shake. Billi didn't think the youth could speak. "Well get your gear off, lunch is waiting." Hektor hesitated a moment and Mandy held out a hand for the spear so he could shed his boots and pants.

Normally there would be a lot of comments about Hektor stripping to his homespun shorts in front of the maids, but all they could do was stare, speechless. One of the biggest moments in a youth's life, the first kill, usually happened out of sight of all but a small hunting party. No youth had ever been blooded in front of his friends and peers, and especially maids. Hektor took a deep breath, reclaimed the spear from Mandy, and started through the bushes.

Hektor paused for a moment to look at where he needed to be, or to steady his nerves before coming close to the monster in the stream. The boar still made occasional abortive efforts to lunge up at Rabbit, but from on his side now and the lunges were getting weaker and weaker. Though the beast still had those long gleaming tusks, and when his head thrashed it became clear the boar didn't consider himself finished yet.

Billi talked through the kill to calm the youth. "Wade out to where you can reach with one step and a thrust. Aim right under his jowls with the blade across his neck, exactly how you killed the pig. I'll have a shaft ready for anything attracted by the noise; the boar won't need it. You do know just how far you can reach with the spear?" Hektor nodded then gasped as he put a foot into the icy water. "Then wade out but don't get too close, and give a nod when you're set. No rush."

The boar's little eye rolled and glared hate as the youth waded out well clear and waited, positioning himself as instructed. Hektor nodded. "Ready, Hunter." Billi looked all around to make sure the noise and blood hadn't brought something else, a hunter from the Wild.

"Rabbit will catch his snout and hang on, so he'll be still for a moment just like the pig at home. Strike fast and sure because he'll try to throw Rabbit off and gore him. Are you sure?"

A pale face glanced back. "Yes Billi. Er, Hunter."

"It's all right, I'm still Billi. Ready?" A short nod and the lad looked back at the hate in that one small eye. "Rabbit, now!"

The words were for Hektor so the youth knew Rabbit would strike. The little song in Billi's head meant that Rabbit already knew when, and the tune spiked sharply as the Hound lunged. A snarl brought the boar's attention back to Rabbit and the Hound sank his teeth deep into the proffered snout. The result came as an anti-climax really but only because

Hektor struck smooth and sure. The beast gave an indignant bubbling shriek, then the wide sharp spear blade went in and severed all the big pipes and arteries in his throat and the squeal died.

Rabbit leapt back as the boar's head came up to try and throw him, and then the big head crashed back down. Three long, strong gouts of blood gushed out into the stream and the boar's legs thrashed and stilled. Billi jumped as a loud cheer rang out. Hektor looked up with a big grin breaking over his face and waved the bloody spear to his peers. Then he jumped out of the stream and started stamping to try and warm his feet.

"Don't forget to blood him." Mandy smiled at the look on Billi's face. "First kill, or the first on a hunt. He'll want the tail or an ear for the memory." She had a bit of a shine in her eyes as well and Billi realised that even Mandy had never been on an actual hunt.

"He can have a tusk. Both. Worth it to save me getting wet, especially in that ice-water."

She laughed quietly. "So nobody saw your stump. Some of us know, Billi, but understand. Even so 'twas kindly done. I can't remember the last youth who took a boar for a first. He'll get a lot of dances at the Springfest, and he'd better start running when the rest of the maids find out." Then she thought a moment. "I don't think anyone ever took a Great-Boar as their first. That's what it is, isn't it?"

Billi eyed up the size of the carcass, easier now with Rabbit and Hektor to help with the scale. "Now I can see the beast properly, it might be. I didn't realise at first because of how deep he'd got himself mired. Though Hektor deserves the trophies anyway, because he really was very steady." Billi chuckled. "Well, I think dinner is ready. We'd better get it packed up."

"You stay up here and watch out, if you like, Billi. If you'll loan us your knives there's enough willing hands to see to the skinning and jointing, and to the packing and carrying I reckon." She sniggered. "We didn't bring our butchering knives because wood doesn't usually need them, but hatchets will serve." Mandy looked around the clearing the stream ran through. "Well memory served me right, plenty of wood here but we'll be carrying meat instead. That'll be a chore even with so many to help."

"We could drag the meat on travois, since we've got the ponies." Billi nodded at the youngsters gathering round the carcase, still a bit wary. "That way you still get some wood and it will let them all earn a bit of pork to take home."

"That's kind as well, I'll sort it out." Mandy headed off downslope and soon ropes meant for timber were being tied onto the boar's legs. It took a bit of doing to tow the carcass upstream and onto the bank, even with so many willing hands, then the youths and maids dragged the boar over to a suitable tree. "Hup, two three four. Hup two three four. The group heaved and chanted until the great head came up into the air and then tied the rope off. The boar's rear stayed on the floor but they weren't getting that weight any higher without proper tackle and a pony.

Mandy stood clear and directed the youngsters. "You've got the tool for the job, Hektor, and you're already stripped so you open it up. The rest watch out for the splashes." Hektor reached with the spear blade and slit the gut open. There were shrieks of laughter as the blood inside the cavities gushed out and then most of the rest of the entrails followed and splashed around the youth's legs.

Hektor laughed. "A bit warmer than the stream." Then he grimaced, braced himself and jumped into the stream to wash down. The rest moved in, knives flashing in the winter sun.

Billi shut the distraction out as he watched the surroundings, though he stopped his constant scanning for a moment because someone started exclaiming over the size of the kidneys. "Will someone let Rabbit have a treat, please?"

"A kidney?" Billi almost said yes since that would be a nice treat, but the laughter meant he looked first.

"That's more like a meal, so I'll share a bit of it with him when we get home. Just a bit of the lungs or a slice of meat will do for now please." More laughter followed and hands threw bits of bloodied meat to the Hound. He snapped them out of the air then quickly wolfed down enough offal to keep him going for a day or so, a real treat considering the size of the prey the pair usually took. Rabbit lolloped up the slope to Billi, still licking his jaws, with a lovely triumphant lilt in his song.

The Hound settled in next to Billi, alert to the two small, cautious shapes already lurking under bushes nearby. The Crows arrived next, then a Raven and another small shape in the bushes. The larger scavengers would hang back because they would see or smell Billi and most of them knew how far a bow would reach. With this amount of meat on offer there would be larger Wild hunters coming as well, eventually.

A polite cough disturbed Billi and he turned round to find Hektor trying very hard to look serious, though a big smile kept trying to escape. He had his hands cupped and Billi realised that the youth had brought the blood. Billi had expected... What had he expected? A Hunter always blooded the youth after his first kill and right now that meant Billi. "A first for me as well, Hektor. I'd better keep my hand steady so you can show the stripes to the maids."

Billi dipped two fingers in the cupped hands, being sure to get them well coated. Then he drew them down one of Hektor's cheeks, carefully so the lines were thick and straight and parallel. Billi repeated the procedure to mark the other cheek, and the youth's smile broke completely free. "It should have been your Da, sorry." Billi was sorry, an important moment such as this should happen on a hunt with friends and family to watch and remember.

"Oh no Hun... Billi, Da'll be right chuffed. He's taken me out three times to try and we found nothing, but the hunting has been bad and. Ah, well, you'd know." Hector shrugged. "Anyway Da worried about that being a sign. That I'd not get a Hound and the Wild was saying no." The youth looked down at his bloody hands. "And now it's all right. Um. Could I have, you know, something? An ear, for memory?" Billi had expected Mandy to tell him.

Billi grinned. "Take a tusk. One of the big ones so you can brag when you're old and grey." Also so the maids would chase and Hektor would have a wonderful Springfest.

"Oh. Oh yes! I thought Mandy was teasing." Hektor looked back down at the group busy with knives and hatchets. "Do you want the head?"

"Why, do you want it?" Shocked eyes met Billi's.

"Oh no! It's just that there's so much meat to pack there might not be room. It's a shame to lose the brains and cheeks and a pity the thing is so heavy." The youth laughed. "It's as heavy as some of the animals Da takes when he's hunting."

"Heavier than most I take. A lot is bone, though there is plenty of meat on it so ask the rest. Tell the others that everyone who helps to pull the load gets a share of the meat. There's only me and Rabbit and we can only save some of that lot for later. Preserving it all would take more salt than there is in the Village at this time of year." Billi gestured. "Go on and show off. If they'll drag the head back, your Ma can have the brains and send me some of her apple pie."

Hektor turned and raised his arms, and the mob down below cheered as they saw his marked cheeks. The youth bounded off down to spread his happiness and sure enough all the maids wanted to inspect the marks. A bloody but busy while later the youngsters were all in the stream washing off blood, with a lot of flirting and comment this time. Though that included a good bit of shrieking and complaining as the ice-water hit their skin, and none of them lingered.

Skirts had been tucked up, blouse arms and trews were rolled up, and the youths had their shirts off. That had been the only way to keep their clothes clean and dry while butchering but also a lot more informal than such a group would normally be. Now they were all splashing in the stream to get the blood and mud off their feet and arms, and teasing each other despite the shivering. Billi looked down the slope at Mandy and the older lasses, now checking over the bones to make sure nothing worth taking had been missed.

The skeletal remains were scattered with the offal though most of the ribs had been taken as well as all the cuts. With so many helpers brought up with Hunters and Farmers, Mandy had pretty much stripped everything edible. Even as the youths were still cleaning up, the less portable pieces such as the kidneys were being wrapped in the cleaned stomach. A chorus of cheers greeted Hektor's announcement about shares for hauling and several of them waved and smiled up the hill. That made a change from grumbling and complaints. Rabbit tensed as something big moved closer. It was time to go.

The older lasses had stayed fairly clean, either supervising or gathering some good long branches. Now the lasses were lashing the biggest together to make impromptu travois, with looped ropes at the front for pulling. Even as the group quickly placed smaller branches crosswise for support and stacked the meat, Billi called down. "Time to go, there are scavengers gathering. We need to get our meat away from the big free dinner." Billi pointed at the bones and offal, then upwards at the big wings circling hopefully.

Mandy quickly organised pony teams of mixed youths and maids, barely enough to pull the nine or ten full-weights of meat. Maybe more, Billi thought, as the four youths heaved the head onto a travois. Since several of the maids weighed less than a full-weight, even eighteen people were going to struggle getting it all home in the snow. Though that would warm them all up a bit after stripping and then washing, because even using snow to dry off with didn't stop some clothes getting damp.

The sheer amount settled any doubts; this really had been a Great-Boar because bulls gave up less good meat than that. There were other oversized creatures of the Wild, Great-Stags and other creatures including the Great Hunter, a striped cat allegedly bigger than a bear. Arguing about if they were outsized ordinary animals or a different, larger species passed many a wet winter evening. Nobody had ever settled the question. Their tracks were seen more often than the beasts themselves which didn't help anyone decide. Well now the entire party had seen one, and chopped it up into dinners.

A sharp crack brought everyone's eyes round to see Edan, red faced and holding his cheek. Mandy glared at him with her hand raised to repeat the slap. "I warned you. Since you have no respect for the Hunter you can carry wood. That's what you came for. Explain to your Ma why there's not pork on your table." Surprisingly, the youth glared at Billi, not Mandy.

Mandy waved at Billi and shouted "not a problem" so he went back to watching the impatient spectators. The little scavengers crept closer to get a mouthful before the larger ones drove them away, while further out bushes moved where larger relatives poised themselves to grab their feast. The first Crows and Ravens darted in for their share, and a Buzzard landed to perch in the tree above the offal.

Within minutes the first travois bumped and skidded into motion and Billi smiled as he saw the huge head perched on one of them. He stumped over next to Mandy. "Boiling the remains of that even after the cheeks, tongue and brains are gone should feed a family for a couple of days."

"That should make you a complete set of leather clothes." Mandy pointed at the bundle under the head. "We more or less got the whole hide." She laughed. "Just in case someone still doesn't believe that head is a Great-Boar." She moved forward to get the ropes from one travois untangled. The triangles of big timbers with smaller branches across weren't easy to pull, but made moving this amount of meat much easier in snow.

Billi slung his bundle of thick sticks over his shoulder and set out just behind the group, while Rabbit hopped up one side and back down the other. This amount of boar meat could tempt a really big predator or scavenger, and Billi sighed in relief when the Wild concentrated on the heap left behind. A cacophony of growls and caws and snarls announced the negotiations over sharing.

Whatever the spat had been about Mandy stuck to her word and Edan didn't pull any meat. Instead he stamped along beside or in front of the rest, hauling a big bundle of logs with a rope tied to his waist and trying to ignore the whole party. The others traded off, switching from the heavy loads of meat to pulling smaller bundles of wood, and now the snow helped the loads to slide. Almost as welcome, the hard work warmed them up after that stream.

* * *

The older lasses took their turns on the heavier pulling and before dusk the group broke clear of the trees and the Forest. Two of the youths dropped their ropes, leaving the logs for later and running across the fields towards the Village. Shortly afterwards three ponies and several men were trotting the other way, towards Billi.

Steban, the first to arrive, stopped and stared. "Hektor! You've been blooded." He saw the head on top of one load. "Forest and Farm, what did you catch Billi?"

"A Great-Boar, I reckon. Luckily there were plenty of helpers to haul it back." Billi waved to where the last travois was coming clear of the trees.

"More helpers now. We've brought ponies though I don't reckon anyone truly believed the youths. They usually exaggerate but not this time." Behind him willing hands moved meat from the travois onto ponies, or in three cases replaced the people pulling it with a pony.

"Here's Barimar. I haven't seen him move that fast since he stepped on a stinger's nest." A ripple of laughter greeted the man running across the field towards them. One of the youths must have gone on to let Barimar know because he ran straight to Hektor and stopped to inspect the youth's face. Then Hektor's Da picked him up in a bear-hug and swung the youth round, laughing.

They talked quickly for a few moments and then Barimar strode across to Billi, arm outstretched, and Billi extended his for the clasp. Barimar clasped firmly and pounded on Billi's shoulder, a huge smile on his face. He stopped suddenly. "Ah, sorry Billi, I'll be knocking you down." Barimar glanced back at Hektor. "We've been worried about him. We tried to get him blooded and the Wild hid." Barimar did really look relieved.

Billi shrugged, a bit embarrassed. "Just Hunter's luck. You search for a week and then one raids the cabbage patch. It's how it is."

"It's how it is now, but it was worrying. D'you really give him a tusk?" Barimar looked at the great head. "That's some tusk!"

"All of them I suppose. I told him if he could persuade them to bring the head he could take it for the brains, in return for one of his Ma's apple pies." Several of the nearby men laughed.

"Start that and you'll be buried in pies on the off chance you find another." The round of agreement included some laughter and speculation on just where to find another of those.

"Good job that one didn't turn up in the cabbage patch though, there'd be no cabbages." They all agreed with that comment as well.

The excited group around the meat called out and Billi went over to explain that yes, the Hunter did say they could all have a share. He confirmed they'd seen Hektor blooded and a half dozen different variations of that seemed to be already doing the rounds. Now those repacking the boar wanted to know the shares. Billi shook his head, at a loss because he had no idea what to give. "Didn't Mandy sort that out?" He looked around to find Mandy, who grinned then said something to her man, Steban.

He came over, smiling, and explained. “Mandy told them that if they pulled the meat they'd get a share. She says they would have probably done it for nothing, for the sheer excitement of being on a real Hunt. Except Edan.” Steban scowled.

Since he'd been reminded, Billi looked round and a lonely figure trekked across the fields, towing his logs. Damn, he'd meant to send some meat anyway because the youth was just that, a youth with his brain still catching up with his mouth. Then hands dragged Billi into the group for the sharing. Eddmune, another of the Hunters who had come to help with the meat, followed Billi's eyes. “It'll be a good lesson.”

“Why?”

Eddmune looked surprised. “Ah, well from what these are saying, Hektor and Mandy told them you'd offered a share for getting the meat carried?”

“I did.” Billi waved a crutch. “That's a bit too much for me to manage, even if my pack was big enough.”

“I'll bet. Seifort, Billi doesn't know what Edan said.” Eddmune beckoned.

Seifort came reluctantly, embarrassed and probably hoping Billi hadn't remembered some of the complaining on the way out for the wood. “Well, Edan thought he should have had the spear. That he is older, so he should be the one blooded.”

Steban interrupted. “Mandy said you asked for the steadiest.”

Billi nodded. “Yes, I needed someone to look out for the others, not be busy watching me hunting. Hektor did a good job so I told him to finish the boar.”

“Mandy thought Edan too excitable and he'd been acting up on the trip, that's why she suggested Hektor.” Steban looked at Seifort. “Then when the loads were being sorted out, Edan claimed they were all entitled to a share. Entitled, not as Hunter's gift. That's right, isn't it?”

“Yes, he said Billi, er, the Hunter, didn't do anything, so everyone was entitled to a share. That he couldn't even, um, sorry Billi, er Hunter, but you couldn't finish the beast yourself.” Seifort blushed and looked round as if weighing up his escape route.

"Billi. No point changing it now." Billi was still puzzled. "But why no meat?"

"Er, there's more. Edan said you fell over the meat, that it was bogged down and trapped. He said, um." Seifort stopped.

"Go on lad. Billi ain't mad at you, but he needs to know why Mandy slapped Edan, and stopped him getting a share." Barimar nudged the youth, probably because he, and all the rest now listening, also wanted to know.

"He said he could have done it on his own with just the spear and wouldn't have needed a three legged Hound." Seifort shut up again but he'd said enough and laughter rippled round the group.

"If he ever gets to make a Hunter, I don't reckon Edan will last long." Eddmune laughed again. "Not if he thinks any bogged boar doesn't need a couple of arrows and a Hound at least, never mind a Great-Boar."

"Don't worry Billi. We aren't stupid, and anyway the rest are all telling what really happened. They won't shut up, probably until after next winter." Steban slapped Billi on the shoulder. "So what are the shares?"

"I don't know." Billi looked at the meat. "Hektor gets the head anyway. Then I'll take a third of what's left, and everyone gets a share of the rest with Hektor getting double. Does that seem fair?" Billi laughed. "If I took any more me and Rabbit would be too fat to get firewood, let alone hunt."

Barimar shook his head. "Too fair Billi. Getting blooded is a privilege, not something to earn extra shares."

Billi shook his own head. "The extra isn't for the kill. That youth stood at the rear while I stalked so I couldn't have done it without him. Hektor's were the only pair of eyes not following the hunt. I checked a good few times and Hektor stayed alert and looking back, away from me, so he earned an extra share."

Hektor had his shoulders pounded by a few more people after that. He also had a couple of maids who had come from the Village congratulating him. Hektor came over with a tusk. "Here Billi. You should have one at least."

Billi smiled and took it. "You'd better watch out or some maid will be running off with yours."

"It will be a lot of fun letting them try." That sounded casual enough, but Hektor eyed the maids with definite anticipation afterwards.

As the crowd neared Billi's hut on the outskirts of the Village, Mandy and Steban came over with a request. "After the head is boiled, everyone wants to put the cured skin back on the skull."

Mandy smiled. "Including the bit over the hump if you don't mind, Billi."

"Then we'll put it on the wall of the alehouse, next to the Wolf. Syman volunteered to carve the right sized replacement tusks out of cow horn or bone and Viktor has offered to cure the hide to put back on the head." Steban waited hopefully.

That puzzled Billi, again. "I don't mind. I gave Hektor the head anyway."

"But not the hide." Victor, the tanner, had moved closer and put in his copper's worth. "I'll cure the rest of the skin for you since I've got a house full of layabouts doing nothing better in this weather. Hungry layabouts, and the share of the boar for Bliss will be welcome at the table." He moved off to join his daughter. Soon afterwards a bemused Billi stood outside his door with Rabbit and a heap of meat and watched something close to a party heading up the track to the Village.

Billi hadn't spoken to so many people in one day for longer than he could remember, and for the first time in many years Billi felt he actually belonged. While he packed most of the meat in snow and put it in the cold store to stop the critters stealing it, Billi thought about belonging. He'd always steered clear of the Village because he knew they thought him a freak, and Rabbit as well. He rarely went to the alehouse because Billi felt conspicuous there, and only felt sorry for himself if he had too much ale. Even before he ended up in his hut, Billi didn't really have many friends. Not even as a littlun.

Well, not after his eleventh summer when the cart went over him and they cut off the mess that had been his left leg. It had been an accident. Billi ran behind the cart, chasing his Bro, and the pony had taken a couple of steps back for some reason or other. Nobody thought he'd make it, his Ma and Da both confessed when Billi was older. But they'd nursed him through the winter and in spring he started learning to use crutches properly and never stopped. Billi still had the chair his Da had made during that winter with its big solid wheels. No wonder he'd built strong arms and shoulders!

After that Billi stayed at home while all his sibs and their friends raced about the countryside growing up, and he just lost any real contact with them. The older folk tended to try and pretend Billi wasn't there, and the younger ones knew Stumpy Billi couldn't play with them. That all changed the day a Hound with a crippled leg limped down the Village street and whined at his Da's door. Rabbit stuck a wet nose into Billi's hands, and moved into the house and Billi's heart. Billi remembered that all right, the first moment when the song filled his head, happy and welcoming. The whole affair had been a big sensation and even the Tinkerers who came through four or five times a year and the Trader caravans had never heard of a crippled Hound.

Not really crippled because Rabbit stood full size for a Hound. Big, intelligent, powerful and surprisingly quick over a short distance even on three legs, Rabbit could hunt and loved to. Some resented a cripple getting a Hound, even a three legged one, but to no avail, Hounds never wavered in their loyalty, never changed their allegiance, and with that sort of incentive Stumpy Billi became a Hunter.

He and Rabbit learned to be slow and patient, and became true if small scale and inconspicuous Hunters. Nobody saw his first kill, because Billi couldn't keep up with the rest out in the Forest so he hunted alone. Billi put the blood on his own cheeks and stumped home with the small deer, proud as punch. Ma had hugged him and cried and Da took the antlers down to the alehouse to brag. Billi still had that little set of antlers.

Billi sighed and finished putting away all the pork, or most of it. Even that took longer than it should, cutting everything into pieces he could carry, hopping up and down the steps to the cold room. Billi realized just how much meat he'd just caught, since his third must be over three full-weights, over forty stone-weights. Then Billi's little family helped him to eat a fry-up of liver and kidney, since Rabbit hadn't eaten it after all. One-shut even deigned to leave his warm spot by the fire and clean up scraps as the raw chunks were sliced.

Billi thought he would trade some of the extra meat for a couple of loaves of real bread, and use the crust to make sausage. He'd never got the knack of baking and Billi's loaves were just about good enough to soak up gravy. Since Billi had no cow, he didn't have butter to soften it enough to eat his bread any other way anyhow. Now he had enough of a surplus to trade for a proper loaf and a pat of butter tomorrow. Billi fell asleep dreaming of soft bread, melting butter, and bacon and eggs.

* * *

The next day Billi traded for fresh bread, and some butter, and the number of smiles and greetings he received in the Village were a pleasant surprise. Better yet, the smiles and greetings continued in the following days. Bliss, Viktor the Tanner's daughter, called by the hut two days after the hunt. "I've brought you this Billi. If you want it?"

"A gift?" Billi looked at the tiny rough stone. "Don't you want it?"

"It's not that. It's just that when we washed in the stream, a few of us found stones with our bare feet." Bliss shrugged, embarrassed. "I just thought that, since you shared the meat?"

"Thank you, Bliss. Really. It's lovely." Billi looked at the little stone in his hand. It didn't look much but they both knew the Tinkerers might trade for it, which meant that it had real value as well as being a kind gesture.

"In that case, I'd better be off." With that Bliss ran out of the little gate and off towards the Village.

Billi looked at the little rough stone for a long time after she'd gone. He couldn't remember a Villager ever giving him a gift, and would keep this one as a memento regardless of the value. The Traders took all stones, good or bad, and traded them on. The Tinkerers paid more but only bought some, and did something to the stones they bought. Something to make them shine with a deep inner fire, as if a star had been dragged from the night sky and imprisoned in the tiny sparkuls. That's what they were called afterwards, sparkuls. The Traders offered huge sums for the secret, because if they wanted sparkuls they had to buy them from the Tinkerers.

The stones intrigued Billi, or maybe just the mystery of where they came from. Once the stones or nuggets in a stream were taken, no more appeared except after a flood when a few might turn up. Sometimes more turned up if a bank collapsed but not every time. That meant there had to be a source somewhere upstream where both stones and nuggets came from, a place Billi wondered about. Because he preferred the Forest to the lonely little hut, Billi often went much further than necessary for hunting, just to see something new. Only Billi ventured up the streams and rivers for any reason except to find the watering places and hunt, but his leg put him off any proper exploration.

If the maid found stones with her bare feet, the stream had never been searched, and so if Billi went up that stream he might find the source. Such a small stream couldn't go very far. As long as they found a clear spot to build a fire at night and took care, Billi could travel for days with Rabbit. The Forest truly did hold danger. The number of Hunters who didn't return from a hunt proved that but Billi didn't mind being out overnight. Billi and Rabbit never took chances in the Forest. They travelled slowly and steadily, and always camped early in a clear space with a big fire. Even if Billi reached the end of the stream and never found where stones came from, that would scratch his itch and he would know that such a place didn't exist.

The idea had popped up several times before and Billi hadn't followed it up. Maybe the upheaval or perhaps just the right stream being found lit a spark in Billi, a determination to find out for sure this time. As usual he spoke his thoughts aloud and Rabbit watched and listened. Billi wondered once more just how much a Hound understood? Maybe just that it would be a trip into the Forest, which would certainly explain the sparkle in Rabbit's song as Billi talked.

Billi told those bright eyes that if he found a lot of good stones the Tinkerers would be very interested. Then he could add to his nest egg, the one for the day his only leg or one of Rabbit's gave out and Billi had to buy meat, and everything else. Unfortunately, the beguilers would also be interested and they didn't pay for stones. Well they did, but not with silver or gold because beguilers could be a lot more casual with their favours than other maids. Tinkerer maids were notorious for that, beguiling a man out of whatever they'd taken a fancy to rather than buying it. Though in the depths of a long hard winter the idea of being beguiled out of some pretty stones had a certain attraction.

Not too much of one because his stump made Billi very self-conscious, especially around maids. A couple of times Billi spent the silver to visit

Anise in the back room of the alehouse, but once they undressed she spent too much time looking at Billi's stump and stroking it. Anise had dealt with his other needs well enough but there was no real feeling there and with her strange interest he'd stopped going. Since then Billi had been alone, something that rarely bothered him anymore. The occasional maid liked a bit of fun with a youth, but not with Stumpy Billi. A few maids were kind, a few were disgusted, and the rest ignored him.

Though as the days passed it became clear that people were paying attention now, all because of one bit of luck at hunting. Billi hadn't realised just how bad the local hunting had been as he didn't often go out in winter except to catch the small hunters for their lush pelts. Snow made hunting even more difficult with crutches so Billi had dried and smoked enough meat and fish in better weather and didn't need the fresh meat. Now, in addition to the large quantity of welcome meat landing on a good few very surprised tables, the boar came as a badly needed morale booster for the Village. The trickle of visitors didn't stop, as Billi had expected.

"Hello Billi. My Ma said that she heard your oven isn't any good for bread."

"No Seibert, I'm useless at making it."

The youth shrugged. "Anyway, she sent two loaves, if you want them?"

"Tell her thank you. They'll be a really nice change." Billi watched Seibert go off towards the Village and scratched his head. He'd had apple pies and two meat and tater pies arrive from different kitchens with a similar message. Billi had actually asked Hektor why since the youth made a point of calling by now and then.

Billi's success had been followed by a definite improvement in the amount of game taken by the other Hunters. They claimed that he'd broken the bad luck, not just by killing the Great-Boar but by the sharing. Hunters were a generally superstitious lot and certain that Billi had spread his good luck. It didn't make Billi exactly popular but he had visitors and they were all smiling.

* * *

Despite having just been wood gathering, Billi needed more firewood and now knew where there would be plenty. He told the Village families they could come if they wished, and defer payment if they wished. Billi had enough boar meat to last the three in his hut for over a moon, maybe two, and much longer than that with what he'd already got frozen and salted. Someone had even put a long length of intestine in Billi's share to make sausage from the scraps, meaty sausage as Billi had no spices, herbs, bread or flour.

This wood gathering trip Billi still had to put up with some banter, but about not finding any meat to cook with the wood they collected. The boar had been reduced to a few chunks of spinal column and some villagers brought back souvenirs to show the size of the teeth that had been at work. The elders quickly took a couple to show as a salutary reminder to littluns of what lurked beyond the Forest edge. The chewed bones also renewed interest in the story and helped cement the new status Billi seemed to have. Coming back Billi had to deal with comments about the lack of anything to eat, but just banter, not complaints about Billi's speed. Remarkably the change in attitude continued.

Perhaps nobody had actually considered Billi a real Hunter before since they'd never really seen what he caught, whereas now even the youths showed some respect. Hektor kept up his usual cheerful chatter but treated Billi with the defence due a Hunter, and since the youth's trophy gave him real status among his peers and the maids that attitude rubbed off on the rest. Almost all of the rest, Edan still bore a grudge and completely ignored Billi the whole trip.

With such a really different start to his year, Billi and Rabbit began to go out hunting more often and traded the larger surplus. Billi wondered if maybe he hadn't considered himself a real Hunter either? Though as he laid by a stream catching unwary fish with Rabbit watching his back, Billi realised he still didn't hunt the same as the rest. No big beefy prey, just small deer or pigs, wildfowl and fish, and the occasional greedy predator or scavenger trying to steal Billi's prey. Gradually, for the first time ever, his meat cellar began to look decidedly crowded.

Billi enjoyed meeting more people and from his song Rabbit enjoyed meeting other Hounds, though both still preferred the Forest to his little hut. Life wasn't all sunshine in the Village as although the youth's family didn't seem to bear any grudge, Edan did and he had a few friends. When Edan's Da had brought the meat to pay for the wood gathering escort,

Billi told him not to bother because he had plenty of meat. But that wasn't really what the older Hunter wanted to talk about. An embarrassed Canitre got to it in the end. "I've heard a few versions of what happened Billi, and I've got to ask."

"I didn't hear most of it, but Hektor got the chance to be blooded because he did a good job for me. Mandy had the ruckus with Edan, but a few told me after and they all seemed to tally." Billi didn't want to actually repeat the tales.

"I've heard a few tell it as well, and only one seems to tell it different. That's Edan." Canitre sighed. "Edan really is too impetuous to make a Hunter just yet. He needs to steady down. Maybe a Hound will do that." Canitre was a Hunter and had a Hound, Autumn, so he knew about the song and how a Hound could guide the Hunter. Billi agreed that a Hound would calm Edan down and left it at that.

* * *

But Edan didn't calm down or forgive and not only because of the embarrassment. The maids flirting with Hektor were a constant reminder and to top it off, within the moon, an excited Hektor arrived at Billi's door. "Billi, Billi, look!" When Billi opened the door, Hektor put his hand possessively on the head of a brindled Hound. "This is Dapple and he just walked up to me, out of nowhere, this morning. I showed him to Da and then came to see you. This is the Wild, they were watching when you let me kill the boar. I'm a Hunter, Billi."

"Yes you are Hektor, congratulations. Come in and have an ale, and let Dapple meet Rabbit." The little frisson in the song that settled into a steady hum meant the Hound already knew, but Billi thought Hektor needed to sit down anyway before he burst. That took a while, and Hektor's walk still had a definite bounce as he set off to walk through the Village, the walk any new Hunter made to make sure everyone saw their Hound. Though not everyone celebrated since according to Edan, Dapple should have been his Hound. Edan maintained that as the oldest youth, the kill should have been his, and Billi had robbed him of the chance.

As the weeks rolled on some of the others also said that the Wood Hunt explained why Dapple came to Hektor and not Edan. Most didn't say exactly the same as Edan; they claimed that Edan's actions on the hunt showed him up as unfit to be a good Hunter. Edan spoke of taking prey without a Hound while out in the Forest, in sight of the Wild, a truly stupid thing to do.

The Great-Boar's head kept the story alive. With the skin tanned and fitted, the head went up on the wall of the alehouse, and everyone reckoned the Great-Boar would have given the Great-Wolf some serious competition. They were more certain when the carved bone tusks were put into place. When the first Tinkerers and then a Trader's caravan came through, the visitors were taken to see the trophy.

Both Billi and Hektor came to the alehouse with their Hounds to show their personal trophies and confirm the story. Their trophies confirmed the size of the Great-Boar and that its original tusks really were the same size as those Syman had carved. Both refused the Traders' offers for their trophies, Billi because the tusk had become a talisman of some sort to him, of the moment his life changed. Hektor seemed to be well attached to his and the number of maids who wanted to see it, though none charmed the trophy away from the now eligible young man.

While there, Billi found that the whole affair had passed into the Village lore as a tale entitled The Wood Hunt. The elders recited their version to the Traders while Billi listened, and had kept the facts straight, though the way they told the tale emphasised two lessons about how to treat the Forest. Hektor had held his place as the rear-guard and then made a clean kill, and he received a Hound. Edan had been impetuous and disrespectful to the Law in sight of the Wild, and he had no Hound. That made such a good example that the Eldest would no doubt trot the Wood Hunt story out now and then for years to come.

A New Beginning

Adalmar the Carpenter called by Billi's hut one morning, and sort of hesitated on the doorstep. "I'm feeling a little foolish Billi, and a little bit embarrassed."

"I can't think why? Come in Adalmar." Billi opened the door wider, puzzled because he barely recognised the Carpenter so couldn't work out why the man might be embarrassed. Adalmar came in and took the chair Billi pointed to, while Billi sat on his bed. He'd need another chair if many more people came visiting, and Adalmar could sort that out. "Now you're here, I could do with another chair. I've not had many visitors before."

"No, nor did ye come into the Village very often, which is why I never put the two together. I mean your stump and a man I saw in a Trader caravan." Adalmar shuffled a little uneasily. "I'm sorry Billi, you sort of slipped my mind. The man had a leg missing the same as you, but he had a peg instead." Adalmar pointed at one of Billi's crutches. "The thing looked like the bottom part of that, a bit thicker, and he had it fastened to his stump with a leather cup and straps."

Billi tried to imagine that. "Did that work?"

"Really well. He could stand without any support if he stayed still, and get about with a crutch. Better than get about, he could move at a fair lick with just that one crutch. I should have thought. Then I saw ye about, so here I am. Are you interested?"

Billi didn't really have to think long, he could see too many advantages of having just one crutch and being able to hold his bow ready to use came top of the list. That and being able to stand and use it without a tree to lean against. "I am, Adalmar, and I thank ye for the thought. Can you make the thing?"

"I believe so, but it'll take some working out and you'll have to let me measure your stump and maybe take a cast to make the leather cup?" Adalmar spoke cautiously, because Billi didn't like anyone seeing his stump. The villagers hadn't had much to do with Billi in the last eight or nine years, but most remembered how he always tried to hide his stump through school and adolescence.

"For this I don't mind. I'll be in to see you tomorrow if that suits?" When Adalmar left Billi sat and thought more about it, but couldn't quell the rising hope. He wasn't the only one, Rabbit's song rang out with an extra happy note. Billi went into the Village as promised and sat while the carpenter measured and drew on the slate to show him, and dunked his stump in clay. After all, what was there to lose? The Carpenter seemed happy to trade the work for meat and hides, and Billi had even more of those now he hunted more often. Billi could even afford the extra chair without dipping into his nest egg, the little silver and occasional gold ingots buried here and there on his land.

The leather straps left sore patches to start with. Billi's stump hurt even with the padding, and he had to soak it in cold salty water night after night, but eventually the scarred skin toughened. The arrangement still wasn't easy to use, not least because Billi had trouble reaching the peg end once it was on. Billi had to remember to put the wooden peg into his trews before his real leg as the stick didn't bend of course, and eventually found the answer. He put the peg into his trews before strapping the leg on. More difficult still, Billi also had to get used to a bit of wood flailing about when he moved his thigh and stump.

For a moon Billi hunted less, because he couldn't manage the peg out in the Forest so he stayed home as much as possible to practice. Billi fell over, and he knocked mugs and pans over, and he even hit Rabbit a couple of times, but eventually he could stand without his crutches while he cut up meat at the table! He could even take a few careful steps if there was somewhere to grab onto or fall onto, inside the hut. The wooden limb came as a revelation and a release.

By the end of that first moon Billi could manage out in the Wild, and found he could move faster without noise and even manage undergrowth. As he progressed, Billi began to carry a bigger pack, a real Hunter's pack, and held his bow or spear in one hand while out in the Forest. Billi started to hunt more and bigger prey and the Forest seemed to welcome them. Rabbit loved the extra hunting and his happiness echoed in Billi's head.

Rabbit would even stand nearby bracing Billi's peg to help at first, so Billi could concentrate on his bow, and Billi felt certain the song had an extra bright note all the time now. Billi took larger and larger prey with a much bigger pack and the stump became less painful with continual heavier use. The possibilities opened out and Billi ranged further on overnight trips and then two or more nights at a time. Places that had taken two days to reach he could now reach in a day or maybe a day and a half so he pushed further, scratching that curious itch that wanted to see more.

Rabbit knew the difference in the amount Billi could carry. He began to sound that hopeful hunting note in the song for bigger, plumper game, pushing Billi to carry more and more. The Hound seemed to grow, to become stronger, more confident, bouncier with all the additional time out in the green. Perhaps Rabbit didn't think they were real Hunters before? Billi stayed out on double or even triple overnights more often and found new streams with unwary game. After all, apart from One-shut nobody would even notice him gone. He really began be a true Forest Hunter, not just sneaking around the edges after small prey.

An early summer wood gathering trip went out as far as the stream and this time Billi moved faster. The wood gathering went well and Billi felt relieved since this was the first time he'd worn the peg in public. Everyone seemed interested but pleased he was getting around better and curious about where he'd come up with the idea. Meanwhile the youths were staying a little respectful, treating Billi as a real Hunter, and that still seemed very strange. Except for Edan, and now two of his friends, who still ignored Billi.

The following morning Billi and Rabbit made their first attempt at following the stream back into the Forest. They didn't reach the end or any heap of stones even though they stayed out three nights. Billi returned to find his goats in the neighbouring field and munching the growing crops. Billi apologised and gave the Farmer some fish and a small hide in compensation, grateful that this Farmer was bonded to Sis so he'd not complain too much.

He didn't have much to do with his sibs because he always felt embarrassed that he'd let them down and caused them extra work. Billi knew he should have been more help on the farm as a youngster, and brought more meat to the family as a Hunter, so he kept out of their way as much as possible. He replaced the worn strap on the gate that had given way, but three days later his chickens were out. If Billi had stayed away overnight as planned, he would have lost most of them to the little night hunters.

Deciding to return early to empty his pack and top up the feed for his animals was pure good luck. Billi had decided that this overnight method wasn't working, even with two overnights, and had come home instead. The next time he meant to set out prepared to keep going for a few days so the pair of them could make a real attempt to find the spring or swamp that must be the source of their little stream. Somehow that had turned into a real urge, and Billi thought the bright spark in the song meant Rabbit felt the same curiosity.

But Billi couldn't work out how the chickens escaped, so he stayed home a couple of days instead and the feathered friends stayed in the pen. Billi hunted closer to home for the next few days but the new strap mysteriously broke by the time he came home one day. The chickens also escaped again, twice, despite Billi checking that they were firmly fastened in before leaving. Rabbit tracked the culprits straight to Canitre's farm, or to the track leading to the house. Edan and his friends had decided to go beyond talk.

Even if he stayed hidden nearby and caught Edan or his friends causing mischief, what could Billi do? Chase them? Actually Rabbit could, and he'd run them down even with three legs but as a hunting Hound Rabbit would pull down what he chased. Especially since Billi could feel an unhappiness in the song; Rabbit would have been too keen to catch the culprits!

Taking the idiots home slightly chewed wouldn't help matters though that briefly tempted Billi. A chewed Edan would just cause more trouble. From the glare she gave him the last time they'd crossed paths in the Village, Edan's Ma now seemed to be in the camp that blamed him for her son's misfortune. Billi and Rabbit enjoyed their new freedom, and didn't want to be tied to one-day trips again but if Edan kept this up and couldn't be chewed, that presented Billi with a bit of a dilemma. A bit of thought and a long talk to three bright eyes provided an answer, Billi needed a housekeeper.

He had a good idea who to ask as well, someone who might want to practice housekeeping and earn a little extra. Bliss looked to be making a determined run at Hektor, and despite her being the Tanner's daughter and not having much of a brideshare he wasn't running away fast enough to mean it. Better yet, Viktor had a large family with plenty of potential hut guards even if Hektor and Bliss caught each other. Billi set off with his latest collection of hides that needed tanning before he had second thoughts. While he discussed the curing of his hides Billi brought the subject up. "Viktor, I've got a problem with my chickens."

"Yes, I know. Somebody thinks he's funny. I've had to tell my pair, Perry and Timath, that thumping him won't fix it." Viktor grinned. "They enjoyed the pork and are taking it personally." Then he eyed up Billi's arms. "Maybe you should thump him?"

"I'm a lot older and bigger than Edan so it isn't worth the uproar and mud-throwing that would follow. Though I've maybe come up with a solution? It's up to you, and Bliss."

"Bliss? She's not big enough to thump Edan or she might have." Viktor kept smiling, but now looked intrigued as well. "So how can she fix him?"

"By spending the days keeping an eye on my chickens while I'm out in the Forest? Maybe she can weed the garden and such, and I can let her have some meat or fish depending on what I've taken. I could let her have a few stones if she prefers, since she collected some from that stream?" Billi waited while Viktor thought about it.

Viktor nodded, slowly. "She'll probably do it to get out of the house, since it's a bit crowded in here with Ellibeth back home. It will just be while you're in the Forest?"

"Oh yes. If possible I'd like her to stop overnight sometimes but I'll warn her first. I can't move fast so it takes me two days at least for a proper hunt." Billi sighed. "With this new peg I fancy going further."

"But you can't because of Edan. He just won't let it go and he's found a few who are encouraging the idiot." Victor waved behind him. "His Da and big Bro are Hunters, and I've got a house full and no Hunter but that's how it works. No point worrying about it."

"In that case a bit of extra meat will come in handy?" Billi liked Viktor and would be pleased to help him out. The Tanner had always treated him fairly when Billi needed his pelts or hides prepared, even before the Great-boar, and Viktor was one of the few people who didn't seem to notice Billi's missing leg.

"Hah, it isn't me that needs convincing. Bliss has her own mind, though I appreciate you asking me first, Billi." Viktor turned towards the rear of his workshop. "I'll get her now so she knows I know, if you see what I mean."

"Thank you Viktor."

* * *

Two days later as arranged Bliss turned up with a little bundle of food. Billi showed her the food for the goats and chickens, and One-shut if he complained too much. "One-shut usually catches his own, but sometimes the rats are shy. That food for yourself, it's not really necessary."

"I thought I'd be stopping over?" Bliss looked puzzled.

"It's easier to show you. Here, if you can lift the hatch."

"Why is there a hatch in your garden shed, Billi?" Bliss bent and heaved, and it came up. "With steps?"

"This is a cold store."

Bliss laughed. "Put anything outside in winter and it will freeze anyway."

"But down here you'll see it lasts a lot longer. There's still ice down here because I pack it in winter. Then this place is chilled most of the year, and cool even when the ice is gone." Billi gestured. "If you go down you'll see."

Bliss stared round the stone lined room at the bottom of the steps. Billi's sibs had dug a proper cold room for him, deep and tightly walled. "That really is ice, and frozen meat."

"Yes, and there's salted and dried and smoked meat here, and a few beets. There's dried and smoked fish over there for a change. As you can see, unless you've got the appetite of a Great Hunter you won't make a lot of impression." Billi waited, because Bliss wasn't answering.

Eventually she stopped looking around. "Where's the flour, and herbs and taters and such?"

"Ah, well, I'm a really bad baker so I stick to meat and fruit. There's a few taters here, and there's some fruit at the back there. I usually get fruit from the Forest so maybe it isn't what you're used to. The wild plums and berries and apples are usually a bit smaller but I like the taste." They were also free since Billi wandered past the trees and bushes while hunting. Billi looked in his belt purse. "There's a couple of silvers here if you need to get flour and things to eat properly."

Bliss laughed. "Eat properly? The reason for the flour and taters and roots is to make the meat go further. The herbs are to make a bit of scraggy meat taste better. Though with a bit of flour I could make some pies with some of this if you wanted a change?" Bliss looked around the room again. "I've never seen this much meat all in one place. If you bought a bit more salt you could sell the surplus to the villagers in winter or summer. We prefer it to dried, or smoked unless it's done right." She laughed. "We don't have cold rooms in the Village, or not that I know of."

Billi stared. Five minutes and she was starting to organise him, though Bliss might be right. He felt the humour from Rabbit. They'd better get out before the pair of them were organised and dusted and polished as well. One-shut would get a shock, and so would Hektor if Bliss caught him. Billi picked up his pack and headed for the Forest still smiling. Rabbit's happiness might be that, or just being out in the green again.

* * *

Billi stayed out overnight, and then spent a day at home, then went out just for the day. This time Bliss met him at the door looking worried. "I heard noises outside, in your garden. Voices. I shouted and then they were quiet."

Billi looked around, relieved that the chickens and goats were still safely shut in. "Did you see anyone?" He looked at the small, thick glass pane in the door. "Not that you'd see much through that."

"No. I went outside after a little while but couldn't see anybody about. The catch on the goat pen had been undone but the gate stayed closed so I put the loop back over to keep it shut." Bliss looked more annoyed than frightened now. "It was Edan again, wasn't it?"

"Yes, or at least I think so." Billi sighed. "I'm sorry Bliss, I'll just have to find another way. We can't risk you being alone if he's bringing friends."

"Ha! I'm not being frightened away by the likes of him. I put the big iron stew ladle by the door." Bliss hesitated. "That's if you still want me to clean up and that?"

"Yes, but I'm still worried."

"I'll ask Da if I can bring a dog. Spots is only young but he knows to bark at strangers and he'll be good round Rabbit. All the dogs are." She giggled suddenly. "He'll be good around One-shut as well because there's a big tomcat next door. All our pups end up with a scratched nose and learn respect." Bliss stopped smiling and looked worried. "You don't mind do you? Rabbit won't mind?"

"No. Some of the Hunter's families have a dog. The size difference means there's never any trouble." Billi didn't feel sure about leaving her here alone. "Do you mind? It would help me a lot."

"It will help Da a bit as well. Since Ma went to the rock, and then Ellibeth came home with Rubyn to look after, things are a bit tight. Ma used to help with the work, the tanning, so Da can't earn as much. Ellibeth is a widow, and she can't claim her brideshare from her man's family until the olduns pass on, so she has to raise her Rubin alone until then." Bliss laughed. "Sorry, I'm gossiping again. Da says it's a failing of mine."

"I don't mind. I don't hear many voices." Billi heaved a sigh of relief. "Just check with your Da first."

"I will. Thank ye, Billi."

"I'd better get ye home now. 'Tis getting dark." Billi and Rabbit walked Bliss home, and left her with a haunch of deer. On the way back Billi resolved to give her a little bit more, to make up for the trouble. It would help to feed Spots since now the dog seemed to be working for Billi as well.

* * *

A young, eager Spots seemed decidedly wary of One-shut and very respectful of Rabbit. When they were together Spots followed Rabbit around, sniffing where he did. Bliss thought the young dog wanted to grow up to be a Hound, a joke since Hounds came from the Forest full-grown. It didn't take Spots long to work out that the bit with a fence round needed guarding, and he soon started barking at anyone who came past. Bliss said she left him outside a lot of the time to wander about the plot, and that seemed to do the trick. There were no more noises or voices.

For the next half-moon Billi went out most days and a few nights. Bliss settled into her task very well, and his scruffy little hut ended up with a bit of a transformation. Billi had to laugh the day he came in wet and muddy and slumped in his chair still in his wet gear, and distinctly heard her huff of disapproval. His diet became a bit more exciting as well since there were herbs and one day a bit of something spicy. Bliss seemed to think her duties included cooking a bit of stew or bread or even a pie a couple of times.

Billi didn't complain because Bliss really could cook and bake, so he couldn't blame his oven any more. He asked about the spice and that came from the Traders. Ellibeth had sent it as a thank you for the amount of meat Billi sent home with Bliss. He gave Bliss a silver to get some and a few days later Bliss asked if she could plant some herbs. A little herb patch appeared outside Billi's door. The meals soon gained even more of a tasty tang, mint and some sage, and herbs Billi had never tasted before. Well not since his Ma did the cooking, and he'd never asked for names then or why her pies tasted that way.

During the entire half-moon Billi's animals stayed safely shut up and no catches or straps broke. The amount of meat or fish he gave Bliss made absolutely no difference to Billi's own eating, though her cooking did. Billi considered the meat or fowl a fair exchange for his animals being safe, and for some decent bread and pastry. He even made an arrangement to get a regular pat of butter from one of the farmers. Rabbit seemed to like Bliss, and the song definitely rang out much happier now they were spending more time in the green. Billi finally took the plunge. "I'd like to stay out longer, if ye don't mind?"

"How long, Billi? I don't mind but Da will want to know when to start worriting." Bliss smiled at that.

"That's a Da's job, worriting, or so my Da told me. I'd like to stop out six nights, but it may be seven. Sometimes this acts up." Billi tapped his stump. "Then it takes me a bit longer to get where I'm going."

"Six nights? Nobody stays out six nights, or seven. Leastways I think not. Will you be all right out there, with it being the Wild and all that?" Bliss actually looked worried which shook Billi a bit. Nobody had ever cared about where he went or if he was all right.

"I'm fine out there because I have the very best lookout. Rabbit keeps an ear, a nose, and possibly an eye opened all night." Billi laughed. "Though we always find a good big clearing away from convenient bushes and trees so nothing sneaks up. I never camp near a kill, or carry fresh meat unless I'm headed home, and a big fire helps. Most of the Wild is wary of fire."

"I'd be frightened out there, in the dark." Bliss shivered. "Surrounded by all those trees and who knows what in them."

"But with a Hound it all feels right. The stars are brighter out there, somehow, and the green itself isn't unfriendly. Some of the Wild are dangerous but as long as we're careful we're safe enough and I prefer being out there, and so does Rabbit." Billi paused, then teased her just a little. "You could ask a Hunter about it. Maybe Hektor now he's got a Hound?"

Instead of blushing, Bliss looked thoughtful. Then she smiled. "I might. When do you want to go, Billi?" She frowned. "I can get one of my sibs, Perry or Timath, to call by now and then. Just so Da don't worrit."

"Tomorrow, if that's not too soon and you don't mind?"

"I'll bring clothes and bits with me." Bliss smiled again. "Since I'm not to bring food." Not only had Bliss not dented the meat in the cold room, but there were now several big pies on the shelves.

Billi walked Bliss home, left a pelt and a hide for Viktor to cure, and half of a small deer since Bliss had been there two days and a night. Billi confirmed that he would be going for up to seven nights, and Viktor confirmed that his layabouts would keep an eye on Bliss. Then Billi spent the evening making sure he had all he needed in his big pack, sharpening the spear, and talking through the trip with Rabbit. This time he intended finding out just where that elusive stream started.

Bliss turned up early in the morning with her bundle and Spots. Billi asked again if she'd be all right for so long and Bliss seemed supremely confident. She assured him her family and friends would come by so Billi called to Rabbit and off they went. Billi could understand why Rabbit's song sounded so happy because he felt the same, they'd have eight whole days out in the Forest!

* * *

Mid-afternoon four days later Billi didn't feel quite so happy. He felt tired and a bit sore and now Billi began to wonder when this stream actually ended, or started really. For a relatively small but swift flow it went on and on winding through the Forest. He'd paused to turn back twice today but Rabbit's song urged him on each time. Billi began to wonder if the Hound knew where they were going? Hounds came from the Forest, full-grown, but nobody knew more than that. Despite his misgivings Billi pushed on.

At least camping for the night had become easier. The trees had thinned, no longer tangled together with webs of vines and creepers. Now there were more open glades, areas covered in lush grass, and the small herds grazing them seemed much more wary of the Hound than the bow. Another bad winter Billi would have a word with a couple of the other Hunters, and maybe organise an expedition up here. Hunting would be good if they took care since the glades provided plenty of open grazing for deer, with cover close by. So far Billi had fished for just enough to eat, except for taking one small deer for Rabbit. The fourth night felt strange, in the middle of a wide open stretch of grass, though the eyes in the bushes catching the firelight warned Billi that safer didn't mean safe.

In the morning Rabbit bounded away upstream, and Billi sighed and followed. Midday today he would stop even if Rabbit didn't like it. Though before then he'd changed his mind. Ahead, above a few lower trees, Billi could see glimpses of higher ground! Billi had never seen hills that showed above the trees, even though these were no longer true Forest giants. He racked his brains but nobody had ever talked of hills this high. Now Billi pushed on with more determination even though he began to worry the stream would end at some waterfall, just to remain elusive and annoy him.

That would end the search as Billi couldn't climb anything remotely difficult and it would be pure foolishness to try. If he fell there would be no rescue, and then Rabbit would stay with him and die as well. There would be no other Hunter this far into the Forest so the two of them would never be found. The changing types of trees, birds and flowers drove that home. Only Billi, with no real responsibilities, would come so far for curiosity. Billi smiled because his curiosity had paid off a little as his pouch now contained a small collection of stones from the stream. Those included a couple of quite large ones, larger than any Billi had found elsewhere.

Billi had stuck to fish as yet because fish were easily found and caught. These fish were unused to the careful hand that gently stroked and then flicked them onto the bank. Billi had his line of course but that wasn't necessary and he thought it a pity this place lay so far from the Village. Around here would be a lovely place to live. Unfortunately, here definitely classed as Forest so the Wild wouldn't allow any man to live here, though the idea of that definitely appealed.

Fishing by hand meant spending a good while watching the water very carefully, and explained why Billi had so many stones. Each time he spotted one while sneaking up on a fish, Billi searched the sand or gravel and usually found at least one more. Rabbit had a wonderful time, especially helping with the stone hunting. He would scratch up the gravel after Billi had searched and when the disturbed silt washed away Billi would look again. Rabbit uncovered both larger stones and several small ones. In a small way the stones might pay for the trip, even if Billi didn't really care about that.

Or perhaps he did, because all these stones seemed to be the ones the Tinkerers wanted. If he could find this amount elsewhere, maybe his nest egg would grow faster than with meat and hides? Billi tried to imagine the small collection shining with an inner fire, but he'd not seen a sparkul close up so as he ate Billi watched the flying sparkuls instead. The Hawkflies shone with a myriad colour as they hunted insects over the water, more colours than Billi ever saw on the Farm. He finished his fish and put the scraps under a bush for the Wild, sat by the fire, and thought about that high ground ahead

Billi wanted to see that hill, just because of how high it seemed, so he'd go that far. Then he would stop, Billi promised himself and Rabbit, because he'd told Bliss seven days and even moving fast enough to hurt he'd not get back that fast now. Though Rabbit seemed perfectly happy to keep going as long as Billi wanted to. If he couldn't find the source by midday tomorrow Billi would go home and maybe reconsider. He would decide if knowing about the stones, and that hill, was really worth a longer trip.

Billi hoped that Bliss really would be all right and not mind him going on another long trip. Her family, her sibs, could come and see her so the maid shouldn't be lonely. Billi smiled, if Hektor truly had stopped running and started chasing Bliss wouldn't be lonely anyway. As well as stones, Billi kept an eye open for other signs as well. If he found ironstone or greenstone here, or the black rock that burned, he would take note of the place. Then the villagers would pay a Hunter well for the information and to stand guard while they came and dug it up, even this far away. The blacksmith bargained with the Traders for blackstone or he used charcoal made from precious firewood. Greenstone would produce copper once the smith got to work smelting the strangely coloured rock.

Would it be worth Billi spending a week or so out here to turn the big deadfalls into charcoal to trade? No wood gathering ever came this far out so some really big branches lay undisturbed and even a couple of small trees. Though this would be too far to drag full tree trunks all the way home with ponies, despite their value. Villagers didn't like being out overnight so four or five nights would be out of the question.

Billi tried working out the time it would take to build a turf oven against how much charcoal he might get and the time taken to trek it home. Then he worked out how much it would cost to bring and guard someone who knew how to actually do that properly. Because of that Billi didn't quite register what he was looking at for a few minutes. He'd finally reached the hill, as the ground ahead rose sharply except for a huge bite out of the slope, a bite that ran back into the hillside.

* * *

Not really a hillside because Billi had found more than a hill. The height of the ground stretching either way came as shock all by itself. The trees had disguised the real height and extent, but now Billi took a moment to grasp what he could see. The only high ground in the Forest that he had heard of or seen came as occasional small rises, usually crowned with trees or sometimes bare rocks. This steep, rocky slope went as far as Billi could see in each direction, and had no trees on top. The only break looked to be ahead, a deep bowl somehow gouged out of the upland to form an almost square-ended valley.

At the far end of the large valley now visible beyond the bushes a waterfall appeared, just as Billi had feared, but only a trickle. The flow looked nothing like enough to form the stream rushing past so Billi moved forward to see where the water came from. He already wondered why there were no trees in there, or none with leaves. There were a good few trees but those were dead and bare of even smaller twigs.

An untidy collection of branches and twigs packed in around a huge fallen trunk sealed the exit for the stream. The obstacle had been concealed by the bushes when Billi first approached but now he could see that the original stream bed had been dammed. The water still escaped over the top of the dead timber and kept the stream flowing, but behind the trunk there must be a pool, possibly running right up the valley. Billi remembered what Mandy had said about flooding probably killing trees, which explained all those bare branches.

Billi came up the slope past a hollow and up-thrust roots marking the original position of the tree, where the sides of the valley began to rise. The unfamiliar hump of a beaver lodge jutted from the pool behind the dam, he'd only seen two before and one had already been broken open by a bear. The beaver had flooded the valley or possibly just spotted the chance and improved the initial blockage, and that had killed the trees. Normally beaver would have encouraged the secondary, more easily edible growth but Billi could see they hadn't been here long. Though perhaps the local browsers were persistent since the secondary growth looked stunted and chewed back in most places.

There might be plenty of browsers visiting because the pool didn't go back to the waterfall or right across the valley, leaving plenty of ground covered in grass. The beaver pond went less than a third of the way up the valley, then a wide gravel bank cut right across the valley bottom, the lower part. At the other side of the gravel a larger, wider pool spread back to the cliff behind. That pool seemed to be the source of the stream. "It still doesn't look right, Rabbit. There's more water coming over the gravel than comes down the cliff." Billi pointed. "Maybe there's a spring there, where the small pools are at the side of the main one."

Billi looked around the rest of the valley. "Look at the amount of grazing in here, Rabbit. Thick grass, and lush with all that water even in the driest summer. There'll be ducks and geese come to these pools, and the reeds make good cover for hunting. This would make a good living for a Hunter and a Hound." Billi realised he'd been out in the Forest so long he'd reverted to his usual habit when chewing over a problem at home, talking it through aloud with the Hound.

Then it hit Billi. He could live here, away from the Village. Those dead trees would provide more than enough timber for a hut, for several huts. "There's only small new growth by the pools, and scrub on the hillsides. All the rest of the trees and older bushes are dead. That pool must have come up higher at some time before breaking out." Billi looked at the remaining growth with new eyes, and Rabbit's song sounded hopefully cautious.

"That's less growth than there is after a fire, when the farmers claim land from the Forest. This side never had trees, but I reckon it's because there's only enough soil for grass. You can see the rocks coming through. That soil side, with the big tree stumps, must be deep enough for crops, for some roots and maybe a bit of barley or wheat. Maybe the Forest would let us take it, Rabbit? You and I, living out here." Rabbit's song definitely liked that idea, or maybe the enthusiasm in Billi's voice.

Billi finished the thought, they would get right away from Edan and his friends. Edan would need a Hunter to escort him this far, and Hunters wouldn't do that just to let out the chickens. Thinking of the chickens ruined the whole dream. Billi couldn't live here. When he went to hunt, the Wild would take the goats and chickens, and eat any crops before they got above shoots. He sat down, deflated. This would have been perfect. The sloping land, though fairly steep further to the sides, had a covering of wiry grass that would have fed sheep or goats, and he could have had a milk cow on the good pasture.

The song rose, interested, and Billi looked up to see what had caught Rabbit's eye. Lazy ripples in the pool, both pools, spoke of big fish, certainly big enough for a meal. That just made things worse. Given the size of the pools there might be enough fish to feed one man and his Hound all by themselves. Nothing much would predate the fish if a Hound lived nearby, with little cover near the pool to conceal the furry fishers and the tangles of dead branches in the near one to stop fishing birds.

Billi sighed, but his head still wouldn't quite let the idea go. "Look Rabbit, we could have dug out the sediment in some of those pools, and laid it on the higher parts to enrich the soil over there. A garden there, fields here." Billi waved his arms about, still picturing it. "Dig out a bit across that part and the chickens would be on an island so they wouldn't stray. The boulders in that gravel are enough for foundations to keep a hut firm and dry." Billi paused, because his eyes had returned to the steady wash of water over the gravel.

He remembered his original impression, more water came over here than came down the cliff so where did all the water come from? Even as he stumped slowly along the side of the valley Billi reluctantly let go of his dream. With his crutch and stump it would take too long to carry meat and hides back to the Village to trade. He'd need arrowheads and salt, herbs and clothing, or a new pan, and Billi couldn't keep the animals locked up in a hut for the length of time that would take.

* * *

Then Billi saw where the water came from and had a new puzzle to work on. A deep cleft in the rocks spilled a steady flow into a small deep pool that then overflowed to form a short stream into the big lake at the valley head. Now that his brain worked properly instead of dreaming Billi remembered his original mission, which doubled his disappointment because he'd never get to the source of the stream now.

Billi had no intention of trying to wade into that low, dark hole. "That's done it, Rabbit. A complete waste." Rabbit's song disagreed, but he enjoyed being out in the green anyway. So did Billi when he thought about it, so the trip wasn't a complete waste. Rabbit whined and looked into the little pool, then hopped towards the lake.

Billi laid on the edge of the small pool and shaded it with a hand, peering into the dim depths. The pool seemed to be more or less bare rock with no gravel, though the moving water and surface ripples made it hard to be sure. Maybe the stones didn't come from the cleft? Billi put a hand into the water to collect a sip and knew that nobody would be trying to wade into that opening even with two legs. The bone-chilling cold in the water would numb and then drown them.

Rabbit's inquisitive itch still sounded in the song and even if it wasn't to do with stones Billi wanted to check if anything came in this way. He smiled and looked over at Rabbit. "This is your fault." Billi sighed, took a deep breath and put his face under the surface. Then he opened his eyes and waited a moment while they recovered from the icy shock. Now he could see better and in the short while before the deep cold forced him back Billi had a good look. Either the stones and gravel came in here and were flushed straight out again or they came from elsewhere. The bottom of the rock pool had been worn in whorls and smooth bumps but looked clean apart from a couple of big rounded rocks.

Billi rubbed the feeling back into his face and ears and headed for the gravel bar. Rabbit sounded happier now, but still very curious about something. Billi searched for suitable sized pebbles and had a surprise result, a nicely sized shiny stone. Or one that would be shiny when the Tinkerers had finished, because Billi knew this was the type the Tinkerers would buy. The stone also decided the size of pebble Billi needed for the test. He took four pebbles the same size, dropped them into the pool and left them while he scooped three fish from one of the smaller pools and chopped enough wood from a dead branch for a small fire.

Billi left the fish on their sticks to cook while he went back to the pool. Now Billi knew how cold the water would be he didn't fancy a repeat but the urge to know had him firmly gripped. Once again he suffered the cold, then pulled his head back out and sat rubbing to get the circulation moving. "You were right, Rabbit. The pebbles are still in there so the stones come from someplace else."

Billi eyed up the waterfall. Maybe a spring flood came over there but surely that wouldn't wash some of these rocks down. The way the larger rocks were smoothed and half buried, they had to have been here a long, long time. There wasn't a regular flood anyway or the beaver wouldn't be living there. A decent flood would destroy the dam which meant this cleft had to be the source or as near as Billi would get.

He sat sharing the cooked fish with Rabbit, who had already caught a couple of his own and wolfed them down raw. Billi looked around to work out why the small stones were washed downstream without a strong flow over the cliff. A heavy downpour could gather on the hillsides and perhaps before the dam tamed it the swollen stream had the power to carry stones. Maybe the cleft had a stronger flow then?

So the stones could still come from there. Billi laughed at himself and cleaned his hands. It didn't really matter since that lovely big gravel bar lay right there, and if he'd found one already there would be others. He'd spend the rest of the day searching and head back tomorrow. Billi could make a faster trip back since he'd been stone searching and fishing on the way here and he would hunt for some meat near the end of the trip for paying Bliss. Even if he found none, the maid would probably take stones to trade on.

Billi looked at the remains of his meal. Maybe he'd take some fresh fish from the lake on the last morning to pay Bliss, who would be wondering by then if she'd 'inherited' a hut. Billi took the entrails and remains to the edge of the valley and threw them into the undergrowth as the tithe. A tongue of trees came along the bottom of the escarpment and curled round and up, just into the valley that side. That came near enough to class as the Forest, and far enough from Billi to keep whatever took the tithe from getting greedy. Then Billi set into some serious gravel searching with his enthusiastic assistant.

By the time dusk lengthened the shadows, and he'd shared more fish with Rabbit, the pair had collected a pouch full of possible sparkuls. As he built up a big fire and gathered dry grass and leaves to pad a spot to sleep, Billi wondered how fast he could build up his nest egg with stones. After all, he'd started using his leg more now so it might give up sooner. Billi nagged away at his old worry, about not having enough for his old age, then the stars and the crackle of the fire worked their magic and he calmed and slept.

* * *

First thing the next morning they headed homewards and travelled fast, or as fast as he could stump along anyway. Billi made a late camp in the dark and set off the following morning before dawn, catching a fine plump buck taking an early morning drink. Billi quickly dressed and packed the meat, tying the lot in the hide with the antlers across the top. He had been travelling light, so the meat still wouldn't slow him too much.

The antlers weren't very big but Bliss could take them home for her Da to use for knife handles or whatever. Until he'd employed her and listened to what she said about his home Billi had never thought about such things. A Hunter's home always had plenty of horn, though Billi hadn't always lived in a home with a Hunter. Thinking back to his childhood Billi realised why he had fond memories of fresh bread and butter and crumbly, tangy cheese. His folk were farmers so the only meat came from slaughtering stock, a rare occurrence.

Few farmers raised meat beasts on the Farm as the good land grew the food crops, so only the rougher parts were grazed. Sheep and goats did best on that and mainly supplied wool, hair and milk, not meat. Billi hadn't even thought about that even when he'd been blessed with a Hound. Rabbit played with his sibs and generally fitted around the family dogs without making any ripples, and Billi hadn't been a proper Hunter. No wonder Ma cried when he brought home that deer, and made such a fuss over the succession of other small animals. That meat must have been a big help in the three winters before the croup went through the Village in the winter and took both Da and Ma.

His older Bro took the house for himself, and his lass of course, and the landshares had been sorted out as Da had already determined. Sis had captured a Farmer with her brideshare, or maybe her laugh, and with his landshare they had a good living. So did Billi's other Bro and his lass with his landshare, and her brideshare still to come. They had enough for their families, but only for that which was why Billi kept building his nest egg. He'd been a burden to his family as a littlun and didn't want that again in old age.

Thinking of the differences between a Village home and a Hunter's house kept Billi occupied through the third gruelling day. When he recognised the site of the Wood Hunt Billi realised they wouldn't make it home before dark, and he had been a bit ambitious even trying. Billi debated with his best advisor. "We shouldn't really travel by night, Rabbit, but at least we know this path. I'd rather push on and get a decent bed."

The song soared at the idea of a decent bed, and Billi wondered if the travelling had made Rabbit sore as well. He'd only got three legs, after all. "It'll be full dark when we get out of the Forest, but I'm up for it. You'll have to be extra careful since I've got this pack to lug about." Rabbit bounced ahead a bit and looked back, and cast his vote for warmth and comfort. Billi laughed and set himself for the trip. His Hound thought he'd be safe enough, or at least as safe as camping out in the Forest was anyway. The larger Wild hunters didn't usually come near the Farm so this bit would be safer than the last eight days. "I'll walk Bliss home and apologise to her Da for how late it is, and we'll sleep late tomorrow."

With home in mind Billi pushed hard but sure enough he came out of the trees with only a bit of moonlight to show the clouds in the sky, the sun had long gone. Nearer to home he exchanged greetings with the night guard and his Hound, sleeping by the corral. Billi had been gone much longer than expected, and the hut really was a welcome sight. He opened the gate. "Well at least Bliss hasn't gone home in disgust." He could see a chink of firelight around the shutter, but Billi didn't expect to hear the deep tones of a Hound from inside and raised voices!

Moments later, even as Rabbit answered the baying with his own, the door opened and a tall figure stood there with a spear. "Who is it?"

"Billi and Rabbit." That caused some confusion and as he came closer Billi realised Hektor stood in his doorway, with Dapple of course. During the fulsome explanations with the slightly flushed faces, and Bliss rushing round plumping up and smoothing down and putting on water, Billi realised that they hadn't expected him back. That meant that Hektor calling round to make sure Bliss felt safe had a slightly different connotation.

Billi thought it a safe bet that Viktor had no idea just how late Hektor called round to check on Bliss, or how long he probably intended to staying given that he was in shirtsleeves. Hektor had brought meat as well so intended being here long enough for a meal, and not tonight. Billi had a hard job keeping his face straight. Bliss seemed to have found a Hunter to answer her questions, and trapping seemed to be a better solution than chasing.

While Hektor explained for about the fourth time that he had just called past on his way home Billi saw the skinned knuckles. "Who have you been punching? Did one of the maids try to steal your tusk?" Billi meant that as a joke since Hektor would never hit a maid. Anyway, looking at the current situation only one maid had a chance of getting the tusk as a necklace, and might not have to steal it. Both blushed scarlet and neither wanted to answer. "Well that stopped you talking, but now I really am curious?"

"Um, well. You should know. It's er." Hektor kept glancing at Bliss.

"I'll check the chickens, Billi." Bliss left with both Spots and Dapple so she'd certainly be safe out there, though the chickens were safely locked up anyway at first dark.

"It's well, someone. They. Well, you give Bliss meat. Er." Hektor still struggled and still blushed bright scarlet. "Someone said it might be because she didn't always leave when you come home." That came out in a rush and Billi felt his own fist clench.

"Edan. I give Bliss extra meat because she makes pies and cleans up. If 'twere not for Edan I'd not need anyone." Billi opened his fist and clenched it again. "I'll deal with it." This time he'd thump Edan and worry about the mess afterwards.

"We know why you give Bliss the meat. Everyone decent knows." Hektor stood up very straight. "No need to deal with it. Nobody will be insulting Bliss in future." Billi looked at the youth's knuckles and understood.

He turned enough to open the door. "You can come back now, Bliss." She came in and glanced at Hektor. "Hektor explained, and that there's no need to worry about it." Billi thought the proud look from Bliss might set Hektor on fire. Nobody would be insulting Bliss, but if her Da saw the maid's look he'd be expecting a bit more room at home soon. There didn't seem to be much chasing or running left to do and Billi might need another housekeeper sooner than expected.

"Since you're here, maybe you could walk Bliss home. It'll be a help because I've pushed hard today." Billi turned away to his pack to avoid laughing at them because Hektor looked relieved, probably because Billi wouldn't be talking to Viktor and mentioning finding Hektor in the hut. "I fell over a plump buck. Unless someone will think it's too much?"

"Someone will be keeping away from me and will never know." The mixture of pride and satisfaction shone through Bliss's voice. "So thank ye, Billi. We appreciate it, all the family do. The pantry is full of meat these days." She glanced at Hektor so maybe he'd contributed. "Have ye any hides to be dealt with?"

"Just the one, but I do have an extra something if you'd like one. I followed the stream this time, and looked for stones. Here, pick one." Billi smiled. "To make up for me being late." He thought about the look and Viktor's pantry being full. If Hektor really had started chasing Bliss, openly, there probably would be extra meat going there. "Take stones instead of some of the meat if ye like."

"I'd like that Billi, thank ye. Just a few stones because as Da says, we eat more than a pack of Hounds." Billi held out a dozen small stones and Bliss picked out one, then another, and carefully unwrapped a haunch of the buck. "If that's right with you, Billi?"

"That's seems fair to me, Bliss." The meat or the stones were all found goods to Billi, though the maid certainly knew her stones and chose quality not size. Once they left Billi relaxed and had a long laugh. Bliss hadn't even asked how he'd got on with following the stream to its source. He used the water Bliss had put to warm for a good wash and both Billi and Rabbit slept long and late.

* * *

Three days later while trading a few low quality stones and skins and collecting a dozen new arrowheads, Billi saw Edan. The youth would have trouble insulting anyone for a while. Certainly until the split and swollen lips healed, and he'd have trouble seeing as one eye had turned rainbow coloured and swollen firmly shut. Edan didn't see Billi and looked to be trying to avoid seeing anyone, as did the two youths with him. Billi did wonder if that would work. Probably for Bliss, but Edan would just go back to making up tales about Billi.

One thing, Billi needn't worry about the poor girl being all alone in his hut. He stumped home with a little smile on his face. Nobody discussed Billi finding Hektor in his hut but Bliss took care to check if Billi really would be out all night, or if he might be home so she could let her Da know she might get home late. That put a bit of a smile on Billi's face as well; it was sweet really.

The summer moved on and this year the kids Billi's goats dropped grew bigger and stronger with someone actually keeping an eye on them. Usually the goats stayed in the pen while Billi went hunting, but now Bliss let them out in the day and the young blossomed. The chickens were allowed to hatch a few chicks since with all the extra hunting Billi could afford the feed. He liked eggs, especially when cooking for himself because they were easy to fry, and they tasted even better if Bliss had left a bit of fresh bread.

"Billi, where does your goat fodder come from? This stuff, because there's nothing like it round the Village." Bliss held out a few long, thin leaves and stalks.

"Those are half grown green reeds. When they get older and stiffer I use some for the goat bedding and the roof of the chicken hut. I don't grow corn and don't have enough grazing so there's never enough straw and hay." Billi laughed. "As usual, I just pick some up on my travels. You must think this is a very strange place."

"Not strange." Bliss giggled. "Though your hut really is very different." Then she sobered. "So the bedding is the same plant as this? Would you mind if I take a little bit of bedding, or could you tell me where it is, Billi? I'd like some for repairing the thatch on the chicken coop at home. Your goat bedding is tougher than straw and the hens might not steal reeds for nests. They keep pulling on the straw we use for the roof."

"Take some of what's there and I'll go that way and collect some more old stuff, though you'll end up with ducks or geese for your pay if I visit the reed bed. Will that matter?" Since the reed beds always had plenty of wildfowl that would be easier for Billi.

"Oh no, Ellibeth will appreciate the feathers." Billi took a trip to the reed bed along the river, gathered some old reed and collected a goose and two ducks.

Bliss took some reed home and announced that the chickens didn't seem interested in the thicker, stiffer stalks. A few days later Bliss asked if there were a lot of reeds, because Fellip the Thatcher had noticed the new roof on the chicken hut. The Thatcher wanted to know because there weren't many by the river and reed made stronger thatch. Billi told her, yes, there were a lot. He asked if the Thatcher wanted an escort to get some.

Two days later a giggling Bliss came with a reply, giggling because the Thatcher almost choked when he found that reeds were being used as goat fodder and bedding. Could he come and talk to Billi about it all?

Billi sent a message back that he didn't mind at all, and the following day the Thatcher turned up at Billi's hut. Billi invited Fellip the Thatcher inside, and the tall thin man immediately asked about the reed, any reed in a sizeable bed. Billi offered him some ale, and considered getting in a bit more ale for visitors. Fellip slowed up for a moment while Billi sat, then set straight in again. "Is it true you use reeds for goat bedding and fodder?"

"Yes. I use the old stuff for bedding but the goats eat the young growth. They seem to like it well enough." Billi kept the smile from his face.

Fellip sipped his ale. "I'd have swapped you straw for reed, especially if it is cut properly. The reed is worth more if it is cut and stacked properly. How much reed is there?" He sipped his ale, waiting while Billi tried to estimate.

"It's hard to say exactly, because it's the shape of a drawn bow, with the curved edge being the river." Billi frowned. "Perhaps the same area as my bit of land? Are you all right?"

Fellip coughed a bit more and put down his ale, then wiped his lips before replying. "Have you any idea of the value of reed?"

"No. Most houses have straw thatch, or all of them I thought up until Bliss mentioned reed to you." Billi definitely wondered about the value now and Rabbit's song had a query in it.

Fellip rolled his eyes. "Hunters. If it doesn't crawl, swim or fly?" He chuckled. "That's unfair because everyone to their own, after all I have no idea what claws or hides are worth. Only the wealthy have reed roofs because reed is expensive. I take some from beside the river each year, but always have to buy more from the Traders. They always try to cheat me of course."

"So is the reed worth a finder's fee?" That would be a handy bonus for Billi, and he could hunt for waterfowl.

"That amount is worth a decent fee depending on what is useable. There would also be the escort fee for guarding the cutting and carting. Similar to when a tree is found?" Fellip picked up his ale. "Is it safe to drink again or is there a second one the size of a farm?"

"No more, and you won't get ponies there easily." Billi chuckled. "I find it a good place for wildfowl, and bring some reed for the goats to save buying straw. I go along the riverbank and that's a bit marshy for laden ponies, but to avoid that we'd have to take ponies right into the Forest. When will you want to go?"

"I'd like to go and look at it as soon as possible, and we shouldn't need ponies at all. We'll use boats for carting any reed since it is by the river anyway, though poling will be a bit of a job." Fellip thought about it for a few moments. "I'll pay you for an escort there as soon as possible to see the state of the reed bed. Then a finder's fee for what we take, and a fee for escort during the cutting and hauling some time just after the Harvestfest, if that is agreeable."

"Finder's fee? Will that be the same as for trees? One tenth but you pay haulage?" Billi shrugged. "That's only one fee usually but I'd want the contract for escort if you go back." He would also be pleased of an escort job every year or three after Harvestfest when hunting became more difficult. With the leaves gone prey became harder to sneak up on, especially with one leg.

"If there's a reed bed that big I'll go back every year. Do you know a couple of local youths who will keep very, very quiet about it?" Fellip scowled. "So that nobody decides to cut what's there early because the reed will still have a value to the Traders, just not as much because the quality won't be as good."

Billi smiled. "Perry and Timath, Bliss' Bros, will be very discreet. They are both hoping for a bit of work from me." Billi almost laughed since they were both angling for the caretaker job if Bliss landed her Hunter. Not only that but Viktor would probably skin them if they messed up the meat supply for hut guarding.

Viktor still seemed unaware of how well Bliss' campaign had progressed. He thought the gifts of meat and hide were a brash young Hunter showing off, a youth impressing a maid he wanted to chase. Viktor definitely approved of the chasing part since a Hunter in the family would be very handy. Viktor just didn't realise that they'd gone past chasing to catching, as far as Billi could judge.

Billi took Fellip out to take a look. The Thatcher rubbed his hands at the extent of the bed, but sounded dismayed by the state of some of the reed. He announced there would be work needed after the first cutting to ensure a much better crop the next year. He would call on Billi sometime after Harvestfest to arrange everything.

* * *

Billi went out to his new discovery, the valley, once every moon during the summer, staying away an eight-day each time. Since Bliss now knew he might be home late on the last night or early the next morning, Billi never found Hektor in shirt sleeves again. Billi found the young Hunter at his hut a couple of times, but still in his jacket, just checking up on Bliss. Billi hoped the pair made their match official before they made a mistake. Not that anyone considered a mistake too serious if they were going to bond anyway, but there were always waspy tongues that would hint at traps. Or maybe cast doubt on the father, that sort of thing would appeal to Edan and he would make the most of it. He hadn't stopped muck-spreading, and a few in the Village still scowled at Billi or muttered 'cripple' behind his back.

While in the valley that Billi privately thought of as his own, he improved the smaller pools by taking out sediment because that kept the water flowing through them and stopped any stagnation. Then he put the sediment on a patch he privately labelled garden, for herbs and maybe a gooseberry bush. "We can bring some blackberry shoots, Rabbit, and gooseberries will go well with the fish. There'll maybe be geese here in the winter, with the open water, and blackberries will sweeten them up a bit."

Each time he visited Billi would smoke or dry some fish to take back or occasionally to store there. "I reckon a heavy stone like this, over this hollow in the rocks, will stop most things, Rabbit." Rabbit inspected the impromptu food safe and tried to nudge the cover aside with his nose. Billi put smoked fish in a greased hide under the large flat rock, handy if they arrived late in the evening.

Billi still toyed with how to make this valley into Farm. "To make a piece of Forest into Farm, it must produce a crop. Do you think fish might be a crop?" Rabbit's song seemed uncertain but hopeful, or maybe he didn't understand what Billi meant and just hoped for some fish. Billi knew that taking a regular crop went right up on top of the list of requirements when making a piece of land Farm, not Forest. So Billi took his crop, assuming that taking a regular amount of fish from a pool counted as a crop.

That worried Billi since without the fish, the valley produced no crop, unless the stones for Tinkerers were a crop because Billi always spent some time digging through the gravel. Rabbit sometimes spotted the stones first now that he'd seen enough to get the idea. Billi listened carefully to that song in his head when they sat by the fire in the valley and he explained what he was trying to do, but the song never faltered.

If he aimed the bow at game, a shot Rabbit thought risky, he could feel Rabbit warning him of the risk. If something dangerous came near there would be a different warning note inside Billi's head. If the pair of them came across prey, something worth hunting, Billi would hear that too. If only Billi could be sure that Rabbit understood what his Hunter intended, then he would know that the Hound agreed with his assessment. Billi certainly couldn't ask anyone else without disclosing what he'd found, and then other Hunters would come here. Rabbit's song definitely said he agreed with keeping this private.

There were a couple of strong downpours through the summer and the efficiency of the big tree anchoring the dam became clear. The waterfall from above the cliff never grew much, but a couple of days after the rain, an increased flow of water gushed out of the cleft and into the lake. That increased the flow over the gravel, but the extra rush of water caused the dam no damage whatsoever. The beavers had built up the sides higher, and the increased flow across the timber centre would take a lifetime to wear it away.

Billi found that he wouldn't be losing any stones due to the downpours. Whatever had been washed downstream from the valley in the past, nothing would be lost now because the beaver pool behind the dam killed the force of the increased flow. Billi actually found a small shiny type stone that had been brought into the lower pool, one embedded in the mud used by the beavers to apply a patch.

After the first downpour there were huge pug marks at the edge of the strip of forest, and scattered fish scales. A Great-Cat came there to drink sometimes and, from the evidence, fish. Billi looked at the marks and wondered if they belonged to a Great Hunter, allegedly the biggest cat of all. That could be a problem if the beast decided it didn't want neighbours though it had tolerated the visits so far. Billi wondered if the beast took all the tithes that he meticulously threw into the bushes there, though Rabbit showed no alarm so the Great Hunter probably didn't come while Billi visited.

Billi could see no indication that the beast hunted any of the game that still helped to keep the plant growth subdued, nor did it fish anywhere else except the pool near the trees. The beast certainly settled one subject;

the goats and chickens wouldn't last one day if Billi left them here unguarded. Billi smiled quietly when Rabbit lifted his leg and accurately marked the pug mark.

Billi built up a good collection of small stones during the summer, despite selling a few to the Tinkerer and Trader caravans that came alternate moons. Most of the stones now came from the gravel bar in the valley and those were the better quality type, the shinier ones the Tinkerers wanted. Despite the amount of searching Billi carried out in the gravel, it would be a long time before he would need to move on to the mud of the dam or even the lower pool.

When Billi dug a hole straight down in the gravel bar he went to the length of his arm. Even then his fingers could feel gravel at the bottom though he couldn't see for the icy, muddy water. After one big downpour his pebbles were gone from the rock pool, which meant that the source probably lay deep in the hill somewhere beyond reach. Billi didn't mind considering the size of the gravel bar, since he only had one life to live and could probably spend it searching there.

* * *

Through the summer Billi let himself be beguiled out of some small stones by the maids of the Tinkerers when they visited. Letting them see his stump came as a real test and reassured Billi since these maids didn't seem to mind him being crippled. He traded the rest of his stones and goods for gold despite their flashing eyes and breathy promises. The little gold ingots, the result of trading a larger number of stones and pelts, were buried under the scree near the waterfall.

Billi also had new cooking equipment at home purchased, with the extra pelts his increased hunting produced. The extra pots, pie dishes, baking and roasting tins and the kitchen implements were very important, according to Bliss. If they kept the pies and occasional loaf of fresh bread coming they were important to Billi as well.

Buying new cooking gear in the hut led to another change in his valley. That started as an old iron pot and a big ladle now surplus at home, left permanently so he could make a bit of stew. Then Billi improved the rocks arranged to hold the pot over the fire, making a permanent fire-pit sheltered by a large boulder. After a couple of blustery days, Billi drove in some stakes and plaited a windbreak from willow shoots. In later visits he improved, enlarged and strengthened the cooking area while sitting under the stars, talking to Rabbit.

"Nothing knocked down our windbreak. Shall we try for a roof, Rabbit? Just a little one, just a shelter as a test? Just to see if the Wild thinks this is Forest or possibly Farm?" Rabbit's song never faltered, and Billi set to with his hatchet and some dead branches to make a sort of plaited wall clear of the fire-pit rock. He laid a few branches between top of the wall or stout fence and the rock. "Since Fellip says they're better than straw, we'll use reeds, Rabbit. Though we haven't got any straw anyway." Billi used the reeds left along the lake banks from last year, and attempted thatch.

Some reeds were waterlogged or part-rotted and the result wasn't truly water-tight. "This is definitely a crop, Rabbit. If we watch the Thatcher, and improve the reeds, we can do better next year." Billi felt happier with that idea because it gave him a true growing crop. He'd half expected the thatch to be torn down and trampled on his next visit but the structure stayed intact. Billi began to wonder just how far he could take this idea. After all, apart from not being on the edge of the existing Farm, this valley matched the rules for claiming new land.

More of Billi's old cooking gear made the trip out to the valley. He made a rough, low enclosure of rocks, then heaved and slid a larger flat one across the space created. A few more rocks, under the edges, and that became a low, very solid stone box that also doubled as a table. Billi put his cooking gear and a bit of food wrapped in hide under there when he left. If he finished constructing a waterproofed wooden lining, he would have a food safe. Billi plaited a willow windbreak across each end of the lean-to. The shelter, "still a shelter, Rabbit, not a hut yet," also gained a small but robust iron mesh that went across the fire to cook on.

Next Billi put together a rough bed to lie on instead of a layer of grass and thin branches. "This place is almost a hut, Rabbit. After all it has a bed if I stuff this hollow in the middle with heather and dry grass, and bring a thick fur? Maybe we can still visit over the winter? We could take another crop, of the small hunters in their winter fur. The shallow water and fish will bring them." The winter pelts on the small fishers and hunters brought the best prices and if he stayed a week Billi could run a trap line and take a good few.

One visit Billi set to and spent two days fishing and smoking the catch. He carried nearly a full pack of freshly smoked fish home, because the local hunting hadn't recovered properly after such a bad winter so food wasn't plentiful. Bliss told him to trade the lot immediately because the local fish run would be in three moons, so right now fresh smoked fish would bring a good price. Sure enough Billi was astounded by how keen the villagers were to trade for the fish. That went into his mental picture of how his valley could provide a living.

The dead trees, bushes and deadfalls provided plenty of firewood and Billi built up a woodpile. Another visit he looked at the size of some of the branches in the woodpile, and ambition stirred. "D'you reckon we can shift a tree, Rabbit? A small one? Maybe if we pick one that will float part of the way? It will dry out once we get it out of the water." The question in the song meant Rabbit knew this would be new, and these days Rabbit liked new. Billi tied his rope to a fallen sapling and tugged, and felt the excitement as Rabbit caught on.

The Hound leapt forward gleefully to seize the rope and heave. A pulling game! Moving even a small tree turned out to be hard work because that still added up to a lot of timber, and without Rabbit and the water to help the task would have been impossible. Despite his three legs Rabbit seized the rope and pulled for all he was worth, and seemed to have a tremendous time. Billi loved the sheer excitement in the song as they worked, and it encouraged him to keep trying. Rabbit's size made the job possible in the end. Billi had a slim, very intelligent, very excited pony helping him.

The pair laid for a little while, exhausted, once the timber came clear of the water near the shelter. Billi talked about how they could spend more time here with a warmer, stronger shelter and Rabbit's song soared. After a rest Billi went to find another suitable tree, and this time Rabbit bounded around as he tied the rope, eager to go for it. By the time they set out for home, three small trees and several large boughs littered the water's edge, drying out.

The next visit Rabbit headed straight for the timber, ready for more, but this time Billi needed big rocks for the foundation. There were some embedded nearby so Billi started tossing the boulders out of the gravel. Rabbit couldn't move the big smooth rocks but proved to be an enthusiastic digger, undermining the edges so Billi could get enough purchase to roll them. The Hound also pounced on any shiny type stones they uncovered, and Billi's collection grew rapidly.

Eventually, as the leaves began to take on hints of gold and crimson, they had enough of both rocks and timber. Billi had to do most of the lifting, but Rabbit provided enthusiastic encouragement both by barking, and in the sheer excitement in his song as the walls started to rise. Billi hacked away with his hatchet, and heaved and rolled boulders, and then Rabbit leapt in to add his brawn to heave on the ropes, and the walls crept higher. Eventually the construction completely surrounded the old shelter, much larger, with one narrow gap for a doorway.

Anyone in the Village who saw the proposed hut would tear out their hair in despair at the construction. Billi built with an odd mixture of whole rocks and tree trunks or thick boughs, then used a rock to hammer home smaller rocks or chunks of timber to brace or fill until the structure stood firm. He gathered mud and grass and used that to plaster the chinks until he thought the result might be windproof. The villagers would weep at the sheer size of the timbers, a terrible waste considering the scarcity of firewood in the Village but Billi had neither the tools nor the skill to split trees into planks.

Billi relaxed, because this new hut, "definitely a hut now, Rabbit," should resist a bear or even that big cat. Billi kept remembering the size of those big pug marks. Those were why he'd used such a heavy flat rock for his food store lid, now providing a table inside his hut. Inside because Billi and Rabbit hauled branches up to lay across as roof timbers, with thinner ones laid the other way to keep out animals and birds. Rabbit could fetch the latter without a rope, and raced up and down the valley collecting them as fast as Billi could put them in place. Finally, the pair collected twigs, leaves, reeds and grass to seal the covering, more or less, with several hides and more thick branches to hold the lot down. The result leaked, but not too badly and Billi moved his bed to a dry spot.

One of the dead tree trunks had split along its length, due to either lightning or frost. Billi gave the Carpenter two small furry pelts for the loan of three wedges and a hammer, and split the long timbers further into thick rough slabs. Hacked into lengths with his hatchet, and with three cross-pieces fastened using a score of iron spikes from the Blacksmith, the timber made a rough, heavy but solid door. Billi used leather hinges but in truth the sheer weight meant the door wasn't really hung, it scraped open and shut. Billi felt his own satisfaction echoed in Rabbit's song the day he could finally heave the door into the opening before leaving their hut really closed up, a proper dwelling, sort of.

* * *

During the other twenty days each moon, back in the Village, Billi spent most of his time hunting, fishing, and taking parties of villagers for wood. He found himself busier than ever before, and despite being away in the valley a third of the time had to trade more meat than ever just to keep room in the store. Billi sometimes went on a three- or four-day trip even when not visiting the valley because the constant heavy exercise made him even stronger, or his leg and back at least. Billi already had very strong arms and shoulders from the wheelchair and then crutches, but the continual travelling with a pack now built the rest of him up to match. Villagers commented on Rabbit putting on weight because Rabbit also built solid muscle, helped by the constant exercise and plentiful fresh meat. As a result, even their two day trips went further than before. Both were now revelling in travelling further than anyone else, being the first man and Hound to see a glade, a stream or a gnarled, ancient tree.

Twice their wider travels revealed fallen Forest giants, great trees that had died or finally been pulled down by storms and the vines and creepers choking them. New big timbers were rare now since any big trees that had fallen within a day's travel of the Village had been brought in long ago, and new falls were rare. Billi's trees were expensive but worth the extra cost of three Hunters as guards, especially since both were true giants. Three Hunters because such a distance meant ponies and villagers out in the Forest for three nights, and both were a temptation for the Wild, especially the plump ponies. The distance to the trees drove home to everyone how far Billi must be ranging, that and his going missing for up to ten days once a moon.

Billi stopped dead in surprise the first time a villager raised a hand in greeting and said, "Ho there, Wanderer." Syman the Stonemason laughed at Billi's expression. "What else did you expect?"

"Stumpy or Billi?" Billi smiled. "Or Stumpy Billi, though a few youths call me Hunter these days."

"The youths have a problem now. They like the idea of a man with crutches being the Wanderer, but fitting it with Stumpy is taxing a few brains." Syman waved a hand down the Village street. "It's good for them to think of something other than maids now and then. Since I've caught you not wandering, Kravitt the Blacksmith would like a word."

That fitted well with Billi's needs as well, since he needed some bits from the Blacksmith so he went straight there. "Ho there Kravitt. I'm after some arrowheads and a bit of ironwork, but Syman says you wanted a word?"

"Yes Billi. How often do you find smaller timber out there? Not big enough to be worth hauling back, but big enough to make into charcoal."

"All the time. That sort of timber is too big to strap on a pack for firewood, and too small to be worth a pony and guards." Billi smiled. "Some is because I'm wandering a bit further than most."

"Hah, yes. Most of us like the name. Some find it funny but watch your back, Billi, there's a few getting very angry about you and your successes." Kravitt sighed. "Angry enough to maybe do something truly stupid out at your place. Maybe not while Bliss is there, but when you stay home, maybe at night."

"With Rabbit there? They must be crazy."

"Maybe one of them is." Kravitt glanced at Rabbit. "He's a brawny lad these days, and so are you, but there's them as can't get past calling the pair of ye cripples. No offence meant Billi."

"None taken. I'll keep a length of firewood by the door, since it wouldn't do to stick an arrow in one of them." Billi stroked Rabbit's head. "Though that might be better for them than Rabbit catching one. He's not best pleased." Billi could hear the edge of annoyance, not quite anger, in Rabbit's song. Either he'd picked it up from Billi or understood what had been said, and Billi still didn't know which. "Was that what ye wanted me for? The warning?"

"No, I wanted to ask about the timber. The thing is, all the timber found close to Trail's End is needed for fires to keep everyone warm over winter. This summer is worse because every scrap had to be collected and burned over winter. I wondered about the costs of a Hunter guarding a youth further out there to watch over some charcoal making?" Kravitt pointed at his forge. "It'll be better than the rubbish the Traders sell me. We're at the end of their route so all the best has gone. Hah, the Village name is a big hint of how they see the world. Trail's End, the Traders think the world ends here."

"How long would the youth be out there? You'll have to hire the Hunter for the whole time." Billi could see Kravitt's face fall. "What about if I built the kiln and made the charcoal? If you advise me how, we'll sort out a couple of lads with ponies and then it's a straight trip out and back to collect when your goods are ready."

"Really? I'd find you a decent saw and a couple of wedges to help with that. Won't it be more profitable if you hunt instead of tending charcoal?" Billi could see Kravitt working through the proposition in his head. "If I tell you the best wood to use, and how to do it, I'll expect first chance at the result and cheap charcoal?"

"We can work the cost out easily enough because I won't tend it. If I set the burn up in a clearing, I can go off and hunt. The Wild won't bother a fire." Billi smiled. "That's a big part of how we keep safe out there at night. I'd actually thought about making charcoal but didn't think 'twas worth it for the price, especially the sort of charcoal I'd end up making. I've never made any nor bought it because wood collecting isn't a problem."

"For good charcoal, decent pieces, the price will make it well worthwhile. After all, the Traders cart the rubbish sort miles up the trail." Kravitt bent and thrust his hand into a sack. "Look at this, tiny bits and dust. It makes my work a lot harder and affects the quality of my ironwork. Now, if we're going into business, did ye want to buy the saw and wedges and a good sharp spade for cutting turf, or hire them and knock a bit off the charcoal?"

"I'll need to talk through how both work out. A big saw and a couple of decent wedges might be handy sometime." Billi meant in his valley. The pair of them set into some serious bargaining and Billi ended up owning a big saw, a medium sized axe to use instead of his hatchet, three wedges because three worked better, and a small but heavy hammer as well as the sharp spade. Billi felt content he'd made a good deal, because the wood came free and he'd not spend that long building a kiln. The tools would actually cost him nothing but a bit of time and would come in handy at his new home from home.

"That hammer will save ruining the back of the axe banging in wedges." Kravitt sounded happy as well since paying in iron worked out cheaper for a Blacksmith, a bit like a Hunter paying in meat. "Keep an eye open for blackstone or ironstone while ye wander, Billi."

"I do, and greenstone. No luck yet."

"You'll trip over some one day. Dig up a turf to set the fire into, or find a place a stream cut through it. That's the usual way." Kravitt laughed. "Ye could teach Rabbit to sniff it out?"

"That would be some trick." One the song said Rabbit wasn't interested in learning.

"I can hire ponies cheap enough if we need them for this charcoal, and pay in ironwork. Do ye want me to find the youths to come out with them?"

Billi laughed. "Not unless you've someone in mind. Perry and Timath will be keen enough and not give me any trouble, or Viktor will want to know why. I can catch the meat to pay them on the trip."

"It'll stop them teasing that Sis of theirs. Not that she cares, I reckon she's already caught her Hunter." Kravitt smiled wistfully. "Brings back memories, a maid or youth running slow enough to be caught by the right person. Most reckon young Hektor is running awful slow for a Hunter."

"I reckon I can run faster." Billi tapped his stump. "Even without the crutch. It won't be too long before I lose my housekeeper."

"Judging by the amount of spare meat Hektor is dropping off for Viktor and his family, most reckon it'll be before Harvestfest." Kravitt sighed. "Though it'll be the usual problem then, which house to squeeze into." He smiled. "Though I doubt they'll mind squeezing at first."

"Probably not." On his way home Billi thought about a new housekeeper and Perry and Timath. He somehow didn't think their pies would be up to much, and he'd be buying bread if he wanted any worth eating.

* * *

Eleven days later Billi hired Bliss' Bros for a fast overnight trip using packs and two ponies with travois to help him carry the charcoal back. Kravitt sounded a truly happy man, exclaiming over the big, clean chunks in the rough sacks. “There’s more than enough for me here Billi, or more than I can afford in one payment. What will ye do with the rest?”

“I suppose I’ll find someone to buy it. I’d no idea what ye needed, so I built two kilns. I picked a spot where there’s plenty of hardwood trees in the area. If I cart some wood to the kilns each time I go past I can make the same again in a moon or two?” Billi had expected Kravitt to take the lot.

“There’s others in the Village will buy some of this because ‘tis good stuff and even the remainder will sell, the little bits, though that’ll fetch less.” Kravitt tipped a bag out. “There’s no dust at all, really.”

“We left that scattered in the Forest because you said ‘twas useless.” Billi felt that counted as a sort of tithe, somehow, though he’d not say or folk might think it odd. “Can ye sell the rest of the charcoal, Kravitt, on commission? Then when I finish the next burn ye can keep enough to last the winter. On credit, since I could be needing some serious ironwork in the spring.” Billi had started considering the benefits of a small stove out in the valley, and could afford it now since this charcoal seemed to be valuable.

“That’s generous Billi. I’ll make sure you get a decent price for the rest, in copper or silver?” He laughed. “Since meat, hides, and stones aren’t a lot of good to you. Unless ye need some extra mugs and dishes, since the Potter will want some of this I reckon?”

“I’ll take some mugs and dishes, and a four pie dishes since if Bliss will be leaving I’ll get some extras made.”

“Good idea. You’d better get her at it because Hektor is looking keener every day.”

* * *

Rabbit and Billi went out hunting the following day but when he arrived home Bliss and Hektor were waiting, looking very serious. “Could ye give us some advice, Billi?”

Billi laughed. “If ‘tis about chasing and such, I reckon I’m the wrong one.”

Bliss blushed but Hektor answered. “The chasing is done, really. I don’t reckon anyone’s running now.” Bliss smiled happily and took hold of his hand, the first time she'd done so where Billi could see and Hektor didn't object so the running was definitely over.

Billi made shooing motions with his hands. "Well get off and give your families the news then. They'll have lots of advice."

Both Hektor and Bliss looked really worried. "It's just that I'm not sure how my family will take it, or how it works. Bliss will bring no land with her brideshare, and a share of a Tanner's business is no good to a Farmer or a Hunter." Hektor stopped and took hold of Bliss' hand between his. "I don't care if there's no share at all as long as I've got Bliss, but the family worries about the holdings getting smaller. My two Sis's will take land away as their brideshare when Ma and Da go to the rock."

Bliss broke in. "I don't want to cause trouble betwixt Hektor and his family, and a Tanner brideshare, only a sixth, isn't much. What are we to do, Billi?" She looked at Hektor. "We don't want to tell anyone until we know it won't cause strife."

"Most of the Village are just waiting for the announcement anyway. Don't worry." Alarm had shown on both young faces. "They've just noticed that the rest of the maids have given up on Hektor despite him being a Hunter, and your Da has enough meat to trade some these days."

"I'm sorry Billi. Do you mind us trading a bit of your meat?" Now Bliss looked worried about that.

"Not at all, is there anything else you want for looking after this place?" Billi didn't mind, he would give Bliss stones if that's what she wanted as long as he could keep going out to his valley.

"A goose or two would help, Billi, for the feathers. For cushions and er, suchlike. Hektor isn't good enough with a bow to knock down birds yet, though he practices really hard." Hektor nodded agreement.

"I've been hunting for years and knocking them down still isn't easy, though it'll not take long for Hektor to get better." Billi kept the smile from his face because suchlike would be pillows. "Hang on a couple of days and I'll ask around." Billi let his smile come because now he had a reason for it. "Nobody will think I'm asking for anything other than curiosity. Not unless a one-legged maid turns up."

"Thank ye Billi. Oh, look, it's nearly dark so I'd better get on home. If

Hektor will walk me?" Billi did laugh this time, and after a moment they both joined in.

* * *

Over the next few days Billi did actually get a bit of teasing, asking what maid he might be eyeing up, but only in jest. The answers meant there wasn't a problem for the couple, a relief for him and 'twould be a bigger one for two other people. When he set off hunting Billi asked Bliss if Hektor could be here when he got back, since he'd got some answers. The quick agreement that Hektor would be waiting confirmed Billi's opinion that the young Hunter spent a lot of time in Billi's hut, when there wasn't a Billi about.

The two apprehensive faces that greeted him stopped all Billi's notions of a bit of teasing. "Relax you two, there isn't a problem. Just let me get my coat off and pack settled and I'll explain."

"There's hot meat and tater pie here, Billi, and I'll make a bit of brew if ye want?" Bliss started fussing, probably to settle her nerves.

"Ale will do, for Hektor as well. Did ye want a drop for a change or there's berry juice?"

"Berry juice, thank ye Billi." As Billi sat a plate with his big slice of pie landed in front of him and two expectant faces looked from across the table. Billi gave up on pie for now.

"First off, the brideshare isn't really a problem. Someone who is due a landshare will want to be a Tanner or something similar and will trade land for a part of the business. Your brideshare, Bliss, to be exact. Maybe a Hunter will want a share in a business in the Village rather than farm their landshare as well as hunt. Sometimes whoever trades will trade again until they get the whatever they are after." Billi started on his pie while the two of them worked that through.

A lot of working through it seemed to involve staring into each other's eyes with happy smiles. Though they did talk, quietly, and came up with another question. "Hektor says he doesn't care, but his Ma and Da might. I don't think a share of my Da's business will bring much land."

Billi swallowed his mouthful of pie. "It might not be a big piece of land but shares aren't always the same. Folk from different families don't bring the same but that doesn't stop couples getting bonded. Over time the farms become split up into smaller and smaller brideshares and landshares and then there's a bit of sorting out, swapping back and forth, to pull it back into a lump around the farmhouse. The result might mean the overall size has shrunk, or maybe grown a bit."

Hektor still seemed worried. "Ma and Pa might worry if the result is a bit smaller."

Billi nodded towards the young Hunter. "As a Hunter you can build up a bit of silver, so you could even buy a bit of land from someone who doesn't need as much." Billi thought this couple had better get on with the official bonding part regardless of brideshares. They had both sat down on the edge of his bed and were holding hands, despite there being one empty chair. Once again discussing seemed to involve mostly looking and smiling a lot. Enough of that for Billi to finish his pie.

"We're still a bit worried, Billi." Hektor glanced at Bliss. "My Ma and Da are crowded already. I've got two Bros at home with their lasses, because they can't build a house or take landshare until Ma and Da go on."

That always caused problems on the Farm. A property couldn't be split up into the landshares until the skulls of the oldest members were on the rock. Until then, couples lived with the man's family, which meant another couple in Barimar's home if Bliss and Hektor bonded. At least with a Farmer there'd be some space outside whereas in Viktor's house, for instance, they'd all be cooped up together. If babes arrived that just made the problem worse.

"I'd ask Da but with Ellibeth coming home and bringing Rubyn, we're crowded as well." Bliss looked down. "Not so much now since I've been here so much Billi, but there's not really any room for Hektor as well. We, er, I've got used to a bit of quiet time to myself."

Billi opened his mouth to point out what Kravitt had said and realised telling them squeezing was a plus might not be a good idea. Not since they were now holding hands on his bed. He sipped ale and thought about what Bliss had said. Actually Billi thought Viktor would welcome a Hunter in the house, but that might not be the problem. Likewise, if Hektor had a room at home now, squeezing Bliss in wouldn't be that hard.

The last bit bothered this pair because when Bliss had mentioned having a bit of quiet time to herself, Hektor had nodded even if he hadn't realised. Though they wouldn't exactly say it the couple wanted privacy when they finally shared a bed, officially. Billi kept his face straight since that was his fault. He had given them privacy and they didn't want to lose it. Despite Bliss wielding a ferocious broom and duster there were quite a few odd corners with a couple of Dapple's hairs caught in them. At least the young Hunter had been discreet, since most of the Village seemed unaware and there were no rumours. Well, if they liked the hut, that could provide a solution. Billi smiled. "I suppose a home of your own would be the best answer."

Yes was written on both faces, but Hektor answered. "That would be perfect, but it can't happen until the landshares are sorted out. That could be years yet." Years sounded like several lifetimes said like that.

"It doesn't have to be a full landshare. If your Da really is crowded, I'm sure your Bros will help you put up a little place. You're a Hunter so you don't need much land to get by. After all it only has to be...?" Billi spread his hands and indicated his plot and hut. After all, Billi lived comfortably with this amount. He watched the flint spark in two pairs of eyes and the tinder flare, and they looked at each other. "Buss her, idiot." Billi got out of there before they made him remember his own situation and feel particularly lonely.

* * *

Two days later, Bliss let Billi know that he would be losing his part-time housekeeper. She had been booked full-time, once the formalities were completed. Neither one intended dragging their feet so that wouldn't be far in the future.

Billi asked Viktor and Barimar for advice and good solid iron pans and roasting dishes would be handy for this couple as a present. Hektor's Ma had to supply two maids with their sets along with their brideshare so there were no spares available. Viktor used every pot and pan he had for his brood since the Tanner didn't have all that many anyway, so he couldn't supply enough for the couple. The next caravan through wasn't Tinkerers and there wouldn't be any more until after Harvestfest, a shame since their wares were prettier somehow. The Traders sold Billi a good solid set of pans, a kettle, and the same selection of ladles and cooking gear Bliss had told him were essential. Since this would be the first bonding gift Billi had bought since his sibs left home, he wanted to do this right.

* * *

Perry and Timath were both negotiating hard for Bliss' job without appearing to do so. They were turning up to help out as they allegedly had nothing else to do, which meant that Billi's garden had been well dug and weeded and his fence put in tip-top shape. The goats were shining with health, the chicken coop in good repair, and the little plot had never been so well tended.

Billi thought that Perry, Bliss' older Bro, had realised the benefits of having a place he could take a maid to practice his own chasing. That might be a trap that shut both ways if the maid suddenly decided to stop running, or even do some chasing of her own. Timath, a bit younger than Bliss, probably fancied the idea of some peace away from the crowded house and the two youths had a strong filial rivalry running anyway. Timath had only just started to wonder about maids.

For either youth, the job provided a chance to get a start on a little nest egg, since Billi found they considered him a generous employer. Not deliberately, he just had a lot of meat and not many mouths to feed. If Billi brought home a goose for example, he didn't chop it in half to pay Bliss. Billi just used another arrow for another goose and gave her a whole one. Viktor had, Billi realised after some time, made sure that a he gave a little something to Bliss for her own nest egg when she put meat on the table. Not the full value or Viktor would have been able to buy meat himself more often, but that he gave her anything when the family only just rubbed along spoke well of the man. Whichever of the youths ended up the job would no doubt benefit from the same arrangement.

Viktor's family only rubbed along because his after his lass went to the rock he had no help with raising the family, or with the work. Perry simply couldn't help as much as his Ma had, not yet, because he hadn't the skill. Billi insisted that Viktor dealt with any pelts or young hides he took though the tougher hides gave Perry some practice. Ellibeth, the eldest maid, had bonded and left home once, and then her man had died. Now she'd come back home but with a littlun of eight summers, as more a burden than help though she also took care of her youngest Bros well. Billi thought Viktor must truly love his six littluns to keep so cheerful about it all.

* * *

The new hut idea worked out well for Bliss and Hektor, since Hektor's Da and Ma were happy to relieve the pressure in the house instead of adding another. His Bros were told they could all squeeze up or they could help Hektor to build himself a 'Billi hut' and they set to with a will. The dwelling would be tight and warm by Harvestfest, and probably in use by Midwinter. The chickens and garden would come with the spring while Hektor's hunting should keep them well enough until then.

There were a couple of current jokes about the couple. One that Bliss would have to let Hektor out of the hut now and then to hunt or they'd starve, since they did tend to be stitched together at the hip. Another joke claimed 'twas the other way about, she'd have to drive him out to get some peace. Neither of the couple cared about any of the jokes when Bliss began to flaunt a secondary tusk from the Great-Boar on a fine chain. With a big smile she told them all that she couldn't wear her other trophy as he was too big. The other trophy wore a smug smile.

Edan had healed up but kept his mouth shut and stayed well out of the way. He seemed to be settling down to guarding cattle and training four guard dogs for the farmyards, burly beasts he'd bought from a trader. Edan intended breeding them as he claimed the beasts would be more help for those without Hounds than the Village ratters. He kept them by the stockyards where they definitely raised a racket if anyone or anything came near and the dogs were big enough to keep small predators off the new-borns. That worked well enough for the stock owners to pay Edan to guard the stockyard at night, though less than a Hunter would have earned.

Opinion split on whether the project would work, because the dogs were going to take some feeding in the winter. The smaller Village dogs kept themselves partly fed by hunting rats and rabbits, but Edan's dogs weren't really agile enough for that. Worse still, Edan had moved out after some strife with his Da so he wasn't in a family with a Hunter and spare meat.

The strife might have to do with the number of times Edan drank too much with his friends. He would start bad-mouthing then, stirring trouble about that cripple, Billi, and the sort of people who befriended him, or stole Hounds. The latter meant Hektor though Edan took care to never say so near the young Hunter. Unfortunately, until recently Billi had been a recluse, so some did wonder if the stories had a real basis.

Billi still didn't see many people. He hunted every day now, for the fat young animals who had plumped up for winter. Even as he laid in more meat and traded the rest Billi wondered why he worked so hard at it. Perhaps because this was just how a Hunter should be and now Billi really had grown into being the real thing. The stack of prime pelts and furs in the rafters above his bed grew and Billi had traded for extra salt so the meat store bulged as well. Billi had never had so much food stored, more than he could eat himself over two winters.

The salted meat sold well to the Traders because that worked out easier than trying to do the job themselves on the trail and meant no wastage. Billi bought more salt with part of the proceeds. Bliss had been right, again, so he would salt more to sell to villagers later in the winter. Almost everyone ran short of food by the end of winter, which explained why the whole Farm worked so hard in the summer to gather in every scrap they could. Now, for the first time, Billi had winter meat to trade and help everyone through the lean times. Perhaps part of that was Billi still being single, since any other Hunter of twenty-five summers had a lass and littluns to support.

* * *

Billi still found time to go out to 'his' valley with some blackberry cuttings to plant along the bottom of the hillside, so that the good grazing would be almost cut off. Eventually, when they grew into a hedge, that would form a trap for grazers or an enclosed pasture for stock. As a bonus the brambles would provide Billi with a lot of convenient blackberries, which he loved. Billi knew he could trade berries for pies and a bit of jam if there were enough, because all the villagers wanted berries.

The villagers organised raids on the Forest berry patches in the autumn, always with extra Hunters and Hounds because the bears loved berries as well. If the bears raided Billi's patch while he happened to be here, they would provide the occasional big fur throw for the bed or a heavy winter coat as well as thick juicy steaks. Bears were definitely plump at this time of year, just before they disappeared for the winter.

Billi had salt in the shelter now as he couldn't carry or eat a whole bear, and the Law said no waste.

The Great Hunter prowled around the rough hut while Billi wasn't there. There were pug marks to show that, but the beast hadn't tried to get in or damaged the roof. From the way Rabbit lifted a leg the cat had marked the place so a competition started with what must be a male. The beast hadn't hunted anything in the valley, or had cleaned up every scrap, but Billi still wouldn't leave stock in here without a guard. Billi felt uneasy but he wouldn't be driven away by pug marks and the beast apparently wouldn't be driven away by a hut. Maybe they could learn to get along side by side? Billi had a bit of a smile at that idea because Man and any Wild hunter, let alone a Great Hunter, didn't exactly share well.

Billi kept the bushes beside the water from growing back and now the beavers helped him by collecting and storing leafy branches underwater. Billi could see the branches down there in the pool with the fish swimming in and out of the foliage. That would stop any fishing with lines in this pool. Because no bushes or saplings were growing to any size the beavers took smaller bushes almost entirely, accelerating Billi's efforts to clear the valley. Billi deepened some pools, putting the silt in others to create a thicker, neater reed bed, more work that might be considered farming.

The Wild didn't seem to be objecting to the hut, and again Billi considered the place as a permanent home. That still wasn't feasible without someone living here to watch the stock while Billi hunted or went into the Village. Though Billi would have to kidnap a maid if he wanted one out here because she wouldn't be impressed by the accommodation. He had fairly basic needs, but having Bliss around the hut made it clear that a lass would expect a lot more.

* * *

"Billi, Billi! Come on, fish run. The fish are here!" Perry already sounded breathless with excitement and he hadn't even started fishing. "I've got to go, see you there." Billi had barely opened his door to answer when Perry raced off towards the river with most of the youths from the Village. The villagers were coming along behind bearing nets, clubs and their thin fishing spears. Rabbit dashed off around the plot, infected by the excitement as Billi gathered his fish spear, bow and the thin barbed fish arrows.

By the time Billi reached the river the youths were in the water, splashing about. They were also guiding the big net out across the flow as a team of villagers heaved on the rope, hard work because of the rocks weighing the bottom of the net to keep it down despite the current.

"Billi, Billi. Over here." Viktor waved from the near bank. "We need a strong arm." Viktor held up one of the round nets that could be thrown out then drawn tight. "You can reach the middle." Billi knew he could. Even when few ever spoke to him, they always made Billi welcome at the fish run. His strong arms and shoulders could propel the small nets out to the middle even with the flick to spread them. This year more people called out to welcome him, almost a half, though a small group of youths on the far bank glared. Edan and his friends kept their grudge alive and well.

Everyone joined in, Hunter or Villager because there would only be three days like this, at most. The silver and gold flecked bounty came once a year, and every possible fish must be caught. Then the whole Village smoked, dried, or salted the surplus and shared the lot between every family there. Billi threw and hauled, threw and hauled, and villagers clubbed the wriggling catch and tossed them onto a growing heap.

The lasses and maids arrived, and knives flashed in the sun as they began to clean the fish. "Hektor's in." Bliss laughed as she pointed, at Hektor trying to climb back onto the raft in the middle where he should be clubbing the catch from the big net. Perry gave him a boost, then dived again. The youths dived to take fish trapped in the big net, and throw them on the bank or the raft.

Even the littluns joined in, those old enough to seize a fish and drag it to the pile after an adult clubbed it. Some were being fed with fresh roe, quickly fried on a metal plate, because lore claimed the treat helped to strengthen littluns against the winter. The maids and lasses had brought watered ale and berry juice, and a few of them cooked fish on a skewer or a mesh using the frying fire. One at a time or in small groups the men and youths stopped to eat, then went back to the harvest.

'Twas nearly dusk on the third day when the elders and Eldest called a halt because too few fish were still coming upstream to the net. Billi and other Hunters were reduced to fishing with bows and fish spears since there weren't enough to be worth a thrown net. "Enough. The rest is for the Wild." A great cheer went up but not as loud as it might be because everyone felt exhausted. The fishing had gone on through the night, with torches blazing above the net and on the banks.

Now the catch had to be saved for the future and already smoke rose from the turf smoking ovens. More fish lay on the racks, drying in the sun, with the littluns shouting and waving to stop the birds stealing any. Ponies were brought out with the empty boxes and the barrels of salt belonging to those who could afford it. That included Billi this year and Viktor and his family agreed to salt Billi's fish for a tub of the salt. He seemed to be turning into some sort of distant family member.

Another two days of work and there were only the drying racks left. The Village cats had staggered back home, bellies swollen, as had the Village dogs. Even the Hounds had eaten enough fish scraps. The rest of the entrails were taken by a dozen Hunters to scatter along the edges of the Forest, as the tithe. The river counted as neither Forest nor Farm, so the Village preferred to play safe and make an offering as if it was Forest. A dozen Hunters and Hounds were needed for safety because the fish always attracted the Wild.

This had been a better year, and the extra fish would make a big difference to many poorer families deep into the winter as food stocks ran low. The heap of timbers built up through the year for smoking fish had almost gone, but now everyone who brought wood from the Forest would throw in a branch or a log to rebuild the stack for next year. A few Village dogs, some youths and two Hunters with Hounds stayed to guard the drying racks and to cover them if the rain came. This had been a good year for another reason, as it only rained for a brief period on one day.

Billi, and probably everyone else, slept late the next day. At least during the fish run Edan and his friends hadn't been able to take advantage of his hut being empty, because their absence would have been noted. Billi spent a slow day recovering, as did Rabbit, but by evening they could both feel the pull of the green. Six days without being in the Forest had become a long time for them, now.

* * *

Billi had intended going into the Village to talk to Bliss but didn't need to. Rabbit raised his head, and Billi heard the welcome in his song.

An excited barking and voices told him Spots, with at least two people, had arrived. He opened the door to see Perry and Timath with a hand cart, and Bliss, Hektor and Dapple.

"Come in. With all the visitors, it's a good job I've got plenty of fish."

Groans greeted him. "It'll be a ten-day at least before I can face fish on a plate." Hektor smiled because everyone felt the same after the fish run. Five or six days of eating fish almost exclusively left everyone sated. "A nice bacon sandwich would go down well, or even dry bread?"

Billi smiled. "Bacon yes, but my bread is very dry. My baker ran off for the last six days."

Bliss laughed. "I can come back tomorrow if you like, Billi, if you want to hunt?"

When Billi saw the glance at Hektor he realised that Edan wasn't the only one in full view of everyone for five days and nights. Bliss and Hektor, even though everyone knew they were to be bonded, had been reduced to hand holding and occasional hugging. Even a quick bussing now and then was frowned on by some of the villagers, and everyone had been at the river. Billi and Rabbit might be missing the green, but Bliss and Hektor were missing Billi's hut. "I wanted to go out to the valley for seven or maybe ten days if you wouldn't mind?" Billi tried not to laugh when the smiles lit up both faces. "Once I've put that lot away."

That lot meant the stack of boxes of salted fish being brought through the gate by Perry and Timath. Perry paused. "Half this load is yours, Billi, since you sent all your share to be salted rather than drying or smoking them."

Timath butted in. "We can put them straight in the cold room, Billi, if you like?"

"Thank ye Timath, that would be handy." That would be easier than Billi doing it with one leg, and both youths knew that.

"Are you still trying to get my job?" Bliss had her hands on her hips trying to look stern.

"Why, are you leaving? What will you do with your time?" Perry ducked because Hektor made a half-hearted attempt to clip him round the ear. The two youths went back to the boxes, laughing.

"Ale and a bit of pie when you're done?" Billi smiled. "If someone will nip down there and fetch a pie since if you wait for me it'll still be cold when you want to eat it."

Bliss smiled at that. "I might be able to find my way." Bliss brought up a pie and they all sat and had a slice and talked over the fish harvest.

"I thought about following the river, to see if I can find a few extra fish. I haven't had chance to build up a big reserve of anything for winter." Hektor sat on the bed with Timath and Perry, and Bliss sat in Billi's spare chair. Billi kept wanting to smile since that only happened when Timath and Perry came in, until then the couple had been sat on his bed holding hands.

"I wouldn't if I were you, Hektor. I do go along the banks the rest of the year, but not just now because the fish run brings the Wild hunters to the banks and some will still be there. They are very jealous of fishing places." Billi never laid his riverside traps until well past the fish run, because either he'd have to fight something like a bear to empty them or the Wild would simply eat whatever the trap caught.

Though he wouldn't mention the traps, since over the years Billi had found a chink in the Law. He'd started by trapping the river banks in the Farm, and gradually extended past the edge of the fields. The river banks seemed to be neither Forest nor Farm, so if he emptied them every day the Wild seemed to accept trapping. Unless something felt hungry of course. "Da said to ask you, since you spend more time along the river banks than most." Hektor sighed. "I'll need to get a surplus built up somehow, because with luck, well." He glanced at Perry and Timath.

"With luck he'll run off with Sis before winter's done, and I can have a room to myself." Perry ducked as Bliss threated to throw her shoe at him.

"You can put any surplus in my cold room, Hektor. If you need more than you've stored, help yourself, then you can put it back next year." Billi hadn't thought of that. Hektor had only just started Hunting, and what he brought at the moment went to his family or to Viktor.

"Next year we'll have our own share of the fish as well, once we're in our Billi-hut." Bliss smiled. "A full share." The Village shared the fish out by the number of those actually fishing, one share for each man or youth, but this year Hektor's share would go to his Da since he still lived at home.

"In your what?" Billi wasn't sure he heard right.

"Our Billi-hut. That's what all the youths and maids are calling it and there's a lot who are very interested in the idea. If it works, there'll be a few more built in the spring." Perry shrugged. "There's also one or two who are bonded and living with their Ma and Da and fancy a bit of space. There'll be no trouble getting help to build since their sibs will be keen to get more room as well."

After a Billi-hut discussion, including gossip about a few that ought to get one as soon as possible, Timath and Perry set off to deliver the rest of the fish. Bliss wanted to make sure about her hut-minding. "Are you sure about a trip, Billi. You're not too tired after the fishing?"

"Thank ye Bliss but I'll head off tomorrow if I may. I'll relax better out there, in the green and in my valley." Billi sighed happily. "The place is so peaceful."

"My valley, Billi? Are you claiming it?" Hektor glanced at Bliss. "Er, Bliss talked about you going there so often, and now, the way you talk?"

"I'd love to but it's a bit far. The neighbours might not be happy if I moved in permanently." Billi meant the Great Hunter. "It would be a bad place to have an accident."

"Well if you ever decide to try, and there's room for two huts? A bit of extra landshare never hurt anyone, nor did a neighbour if there's strife." Hektor got to his feet. "We'll be off now. I'll walk you home, Bliss."

Billi watched then down the path, holding hands and with heads together. They'd be bonded at Harvestfest, only weeks away, and then by rights there would be a moon for either to change their mind. Billi thought the new hut would be occupied long before then, so he'd best make the most of the pies and bread right now.

* * *

Billi took under three days to get to the valley, without stopping to search for stones or even food because he'd brought one of Bliss's pies. As the valley came in view Rabbit had that extra added happy zing to his song and dashed forward. Usually the Hound jumped about in the small shallow pools either scaring the fish or collecting a few for himself but this time Billi heard barking and a small flock of ospreys and eagles rose into the air, mixed with crows, ravens and a few buzzards.

"What have you been up to?" Billi stopped on top of the rise because he could see. A bear lumbered up the slope to one side, and a last few birds finally abandoned branches near the water. "Why are they all here now?" Then Billi saw the dead fish floating in the pool or laid on the banks, and the way the water churned slowly. He moved for a better look, to an angle that let him see beneath the surface.

"We've had a fish run, Rabbit." The familiar fat silver and gold shapes were moving slowly, many apparently dying or already dead. Billi realised that the pool scooped out at the base of the dam by the water spilling over it must be deep enough to allow the fish to jump, which meant this must be where these fish spawned. That was old lore, handed down from the earliest days, that the fish came up the river to breed and die. Then in the spring the tiny young fled downstream but they were never caught, in the hope they would return as big fat adults. Legend and lore claimed that if the young fish were taken, the fish run would never return.

"We'd better get some wood, and smoke a few." Billi looked up and birds were perched on the branches of all the dead trees. "I think we've got competition." Though none of the others were interested in the healthy fish Billi caught. The birds and the occasional bear didn't care if their catches were dead or dying and those were easier to catch. Billi noted that the small pool by the trees had a scattering of scales and bits of fin and tail nearby, so the Great Hunter had been to take his share.

Oddly, despite having just finished the fish run at the Village, Billi found this fishing relaxing. Maybe because nobody rushed about and he didn't need to hurry since these fish weren't going anywhere. The resident fish, a smaller version of the new arrivals, seemed happy to help with clearing corpses but wouldn't get them all and now Billi felt relieved he took his fresh water from the outlet, and not either pool. The rear, larger pool held its own share of fish, though that pool wasn't as crowded. The fish must have wriggled up the wide, shallow flow across the gravel. On the other side Billi could actually see the roe scattered among the gravel until the water deepened and the bottom fell out of view.

Twice in the next few days Billi opened the hut door to find a bear snuffling about nearby, but both times the bear moved off. They were wary of Man and Hound, or maybe of something different because these bears didn't understand the range of a bow. The neighbourhood animals set into this feast under some sort of truce, with smaller cats and the little furred hunters joining in among bears, a few larger cats and the large aerial predators. Trapping a few of the little furred hunters would be easy, but Billi knew the colder weather would thicken their pelts and improve the prices.

* * *

Billi felt trapped when he returned with a pack full of fish, by Viktor. "But I never come to the dances. I'll look stupid with only one leg. I can hardly hop round the garden." Billi felt both embarrassed and panic-stricken. He'd never been to a Harvestfest because by the time he was old enough, he'd only got one leg.

"If you don't come, Bliss and Hektor are going to round up a gang of their friends and kidnap you. I'm sure Dapple will persuade Rabbit that it's a good idea." Viktor grinned. "You've got to be there since you're giving them a well-wishing gift, or I hope you are after what you said. Otherwise they'll be eating everything off skewers or Hektor's spear."

Billi glanced over at his Hound. "What will Rabbit do if I go there?"

"The same as all the other Hounds. He'll hang about at the door and scrounge scraps, or whole pies if anyone leaves them too close. We all know a Hunter won't leave his Hound behind." Viktor slapped Billi on the shoulder. "Come on man, you'll enjoy it. You can sit on a chair with the others who aren't too spry, and poke fun at the rest."

"But they're old men." Billi looked down. "Though I suppose they're still better on their feet than me."

"Older, not yet elders, though they'll be there as well. Look on the bright side, the men sit near the ale and cider table. The older women sit the other side of the dancers." Viktor sniggered. "That's to give them a break, they reckon, but I think it's so they can tell lies about each other. You'll have to judge for yourself though they'll bend your ear about where you've been wandering."

Billi gave up, because Viktor meant well, and maybe he should take a look at how the rest of the Village lived. A little bit of him didn't fancy sitting here all alone again while everyone had fun, though now he had another problem. "What would I bring? I don't really have anything suitable, no ale or such, and I've no oven to roast a big joint." Billi remembered his Ma baking because everyone took something to the Harvestfest.

"Bring one of those big pies that Bliss made. She reckons she made a couple that were the right sort of size, for if you came this year. Bliss also said your pies have a lot more meat in than some, and will be welcome." Viktor stopped a moment. "Ah, no offence but would ye like Perry to nip over and give you a lift with it? 'Twill save the pastry being bashed if you're bringing the pots and pans."

"I'd be obliged." Since if Billi tried to bring a big pie up the steps he'd either drop it or squash it. Billi realised he'd just said he would go. "What do I wear?"

"Have you never been to a Harvestfest Billi?" Viktor's face fell. "Sorry, I never realised. Just wear something clean. There'll be some with fancy embroidery on their coat or dress, but most will wear their best plain." He grinned. "Just in case they dribble pie or spill ale while dancing."

"I'll do both if I try to dance. All right Viktor, and thank ye."

"Not me, Bliss and Hektor won't let you say no, not at their bonding. I'll send Perry down in time to get you there for the grand entrance." Viktor stood up. "Now I'd better get back to see if the layabouts have eaten me out of house and home or wrecked the place yet." Once Viktor went out of sight Billi went through his clothes in a panic, trying to find something he hadn't sewn a rough patch on at some time. He ended up heading into the Village himself with a roll of leather, to see if he could get some new trews made.

The tanned hide from the Great-Boar came in handy after all. The Seamstress thought it would be a shame not to have a jacket to go with the trews, with all that matching leather. A bemused Billi ended up agreeing, then sat or stood as directed while she measured and took notes. Sythyl promised the clothes would be ready for the Harvestfest, and happily traded her work for salted meat and the rest of the boar skin. Billi went home and set into trying to make his better boot look fit for company.

* * *

Perry came through the door to collect Billi and the pie and stopped, and a big grin spread over his face. "Very fancy, Billi. Who are you chasing?"

"Nobody, idiot. Does it look all right? It's not too fancy is it?" Billi had been surprised by the jacket and trews. They were a lot better fitting than his usual clothes and Sythyl had kept the stitching plain coloured but put in a double line of it, weaving through each other.

"No Billi. You look like a Hunter who can bring a pie big enough to feed the Village. That's according to Bliss." Perry gestured. "Shall I get it?"

"If you will, please. I'm not sure which one because she made two really big ones. I did wonder why." Billi had decided he'd have to bring them up a slice at a time when he'd seen them.

"Bliss made two in case you started one of them. If you haven't you've to save the other for the next dance." Perry laughed at Billi's face. "She does this all the time, her and Ellibeth. Organises us and lets us know after."

"That'll be a shock to Hektor."

"Hektor still thinks he chased Bliss instead of the other way round. He'll realise eventually." Perry sniggered. "But I don't reckon he'll care." The youth went off to get the pie and Billi put on his big coat because he could feel snow, or frost at least, in the air tonight. By the time Perry came back Billi stood outside ready. Rabbit's song definitely felt excited, and he ran around them in circles as they went down the track to the Village hall.

The hall usually served as a big storage barn where folk put things they wanted to trade with the Tinkerers or Traders, but the sacks and bales and boxes and bags had all been put into other barns and sheds for the night. The youths had done the carrying and the maids the sweeping and dusting, and both had hung some evergreens around the walls to liven the place up. Now tables were set up at the far end, with chairs for the musicians and those needing to rest.

"We've not done too bad tonight for music. Werne is a proper fiddler, and Guthra has his horseshoes. He can bang out a good stomping tune on them. The cowbells are here, so one of the lasses will be playing them as well." Perry definitely sounded excited. A lot of the preliminary teasing prior to any real chasing happened at the dances, since maids and youths were allowed to dance together and often met young folk from the other end of the Farm. "You'll have to come with me Billi, since the pie is yours."

Perry led the way to a table already bearing pies and a variety of pastries, cheeses, fruits and skewered meats. "That's a beauty Billi. You seem to have skinned it as well." Mandy smiled as she made her joke about Billi's usual way of paying for anything, with big bits of meat and sometimes with the hide or fur still on them.

"Bliss has been practicing her cooking on me. Where do I put this?" Billi swung off his small pack and it clanked as it hit the floor.

"If that's a well-wishing put it by that table, or unpack it and place the gift on the table. Ye can hang that coat on a peg along the wall there." At least Mandy had realised Billi felt lost, and let him know where to go. "If you want to sit it'll be here, in front of the food and drink. If you sit on the chairs over there, among the older lasses, you'll cause a proper scandal."

Billi took off his coat and headed for the chairs then hesitated a moment, unsure of where to sit. "Over here Billi." That came from Devved, an older Farmer, and he waved to a chair. "Get an ale and sit thee down. Otherwise, with a jacket like that, the maids will think you're here to dance." Billi collected a beaker of ale and sat, hoping the bit of a blush didn't show in the lamplight. "Now ye can tell me what that's made of. It looks like pigskin but since it matches the trews, it must have been some pig."

"It was, a Great-Pig." Viktor, heading for the ale, laughed. "I'm pleased you found a use for it, Billi."

"That's from the Great-Boar? Well since you're sat here with nothing better to do, you can tell us the truth of the tale." Billi soon found out that the men seated here really did like to gossip and seemed pleased to get a new victim. Billi's three sibs came over with their bonded to say hello and compliment his new clothes, and seemed pleased to see him at the dance. That came as a bit of a shock, two of them lived across the Farm and sometimes Billi didn't see them from one summer to the next. None of them seemed to be upset about him showing off his stump and peg. Billi always harboured a suspicion he embarrassed them, with him being crippled. Hektor came in with his family, bearing big cooked joints since as a Hunter he should provide meat at his bonding. Traditionally that proved he could support a lass.

Everyone quietened when Bliss came in with her Da and Timath and Billi saw Ellibeth for the first time. She looked younger than he expected, since Billi knew the lass had a littlun of eight summers. He briefly wondered if she'd be lass or maid now her bonded man had gone to the rock. Bliss looked over at where Hektor waited with his family, wearing a very clean set of hunting leathers with a bit of fringing.

Bliss smiled at Hektor and took off her coat to show a string of claws and teeth around her neck, a traditional Hunter's bonding gift. What brought the gasps from the maids were the smaller tusks and the big one in the middle, all from the Great-Boar. That brought a rush as the maids and some lasses swept in to take a closer look and ooh and ahh at the Great-Boar tusk. Not everyone had actually seen the real thing, and only men saw the carved replacements in the alehouse.

The crowd parted, leaving a clear lane to Hektor, and Bliss held out her arms. Not strictly right, and that brought a ripple of laughter, but Hektor didn't care. He strode over and picked her up then carried her back to his own family, waiting with big smiles. That showed everyone whose family Bliss belonged in now.

Her beating on his shoulder and calling to her Da and Bros for rescue was traditional as well though none could have done so anyway because they were too busy laughing. In fact, Bliss had a lot of trouble calling out through her own laughter. When he put her down, Hektor received his first, fairly restrained, public bussing. As their lips parted the whole room cheered and stamped. The bonding was official!

Or almost, as Bliss went off to bring a bit of pie she'd made to show she'd be feeding Hektor in future, and Hektor ate it and assured everyone it tasted delicious. Then the elders got their moment, warning both of them that this was serious, that there were responsibilities involved. Both were told they had a moon to change their minds before moving in together. Near Billi the men were betting on how many days 'twould be before they were both in the Billi-hut.

"Watch out Billi. You'll be next if ye dress like that." Devved laughed, as did the rest, but without malice.

"I reckon I'd have trouble carrying her off." Billi grinned. "Unless she got in my pack?"

"Pick a good strong one, Billi, then she can carry you." Billi laughed with them, because humour helped that little stab at the reminder that he never would have a lass. None would want a one-legged man, especially as she'd have to care for him when that leg gave out. As usual Rabbit's song strengthened and soothed him and at least here was a better place to get over the pang than sat alone in his hut.

Judging by his song, Rabbit thoroughly enjoyed being at a dance. He stood in among the other Hounds at the door, and both Hunters and others were throwing scraps that way. The Hounds didn't squabble over them, as a pack of dogs might, and there'd be no dominance issues despite Rabbit only having three legs. All Hounds seemed to be supremely self-confident without proving anything to each other. Some thought that might be because there were no Hound bitches, others thought each Hound had their Hunter and needed nothing more.

Billi didn't have time to mope if he'd wanted to. "Come on Billi. Da says you're to come with us."

"I'm not family, Perry." Bliss's and Hektor's families were coming together, to show the couple had united them.

"Bliss and Hektor say you're to be there. They say this is your fault." Perry mock-shuddered. "If you want Bliss and Ellibeth to come and drag you over, I'm getting out of the way." By now one of the men nearby had picked up Billi's crutch and another had a hand under his arm to help him up, so Billi shook his head and gave in.

He knew Barimar, Hektor's Da, and Viktor and Perry of course. Timath wasn't old enough to be here by rights but allowed to see his Sis bonded, though he'd leave before the dancing. Billi got to meet Barimar's lass and all Hektor's sibs, and Ellibeth. She complimented him on his jacket as had several others, then Billi went back to sit down as the floor cleared ready for the dancing.

Billi sat among the older men who had their fun laughing at the youths, criticised their dancing, and speculated on who was chasing who under cover of the general merriment. Billi soon found out that the older men were just as keen spotting potential scandal as the youths and maids. The older men also discussed crops and the hunting this year; this had been a good year and larders were stuffed which made for a really cheerful Harvestfest. As the men included him in the conversation and jokes, and asked his opinion on this and that, Billi began to relax. This new social life had turned out better than expected.

Better still, Edan stood there laughing with a group of others without a single glare at Billi. He even flirted and danced with a couple of maids so maybe he'd finally got over it all. Having those dogs might be helping. Billi hoped so, because the happy couple dancing in the middle included his usual hut guard.

A Different Sort of Landclaim

Bliss clung to Hektor, torn between happiness and a little bit of embarrassment. "I'm sorry Billi. I should have been looking after your hut a bit longer, but, well." She looked up at Hektor and "but" and "well" didn't really need explaining. Those who'd bet on six days were in for a payday.

"Don't worry. It'll give me a chance to get ahead of the pies before I'm buried in them." Bliss had been baking every day, and being buried in pies looked a definite possibility.

"Thank you Billi. I'm sure Perry or Timath will look after the hut for you." They all laughed because both youths were waiting about twenty paces down the track to make their bid.

"Get you gone then. You'll need to get settled in quickly else there'll be no pie for Hektor's tea." Billi smiled and shook his head as the pair headed off down the track with Dapple. Pie wasn't really on either of their minds. A voice soon interrupted his musing.

"Ho Billi." Perry wore a bright hopeful smile. "We noticed there was nobody looking after your hut, and Da said we should ask if you needed someone?"

Since Billi had already cleared this with Viktor, the Tanner might have put it like that. "If you'd like Bliss' job you can take it in turns, though you'll have to check with your Da about Timath staying nights." Billi tried to frown and look serious. "I'll expect more work on the land, since I'm told your bread and pies are terrible so you'll not be cooking."

Both broke out laughing which spoiled Billi's attempt at being stern. "Da says the only reason he'd let us cook is to scare the rats away." Not that there were many rats since Viktor's house had an older, wiser ratter than Spots, and that feisty tomcat next door. "When would you like someone?"

"Tomorrow for a couple of days, please. The pair of you had better come in and find out where everything is."

* * *

Billi went hunting three times in the next eight-day, including two overnights, and now knew that dusting and polishing weren't very high on the priorities of either youth. They swept the floor and the place wasn't dirty, but Bliss had left a hard example to live up to. The place still looked no worse than how Billi kept it before his hut had been Blissed, so he didn't mind too much. Warned about the youths' cooking, Billi arranged for fresh bread now and then from the Village and cooked his own meals. He supplied flour, meat, hide, or horns to a villager and a warm, plump loaf arrived in return.

Fellip the Thatcher arrived on the doorstep soon after Billi's latest trip. "Young Timath said ye were back Billi. I wondered if we might look into taking that reed now, before the snow really starts?" There had been a proper dusting on the fields that morning, more than heavy frost.

"That'll suit me. When did you want to go?" When didn't matter to Billi.

"If you'll leave it another four days, then I can take my bit of reed from near the river and make sure everything is left tidy at home. I'll need to get any jobs finished since it'll take four or five days I reckon though not all of that will be reed cutting. Some will be clearing the place for next year." Fellip smiled. "I'll need at least one of the days to arrange borrowing the boats. The elders will want to know everything and I won't tell them else they'll gossip." The three boats were held for the Village to use, either for Hunters to cross the river to hunt to save wading across further downstream, or for the fish run.

"In four days' time? That's fine. Do you still want Timath and Perry? Oh." Billi realised his problem.

"Is there a problem?"

"Not really Fellip. I'll just have to sort out another hut sitter so the four days might be handy." Billi wasn't sure who to ask. He'd check with Viktor since the Tanner knew everyone in the Village, and would know who would be reliable.

* * *

Billi went the next day, and Viktor thought a while. "That's a bit awkward, Billi, since I wouldn't want to take advantage."

"In what way, Viktor?"

"Well, I know a maid who would probably take the job, and do a good job, but it's my Ellibeth." Viktor shrugged. "You've already been very generous and both the younguns will be earning on the trip, so I don't want to look greedy."

"Reliable is reliable, Viktor. I've no problem with Ellibeth coming while the other two are busy with the reed." Billi smiled. "With a bit of luck I'll get some fresh bread without coming into the Village."

"Ha, yes, I'm sure you will. Oh, there might be another problem. Can she bring her littlun, Rubyn?" Viktor gave a little smile. "He's lively but well enough behaved."

"As long as he don't let the chickens out or anything like that?" Some of the littluns in the Village were a bit careless like that.

"No, he leaves ours alone and Ellibeth won't stand for that sort of nonsense. He'll be too busy running about getting the kinks out anyway." Viktor turned to the back of the workshop. "I'll get her in here so you can ask, since she's another with a mind of her own." He raised his voice a bit. "Ellibeth, have ye a minute please."

The maid didn't take long. "Yes Da. Oh, hello Billi."

"Hello Ellibeth. I'll be taking Timath and Perry out all day for probably a five-day. I wondered if ye could care for the hut, same as Bliss did? I'll be back each night." Billi glanced from Ellibeth to Viktor and back. "The pay would be waterfowl since we'll be by the river."

"Do you still need someone, Billi? I thought Edan had stopped all his nonsense?"

"Maybe Ellibeth, but he's still talking in the alehouse, and some are still listening." Billi had heard an anonymous 'cripple' from behind him on the way here, but didn't even bother to look back. That would just encourage whoever 'twas and they'd be hidden or looking innocent anyway. "I'd rather be safe than sorry if you don't mind?" Billi also liked coming home to a lit fire, the chickens being fed, the eggs gathered, and the goats milked. He might be getting soft but a note in the song said so was Rabbit, and he liked the idea of a warm fire waiting.

"As long as Rubyn can come? I'll keep him in hand." Ellibeth glanced at her Da. “You did tell Billi.”

“He doesn’t mind, Ellibeth.”

“Then yes, Billi. Let one of my sibs or Da know when you want me. Rubyn will enjoy running about in the fresh air even if it’s cold.” She went back inside the house.

“That will be odd. I can’t remember the house being empty.” Viktor smiled at Billi’s look. “No, I don’t mind. Thinking about it I’ve never known the house empty. I bonded before my Ma and Pa went to the rock and then there were littles. I’ll find out how you live.”

“Not really. I’ve always got Rabbit, and sometimes One-shut.”

“Of course, and since Mouse will be here I’ll not be alone either.” Viktor laughed at Billi’s look. “He’s a dog and a ratter, but caught his first mouse young enough for it to be his name.”

On the way home Billi thought about that, being alone. Since that day, nine summers since, he always had Rabbit and his song. Rabbit kept him informed of how the Hound felt, what he thought of what Billi was doing, if sound or scent suggested danger, and if he’d gone off chasing a flutterbye. A whole conversation in a song with no words, running through Billi’s head every waking moment. Billi felt lot better off than most, despite his leg.

* * *

Ellibeth turned up with a little parcel of food because with Rubyn along there were two to feed, a replay of Bliss turning up so Billi just showed her where everything was. Then he explained not bringing food and showed her the cold room. Her eyes widened when Ellibeth saw the buried store, much better filled this year, so Bliss hadn’t been telling anyone tales. They came back up and Perry let Rubyn, kept by the gate until his Ma had done with business, come to greet Billi.

Although Ellibeth seemed quite young, Rubyn really was eight summers of barely suppressed energy. Excited and curious, and obviously struggling to obey instructions to be good, he almost bounced up and down while being introduced and his eyes were devouring everything. Then he met Rabbit and Rubyn went very quiet.

“That has quietened him for once, and me a little bit as well. We see

Hounds round the Village and they are always so well behaved but I never realised just how big a Hound is until now, in among ordinary furniture." Ellibeth sounded awed and Rubyn had been struck speechless, probably because even at a tall eight summers Rubyn still only stood eye to eye with Rabbit. Billi got out before the littlun exploded again. He could hear Rubyn's excited voice before he made it out of the gate.

* * *

When he arrived at the river there were three youths, Perry, Timath and a stranger. Fellip called the youth over. "This is Gordi. I thought about those reeds, and the state of them, and we'll need the extra hand this time because a bit of digging to keep the water flow right will stop the edges drying out." Fellip smiled. "He's one of my nephews so he'll keep his mouth shut, sort of keep it in the family."

Billi opened his mouth to say Perry and Timath weren't family, but Bliss and Viktor had both treated him as a sort of family. Instead he nodded towards the boats. "Another youth means we don't have to spell them pulling a boat." There were two, and each held big coils of rope and a selection of tools. "Will two boats be enough?"

"Now I know 'tis upstream we only need the boats to carry the tools, and us on the way back. We'll make reed rafts and use the boats to control them while float home." Fellip rubbed his hands together. "Right, let's get moving. Will the snow bother you?"

"No, not a little bit like this. I could do with a foot on the end of the peg when it gets deeper, and on this thing." Billi waved his crutch. "But 'twould be clumsy any other time." He struck off upstream along the bank. "The boats will be handy to get across without going downstream and wading. The other side of the river is soft here but easier going further up." Billi concentrated on picking a good path. Behind him he could hear the three youths chattering and commenting on the new scenery, and taking turns to have a break since one could tow each boat. Fellip soon started asking questions about the birds and the plants which weren't really very different from those on the Farm, though the birds were a bit bolder.

Villagers didn't travel along the riverbanks. Although clear, the banks definitely weren't Farm, but weren't really Forest either. The Wild used them to travel, or where the banks were low enough to drink or cross over. Billi pointed out the marks of deer and boar, of fox and badger and rabbits, of three wolves where they crossed, and once a big cat had come down to drink. Fellip looked entranced, which once again reminded Billi that most villagers never went anywhere new. The boats did make crossing over much easier, and the better footing on the other bank meant they made good time over the second part of the journey. "It isn't just snow you need a foot for, Billi. The swampy sections on the other side slowed you up on our first trip."

"True, but once again I only need that now and then. I can hardly pack another crutch and peg leg along just in case." Billi glanced back. "Those three should be pleased we crossed over."

"Oh yes. They would have sunk up to their knees in that mud with the strain of pulling the boats." Fellip smiled. "Even so, they're saving their breath now for pulling instead of nattering. Though we're close now, aren't we?"

"We are, another bend and we'll see it. I hope it didn't catch fire. All that dry reed would only need one thunderbolt." Billi had only just thought of that.

"No, it'll be there. If it had burned we'd have seen the smoke from the Village. Not only that, but low reed beds next to the river won't attract the thunderbolts. Ye know yourself, it's the tallest trees." Fellip eyed up Billi. "You'd best not stand in a field when there's thunder, Billi."

Billi held up his crutch. "I wouldn't want to get my branch scorched. We can see the beginning of the reed now so it would be best if you all wait here a while. I'll just sneak along the edge of the trees and deal with dinner and pay, though I won't get out of sight." Billi took off his pack and only took his bow and a dozen thin arrows. "Does anyone care if it's duck or goose?"

Nobody did, they were all more impressed by Billi's sheer confidence that there would be one or the other, and that he'd get one. A Hunter wouldn't be impressed because a reed bed kept the Hunter and Hound concealed from wildfowl, and such a place always had plenty of such feathered diners. Billi moved along the edge of the trees, slowly and quietly, and soon had four ducks. The fifth duck flapped and made a racket, but Billi had an arrow in the bow fast enough to take a goose as it rose, alarmed.

"Come ahead now." At the call the youths heaved on the boat and Timath, not currently pulling, came running up to see what Billi had caught. Rabbit splashed into the shallows and came back with the goose, carried carefully to preserve the arrow. Then he went after the ducks.

Fellip stood, hands on hips, and had a good look at the reeds. "Just in time Billi. A few more years and there would have been proper saplings along this edge as it dried out, and bushes among the reed further in. Not now. We can clear seedlings and creeping weed without breaking any Law." The boats were tethered and a selection of different shaped blades, forks and spades came out of them. The three youths were soon pulling and cutting as instructed.

* * *

By evening there wasn't much reed bundled despite the amount of work. "We've cut enough to make a couple of rafts, but most of today has been weeding and clearing. I've had a better look now, and this really will be a good bed when its sorted out." Fellip chuckled. "Another year we can sell some to the Traders. That'll be a shock for them when they produce their rubbish and tell me how good it is." Billi got the impression that showing the Traders up might be at least as important to Fellip as selling the reed. The Thatcher produced a small scroll and made notations. "Usually the cost of the labour is added to the price of the reed. Since you've paid them, I'll owe you that."

Billi looked at the selection of ducks and two geese laid on one of the two big reed rafts. "I didn't even think about that. I usually pay my way like that, with whatever comes in front of my bow and here it will be waterfowl. I could find some fish as a change?"

Fellip pulled a face. "Not really, not so soon after the fish run. Even us villagers have had enough at the moment. Gordi is really pleased with a brace of ducks and says his Ma will want the feathers so there'll be no waste." Fellip nodded towards Perry and Timath. "Viktor will get a new pillow if you do that on the other days."

"Are you sure one is enough for you?"

"I'm the employer so I shouldn't be paid Billi, but yes, the duck is very welcome and plenty for me and my lass. Being in business with a Hunter is definitely different. Now climb into the boat and relax, Billi, the Wild can't reach us so you can have a little snooze on the way back." Fellip waved to the other boat. "Cast off, let's get home." Rabbit jumped into the boat before Billi.

* * *

The ride back definitely felt restful. Billi took his two geese home and as he came through the gate breathed in the smell of fresh bread. The warm hut had been polished to within an inch of its life and all the spiders were homeless again. Billi smiled quietly, as he could see a definite hint of Bliss in the way Ellibeth bustled about. Their Ma had taught her maids well before she went to the rock. Ellibeth had a hot pie waiting in the oven and warmed ale in a mug, another Bliss-like touch.

Rubyn still looked wary when Rabbit came in. "Come and say hello, Rubyn. He won't bite. In fact, if you sit there, where there's a fur on the floor, he'll come and lie next to you." Rubyn looked at the big fur and the Hound. "That's his bed."

"Go on Rubyn. If Billi says it's all right, it will be. Bliss says the Hounds are very gentle." Rubyn looked at Rabbit, and his Ma, and she gestured towards the fur.

Billi offered a piece of pie crust with gravy on it. "Here, give Rabbit that once he's laid. He'll have a bit more later." Billi offered another piece. "One for Spots, or he'll be jealous."

"I kept the scraps from cutting the meat. One-shut had some and Bliss said the rest and a bit of gravy are usually saved for Rabbit." Ellibeth pointed at a pot with a lid. "In there."

Bliss seemed to have made a list of what Billi expected or Bliss had taught him to expect, which came as a pleasant surprise. "That's right. Rabbit eats out in the Forest, but always has a bit of mine as well."

Billi finished his pie while talking about the reed cutting. Ellibeth seemed interested, because that world was all new to her. Rubyn sat quietly with a hand on Rabbit, and Spots laying the other side, entranced. Though that stopped once he headed home and Rubyn chattered continually. The littlun marched along with the goose slung over his shoulder for all the world as if he'd caught it himself, right up to when they went through the front gate to Viktor's house. Then he legged it into the house shouting "Ganda, Ganda, look at what the Hunter give Ma!" at the top of his voice.

Ellibeth shrugged apologetically. "He's a bit excited."

"Not a problem to me. Save the feathers from that and you can trade them. Someone will want to fill a pillow." Billi raised a hand as Viktor showed briefly at the door, coming to see what the fuss was about.

"I'm sure someone will want them. Same time tomorrow, Billi?"

"Yes please. Goodnight, Ellibeth and thank ye." On the way back Billi reflected how much nicer his dusted, swept and warm hut had been. He would be ruined again after five days of this and would need a ten-day trip to the lake to toughen again.

* * *

On the fourth day Viktor met Billi at the door when he delivered Ellibeth and Rubyn, looking embarrassed. "It seems a bit ungrateful, Billi, but would you mind if I sell some of the fowl as they are?" Viktor gestured at the brace of ducks Rubyn carried. "Since you've no doubt given the layabouts a brace each, that's six. I can save them, but they'll fetch a better price now, fresh. If ye don't mind?"

"They're yours to do as you wish. Make sure you get a good price mind you, those are prime birds and fresh today." Billi laughed. "Don't go undercutting the other Hunters or they'll be cursing me."

"Don't worry Billi, there aren't enough waterfowl coming into the Village to bring the price down, especially ducks. Hunters tend to go for big meaty prey." Fellip looked at the ducks. "Much obliged, Billi."

"Make the most of it, Viktor, since we'll be done tomorrow. Timath and Perry will tell you anyway when they get back from carting reed from the river to the Thatcher's."

"Oh yes. We'll get a blow by blow of the whole day. They're both practicing with a bow because they reckon with luck the Wild will remember them and send a Hound." He nodded at Rabbit. "Young Rubyn wants one as well, but so does every lad and youth."

"Same time tomorrow Billi?"

"Yes please. Goodnight Ellibeth."

“Good night Billi, goodnight Rabbit.” Ellibeth seemed much more relaxed around the Hound after watching him with Rubyn four evenings.

On the way home Billi turned it over in his mind. He had assumed that Viktor would sell or trade what he didn’t want, as Billi did. The Tanner and the Hunter really did live in different worlds and Billi occasionally understood why Edan had been bitter about not getting a Hound. Edan’s Bro had a Hound as did his Da so he’d seen all the advantages but couldn’t have them. Billi understood, but it didn’t excuse what the youth still said and what he’d done. After all some houses had no Hound at all and did well enough with hard work.

Edan’s reaction over Hektor getting the spear and then the rudeness that led to him getting a slap and no meat came down to arrogance, or just nastiness, and started before the Hound failed to turn up. Actually it still wasn’t too late for a Hound, but the whole Village seemed to have assumed that wouldn’t happen for one reason or another. Even Edan felt that way though it wasn’t his fault of course. At least after the bonding the troublemakers had settled down to occasional lies and insults, though never to Billi’s face.

Tonight, Billi had a visitor when he arrived home. Fellip waited by his gate. “Do you have time for a talk, Billi?”

“Yes, all evening, Fellip. Come on in.” Fellip settled into a chair and Billi supplied a beaker of ale.

The Thatcher brought out his scroll of reed paper. Billi had been really interested when he first saw the paper because he’d seen very little about and this looked thin and quite smooth compared to most. “I’ve been thinking about the reed, long term. We’ve done a lot of clearing and digging, which will pay a big dividend next year unless someone else moves in and cuts the reed early. After all it is out in the Forest, not part of a landclaim.”

“True enough.” Billi laughed because the distance to the reed bed put it well outside the Farm.

Fellip hesitated and took a deep breath before continuing. “I was wondering about making the reed bed a landclaim, then nobody would try to take advantage of our work.” Fellip chuckled. “I can’t do it of course. Only a Hunter can, so the claim would be yours.”

"But I can't work it." Billi gestured to his stump and peg. "That's why I have no landclaim here, bar this little plot and hut." Billi frowned in thought. "I couldn't guard it from the Wild."

The Thatcher leant in, intent. "But the Wild aren't interested. The wildfowl will use the reeds to feed and nest, and now and again something big will smash a hole down to the water, but otherwise it will be ignored. After all," Fellip shrugged, "it's there now."

"But can it be claimed? Other Hunters will have seen those reeds and taken wildfowl there." Billi started thinking it through properly now. Was this so very different to what he'd started doing out in the valley? Was this a way to test his half-formed ideas about the valley?

"But Hunters have taken prey in every bit of Farm, before it was claimed from the Forest. This time we have to claim it before there's a fire instead of after. After that, if you don't mind, Hunters can still take fowl?" Fellip smiled. "I could work out a deal then for me to keep the reed bed productive and take the reed, and you to claim it, guard the workers, and get a share of the profits?"

Billi sipped ale and thought about it. The five days guarding would be a tidy bit of regular work all on their own, and a share of reed would be a bonus. They talked it over and there seemed to be a steady bit of business here, year after year. "I reckon yes." Rabbit seemed excited, despite a little caution, but no real dissention showed in his song. Billi smiled "After all, if it doesn't work, the reeds can be left for the Wild and the Forest to reclaim."

"So would you prefer me to buy out your share of the reed, or pay you as the reed is used or traded?" Fellip shrugged. "You will get guard pay anyway for all the visits unless you let another Hunter stand guard. That will come out of the profit, as will the pay for the youths." Fellip chuckled. "Or you'll be paid for whatever that bow of yours brings in to pay them."

"I'll need to think on that, Fellip. This is all a bit sudden. I'll also want to check with the elders and see if I can claim the reed bed. I know the tales speak of plots claimed away from the Village, but they are all warnings." Billi sighed. "Which worries me."

"Ah, but those tales talk of a plot surrounded by Forest, a plot the Wild want as well. The tales talk of crops and stock lost, not of what grows there naturally." Fellip unrolled a second scroll. "Take this to the elders. 'Tis a drawing of the reed bed, with the dimensions paced out and a description." Fellip smiled. "Get more patches like this and you'll have a good landclaim, and the maids will pay attention."

Billi laughed, because Fellip's voice showed no malice. "They already pay attention, Fellip. Stumpy Billi, remember."

"You never know. Three or four plots like this, and one may look past that leg." Fellip rose and put out his arm to clasp. "We have an agreement, Hunter?"

Billi clasped arms. "We have an agreement, Thatcher."

"Then I'll leave you to think. It'll take me a few days after we get the last reed home to work out what we've got and how good it is. Then we can sit down to sort out a value, and maybe decide on the rest of the proposition." Fellip put on his coat. "I'd better rest up. We'll try to finish tomorrow."

"I'll think on it, and while you calculate I'll talk to the elders. If they say yes, I'll give them this." Billi indicated the drawing. "If the landclaim is sorted out, we can beat out the details. Meanwhile I'd better rest as well."

* * *

Though it took a long time before Billi could rest. He talked the whole proposition through with Rabbit and One-shut, or at least he talked about it out loud and they pretended to listen. As usual Billi found that helped him to settle his ideas down. Talking out loud got his notions lined up to be beaten into shape. Billi listened to Rabbit's song as he did, in case it changed, but Rabbit seemed very happy with whatever the Hound thought Billi intended.

There must be a limit to what Fellip proposed. Billi had a vision of himself and Rabbit clumping around the forest from one patch to another, trying to keep each one weeded and tended and cropped. He smiled, imagining a line of youths carrying hoes and scythes and following along like ducklings. Rabbit seemed to get that idea when Billi explained it, because a real note of humour showed in the song. Though another thought kept nudging in, about a valley big enough so he needn't wander from place to place.

* * *

The following day Billi found Gordi laughing when he arrived at the river. "You've started something, Billi. Perry says his Sis has a pillow half stuffed with goose feathers and is keeping an eye open for any more in the Village. She says they're softer than duck feathers."

"You should have said, Perry. I would have given her another." Billi had given Ellibeth a goose on two days, and a brace of ducks on the others.

"Hide and horns, Billi, don't tell her I said anything. She'll skin me. Ellibeth is scarier than Bliss, and she told me keep quiet. She's well pleased with the ducks." Perry did actually look worried.

"Well it would be no bother. I only take what comes first, and there's a lot of wildfowl round there." Billi decided to look for a goose deliberately today, because he really did appreciate the clean hut and warm food. That would also finish off her pillow without having to trade for feathers. Billi remembered telling Ellibeth to trade the feathers, and her saying someone would definitely want them. Once again Billi had assumed someone already had an item that any Hunter would own, a feather pillow.

As usual Billi went ahead to see what he could catch unawares. This time when they arrived the rest gathered round to have a good look at his catch. Not the ducks, because they'd seen a good few of those. "What is that?" Gordi looked baffled and so did the other two youths. Billi thought Fellip might know though he kept quiet.

"That's a gobbler. A big prime male. They came for the heap of weed you've been stacking up." Billi gestured at another bird, one with mottled brown plumage. "This other one is a female and that's why it's a lot smaller."

"A lot smaller but still a big bird, though nothing like as colourful. That male will take some eating." Though the way Gordi eyed it up he fancied trying some at least.

"You've maybe had some before but didn't realise. Once the feathers are off and 'tis dressed gobbler looks very much like a swan." Billi looked at the one he'd killed. "Though this one would be a big swan."

"If I'm right, there's more dark meat on one of these than on a swan. I think 'twas Eddmune had some luck at the right time and brought one to the Winterfest a few years back." Now Fellip looked puzzled. "Why don't we see more gobblers with them being that size? Hunters bring in deer that might not weigh as much as that."

"It's a big fowl even for a family so they are often cut up and frozen down if the weather is cold enough. That's not often, they're harder to find then because the males don't make such a noise. The best time to hunt gobblers is when they strut in the Forest glades, attracting the hens. The ones caught then are eaten straight away because that's in the warmer weather." Billi looked at his prize. "Though this can be frozen."

"That's sorted out what you bring to the Winterfest, Billi. Mandy will love that in the middle of her display. Unless you eat it or trade it first?"

"Winterfest?" Billi had only just survived his first Harvestfest. Though a lick of happiness in Rabbit's song caught him by surprise. Rabbit must have enjoyed Harvestfest, or maybe all the treats.

"You'd better be there." Fellip waved an arm over the expanse of stubble and the remaining reeds. "I'm not explaining this to everyone without help."

Billi looked at the gobbler, which he'd decided to give to Ellibeth to fill her pillow and for Viktor to feed his layabouts. Now Fellip had marked the bird down for Winterfest, so he still needed a goose. Billi looked round. That wouldn't be easy because there weren't any. They'd flown off while he'd been busy shooting these. "While you work I'm going to move back a bit to the last bend, to see what turns up to collect the floating weed. I'll still be near enough to guard, and Rabbit will hang back nearer to you and warn me if there's need."

"You're the Hunter Billi, so if you think 'tis safe go to it. Now come on you three, enough of admiring Billi's catch, we've got reed to bundle." The youths moved off with good-natured grumbles about mean, brutal employers.

Billi moved back to where he could see the next stretch of river and settled down with his bow. Clumps of weed were soon drifting down the river as the youths and Fellip disturbed them during their cutting. Billi hoped for geese but eventually three swans swam around the further bend, following the bounty upstream. Billi sat very still and debated. A swan seemed a bit big for a day's wage, but then those feathers would definitely fill up that pillow.

Eventually the swans moved closer and one came in range for a safe shot, one that wouldn't leave the bird wounded but able to fly. He definitely couldn't risk that since Billi couldn't follow until the prey eventually landed, not with four people here to guard. He waited a little longer, but the other two stayed back. Billi raised his bow and drew, very slowly and carefully, and locked his arms. For long moments Billi waited until the nearest one turned to give him a shot that would pin the wing, and then he loosed.

Rabbit had moved slowly closer as Billi took aim, poised, and started running as soon as the arrow left the bow. The Hound hurtled past Billi and into the river, heading straight for the struggling bird. Meanwhile Billi kept one eye on the Hound in case the other swans moved in, and tried to watch the reed cutters as well. As soon as the other two swans took off he stumped back up the bank to the reeds.

Fellip stood up and looked past Billi. "What's the commotion?" The reed cutters could still hear plenty of splashing and growling though the hissing back round the bend had stopped.

Rabbit could take a dying swan with a pinned wing even in water so Billi didn't worry. "I've found something to fill the rest of Ellibeth's pillow."

"It'll take a big goose." Perry tried to look but Fellip nudged him and pointed to the reed, while Billi just grinned and wouldn't say any more. The noises died out and a little while later Rabbit came around the bend of the river towing the swan in the water, much easier than dragging the dead weight. Billi went to help the Hound get the prize out of the water, and Fellip came as well.

"That'll be some pillow, Billi."

"Aye. They're always a bit bigger out of the water and this one's nigh on a match for the gobbler. It was the nearest, or I'd have taken one of the smaller pair." Billi smiled. "Not that Viktor will mind when it's in the oven making gravy." He looked at the pile of fowl. "I'd best get this lot cleaned. I'll take the tithe well into the trees."

"Oh yes." Fellip looked over the reed bed and chuckled. "Away from your new bit of Farm."

* * *

Fellip called a halt mid-afternoon. Billi looked over the stretch of stubble, definitely all stubble now. "Now that's a sight." A huge heap of weed, seedlings and old, rotten reed back inside the edge of the trees showed why nothing grew any higher. "We've even given the tithe to the Wild."

"True enough, odd as that seems." Fellip looked at the heap, which Billi had asked the youths to help him move, with new eyes. "You seem very careful about that Billi. I can't think of anyone else who'd give a tithe of weeds."

"The Wild is good to me, and giving a little back costs nothing." Billi pointed, sweeping his hand across the weed bed. "I find this unbelievable, that this really will all grow back, as tall and thick as it was when we arrived." The wide expanse looked ravaged, stripped until Billi could see the water running slowly between the stubble. Water that ran a little faster in places because of the digging Fellip had asked for.

"I promise this will be back just as thick and strong next year, probably thicker and stronger after the mass of weed and rotten reed we pulled away." Fellip rubbed his hands in what had now become a familiar gesture. "Early finish today, so we'll have this lot landed and in my back yard before dusk." He went to chivvy the youths into tying the last bundles onto the ungainly rafts tethered to the boats.

A definitely festive air descended on the party as they drifted home, with the youths splashing each other and making jokes about each other, the gobbler, and Gordi chasing one of the maids. That continued as the youths laughed at Billi loading up with his day's catch. He probably did look comical with a swan and a big gobbler on his back, even with their wings strapped tight. Gordi looked really pleased with the female gobbler instead of a brace of ducks. He still maintained his family had never tried the birds before, and reckoned his Ma would love the feathers.

Spots heard Billi opening his garden gate and as Billi lowered the swan and gobbler, Ellibeth came to the door. Rubyn peeked past her and his eyes opened wide. "What are they, Billi?" The littlun looked closer. "That looks like goose but a lot, lot bigger and all white but I don't reckon that's a goose of any size." He pointed at the gobbler.

"That's a gobbler and wouldn't swim too well and the other one is a swan. They came a 'calling so I brought them home. The gobbler is for the Winterfest." Billi chuckled. "Fellip says I've got to go to back up his stories."

"And to show off your new clothes. You'll be spending plenty of time explaining the gobbler since I don't reckon many have seen one, me among them." Ellibeth smiled. "Not with the feathers on anyway and maybe not without. You'd better bring them inside or half the Village dogs will be here trying for a piece."

"Not with Rabbit here, but the crows are bolder." Billi pulled the two fowl inside and sniffed at the aroma of roast pork.

Ellibeth chuckled. "Since you'll have no cook tomorrow I put in a joint with roots and taters, and there'll be gravy once I get to it. I thought you could save the rest of the roast to eat cold, with the fresh bread. You could carry that with you when ye go wandering, to save stopping."

Billi sniffed again. "Mmm, yes, fresh bread as well." He sat and pulled off his boot, and put on the soft one he wore indoors. A beaker of warm berry juice landed on the table.

"Now while dinner finishes cooking, you can tell us about that gobbler. Where on Forest and Farm did you find it?" Beyond Ellibeth, Rubyn settled down on the fur with Rabbit and Spots. His hopeful gaze went from the gobbler and back to Billi.

"Well, this one came uninvited and unexpected. But usually…" Billi found that his attentive audience wanted to know all about gobblers. Why the males strutted, why they were called gobblers, and where they usually lived. Eventually, by the time Billi finished his dinner, dusk was drawing in.

"I'd best get you home so I can start dressing that." Billi gestured at the gobbler.

"It'll take you all night just to pluck it. Those feathers are pretty." Ellibeth pointed at the shiny reds and greens on the gobbler's neck.

"If you'll pluck it ye can keep the feathers. They'll go with those." Billi pointed at the swan.

"How do ye mean Billi? You want me to pluck the swan as well?

Though taking the feathers is too much just for plucking. I'll dress and pluck them for the feathers?" Ellibeth estimated, looking at the birds. "It'll take me a while."

"That's a deal for the gobbler, but the feathers on the swan are yours anyway. That's today's pay since I couldn't find a goose." Billi laughed. "That should finish off the pillow. Ah." He'd just remembered. "Don't skin Perry. He didn't tell me, Gordi did."

"I'll skin him anyway for spreading my business about." Though Ellibeth's heart wasn't in the threat because she was staring at the swan. "A swan is too much. Either find something from the store, Billi, or I'll give ye some fowl from home when we get there."

"All right." Billi figured that once the swan was in Viktor's house, it would be harder for her to say no.

"I can't carry that." Rubyn sounded despondent.

Billi knew the littlun enjoyed showing his Ganda the day's pay, so there had to be something small to add in. "I noticed fresh straw in with the hens. Where did that come from?" Billi hadn't tonight, but he'd noticed a bit of fresh straw other days so that was a safe bet.

"I picked it from the fields nearby. Ma said 'twas all right if I took Spots and stayed close." Rubyn looked anxious. "Ma said I could take the straw left by the Farmer after harvest."

"True, but there's only scattered bits so I never have the time to collect enough. Since you spent the time," Billi sighed, "I suppose you'll need paying." Ellibeth started to object but Billi raised a hand to stop her. "Since 'twas for the hens I suppose they'd better pay. I reckon two eggs. What do you think, Ellibeth?" Billi nodded at the question in her eyes.

"Well I don't know. I thought he was playing more than finding straw." A spark of mischief showed in her eyes.

"But it was a straw-finding game? So work as well? Please, Ma?" Rubyn's eyes were bright and excited. He was going earn two whole eggs!

Ellibeth shook her head in resignation. "I'd not be as soft, but since Billi seems to be feeling generous you'd best take advantage." Rubyn's eyes moved back to Billi.

"Two eggs it is, providing we've got two left someplace?" Billi looked round as if searching for them while Rubyn kept starting to get up to fetch them, then stopping because he wasn't sure he should.

"I reckon." Ellibeth tried not to laugh since Billi's hens produced more than that every day.

Billi suddenly 'discovered' the big bowl with the eggs in. "I'll sort out a couple or maybe you should. Brown or white, Rubyn?"

Rubyn shot to his feet as if he'd been sat on a stinger nest. "Brown taste better, Billi, if you don't mind?" The two adults stood, smiling, while Rubyn debated over choosing two out of the five brown eggs. He cradled one in each gloved hand all the way home, and went into the house with no dashing this time. Though he still shouted.

"Ganda, Ganda! Look at what Billi and Rabbit found this time. They're enooormous. Come and look, Ganda." Ganda came and looked, and Billi turned to show what hung on his back.

Viktor laughed. "I'm pleased to see the rest. I'd just wondering what could be standing behind you, peeking over your shoulders." Billi and Ellibeth laughed as well, because the heads were laid on Billi's shoulders. "What are you going to trade those for? A farm?"

"Well one is to save for Winterfest when Ellibeth's done plucking it, and 'tother is Ellibeth's pay for today."

"I'll need to give Billi some back from the larder, Da, if that's all right. A swan is too much for one day." Ellibeth headed for the door.

"Sort something out. We'll need extra room in there to make room if these monsters are moving in." Viktor smiled. "At least they won't be eating anything."

"No, no. I've got a store full of meat including fowl, and a cold roast to see me through the next few days. I've no space either." Billi smiled. "I'll have to eat something before the gobbler comes home for freezing."

Ellibeth turned quickly, and her face flushed pink. "I told ye no, Billi. A swan is too much."

"A swan only takes one arrow the same as a goose. It's a big goose, that's all. Rabbit got a bit more exercise, but that stops him getting fat." At the note of humour in the song Billi wondered again just how much Rabbit understood.

"I don't know Billi, that's an awful big goose. That's even big for a swan, as far as I recollect. 'Tis a lot for a day." Viktor eyed the bird, looking uncertain.

"There were three swans and no geese, and this one came closest. I daren't go for a smaller one in case it got away. I had to guard the reed-cutters so I took the certain kill. That's the Law, Viktor." Billi shrugged. "I'm not carting it home again; my leg is tired now." Billi had started to wonder now because he'd expected Viktor to back him.

"Da, tell him. Explain it's too much. Explain to Billi why it's too much." Ellibeth looked nearer to red than pink now as her blush deepened and she disappeared through the door in a rush.

Viktor looked as baffled as Billi felt. "Why so much, Billi?"

"Because Perry let slip she needed the feathers. I went looking for a goose, and this came along instead." Billi shrugged. "Then I thought why not? Ellibeth has sort of reminded me how poor I am at dusting, and Perry and Timath aren't much better but I expected that. You should see the difference in my hut."

"Yes, both my maids are something ferocious with a broom and duster. But even so, 'tis a lot." Viktor sighed. "You heard her. Ellibeth says it's too much."

"She said you'd explain why." Billi never had been able to sort out values for meat when compared to hut sitting or baking, not really. A bit of care, an arrow, and lugging the result home cost about the same regardless of size. Though he knew what the Traders would pay for the meat, the values in copper or silver.

"Ha, I wish I knew. Maids are a mystery even to their Da. Now I'm stuck in the middle since you won't take it back and Ellibeth won't accept it." Viktor chuckled. "I could camp out here with the thing until I've eaten enough for Ellibeth to take the rest?"

"How about extra pay for the bread and pies, and the goats and chickens are looking happier than since Bliss left." Billi knew he was being stubborn but the swan really had only cost an arrow, and not even that since he'd got the arrowhead back.

"That'll be Rubyn. To hear him talk he spends half the day with them.

What are the eggs for?" Viktor wore a little smile now. "He says he earned them?"

Billi laughed. "Gathering straw, but really just so he had something to carry home. I'm not getting into a tussle over two eggs."

"Nor am I. So bread, pies, the roast, the animals look better, and the quality of her sweeping and polishing. I'll try. Does all that really make much of a difference?" Viktor still didn't look convinced.

"Oh yes. I've come home to a cold hut and set into cooking for a lot of years. Now I find that a warm hut and a hot dinner are worth a lot to me, especially with real pastry or bread instead of my attempts." Billi grinned. "Edan did me a favour, since letting out the chickens led to Bliss spoiling me."

"Don't tell Edan, he'll burst a blood vessel." Viktor sighed. "I'll try and convince Ellibeth her version of hut-minding is worth extra. Just to prove that's true, I'll arrange for her to look after your hut every fourth or fifth time instead of Perry or Timath if you don't mind?"

"I'd like that. The dust and spiders won't have time to make themselves at home. If you don't mind, could Ellibeth be there the last day when I go on a long walk?" Billi smiled. "I really do like warm fresh bread and it smells and tastes even better then."

"I'll see if that flies, though those two layabouts had better work very hard on fences and gardening if Ellibeth is cleaning up inside." Viktor shook his head, then called out. "Ellibeth?"

The maid came out and her blush had gone. "Did you explain, Da?"

Billi tried not to smile as he actually saw Viktor brace himself before answering. "I did, and then Billi explained. Now between us I reckon we can pick up your pay, then we'll come back for the gobbler."

"But Da!" Ellibeth stared at her Da and her cheeks started to darken.

"I'll explain inside. That's if I can make sense of it myself. If not, you can go and see Billi, and cart the swan with you." Billi and Rabbit left while they were bickering, and Billi felt sure about the humour in Rabbit's song this time.

* * *

The following day Billi went to see the elders. The elders didn't lay down the law in the Village, but they were the oldest surviving villagers. As such they knew more lore and history, and had the time to chew it all over and make decisions. He called on Kina, the Eldest, and she sent the nearest littluns scampering off. Then they talked about the crops and weather until a half dozen elders gathered. "Billi the Hunter wants advice. I reckon we've enough?" Kina looked around at the group.

Heads nodded in reply. "What have ye found now, Billi?" Werne the fiddler loved to spread the latest gossip.

"I don't know. A new idea, or maybe an old one, or maybe it won't work." Billi spread his hands. "So I'm here. Does a landclaim have to be in the Village or Farm?"

"No. We can all answer that. Nothing in the Law says where Farm has to be, but be warned, the Wild will want your crop or stock. If ye can keep it, the land is Farm." Kina sounded absolutely certain and all the heads nodded. "How far away is it Billi? You'll need to clear and plant before summer." She glanced at his peg, not the best thing for digging.

"That part is done, providing reed is a crop." Billi waited as they all thought that one through.

"You've still got to tend it, and keep it from being taken by the Wild." Kina stopped, suddenly thoughtful. "Do the Wild want reed? How would you farm reed?"

Billi explained the weeding and clearing the old reed, the digging to keep it healthy, and the yearly crop. This time the elders spent a lot longer muttering between themselves and definitely frowning. "I put the tithe outside the reeds, into the Forest."

Werne stared. "What tithe?"

"All the rotting reed and pulled up weeds, as well as the guts and such when I took birds there." The elders all stared, then went back to muttering. One after the other they all nodded to Kina and sat back.

"We think yes, under the usual conditions. That is, if you let the Wild back in, if you stop weeding and maintaining the land, you'll lose it." Kina sighed. "We believe the Wild will respect that, providing you've got your bow and Hound of course." They all laughed including Billi. That part applied to any dealings with the Wild.

Billi had been thinking hard while the elders did so now he asked, and felt Rabbit's interest spike as he did. "Would fish be a crop?"

"I don't see how?" Kina started frowning again and then she smiled. "What have you come up with now, Billi? How do you expect to farm fish without digging a hole in good farmland?"

Billi took a deep breath. "I might have found a place, and a way. If I cut off a big enough bit of water to keep the fish trapped, then I can crop as I wish. If I do that regular maybe that's a proper crop according to the Law. Keeping the waterways and ponds clear of weed and sediment to preserve the flow might be farming. Keeping the bushes from growing back on the banks is the same as claiming after a fire. Maybe." Billi sat back and waited.

The perplexed faces told him the answer wasn't a straight no, but the storm of discussion meant he'd definitely come up with something new. Unfortunately, the Forest and Wild didn't usually welcome new, and couldn't actually talk to the Farm. Even the Legends weren't sure how the Laws had been agreed in the first place. The elders were intrigued as Billi's description did fit the Law, it had just never even been considered. "We don't know Billi. We don't think anyone ever tried that, but if they did there's no Winter Tale about what happened. That is a good sign, since if it had happened and been a disaster, the tale should be in there." Kina shrugged. "We are happy for you to try because if it works, this is another way to grow the Farm. Don't complain if the Wild doesn't like the idea."

"If the Wild doesn't like it, you'll never find my bones. So far, so good." Billi smiled. He wasn't going to give any hints yet.

"We would like some idea?"

"If the Wild does object it might be best if a Stumpy Hunter found out, rather than lose more Hunters trying to do the same? This way of farming is something only a Hunter can manage, if that makes sense." Billi didn't want some youth pushing the boundaries of the Law along the river and going missing. More so since right now a young Hunter the other side of the Farm had been out two days too long and he'd gone to hunt, not to wander.

"That makes sense, as long as you register landclaim once you are sure. Then your claim will be respected by the Village though we really would like it registered as soon as possible." Guthra and several others were leaning forward, nodding.

"Why does that matter?"

"If your idea works, the Village need to know where and how, just in case you don't come home one day. Then another Hunter can take over so the Village doesn't lose the extra food." Billi felt a pang. Even if he never really expected to have anyone to leave a landclaim to, it hurt that the elders seemed to agree. Rabbit's song immediately rose to sooth and reassure, as always.

Werne frowned. "What about this reed bed? You should register that since we've all heard what Fellip has been bringing home. We all thought you five were pillaging a wild reed bed just the once, not making a claim." All of them leant forward again, expectant.

Billi pulled out Fellip's drawing. "There it is."

There were two low whistles, then Guthra worked out the pacing, to get a true area. "That's as big as some landshares. Who paced the boundaries and drew this?"

"Fellip. He'll be a partner in the reed cutting, but says I have to claim the land since only a Hunter can." The reaction had startled Billi. He knew the reed bed spread much further than his plot and yes, the area looked huge once cleared, but even so he hadn't thought a full landclaim.

"Where is it? One moment." Kina found a quill and a little pot of ink and turned the paper over. "Can ye sketch the river? Is it our river? We'll not need measurements, just the bends and landmarks."

"I can do that. It takes me about a third of a day, and is obvious really." Billi sketched as best he could. "Is that good enough?"

"That'll do it. Right. It's yours now."" All the elders sat back looking satisfied.

"That's it?"

"Oh yes." Kina wore a wicked grin. "The Village will respect our decision and if the Wild won't, that's your concern." Everyone agreed and Kina produced ale to go with the congratulations.

* * *

Over the next two days, before Fellip came back, Billi considered his options. He talked with his advisors long into the night and finally thought he'd got it sorted out. When Fellip arrived he looked very serious, which worried Billi a bit. "I've claimed it, Fellip, all official and the Elders say 'tis settled as far as the Village is concerned." Billi smiled, "Now Kina says I've got to convince the Wild."

"Then we must make a proper on-going agreement. I've worked out what the value of that reed is, or rather what I think I'll get for it. The final value depends on the Traders and how their supplies are, but I'm confident they'll take any surplus. First off, will you be taking your share in silver now, or when the reed is used or sold?" Fellip sighed. "If you want it all now, I'll be selling some as soon as possible because you'll take all my silver."

"Really? Sorry Fellip but that still doesn't really make sense. It's just tall stiff grass to me." Billi bent over the figures that Fellip showed him. Then he sat back and thought it through because all his previous calculations were completely wrong, in a good way. "The top list shows the coppers and silvers I'll get anyway, for guarding and for paying the youths? You'll pay that in silver?"

"Unless you want to trade for some thatching or anything else I can spare? I have a few crops and there's a bit of a surplus that I sell, but I doubt you'll want roots and grain or straw." Fellip smiled, just a little. "Except as bedding for the goats."

"I might take a bit of grain for the chickens and some straw. I don't need the other silver in one lump, not if I'm getting the first part anyway." Billi looked at the larger sum again because he wouldn't spend that. The silver would go straight into his nest egg, a really welcome addition. "What sort of deal will you give me if I take that part over the year, as the reed is used?"

"A better one if 'tis spread out over the year. This price is based on the value the Traders put on their reed, and some of our crop is better quality so I'll use it for thatching on the Farm and get a better price. You'll almost certainly end up with a bit more silver, because if 'tis spread out I'll be willing to give you a slightly bigger share." Fellip really cheered up now. "That's also much better for me, because you really would have almost cleaned me out."

They spent some time working through rates, and costs, and different qualities of reed. That came as an education for Billi and he tucked away the information on getting the best reed, to use when tending his valley patch. Somehow he'd started that, calling the valley his. Eventually they clasped arms on it, enough of an agreement in the Village. If a man broke his word then he would get no more deals with anyone and if he cheated another villager badly enough, a man could even be banished.

Once Fellip left Billi spent more time sitting with Rabbit and One-shut and making sense of what had just happened. He had a steady income even without hunting, a small one, which really did make a tremendous difference. With the hoarded proceeds of selling his stones and pelts, even bad weather and bad luck on the hunt wouldn't be a disaster. Billi always worried about his future. Now, because he couldn't be a traditional Hunter Billi had become something else, part Hunter, part stone and nugget seeker, and part Farmer.

* * *

That relief seemed to give a permanent lift to Billi's spirits, and more so once he'd organised hut-sitting. "Come on Rabbit. Off to the green again." Billi set off in a tremendously good mood, off to the valley again. From his song, and the way he bounced about, Rabbit really looked forward to a valley trip as well. Though this trip winter had really started to bite and the first snows slowed Billi, so travelling took longer and he wouldn't have as long up at the lakes. A skin of ice had formed on the edges of the shallowest parts and Billi had to give up catching fish with his hands. That wasn't a real problem, since Billi had his lines or the long, slim fish arrows with the three thin points and their tiny barbs. This time Billi used packed snow to freeze the fish and save the time it would take to gather wood and smoke them.

There were big pug marks in the snow and two sets of normal sized wolf tracks around the hut. Rabbit carefully re-watered his marking places and the wolves at least would probably take the hint. Wolves didn't confront the much larger Hounds unless they really had no option. Since Rabbit also marked a couple of bushes where the Great Hunter came to fish, marking wars had been declared.

Billi woke on the third morning with Rabbit's nose on him and the bright hunting alert in his head. He crept out of his sleeping furs and strung his bow but when Billi cautiously cracked open the door he found that he needed the biggest hunting head. A bear stood rooting around the outside of the cabin near the flat rock Billi used to dress his fish. Rabbit had it right; this was a hunting opportunity. Billi swapped his arrow and waited, since the scraping as he opened the door further would alert the bear, which stood too close to risk it. If the beast attacked instead of running, an arrow wouldn't stop him fast enough. Billi waited until crows were making a racket fighting over a dead fish and eased the door farther open, just enough to shoot round.

Billi waited for the bear to be in the right position and put a shaft in almost sideways through the big ribcage, then heaved on the door. Rabbit raced out of the hut and danced around on his three legs, just near enough to keep the bear distracted and turned away from Billi. Despite its pain the bear, now reared up on his hind legs, had to turn to face threat from the Hound. Billi planted his second shaft through the bear's lungs as well, trying for the heart. The animal dropped to four legs and lunged feebly, then crumpled. Rabbit backed off, while keeping the bear's attention as the blood poured from its mouth and ribs. By the time Billi had organised his crutch, boot and spear the bear only twitched now and then. Billi probably didn't really need the spear thrust though he always made sure, as the Laws required.

Billi spent most of the day dressing out the bear and cleaning and scraping the potential new sleeping fur. He left plenty of fat and meat scraps on the bones that went with the offal down by the trees, because this bear had been ready for winter. Many of the bears had already gone off to wherever bears lived over winter, nobody had ever found out.

Billi tried to make a point when he put the tithe down by the trees. He tried to show that he'd claimed this part as Farm and that part stayed Forest, and he would deliver the Hunter's tithe to the Forest. Billi didn't even know it that's how it worked or if anything in the Wild would understand. The Village knew the extent of the Farm, and new land became an extension to the cleared area but here Billi had to establish a brand new boundary. Early the next morning, as he came past loaded down with bear meat and fur, every scrap of the tithe had been taken.

When Billi and Rabbit arrived home, Ellibeth had pie and bread baked and the hut warm and welcoming. This time she raised no argument about too much pay because of the sheer amount of bear meat Billi pulled out of his pack, and Rubyn once again earned two eggs. Perry had been hut-sitting part of the time and when Billi took Ellibeth home the youth came outside for his meat.

When he saw the bearskin, the youth asked for a claw as part of his pay. That would go on a leather string around his neck, and Perry no doubt hoped some maid would notice. Early the next day Timath made a point of calling in to see Billi and exclaiming about Perry's claw, so he ended up with one as an advance on his pay. Viktor took more bear meat as payment to turn the bearskin into a sleeping fur, because there were plenty of villagers who would want to buy some.

* * *

Billi had a shock when Ellibeth and Rubyn brought the finished sleeping fur and he unrolled it. "Oh, I'm sorry Billi. I never realised. Da just said footwear to keep the frost out." Ellibeth blushed a little bit. "As a thank you for all the extra meat, and for filling my pillow."

They were all three staring at a pair of big boots. Hairy boots, because Viktor had used the fur from the bear's rear legs with a thick leather sole across the bottom. He'd even brought the fur round underneath for grip, and lined them with fur from the front legs. "Well, they'll last me twice as long this way." Billi didn't mind, he felt flattered that Viktor had managed to forget his missing leg.

Ellibeth giggled, which came as a relief. "Unless you get a wooden foot for the end of your peg for the snow? The boot would stop it sliding about."

Billi explained why a foot wouldn't work. "Fellip said the same for swampy ground, but that would also mean carrying a spare peg and crutch."

"Yes, you'd need three boots so Da would still be wrong. He'll be mortified."

"You tell him I appreciate them. Those things will keep out the worst weather." Billi smiled. "I've even got a spare if one is soaked." Billi noticed Rubyn eyeing the boots. "Do you want to try them?"

"Really?" Billi nodded and they both sat and laughed as the littlun stomped and growled up and down the hut. "Where are the claws? I thought bear feet had claws, Billi?" Rubyn peered at the furry toes of the boots. "Perry had a claw, and so did Timath. Is that why there aren't any?"

"No, they're still on the feet someplace, unless," Billi opened the sleeping fur right out. "There you are. Four feet and most of the claws." Billi glanced from Rubyn to the claws from the front paws, which Viktor had detached. "Would you like a claw, Rubyn?"

"Ooh, really? Perry says I should start saving now, but that chicken claws aren't any good." Rubyn hovered over the claws, glancing from them to his Ma and then Billi, and back to the claws.

"Choose one. I'll only put the others in the box." Billi glanced at Ellibeth, opened his mouth and shut it sharply. He'd been about to ask if she wanted a claw as well since the rest of the family had one. Then Billi remembered that giving claws had significance when it was a man giving them to a maid. "Um. So, there were enough feathers for the pillow?"

"Oh yes. A lovely big one." Ellibeth glanced at the one on Billi's bed, opened her mouth and shut it. Billi looked and yes, his wasn't all that big. Maybe he would save a few feathers and make a bigger one. Billi left them at Viktor's gate with Rubyn and Spots dancing around Ellibeth, Rubyn waving his claw and growling. When he got back to the hut Billi put the claws into the box. Over nine years he'd built up quite a collection of big teeth and claws in there.

* * *

The last Tinkerers came through, their brightly painted wagons pushing along the trails through the early snows to pick up the first of the winter pelts. These Tinkerers always risked the edge of true winter for those pelts and the last summer meat, to sell far to the south. Billi had a good selection of furs, pelts and fine hides this year, which he sold for a few little ingots of both gold and silver. He went to see the man who bought stones with definite anticipation because this year Billi expected to do very well.

During the year Billi had taken his stones to the Tinkerers as they came through to try and work out which ones they really wanted. He sold their rejects to the Traders, and put the slim silver ingots in little caches in his valley. Billi didn't trade all the stones the Tinkerers wanted, because he wanted to inspect most of what they chose, and now he thought he'd got it right. Billi was very happy to find out that many of the stones from the gravel bar were the type they liked, because those would be the majority in the future. More, if the stone were the right type the Tinkerers really did want the larger ones.

For once a Tinkerer made a mistake while negotiating for a larger one and Billi caught the hint of eagerness. He bargained very hard, despite some very intense distraction from the two Tinkerer beguilers with their flashing eyes and exotic tattoos. After the trade had been agreed the Tinkerer told Billi to hang on to any other large ones and he'd give Billi a similar good price, adding that the actual amount depended on how Billi's willpower held. His two assistants, the beguilers, laughed with the men.

Now Billi wanted to sell one of his bigger stones to this man, the last Tinkerer of the year, and see if the price actually stayed better. He'd also brought all his smaller stones, the type the Tinkerers liked, because this man usually gave a fractionally higher price for those even if he seemed a bit choosier. The better the price he could get the faster the nest egg grew, and now Billi might have need of silver and possibly gold before then. If he really intended making the valley into Farm he would eventually need a proper hut, built by a tradesman.

"Greetings. I hear you have a new name. The Wanderer." The Tinkerer waited at his little table, smiling in the bright lantern light from above. Unlike some types of vendors, stone buyers always liked to see what they bought or sold.

"Where do you like to wander?" Her bright smile had a little suggestion in it, and the maid waved her hands at her tattoos to indicate a few possible places. The beguilers weren't wasting time today.

"A long way from here though in the cold, under the stars, I sometimes do think I'm in the wrong place." Billi had a little bit better resistance to beguilers these days after dealing with four other pairs in one year. Both beguilers laughed and moved in closer as the bargaining began.

Billi tipped out a bag of small stones and then a smaller bag in a separate heap. He thought most or all the first bag were the right type, and most of the second weren't. The bargaining became spirited, with one of the beguilers threatening to sit on his knee at one stage. Both were wearing a good few sparkuls, the beautiful polished version of what Billi had brought, though most weren't for sale.

Or so Billi had heard. Maybe nobody had the price? The sparkling stones drew his eye again and again to whichever parts the beguiler thought Billi should wander to, in return for one of his stones of course. Billi refused to be parted from a stone, though he did start to wonder about where some of those tattoos went under the brief clothes, and what they became. Then he would drag his mind back to the bargaining and the beguiler would pout and start again.

Eventually Billi had a small stack of ingots, and slightly more rejects than he had expected so he still hadn't worked out exactly what the Tinkerer wanted. "I have something else this time, something I came across while wandering." Billi pulled out another bit of scrap leather and unwrapped a larger stone. The beguilers swept in to renew their assault while the Tinkerer carefully inspected the stone with what looked like a very short version of a long-glass. Billi had seen a long-glass on a caravan, and paid his copper to peer into it. The distant treetops had seemed to leap forward. This glass fitted in the Tinkerer's eye, leaving his hands free to turn the stone in the lamplight.

Billi expected the dismissive tone in the first offer. "As you know, I'm sure, just because a stone is large it might not have much value."

"But if the large stone is also the right sort, the type that can be made into a sparkul, then size makes it much more valuable." Billi kept his own tone off-hand, as if that were common knowledge.

The Tinkerer took out the glass and gave Billi a long hard look. "You seem to have been wandering in some very different places. Worse," the man glanced at the two maids, "you appear to have kept your wits." He put the glass back into his eye and resumed his inspection while the beguilers treated Billi to some close-up views of sparkuls. They moved onto flaunting tattoos that disappeared behind scraps of cloth, and suggested he might like to see where they led.

Billi held firm, despite being intrigued at the very least, and once the Tinkerer had finished inspecting the maids pulled back. The real bargaining started, at triple the first offer! But Billi knew what the last

Tinkerer had paid and bargained very hard. At last Billi judged he'd got what he could, and he had confirmed the value of larger stones. "I surrender. I just hope I won't lie awake worrying about how much I've been swindled."

"You don't have to lie awake alone?" Billi laughed and shook his head at the young woman.

The Tinkerer tried to sound indignant. "I haven't swindled you. That is my best price, in the hope that you'll bring me any other large ones?" The man definitely thought Billi might have more, and he wanted them.

"There might be, if the prices are right." That pleased Billi even more because the Tinkerers never said that about the smaller ones, so they really did prefer the larger if they could get them. "I have found a small pocket." Billi wanted to tempt the man a bit to increase the price for the next one, but unfortunately he also tempted the beguilers into redoubling their efforts. These two really were very pretty and very distracting.

"You will find that I pay very well for quality stones. Was the first bag from your small pocket?"

Billi debated, but the Tinkerer had caught on that the two bags had been deliberately kept separate, and were very different qualities. "Yes."

The Tinkerer looked very serious, without the usual flamboyance. "Then I will be very interested. We might be able to come to a better agreement on the smaller ones if you save your year's collection, the ones from that pocket."

Billi ignored a whispered suggestion that there might be a small pocket inside the beguiler's brief clothing if he'd like to check, and perhaps put a stone in there as a test? "I'll certainly bear that in mind if the supply holds up. Just to satisfy my curiosity, are the sparkuls on the beguilers for sale?"

"Everything is for sale." The maid smiled and waved at a few items, mostly sparkuls or gold but some were only tattooed.

The Tinkerer smiled. "Yes, but most of those sparkuls are very good quality. If you wished to impress a Village maid, I can trade you some of your roughs for small unmounted sparkuls instead of gold." The Tinkerer laughed. "That would be a sight, a Village maid in Tinkerer sparkuls, though the mounting would cost extra and there would be the price of the gold."

"Do you have a lucky maid in mind? Is that why you are so mean to us?" The beguilers didn't seem to be backing off at the thought of a maid in the background.

"No maid, I just wondered. That might be another way to hold something against the day my leg gives out." Billi slapped his good leg. "Instead of keeping gold."

"A sparkul in a setting would be smaller than the same value in gold, and easily kept hidden. Would you like to buy some now?" The Tinkerer poised, ready for some unexpected extra trade.

"Not this time, but I will think of it. I don't think I should try and trade at the moment after being shown all the possible purchases." Billi got out while the Tinkerer laughed and one of the beguilers assured him he hadn't seen everything. Though later, when his head cleared, he did consider trading for unmounted sparkuls.

Though that wouldn't be until spring at the earliest. In the meantime, the departing Tinkerer caravan reported a problem on the trail into the Village which certainly cleared thoughts of beguilers from Billi's head. The Village were supposed to keep the trail in good repair for a half-day's travel by Trader cart or Tinkerer caravan and Billi turned out with the rest. The villagers spent two days filling in the washed-out section and then cutting back the encroaching brambles and uprooting seedlings along the rest of the nearby trail. At least the trail only came in one side of their Village, not through and out the other direction. Trail's End was a description of the Village as well as a name. Some of the Hunters and villagers grumbled a bit, because nobody would be paid for their time and any meat taken by the Hunters on guard would be shared out without payment.

* * *

On his next trip out, Billi went along the riverbank to set a few traps for the small furred hunters and took four geese with his bow. The geese reminded him about feather pillows and about Bliss and Hektor setting up a new home. Bliss had mentioned cushions and pillows, and young Hektor's inexperience in killing fowl. He sent a message through Timath that he had a short trip to take that Hektor might be interested in. Hektor called by, and yes Bliss did want more feathers, and Hektor wanted fowl as well since still hadn't stocked up enough meat for winter because the cold room had only just been finished. Billi took him out along the river bank, stopping as they came around the bend to point.

"There, that's my new landclaim."

Hektor stood still, taking it in. "That's a lot bigger than I expected. We've been wondering exactly where since the elders are shy as yet."

"It seems bigger because it's wide open next to the trees, I think. The Hunters will soon know when one comes along this way and sees the reed is tended." Billi waved a hand across it. "More to the point, if you lurk in the bushes at the edge of the trees, plenty of waterfowl will wander in front of your bow."

"Slowly, I hope. I'm still having trouble with moving targets, especially small ones." Hektor looked from the bushes to the reeds and that wasn't an easy shot at a small target. "Are you sure you don't mind?"

"As long as nobody hunts it too hard, the birds will stay unafraid, but a few for pillows and such won't change that. Wait until you see the gobbler at Winterfest." Billi pointed. "That came out of those bushes."

"I heard all about the swan and all the feathers, though I'm sworn to secrecy for some reason. Not with you I suppose." Hektor still eyed the distance from bushes to reed bed. "I hope they are slow."

"They'll be stopped, feeding among the reed stubble if you wait long enough. I rarely aim at the moving ones and never at moving ducks. They're too small and if you don't knock them down it's a day gone finding the durn thing." Billi shook his head. "One duck isn't much of a return for a day's hunting."

"You might be right. Maybe I should stop trying to take everything that turns up? Da says it's a young Hunter's problem and I'll grow out of it." Hektor turned with a big smile. "Thank ye, Billi, Bliss will be really happy. Better yet, if I get used to waiting for ducks to stand still, I might slow up with the rest of my hunting. I'll not mention all the fowl to anyone else, or just where this place is."

Billi stayed long enough to collect a brace of ducks and then left Hektor to wait until the disturbed fowl came back. The young Hunter would make the trip a lot quicker than Billi, especially since Billi had to go round by the ford and underfoot had turned a bit icy today. He more or less forgot about the whole affair, but Bliss didn't and just before midwinter a plump new pillow arrived from Bliss with thanks. Better yet her needlework, a lot neater than Billi's, didn't leave marks if it got under his face. Bliss must have noticed the sad state of his pillow while looking after the hut, or maybe her Sis had said something, but either way 'twas a kind thought.

Bliss and Hektor were attracting attention now, but friendly attention. Hektor told Billi there had been several couples drop by for a talk, some not yet bonded. They all wanted to know how the hut idea was working out. From the permanent smiles whenever Billi saw Hektor or Bliss, very well.

* * *

He went to the alehouse a couple of times this winter for a change, since Perry had mentioned Edan and his cronies had stopped going. There were some looks, but folk seemed curious rather than unhappy. Billi had to put up with some humorous queries about his hut being available for those who wanted to practice this independence idea. There were other jokes about the way everyone called them Billi-huts and if Billi would get a tithe for each one built. That wasn't quite as funny to Billi, as his would be the only Billi-hut without a lass in it.

The gossip in the alehouse let him know that at least one couple were planning a bonding in the spring if they could have a Billi-hut. Two other bonded couples were intending to leave home; the Billi-hut idea was spreading. If the couple built the hut on the portion of landshare the man or lass would eventually inherit, and especially if the man was a Hunter, the hut got them out of their Ma and Da's home early. The hut could even be enlarged if a family arrived and if the man wasn't a Hunter he could continue to work the family farm for food and still benefit from some space and privacy. The little huts would allow couples to settle into a proper home life, or so quite a few young couples believed. Hektor and Bliss were the subject of a lot of discussion and many were waiting to see if the next three experiments worked out.

Billi's hut had a maid in every ten-day or so but not while Billi was there, and the number of times Ellibeth came dropped off as winter tightened its grip. This winter didn't tighten as hard or as deep as the last one and the hunting held up better, which wasn't as much of a benefit to Billi as the wet weather meant soggy ground that his peg and crutch sank into. One evening Syman, the stonemason who also did some woodcarving, came and sat with Billi in the alehouse. "Ye can tell me to mind my business, but twice now folk have mentioned you have trouble with snow or deep mud and swamp."

Billi smiled. "That's no secret. Several have suggested a peg with a foot, and a crutch with a foot since I've the same problem with that. They both sink in further than my real foot." Billi chuckled. "Then I'd be a three-legged man."

"That would be expensive in boots, though why haven't you tried it?" Syman smiled but seemed interested, not joking.

"Because they would be clumsy ordinarily so I'd need to carry the spares on my pack in case they were needed, and it seems a lot of extra weight and bother." Billi sighed. "I don't fancy trying to get my peg off and a new one on sat in the Wild in the winter."

"Brr. Nor me. Though how about an attachment to go on the end? Then you'd only need to carry that." Syman leaned back and sipped ale while Billi thought about that.

"Sort of two wooden feet in my pack. Wouldn't they make my peg and crutch longer?" Though Billi liked the principle.

"Not a foot, and not on the end. You just need a flat bit that doesn't sink in." Syman looked at the plain end of Billi's crutch. "Unless you think a foot shape would be better, for the look of it?"

"I don't mind the look of it, Syman, I've been like this too long to fret over how it looks. If it gets me about better, whatever you're thinking of can look downright silly." Billi chuckled. "The Wild don't care."

"Well I wondered about a flat round piece like a small plate, with a hole in the middle. The fastener would take some careful carving, but I'd enjoy that. I don't do much fancy these days." Syman dipped a finger in his ale and drew on the table. "I was thinking of something like this…"

* * *

A week later Billi tried out his new peg end. "You'll need a little hole bored into the end of your peg and crutch, so the screw seats in properly. The screw and the threads in the collar were the hardest parts to carve. It had to be hardwood but precise." Syman sighed. "It's been years since I carved anything really challenging, since my lass went to the rock." Which would have been doubly hard for the man, since he carved the ledges for the skulls.

They argued over price, but 'twas an odd bit of bargaining. Billi felt the bits of wood were more valuable to him than any meat or fish, while Syman confessed he'd enjoyed doing the work and the wood cost coppers. They got it sorted in the end with Billi thinking he'd underpaid, and Syman thinking he'd somehow overcharged. Billi tried the new ends out while emptying his traps on the river bank and he could move almost as fast as in the summer. Billi wore the new attachments and the next firewood trip went a lot faster. He didn't really need the extras paid for escorting firewood collections now but kept taking them out now and then. Maybe he'd become a bit superstitious since his own luck changed on the Wood Hunt.

The wooden plates also made a trip to the lakes still feasible as the snow thickened. On the first trip Billi took his old sleeping fur as he now had the lovely thick new bearskin at home. Billi ran his traplines in the valley and collected a steady harvest of small soft furs and handy meals for three days. While there he sealed the various leaks and holes in his hut that became apparent with the icy winds and put more reed on the roof. He cut his own reed bed and cleared out the weed and seedlings, more farming. The next trip his hut felt much warmer, downright cosy once he'd built a good fire in the crude fireplace at one end.

On the last trip before midwinter, the lakes froze right over except for a few small patches and the level of the lake at the back rose a little as ice built up on the gravel bank. Billi broke the ice dams here and there so there wouldn't be a sudden flood in the spring when the ice gave way. He didn't want any stones washed away from here.

The beavers probably kept the hole clear in the middle of the front lake and the water fowl swimming around on the rear lake were preserving the patch of open water there. The strong current from the cleft kept the little pool and the short flow to the lake clear of ice, and a small area where the flow entered the lake. A few waterfowl risked that, though they had to be wary so close to the bank. The cleft and short stretch of open water were used as a watering hole by a succession of wildlife, and some would have duck or goose in their potential diet.

In the pool down by the edge of the Forest the ice had been broken, and the familiar pug marks could be seen. The Great Hunter also prowled along the pool bank near where the snow covered hump of the beaver lodge showed. If the beavers had gods, they would be praying that the ice stayed just too thin to take the beast's weight. Each time Billi visited, the same distinctive pug marks showed in one circuit around the hut since the last snowfall. Rabbit meticulously watered those and the bushes near where the big cat drank as required by the rules of marking wars.

* * *

The day before Winterfest arrived, and with it a well wrapped up Perry. "Da and Sis, Ellibeth that is, say you'll be needing a bigger oven for the gobbler."

Billi would. He'd already been told that the bird could be cooked at Viktor's but dreaded carrying it now the dressed gobbler had thawed. The fowl no longer had a convenient neck to rope it to his back. Perry marched off with his prize, leaving instructions to come and collect it on the way tomorrow. From all the organisation, Billi suspected Ellibeth's hand in the arrangements and possibly even Bliss'.

* * *

Sure enough, Billi found himself organised when he called at Viktor's house. "Here, Billi, I cooked it in the biggest roasting tin, the one we used for the swan." Ellibeth gave the cooked bird a critical look. "I'm not sure what gobbler should be cooked with, but I put some taters and roots round it to cook in the juices, and some sausage meat and herbs inside." She wagged a finger. "Don't you dare offer me the sausage meat to make up, Billi, since I intend getting a big slice of this to try."

Billi shut up, though he did notice the spray of red and green feathers on the side of Ellibeth's hood when everyone got ready to leave. They looked a lot like gobbler neck feathers to him so Ellibeth had taken her pay for the plucking and dressing. Perry insisted on marching up the street with the big bird, grinning at those trying to work out what lurked under the cover. The guesses went from a whole small deer up to "another

Great-Boar?"

Mandy took the cover off. "A swan Billi? We've not had a swan for a year or two. Was that from your new landclaim?" Mandy grinned. "You'd better stick to berry juice tonight. Judging by the number of people with questions, you'll need a lot of lubrication for your throat." She sniggered. "I don't fancy carrying you home if you drink ale instead. We'd need a pony and travois."

Billi looked around, alarmed, and three men were waving him to a seat. Several younger ones were sort of hanging about near, waiting for a chance to talk. "Thank ye Mandy. Berry juice it is." He nodded at the bird. "That's a gobbler that got careless late enough in the year to freeze. Save a decent slice for Ellibeth, will ye, since she cooked it."

"Did she?" Mandy looked over the bird. "Put some taters and roots to roast as well. Proper job that, which is a relief with you bringing it. We all know you cook with a skewer and a big fire." Mandy smiled. "I'll save her a bit of white and a bit of dark, since I doubt she's had gobbler before. It's been a good while since we had one at Winterfest." She waved Billi away. "Now go before someone bursts with impatience."

The first questions were about his bearskin boot and Billi explained the bear. "Ah, that explains the claw." Arikk waved at the youths trying to talk to the maids. "A few of us wondered where Perry got that claw. He's being mysterious but none of the maids is being taken in."

"Timath has one, and Rubyn, since they all liked the look of Perry's," That brought a round of laughter.

"It'll be a while before Rubyn realises the true value." Arikk lowered his voice a bit. "Now what's this about a bit of Farm out along the river?" Lowering his voice didn't make much difference since the rest just leant in closer.

"Well, I had some reeds, and Fellip wondered where they came from." Eventually Billi had done with explaining, and then the younger Hunters moved in for a repeat.

Hurwald, one of the older Farmers narrowed his eyes. "There's a rumour you're doing the same someplace else? But not with reed." The others looked at Billi, curious again.

Billi sighed. The elders just couldn't keep completely quiet. "Just an experiment, to see if the Wild will allow it. I'm trying to farm fish."

"How would that work? Is it along the river then?" That was young Mikkel, who'd come over to hear about the landclaim.

"No, because it has to be a clear place, and ponds, not the river." Billi shrugged. "I'm still trying to make it work."

"Is that how you found all those fish just before the fish run? A couple of Hunters went up and down the river trying to work out how you did that." Mikkel sounded downright aggrieved.

"That was what gave me the idea, a few trapped fish, though the eagles and ospreys take a tithe themselves." Billi sighed. "The Wild likes the idea of a few trapped fish as well."

"How do you stop that?"

"Make a bearskin boot or three." Farimer, an established Hunter, might be making jokes but he looked interested in the whole idea.

Billi joined in the laughter. "That helped. So do branches in the water so the birds can't dive."

Mikkel frowned. "Won't that make fishing harder?"

Billi smiled. "Yes, but then I get all the fish, or most of them."

"What about the smaller hunters, the swimmers?" Mikkel really fancied this idea now.

"A trapline, and more pelts for trading." Farimer answered this time, with a big smile. "I'll bet you've got some lovely little pelts this winter, Billi."

"One or two but I'm still experimenting." The discussion spun off into whether it was possible to scoop a hole out of the side of the river bank someplace and use willows to make a pen. Others objected, pointing out that the spring floods when the snow melted would set the fish free. Some were wondering if the same could be done but up a smaller stream as the beavers did, to create a big pool without a big flood.

The discussion broke up while the younger members joined the dancing, then struck up again afterwards. This time the talk moved on to Billi-huts and the harvest, and how this seemed a better winter so far. A small group of younger Hunters seriously discussing banding together to look for a big clearing, a pool, or more reed beds. Several of the Hunters asked if Billi would mind them visiting to talk some more, "if we can catch you at home." Billi and Rabbit went home to their beds happy and tired.

* * *

Billi had traded for a second chair so he didn't have to sit on his bed when he began to have more visitors. Now he was a little bemused to find that he needed another and had to trade for a few more pots to deal with more folk at once because the younger Hunters came in twos and threes. Billi now had mugs instead of just beakers so that visitors could have a drop of ale and he even ended up keeping a small keg in the hut, for visitors.

"Can a landclaim like the reed bed be left to littluns?" Mikkel really had become interested in this idea. This time he came with Hektor, who also seemed interested in that part.

"I never thought of it. The elders wanted to know where, so another Hunter can keep the reed bed or the fish pond if it works in case I don't come back." He smiled, "not for leaving as a landshare."

They all nodded, though Hektor grinned. "You might be surprised, Billi. If your fish pond is as big as the reed bed, some lass with a small brideshare might find you a good catch. You won't be able to run very fast."

"If she likes fish that much, she might fancy putting out a line for a slow-swimming Hunter. That might work with the right bait." Mikkel found that hilarious.

"Either that or she'll have to run very slowly." Hektor started laughing now and Billi had to join in because that really was funny. The chasing and catching, as everyone called the courting betwixt the youths and maids, wasn't actually a foot race. If it had been, Billi would have been a very easy catch.

"Not much of a landclaim if the littlun doesn't become a Hunter." Though Mikkel still smiled at the thought of Billi running or swimming. "They'd have to hire a Hunter to keep it."

"Ah no, Billi explained trading landshares, for me and Bliss." Hektor glanced at Billi's bed, barely a flicker of his eyes. "We were worried, but a non-Hunter littlun could trade landshare, a reed bed for instance, for a Hunter's landshare."

"Ah, yes. Maybe if a Hunter had a share in a Tanner's." Mikkel smiled at Hektor, bonded to a Tanner's maid. "Or a bit of farmland that a Hunter didn't want to spend the time putting crops on." Hektor and Billi exchanged glances because Mikkel's family were Farmers so that described the landshares he'd get one day. There'd been no hint of Mikkel chasing, though with Mikkel being a Hunter there would be a maid somewhere considering doing some chasing of her own.

"Tending a reed bed or a fish pond would leave plenty of time for Hunting." Billi shrugged. "I only really need to be at the reed bed four or five times a year, though I call by for wildfowl now and then."

"About that reed bed, I went out that way to look and the wildfowl do like the cleared feeding among that stubble. Would you mind if I take a couple now and then, Billi? For a change, and also because I need to practice on smaller, moving targets." Mikkel glanced at Pointer, his Hound, laid with Rabbit and Dapple. "If I make a mistake in the open reed bed, Pointer will have a better chance of running whatever I've wounded down." He grimaced. "Instead of spending half a day beating the bushes."

Hektor chuckled. "I practiced there. Billi told me to start with the slower ones, the swimming fowl, and work up. That way Dapple only had to swim." Both looked at Billi.

"It isn't a problem to me, as long as you don't hunt enough to make the fowl wary." Billi thought of the pair of swans. "I'd appreciate it if ye leave the swans alone until there's more."

"Thinking of filling some maid's pillow, Billi?" Mikkel sat up, alert for a chance of gossip.

Billi pointed at his bed and the plump new pillow. "I was thinking of a cushion to go with that. A nice new pillow for my head has left the other end feeling neglected." The youths laughed.

Another night Billi's visitor, Eddmune, came on his own. "I've got two sons and not much of a landshare. How much work do you reckon a clearing would take, Billi?"

"That would depend what you tried to grow there, I would think." Billi waved him to a seat and fixed him up with a drop of ale. "I've thought about it and stock, or crops like grain, would never survive. That would take a hut and a man with a bow though not necessarily a Hunter if 'tis Farm, and there'd have to be a Hunter to travel to and from the place. Though if the Hunter had some land here, and maybe used the clearing for hay?" Billi had been thinking of the open ground near his valley, or even the grassland inside. The valley lay too far away to haul hay back to the Village, but a similar, nearer clear patch might work.

"That would mean more stock could be held on the Farm, since no land would be needed for hay. I suppose if seedlings and bushes were cleared, that might be a sort of farming?" Eddmune smiled. "Though it might take a few such clearings to make a difference to the land needed for hay on the Farm."

"I did think of a line of youths with hoes and scythes, following me and Rabbit from clearing to clearing?" Billi chuckled and Eddmune joined in.

* * *

Though the next time he called by, landclaims weren't on Eddmune's mind at all. "The game has dropped off as usual with winter. They're warier, or can see us coming without the leaves, or they've moved off to find more grazing. This it isn't as bad as last winter, but food is shorter every year now." Eddmune sighed. "There are too many folk here now, and there's not a nice convenient clearing full of fat deer or boar to claim."

"I thought about that since I wander about a bit. Not the number of people, because I'd never realised. I did notice places there might still be prey in winter, or where the hunting is easier in summer." Billi smiled. "I've found places the herds don't move until they think Rabbit is a threat, which is well inside bow range."

Eddmune leant forward a little, intent. "But would there be enough animals to make it worth a Hunter travelling in this weather? This isn't as bad as last winter, but some cellars are getting awful sparse, especially in families without a Hunter."

Billi debated for a moment, weighing up what he'd seen on his long explorations this year. "I've seen a place where I reckon there'll be game in winter, though that would take a proper trip. 'Twould take several Hunters and Hounds, some youths and maybe a pony to pull a travois. Enough meat to make the trip worthwhile would also attract the Wild." Billi shrugged. "I'm not too bad for meat myself, but if a couple of the younger Hunters wanted to boost their storehouses I could give them directions?"

"They'd need to more than a couple, because as usual the Wild is hungry in winter. There's another Hunter just gone. Marris came home to let his family know and leave his bow, pack and knives, then went back to the Forest and Lop's body to meet the Wild together." The Hunter sighed. "Still, I'll ask around because a few of us might fancy the idea. Hektor for instance, since that pair wouldn't wait for spring so he's not had chance to store a lot." Eddmune smiled. "That's if Bliss will let him stay out that long."

The Cost of Winter Meat

Eleven days after talking to Eddmune, Billi returned home to find Hektor, Eddmune, Mikkel, and Cynel standing by his gate. "We want to try this winter hunt idea, Billi." The two younger and two older Hunters all looked determined.

"Come in then." Billi looked at the Hounds, wondering how all four were going to fit inside but Rabbit went to join them and the five Hounds wandered off around his plot. Rabbit's song sounded happy with that so Billi shut the door once the men were inside. "It wasn't exactly a plan, just a stray thought."

"How far is this place, Billi?"

"Three long days for me, four in this weather, but you might make it inside three if you push hard." Billi looked them over. "Though definitely three or even four with a pony." Billi smiled because the younger Hunters always boasted they could carry their catch faster than a pony. They might even be right because a pony needed a better path, and the plump pack beasts were always wary out in the Forest.

"Three or possibly four days for a Stumpy Wanderer because you have to come, Billi, to show us the way." Hektor grinned as he said Stumpy Wanderer because the young Hunters still found that funny.

"I can tell you where." Billi had been thinking of different places he had seen, and the one he had in mind should be ideal. There'd be plenty of unsuspecting prey, far enough away from his valley so nobody would see any of his sign, and several options to make sure the Hunters found meat.

"But you're the Hunter's luck, if we're going somewhere new. Everyone knows it needs the Wanderer to try out anything new in the Forest." Cynel stopped smiling. "Seriously, some of us think the Forest and the Wild like you Billi, and maybe let you get away with just a little bit."

"More likely the Wild is waiting for me to drop my guard." Though Billi wondered sometimes, because he did always seem to find pack full of prey or fish out there. Perhaps only because Billi and Rabbit moved slowly and carefully, more so than most because of his leg.

"Aye, which is why you'll need us along to try out this idea. We've talked it through and this will only work by going to someplace such as you suggested, right outside our hunting grounds. We hunt about a day and a half out from the Village, and not often that far since we don't like to stop out two nights." Eddmune paused, then smiled. "You go for seven or eight days, to where the game has never seen a Hunter, you said."

"True, Eddmune. The animals have no idea how far a bow will reach." Billi decided, and from the little lift in the song Rabbit had kept track somehow. "There's a series of valleys, five or six, that run into some upland. I tried getting up there but it's steep and looks to be all scrub and heather and no water. The valleys each have a stream and plenty of trees and grass, but they're narrow enough so a group will get a shot at anything that runs."

"Will the valleys be buried in snow?" Cynel frowned. "Dips collect snow sometimes."

"I reckon not, or rather it won't matter. There's enough trees to provide shelter, yet it's not all choked with underbrush. There's thickets of course but plenty of clear ground under the bigger trees." Billi ran through his memories, to get the place clear in his head. "I saw sign for a lot of game, and both wolves and spotted hunters as well as the smaller ones so there's enough prey to support a pack."

"No fish pond, Billi?" Mikkel wore a big smile and the rest also started to smile.

"No, hard luck, but maybe you can dig one?" The rest joined in, teasing Mikkel about carting a pony load of shovels three days into the Forest. The meeting broke up with promises that they'd be in touch. Billi warned them he'd be gone eight days to tend to his fish, and with a big smile Mikkel offered to help.

* * *

Once he came back from his valley, the Hunters didn't waste any time and within two days were ready to go. Billi felt both embarrassed and flattered when the group assembled outside his gate and insisted that he ride the pony. "I can walk. Well hop, anyway."

"We need to toughen the pony up for all the meat, Billi." Hektor grinned and Bliss, here to see them off, started laughing. Several others made similar comments and Billi gave up. He balanced himself on the empty packs tied to the pony, and off they went. Their departure looked nothing like the usual start to a hunt, with at least a score of relatives and villagers laughing, joking, and waving the party off.

They made a very light-hearted hunting party, mostly younger Hunters who seemed to treat the trip out as more of a holiday than a serious hunt. Though all were serious about the reason, and all knew of at least one family who'd be hoping this went well. With so many Hunters and Hounds travelling together they ate well despite the snow, with the Hounds ranging wide then calling the Hunters in for the prey they found. The older Hunters were interested in how the Forest changed and thinned out towards the end of the third day of travel. The young Hunters were more interested in how game became easier to stalk.

"I reckon a group like this could travel for a moon or more, and they'd not even need to feed their Hounds." Cynel watched six of the Hounds run down a small herd of deer and turn them, trapping the prey against a thicket. Then they moved in and pulled down enough to feed every Hound. "Though the Hounds would have a wonderful time." He looked at where the Hounds were feeding and shook his head. "A terrible waste of hides."

"Yes, I'd be lucky to get a pair of slippers out of one after the Hounds are done." Perry laughed and looked down at Billi's boot. "Even half a pair for Billi. Here's our supper." He nodded to where two Hunters were coming through the trees with deer over their shoulders. Their Hounds split off to join those feeding on fresh deer.

The following morning when everyone rose bright and early, Billi took a good look round. It had been dark when they arrived, so he hadn't been sure how far they'd got, but now he was. "If we go up the rise here, and find a gap in the trees, we might get a sight of the high ground and maybe the valleys."

"We can go up there and climb a tree. Then if we can see something, but there isn't a gap in the trees for the old men, we can shout down." Mikkel still sounded in high spirits. Four young Hunters and their Hounds, and Perry, ran up the slope shouting to each other.

Eddmune shook his head. "We spend so long teaching them to be quiet, and then they go and scare all the game in earshot." Then he laughed. "Though I'm tempted to join them. It's all this new country Billi. I can see why you do it."

"Though it is a bit more peaceful when it's just me and Rabbit." Since Rabbit had started barking and running about the Hound treated this trip as different as well.

"Over there!" Hektor shouted from his tree, and soon other calls joined him. "There's a tree fallen down over there, a big one, so you should be able to see." The rest made their way upslope, and followed the pointing arm. Sure enough high ground or low cloud showed in the far distance, a dark patch just above the trees.

"There's no trees on there, Billi. Is that the end of the Forest?" Cynel thought a moment. "I hadn't thought of there being an end."

"No, I reckon it's just a rocky patch. We've all found them, places with the rock near the surface and no trees and they're often a hill." Billi had considered that idea as well, briefly, and rejected it. The Forest just went on and on until it became too Wild for Man, that was why the Village had been called Trail's End.

"The hills aren't usually as big as that, but your idea makes more sense." Eddmune brought out a long-glass and grinned. "I borrowed this from the elders." He put it to his eye. "I can see where the valleys are or at least six lines of green in the white of the slopes, so they must be decent-sized trees. Is one of the valleys better than the others for a hunt?"

"I've no idea because I didn't go up them all. We'd best get off to reach it today, and we can talk on the way." Billi had come along as a guide, but as the group travelled and talked, found the others expected him to have a plan for the actual hunting. That felt odd with both Eddmune and Cynel being older but willing to listen.

* * *

The group kept going past dusk and camped the third night less than a candle-mark's easy travel from the nearest valleys, and finalised plans. Mikkel had gone ahead with two of the other young Hunters, to see if one valley looked better than the others. "The first two valley entrances showed plenty of signs of game. What animals we saw looked to be plump, and were more cautious of the Hounds than our bows. We could see what Billi meant, there isn't the tangled undergrowth out here and there's open patches under trees like we've been seeing today." Mikkel almost hopped from foot to foot with excitement and Pointer kept running in little circles for no apparent reason.

"Then Billi's idea stands. We hunt the nearest valley, with a pair of Hunters up the ridge each side. The rest go straight up the valley, with Billi taking any that break past us and guarding the pony." Nobody mentioned Billi's leg, but the plan neatly took care of the problem. So did Perry staying with him, carrying a spear to save Billi chasing after everyone's wounded animals to finish them. "We'd netter sleep now, since it'll be a hard day tomorrow."

* * *

The hunt turned out to be pure bedlam. Their Hounds barked, the Hunters shouted, and the trees exploded with action.

"Watch out, it's getting past!"

"Missed, watch out Billi."

"Cynel, something in the tree!"

"Leave that one Tempert."

"But…"

"There, another arrow, let Streak grab it first."

"Leave the boar, Hektor, hit the easy ones."

"But Eddmune... Oh, Dapple agrees."

The majority of the game animals tried to break past the line as the net tightened, relying on speed. Some of the larger such as elk, bulls and boars ran alone but smaller game ran in herds or, as with the female boars, with their young. The bows took a heavy toll as the animals ran past at close range, many dropping before reaching the valley entrance. Billi concentrated on bringing down those already wounded, especially the large loners who might run for hours.

Though his accuracy soon started to suffer. "Hold up Perry, the pony is pulling me about."

"But the rest are getting ahead, Billi." Parry turned to look as the pony panicked, trying to bolt and yanking Billi off-balance so he missed his shot. "Hang on I'll grab it." Together they wrestled the frightened animal next to a tree and tethered it.

"Stay here now Perry, or something will kill the pony." Billi set himself properly. "How are you?"

"I don't know, it's not like the practice." Perry had been practicing hard on the trip, coached in using a spear by Billi and the other Hunters. He'd started off tentative but had begun thrusting hard and true as he realised that did work best.

"Just let Rabbit get in first, but then be quick." Billi pulled and loosed, pulled and loosed as the line of Hunters drew ahead. Now he could see which ones were wounded in time to hit them properly, so they didn't run too far.

Ahead voices called out, warning or sometimes an exclamation as a wounded animal went for the Hunter rather than escape. The baying and snarling of Hounds rose as they pulled down or held the wounded. A Hound howled, a long pure note and Eddmune's voice rose over the bedlam. "Enough, enough. We have enough. Finish the wounded." Billi heard the note of agreement in Rabbit's song and other Hunters raised their voices, agreeing.

Eddmune had told them a warning would sound in the Hound song when enough prey had been taken, so no meat would be wasted. The Hunter claimed that happened occasionally when he hunted with others, especially if they trapped a small herd. "Leave it, Perry." Perry hesitated, and Billi put another arrow into the elk, backed into the bushes with an arrow deep in its side. "Leave it a moment until that takes effect. A big one like that will kill you unless it's weakened a bit."

Rabbit moved up and kept the elk in place until it dropped to its knees. "Now Perry, thrust when Rabbit takes hold." The Hound darted in and seized the elk's muzzle to hold the head still and Perry struck. Not perfect, but the animal quickly stopped thrashing. A crashing in the bushes alerted them to the next prey, a pair of deer with one already hobbling from an arrow in one shoulder. Billi put another arrow into it, and Rabbit and Perry pounced as it stumbled and fell.

Ahead the other Hunters and youths were working back towards

Billi, finishing the wounded. "Are you all right back there, Billi?"

"Yes thank you, Hektor, I had to tie the pony. There's a few wounded got past me."

"How many, Billi?"

"Three, but one is labouring and bleeding badly so he won't have gone far." Cynel and Hektor came back with their Hounds to chase the runners, and Hektor collected the pony to help drag the carcases back.

"Which way, Billi?" Billi sent them to where he had seen the animals and the Hounds soon picked up the blood trail.

Mikkel came off the ridge to pick up the third trail, and report in. "We took mostly hunting beasts, so there's some lovely pelts up there." He set off after the last blood trail and Rabbit checked to see if there were any more, then Billi moved forward to meet the rest.

"Billi?" He glanced back and Perry stood by the elk, and had scooped up a double handful of blood. "Can you? Please?"

"Of course." Billi hadn't thought of it because Perry would be training to be a Tanner. Though every youth hoped for a Hound, and always considered being blooded a good way to catch the eye of the Wild. Billi looked at the elk. "If you take the horns you'll never stand upright again."

Most trophies were hung around a neck, and Perry burst into laughter. Then he assessed the horns. "No, but the maids might be interested in coming to look at them. If a youth found somewhere a bit private to keep them?" Then he straightened his face while Billi dipped his fingers and did the honours.

Both the other youths were wearing twin lines of blood on their cheeks and big smiles as well. One had a boar tusk and one an antler and both congratulated Perry and agreed the elk horns would be a trophy to tempt a maid with. Then everyone set into gathering the animals together before the scavengers moved in. Ice lined the banks of the small, swift stream, but the fresh cold water in the centre turned out to be ideal for numbing, then scrubbing, various small cuts and grazes to stop wound rot. In addition to the usual collection, the water numbed two broken fingers and then a bite that would remind Tempert to never assume any animal dead before the spear made sure. More water went into pots over a fire to boil so a poultice could be heated and bound over the bite.

By the time the three Hunters returned from tracking down the escapees, laden with the hides and meat from two and towing the third, fires were lit and skins were being roughly scraped and rolled. Now the small group were in a race against the night, because nobody wanted to camp next to a pile of offal like this once the bigger scavengers arrived. "These are lovely pelts." Hektor stroked a lush dappled pelt, one of several taken on the slopes. "We didn't get many down here."

"Don't worry, you'll get a share, enough to make Bliss a winter jacket at least. I'm more interested in some of that heap of lovely meat you took down in the valley. There weren't many big prey animals up towards the ridges. That's why we took hunters, especially those with good pelts." Mikkel stopped a moment, puzzled. "Why was that, why didn't we get any elk or boar?"

Eddmune gestured at the spotted hunter he'd been carefully skinning. "These, the hunters, were trying to avoid being injured. The others, the prey animals, were trying to stay in cover and break through into the Forest." He looked round the interested younger faces. "If you give a hunter a way out, it will usually run. Unless it's a Great Hunter."

"In which case nobody will find the bones," Cynel concluded.

"We might attract a Great Hunter, with all this meat." Ewward, one of the newly blooded youths, looked around nervously.

"Not likely, if we get clear of the offal. Even a Great Hunter will take the easy option." Billi didn't say why he sounded so sure. "What we leave isn't going to be bare bones."

"Hide and hair, no. There won't even be room for any trophy heads." Cynel looked over the carcases still to be butchered. "I doubt we'll be taking any of the gristly cuts or offal. The Hounds won't need offal on the way back, or any food I reckon." The Hounds were setting into the feast with a will and some stomachs already looked tight.

Eddmune laughed. "As long as we take all the usual cuts, and the hides and pelts, the Law has been met. Unless you have a particular liking for gristle?" They all bent to their task, only pausing to deal with a long shallow cut in a forearm.

"That'll teach me not to hurry too much. Aaah." Ewward's knife had skittered off a bone, and he winced as Eddmune scrubbed the cut with ice cold water to clean it. He winced again as Eddmune bound a poultice to it, then brightened. "Worth it though." He indicated the bloody stripes on his cheeks and two similar smiles agreed.

Everyone felt bruised and sore, the usual result after a hunt involving crashing through undergrowth. The youths would probably have traded at least another broken finger or two for the experience since they were now all blooded. Just as importantly, all had a really good story and a trophy from their first real hunt.

With everyone working as fast as possible they were finished and packed before dusk. By the time the last Hunter strapped the last hide to the last load the trees were full of eager, hungry eyes, as were the bushes. They'd started gathering even as the Hounds fell silent and the men began to finish those not yet dead. Now only the fires and the Hounds were keeping them back, though even what the party left behind made a magnificent feast for the scavengers.

Eight Hunters with Hounds and three youths staggered behind a pony, all twelve dragging travois loaded with meat, hides and pelts. The ninth Hunter and his Hound stumped along with his pack of meat, leading the pony as the party left the valleys behind. The Law had been kept, and all the good meat left on a travois or inside a Hound even if that meant the party would travel slowly on the way home. The Hounds all had rounded, tight bellies and none would eat for a couple of days at least, though a couple limped badly and others had collected their own scars. As the group came clear of the valley, the noises of fighting and feasting rose behind them. The noises carried clearly, fading gradually as the party opened the distance. It was late in the winter for scavengers too.

The group pushed on until full dark to open the distance between the valley and their own heap of meat, and made camp with five fires lit around them to help keep any opportunists at bay. Even as they finished a hurried meal and curled up in sleeping furs, a long, loud howl echoed behind them. Half the party came erect and reached for bows, but the Hounds just pricked their ears. The volume was due to the size of the beast, not it being close.

"Is that a Great-Wolf?" Hektor sounded awed. Despite the head in the alehouse, few Hunters ever heard one, and the three youths were completely speechless. So were most of the rest when an echoing roar answered.

"A Great-Hunter?" Perry looked and sounded distinctly nervous.

"No, that is more likely one of the other hunters, but a Great-Cat of some sort?" Eddmune couldn't be sure, since few ever heard any call by the outsized hunters.

"That might be a dappled cat. They get pretty big, so a large one?" Cynel frowned. "I've seen some big marks now and then and don't want to tangle with any of them."

They were all back out of their furs now. "This size?" Billi drew the pug marks he had seen in the snow, what he thought might be a Great-Hunter, being careful to get the size about right. This seemed a good chance to find out.

"Forest and Farm, Billi, where did you see that?" Despite being an experienced Hunter, Eddmune looked decidedly nervous. "That's bigger than any I've ever seen. It has to be a Great-Hunter." Eddmune glanced round. "It wasn't near here?"

"No, a long way away. I wondered if I'd come near a Great-Hunter." Billi chuckled. "Now I know not to annoy it."

Hektor pointed at the big shape Billi had drawn. "You needed a name to realise you shouldn't annoy that!" The rest laughed then rolled themselves back into their furs and slept, exhausted, secure in the knowledge that the Hounds would let them know of danger. Billi smiled the next morning to see Rabbit carefully pee on the pawmark as they were leaving. It seemed the marking competition extended to any sign of the opposition.

The group spent a fourth night in the snow on the way home, at least partly due to Billi's speed although some claimed the pony hadn't toughened up enough. Others blamed slowing up to hunt to eat on the way home. Everyone agreed on the extra time spent hunting, rather than waste any of the meat they carried on the bunch of layabouts carrying it home. Those were very tired and happy layabouts when they broke free of the Forest mid-afternoon and the Hounds loped ahead, belling loudly.

The greeting turned into a larger repeat of the return after the Wood Hunt, with happy family members greeting the returnees and taking over the loads. A few looked over and frowned as if about to say something to Billi, but then set into helping the other Hunters. Perry offered to help Billi with his, both the sorting and carrying the meat and skins home. Fortunate the cold meant the meat had frozen on the trip so all it needed was storing.

* * *

Billi's homecoming happiness didn't last long, because Timath met him sporting a black eye and a split lip. "What happened to you? Edan?" Billi knew that might be jumping to conclusions, but usually one person lay behind most aggravation around Billi. Though this looked like a lot more than sneaking around spreading lies.

"Probably. It's been dealt with, but Spots was the real hero. Ellibeth is here and she's made bread in case you came home tonight." Timath smiled which looked ghastly. "She made some yesterday and that was really tasty, thank you." He gestured. "You'd better go in there to get the story or I'll get skinned." He looked past Billi. "Perry! You've been blooded!" The dried remnants were still just about enough to show.

The door opened and Ellibeth clapped her hands briskly. "Come on you pair. Get the meat packed away, whatever there is, then bring the pelts or hides in here so the scavengers don't get them. Billi needs to get his boot off and have a hot drink." Perry opened his mouth to object or point out he'd done the same trip. "Scat. I won't tell him one word until you get back." She shooed them out with her hands.

So Billi got his boot and his big coat and jacket off, and put the bag of claws and teeth in one corner for cleaning. Then he sat in his chair and drank warmed ale while Rubyn explained how he had looked after the hens and how many rats One-shut had caught. Also how many rats Spots had eaten, and how many eggs Rubyn had gathered, and sorry about breaking one. He continued with how much milk Ma took from the goat, how much feed the goats ate, and from the sounds of it had spent most of his free time here.

At last the two youths came back in. "Some of the meat is in the shed because it won't all go into the cold room, Billi."

"I'll trade most of it anyway. Is your share safe, Perry?"

"It's in the shed as well for now. Where do the hides and pelts go, Billi?" Both youths were carrying some, rolled and tied.

"Take them with you, for your Da to sort out if you will, Perry. You'll have some of your own this time." Billi grinned, waiting, and sure enough Timath's, Ellibeth's and Rubyn's eyes lit up.

"I've got a full half-share of what was taken in the hunt so there's a pelt and some hides, and some are beauties. But I've heard some of what happened here and Billi needs to know." Everyone looked at Timath.

Timath sighed. "Four days since I heard a noise outside and Spots barked. I opened the door, and someone shouted to stay in here if I knew what was good for me." Timath shrugged. "I'm stupid so I opened the door and went out, and there were three of them."

"Who. Do you know who?"

"No Billi. None of them was Edan though. You know how tall and thin he is?" Billi nodded. "They were shorter, and all had a bag on their head, a leather hood with eyes cut out. They were going into your shed, Billi."

"After the cold room?"

"I reckon. I told them to clear off and they said no, and if I interfered they'd smash up the hut as well. That I was a hut guard and should stay there." Timath sighed again. "Spots ran forward and tried to grab a leg, and the man kicked out. Spots yelped and I lost my temper."

"That's not hard. He does it all the time." Perry might have been teasing a bit, but he wasn't smiling.

"Shush, Perry, let Timath tell it." Ellibeth gave Perry a warning look.

"I took the bit of firewood you keep by the door. Then I threatened them." Timath gave a short laugh. "I got in one good lick, maybe. Then they took it off me and knocked me down. I reckon Spots saved the day."

Everyone looked at the little dog laid with Rubyn and Rabbit. "Spots?" Billi tried to work out how the little dog driven off three young men.

"He howled, just like a Hound but not as loud or as long. It worked though. A real Hound answered, and then another, and then half a dozen.

The three of them dropped the sacks and ran." Timath blew out a long breath. "They'd got me on the ground by then so I didn't get chance to chase them." Everyone laughed at that and Timath gave his ghastly grin. "So Spots saved the meat and me."

"So what had they brought in the sacks?" Ellibeth probably knew and just wanted Timath to get on with it, but Billi wanted to know anyway.

"They were full of manure from the stockyards. I reckon those three were going to spoil your stores, Billi." Timath wore a big scowl now. "That's a disgusting thing to do with food in the winter.

"They maybe intended stealing some as well, to feed those dogs of Edan's." Ellibeth's sneer had a lot of satisfaction in it. "Well it'll be harder to feed them now because nobody is feeling sympathetic."

"So it was Edan?"

"No. Most folk reckon they were some of that crew that hang around drinking his ale and agreeing with everything Edan says." Ellibeth sighed. "But there's no proof."

"Did the Hounds actually come?" Billi thought of Rabbit tracking Edan before.

"Oh yes." Timath's eyes were wide with wonder now. "Four of them, running like the wind. They came from different directions, then three took off after the men." Timath shook his head. "The Hunters came behind and followed the three. Barimar picked me up and dusted me off, then stayed here with Ripples."

"The tracks went to the stockyards, but the Hounds can't pick out a man. Barimar thinks the men rubbed their clothes with manure before coming, to stop Rabbit hunting them down." The bright anger in Rabbit's song said he would have liked that. Ellibeth glanced at Rabbit, although she couldn't hear the song. "That would have been justice, if they'd spoiled all that food."

"So nothing can be done?" Billi fancied finding whoever had thumped Timath, to dish out a bit of thumping himself.

"Not really. There's a few doors closed to them now that were willing to listen, and Canitre has cut off the silver to Edan. He'll come round and explain." Ellibeth's tone softened. "The man is embarrassed, Billi."

"Fair enough. I'll not blame him since Edan more or less lives in the stockyards now." Billi sighed. "It might be best if I don't go into the Village for a little while. If I bump into Edan and he makes one of those remarks, then I'll be paying a fine." Because Billi would lose his temper, and thump him good and proper.

"You go when you like, Billi." Ellibeth looked and sounded defiant. "It'll be Edan keeping low for a bit, I reckon." Her lip curled in a sneer. "Spoiling food in winter? They're all lucky the Hounds couldn't pick one out because the elders were talking banishment."

Billi smiled at Timath. "Well then, I'd best pay up for the injury, since you were defending my stores. There's plenty of meat in the shed, ye tell me."

Timath shook his head. "No Billi. 'Tis my job and you pay well enough."

Billi's smile widened. "Then I'll pay Spots." He cupped a hand round his ear. "Spots isn't saying no though he'd like you to carry his pay, Timath." Everyone laughed and Timath gave in and accepted extra meat and a hide "So that you can practice without your Da complaining."

When everyone had left Billi talked it over with Rabbit and One-shut but there was nothing to be done. He did decide to buy proper iron locks from the blacksmith, for the shed as well as the hut. They were expensive but Billi had plenty of meat to trade just now. Sure enough, Kravitt welcomed extra trade in the middle of winter, especially when Billi paid him in fresh meat. He promised they'd be good strong locks, since he'd somehow come across a lot of good charcoal.

The visit from Canitre, Edan's Da, turned out to be very awkward. The Hunter couldn't actually apologise for what had happened because that definitely wasn't Edan. What he did promise Billi was that Edan wouldn't be getting any extra silver to keep his friends in ale. Then perhaps, as Canitre put it, "The fools won't be so keen to believe him, or encourage his foolishness." Billi offered him a drink, and talked about the Winter Hunt and other subjects until Canitre seemed to lose his embarrassment.

* * *

Over the following weeks a sizeable part of the proceeds of the Winter Hunt were traded away to the villagers. Some went to other Hunters who hadn't had much luck lately, traded against future pelts, hides or meat that would then be traded on to the Traders or Tinkerers when they came. Some traded meat for future pots, mugs, arrows, sewing or flour, so those who were feeling the pinch could relax a bit. Those with nothing else promised their labour. The benefits spread through the Village and eased the period betwixt Winterfest and spring. Since a lot of the trading from those on the trip went against items not usually bought in the winter, the villagers were doubly pleased with the little boost.

The hunting party had made an agreement before coming home, none of them would trade all their extra pelts and hides at once as that would spoil the market. The first caravans would get a good few, as they always did, but some prime goods would be saved for later Traders and Tinkerers.

The party insisted that Billi had both the spotted pelts from a pair of hunting cats as part of his share of furs. Maybe 'twas because of the euphoria after the hunt, but someone suggested Billi keep them for leading the party. He refused, so then the laughing youths pointed out the furs would be spoilt by cutting them into shares. Billi hadn't anyone else to support so he could keep them until he found a use. Billi had no idea what he'd do with the spotted furs, because they were simply too beautiful to trade. There were several jokes made about being chased in earnest if the maids caught sight of them, or the amount of pies Billi might receive. Eddmune started them all laughing again by wondering what sort of beguiling a Tinkerer maid might produce if a spotted pelt showed up in the Tinkerer camp.

Viktor wouldn't be short of stew or roast the rest of the winter and possibly summer. Hektor had come on the hunt and despite needing most of the meat to see the pair over winter, Bliss sent some to her Da. Perry brought home a full half-share, and in addition Timath and Ellibeth had their hut-guarding pay. Spot's earnings were definitely substantial, and a cause of much hilarity around the Village. Some of that had an edge because those saying it knew how the idea would burn Edan, especially with all the difficulty he had feeding his own dogs.

Viktor also benefitted from extra business, from the sudden influx of fine pelts needing proper attention. Most Hunters also paid for that in meat, and Viktor started joking that he had more meat to trade than a

Hunter. Perry found himself busy for once, preparing the other hides and better still he carefully cured his own share and put them on display. The proof of his improving skills, especially on the pelt, would bring extra business through the summer. Billi refused to let Perry keep the Elk horns at his hut for showing the maids while Billi went hunting. Presumably he found somewhere else.

Billi traded some of his meat against future hides which he intended trading for more salt from the caravans before the fish run. He also traded against two more chairs and a decent bed, all made to split down for carrying. Billi wanted to improve the hut out in the valley, and make it even more of a home. Billi would have a small but snug dwelling by next winter, especially with the pieces to build a small stove that the Blacksmith had started making.

There were a lot of jokes about what Billi intended doing next year to liven winter up. Some were already talking of a repeat Winter Hunt if he couldn't find another Great-Boar or maybe a Great-Bull, as there were half a dozen valleys there. Billi suggested that if a group hunted a different one each year and only made one trip that would make little difference to the prey available. The six years before Hunters went through the first valley again would provide another crop of prime adults. The Hunters took him seriously, and solemnly agreed to do just that but with one definite addition, next time there would be two ponies.

* * *

Eventually the snow started to melt and the first Tinkerer caravan came down the trail in their brightly painted wooden wagons. First visitors and last, the Tinkerers always pushed the winter hard at both ends to stretch their season. That also allowed them to claim the pick of the goods, and they did pay well for quality. Billi withstood the beguiling and parted with a selection of the small plush pelts he'd taken around the lakes to spoil himself with a new set of knives. They were a bit flashy but as he hunted alone nobody else would ever see the beautiful wavy pattern in the blades. More importantly they were superb quality as all such blades were.

Billi also allowed himself to be beguiled out of two of the small white pelts. With all the new Billi-huts planned, his own seemed more empty which had made this a long, lonely winter for him. The Tinkerer maids

Billi thought about it, but unless someone spoke to him directly, he couldn't just thump someone on suspicion. "With luck it will pass. Thank ye, Perry, but don't get in strife over me."

"I don't need to Billi." Perry grinned. "I can find my own."

* * *

But the rumours didn't pass, probably because someone kept feeding them. Going into the Village began to feel unpleasant for Billi, with pointing fingers and whispers following him down the street. Billi gradually gave up his occasional visits to the alehouse after a few started whispering together and glaring. Eventually he only ventured into the Village when going to the traders he needed to see.

The rumours continued to grow very gradually through the summer and some of the businesses in the Village such as the Brewer and the Potter became less welcoming. The majority of tradespeople still seemed pleased to do business with Billi, especially those who did most trade with the Hunters, so he just stayed away from the others. The Blacksmith and Fellip both made a point of letting Billi know they considered the whole thing to be nonsense, as did Viktor. The occasional Hunter still called by his hut for an ale and a bit of gossip, so even as he pulled back from the Village Billi didn't end up in his previous solitary state.

The suspicious stares and hard glares hurt a bit more than before, though Billi felt sure some would be the same old reason. Billi one-leg, cripple, half-man who had a Hound, but a crippled Hound. He and Rabbit were marked by that and some just didn't like anything different, or were jealous about Rabbit even with his three legs. Billi had learned to live with it, keep to himself, but after a year of being accepted and even making friends he'd let his guard down.

Though Billi's life stayed better in one way because through the long days of late spring and summer Billi and Rabbit roamed the green whenever they wished, for as long as they wanted. They made some long trips out in different directions but found nothing exceptional, though they were in unexplored Forest where the game knew nothing of Hunters. They ate well, and new streams meant finding occasional stones and this year a few gold nuggets. Maybe spending so long in the Forest didn't help with the rumours and bad feeling, but it made Billi and Rabbit feel better.

Billi spent a lot of time making his valley more and more domesticated. He took up the reeds where they were thin and planted them where he wanted them thick, and removed the last small shrubs from the water's edge. The bramble shoots he had planted grew riotously so Billi put on thick hide gloves and bent and plaited the thorny branches together into a thick barrier, a real fence now. There were hints from the elders that if this fish farming experiment hadn't failed, it had worked, in which case Billi should show someone where it was? Billi wasn't ready to do that yet so he deliberately misunderstood the hints. He loved the quiet and solitude in the valley, especially with the current attitude in the Village, and felt unwilling to share it.

* * *

Just as the fruits and berries out in the Forest were starting to ripen, Viktor came round one evening for a talk. The Tanner didn't usually come to Billi's hut, and Billi immediately assumed it had to do with rumours and wondered what else had been invented. "This is really difficult, Billi. I hope ye don't take it amiss because 'tis just bad mouths again, but it's affecting my family now." Viktor did look ill at ease instead of his usual self.

"Are they taking trade elsewhere, Viktor?" That was all Billi could come up with.

Viktor actually laughed. "I wish it were. They'd get second best and my loyal customers would benefit in the trading. As it is, 'tis the Hunters bring my trade and they don't believe a word. This is about Ellibeth."

"Ah. The same as with Bliss. It will be a pity to miss out on the hot pies waiting, but Timath and Perry can guard well enough." Billi smiled. "Especially if they bring Spots."

"Oh no, you won't get rid of Ellibeth like that! There's a wide streak of her Ma's contrariness in that maid, and she'll keep coming unless ye actually lock the door." Viktor sighed. "I'm worried about her reputation and future prospects. Enough mud is being thrown for some to stick with those as don't know us well. 'Tis the overnights."

"But I'm leagues away, deep in the Forest. Every Hound knows that if the folk don't." Billi knew he'd never find who said whatever it was, though he had got a definite hankering for thumping someone.

"Ah, the thing is Ellibeth really does sleep in your bed then, even if it is with Rubyn, so the plain statement is true. Then someone hints that maybe you come back early." Viktor sighed, again. "Hints are hard to counter. The Hunters say ye don't but a good few think Hunters are strange anyway, and that's part of the rumours."

Billi sighed as well. He knew all about hints plaguing someone. "Then Ellibeth stops sleeping here and just guards and cleans in the day. That should stop the nonsense."

"Not according to Ellibeth because she says to stop now will hint it's true. I tell you Billi, she's got her heels dug in. These rumours have really rubbed her fur the wrong way. She stood in the mill and pointed out loud and clear that Rubyn is always at Billi's hut with her." Viktor chuckled. "She took Rubyn with her and asked if anyone wanted to ask him, asked loud enough for everyone to hear." Viktor shook his head "Said no sneaking liar who wouldn't stand up plain was telling her what to do."

Billi chuckled. "Bet that pinned some ears back." He sighed again, it was that sort of talk. "But if I say I don't need her overnight, since you're worried about her reputation? Though I won't say that!" Billi added the last bit as he saw the alarm in Viktor's eyes.

"Ellibeth would be upset, Billi. She's stood up now and told the Village she isn't stopping. Ellibeth is mad clear through and won't listen to reason." Viktor sounded completely flummoxed.

"There has to be a way to sort it out. A way so she can stop over, but not in my bed." The two of them stared at the offending bed. "There isn't room for another bed."

"Even then, there isn't room for a wall to split one from the other." Viktor looked around the hut. "This place just isn't big enough for that."

They drank another ale each, chewing around and around it, then another ale and suddenly Billi grinned. "I've got a solution." He quickly outlined it.

Viktor sat bemused. "Well, it would work, there's nobody could say it didn't. But that's a bit extreme, Billi." He scratched his head. "Expensive as well."

"What's the reputation of a decent maid worth? Most of what I'll need will come from the Forest anyway, so the cost won't be that much." Billi chuckled. "I'd love to hear the rumour mongers work their way around that!"

"So would I, especially if I hear them trying." Viktor's eye got a nasty little glint in it at that. He wasn't a big man but Viktor cared deeply for his littluns, no matter how big they'd grown. "Though I don't fancy trying to persuade Ellibeth."

"So don't." Billi wasn't sure if the sudden giggle was ale or the idea. "We'll keep it a secret until it's too late."

Viktor laughed out loud. "That'll be some trick. I'm going to hide while you tell her." He sobered a bit. "But it'll take some planning, and we'll have to keep Timath and Perry quiet." His grin grew again. "But I want to be in the alehouse when the news breaks."

"Good a place to hide as any if Ellibeth blames you?" They both toasted each other with the last ale in the mugs, and Viktor went down the track chuckling. Billi set off to explain to his Sis, because the hut would be hers one day. He'd been a bit apprehensive since he kept out of her way usually, but she shocked him by giving him a hug and wishing him luck! Despite all the changes since the Wood Hunt that had to be one of the strangest things that had happened. Billi went home bemused because Sis seemed to mean it, and didn't seem to be holding any grudge at all.

* * *

On his next trips Billi went back out to where he had seen fallen trees, too far for anyone to haul them home, and scouted a decent route to bring them back. They were only too far unless someone decided to be a little bit stubborn, someone who didn't have to pay the Hunter's tenth or for all the Hunters to guard. Billi felt both angry and stubborn, and even dipped into his nest egg to arrange the hire of ponies.

Then Billi went to see the Carpenter with a proposition. At first Adalmar seemed very cool about talking to Billi, until he realised what he'd been offered. He'd end up with part of a new tree and the location of a second, without paying the Hunter's tenth, and at least one free guard while fetching it. The second tree would be the remainder of the payment for the work, but mostly a bonus if he kept quiet until after the job.

That meant Billi explaining why, and once he realised the reason for the work Adalmar thawed a little and agreed to the deal with better grace. Several days later Billi, Hektor, Perry and Timath took six ponies and Adalmar out into the Forest for six days. That meant Ellibeth sleeping in Billi's bed, but even the worst rumour monger couldn't explain why Adalmar would lie about Billi's whereabouts.

On the sixth day the ponies dragged the tree out of the Forest and up to Adalmar's yard and the whole Village knew where they'd been. The carpenter began cutting and splitting straight away, and fending off enquiries and offers for timber. Perry, Timath and Gordi, the Thatcher's nephew, set into digging big rocks out of the rougher pastures. Farmers never minded that since it improved their grazing, especially when the youths loaded the rocks into a hired pony cart and took them to Billi's plot.

Syman the stonecutter came round to look at the job, extending Billi's hut four paces. "Are you feeling cramped Billi? Or thinking of moving a maid in?" Syman held up his hands, "Sorry, I don't mean the rumours, I meant it as a joke."

Billi believed him so he smiled. "Maybe I am, Syman, and maybe I need a bit more room with the bit of luck I've been having. Can ye do it?"

"Yes, and since you've offered to pay for the best I'll cut good building stone for the corners from Skull Rock. That'll make a few more niches for the next skulls at the same time." Syman eyed up the marks showing the size of the extension. "You'll hire a pony and cart and supply labour to move the stones?"

"Yes, and Perry, Timath and Gordi will dig a foundation and fill the trench with big cobbles from the riverbank near the ford."

"Ask them to put gravel in to fill the cracks and keep it all firm." Syman looked around. "Those rocks from the pastures will do for building the walls themselves, along with some of the ones from the old end wall. I'd best be at it so you can move back in before it snows."

Billi hesitated, because this might let the cat out of the bag. "Leave that wall until the place is weather-proof will you Syman, then I don't have to move out."

Billi heaved a sigh of relief when Syman pointed out the man who paid called the tune. Syman set into cutting rock straight away so the youths started digging. By the time the three walls were up to roof height the carpenter had finished cutting and splitting the tree. He'd kept one thick timber from Billi's share of the tree for the main roof beam and enough long pieces to make a frame for the thatching, then made planks and smaller timbers of the rest, plenty of both for the doors and frames.

During the ten days of frantic activity Ellibeth stayed away, because Billi allegedly went hunting nearby along the river and came home every night. Timath and Perry supposedly kept an eye on the hut since they were digging Billi's garden over and helping him by tossing out rocks. By now several people, mainly Hunters, had called round but Billi hadn't had time to chat. He just told them all that with the extra visitors he needed a bit more room. Perry and Timath were allowed to tell Ellibeth the same when someone in the Village asked her about the construction.

Fellip nearly fell off his ladder when Billi told him what the extension would really be for. Until he saw the door being put in between the two parts Fellip had thought this really was just an extension, that Billi had found a use for some of his extra silver from the reed. Billi had called Syman back to cut out a doorway in the inside wall and repair the stonework around it, and let him into the secret at the same time. The Stonecutter declared that Billi must crazy, and that he'd be in the alehouse when the news got out. He'd keep quiet until then because, like Fellip, he really did want to see the news breaking and how some folk took it.

All the planks, boards and timbers became doors and a little table with two chairs. Billi's new bed, the one he had intended for his second cabin, went into the extension and the carpenter agreed to make another to replace it, a bit bigger but not a proper big bed for a man and his lass. Adalmar kept on about the time, effort and silver going into scotching one small rumour, and in the end Billi lost his temper a little and gave him all of it.

"I'm not allowing the dirty mouthed scandal mongers in the Village to ruin a decent maid's reputation. 'Tis my silver, and my time." Billi gestured towards the Forest. "I spend a lot of time out there hunting, and I've had good fortune this last year. I've got no maid, and no littlun to leave it to, so I'll spend it on ale or beguilers if I want to. If I wish to build an extra bit on my hut to save a maid's reputation I will. I like coming back from a long wander to fresh bread and pies, and that lot are not telling me what to do any more." Billi waved an arm towards the Village.

Adalmar looked a bit shifty by now since he'd been doing some of the bad mouthing, or at least believing some. Billi didn't care because he'd finally got the bit between his teeth. He gave the carpenter the lot. "If that nasty mouthed manure shovelling Edan had a peck of decency none of it would be needed. He broke my gates and let out my stock." Billi pointed to Rabbit. "Rabbit followed him home, and his own Da knows 'tis him. Any Hunter does if a Hound followed him. Edan's silver paid them as beat on Timath and tried to ruin my stores, my meat, in the middle of winter."

Billi threw up an arm. "Nobody with a peck of sense can believe the nonsense about the fever, but Edan and his friends kept it up until folk began to wonder. Then he starts on the reputation of a decent maid. He tried with her Sis and Hektor beat him proper for it, so now he hides behind rumours. Well I ain't standing for it this time."

Billi calmed down because Adalmar looked a bit worried and had backed away a couple of steps. "I won't set into you or anyone else, Adalmar, unless I can catch Edan or his friends with the lie on their lips. But now you know the why, and now ye know exactly who." He let out a big breath. "Now I'd better stick my head under the pump and cool off."

The Carpenter would talk once the secret came out because that was too good a story to sit on, but Billi had gone past caring. He hoped Edan came to brace him and Rabbit. Billi knew Gordi and Perry, listening nearby, would spread exactly what he'd said among their own age group. They'd make sure that anyone wondering knew just what Billi was doing, and why, now he'd shouted it at the Carpenter. Keeping the secret this long must have been burning the youths but their hefty bonus depended on nobody opening their big mouth, a bonus in claws and teeth and silver.

Extra pottery cost mere coppers, and Viktor bought that since Billi wouldn't go near the Potter just now since the Potter had gone from agreeing to repeating the rumours. The bed linens cost silver, because they were better than those Billi usually had. He put up with the stony looks from Sythyl the Seamstress. She took his silver happily enough and she could think what she liked about him buying better quality bedding. Billi smiled as he went through the big bed furs he'd been saving to trade with the Tinkerers. The Tinkerers liked quality, so these were thick and soft and would be warm on a winter night. He put another fur on the stone slabs covering the floor.

The blacksmith traded skins, silver, and some small stones for a couple of little pans, a small kettle and the ironmongery for a hearth and the doors. He came out to fit the new fireplace, and all the door fittings, but only on the day the rest of the work ended. Kravitt might keep quiet overnight as he promised but the alehouse would be busy on the morrow as the Carpenter and the Stonemason would be there as well. By now a few had to be wondering about the little smiles on some folk when the rumours came up again.

Finally, Billi sent a message with Perry, asking for Ellibeth to look after the place the following day because Perry and Timath were busy working elsewhere. The pair would be elsewhere all right, spending their bonus and spreading the story no doubt, but they wouldn't tell Ellibeth tonight.

* * *

Billi asked if she would come early so he could get away and the following morning the Ellibeth and Rubyn turned up. When he came to the hut door Ellibeth stood looking at the extra length of wall and stout door with a furrowed brow. Billi smiled. "That's the new extension."

"I realised that, but why has it got a separate door?"

"Come in, I'll show you." Billi opened the new door and Ellibeth came in, followed by Rubyn.

"You've made yourself a proper bedroom, Billi." Ellibeth looked around at the bed and the little hearth and kettle. "You can even make a herb brew without leaving here on a cold morning. This will be really snug in the winter." She moved to the connecting door and laughed at the big bar across it. "Are you worried One-shut will break in?"

"Who knows who might be trying to break it down?" Billi stood behind her so Ellibeth couldn't see his grin. Rubyn was too busy stroking the big soft bed fur to care.

Ellibeth lifted the locking bar and opened the door, then stopped. She stared through into the original hut for a long while, then finally spoke. "Your bed is still in here Billi. Why?"

"Because that is my bed, and this one is yours. I'm not having your reputation ruined by the nasty minds in the Village. Nor am I going to live in a scruffy hut to make them all happy." Ellibeth had turned open-mouthed and Billi smiled happily and waved an arm around. "If anyone starts again just grab them by the ears and drag them out here, then show them the door and bar. This room is yours, yours and Rubyn's and I'll not come in here again, ever." Then Billi stumped through into his own original hut, sat in his chair, and settled in to ride out the objections.

He expected the first. "But it must have cost a fortune."

Billi sat unmoved and calm. "My fortune. Some would say it's a better use than beguilers or ale."

"That's not the point. It's a waste of silver."

"How do you know? I found the tree for the timber, I found the reeds for the roof, the rocks came out of the rough grazing, and I even found these to pay for anything else." Billi tossed her his largest gold nugget, as big as a walnut. "Furs are free, and meat for labour or ironwork is free. Now how much did it cost?"

Ellibeth waved her arms about. "But you can't just use them for this. It's, it's, too much!" For a moment Billi thought Ellibeth would stamp her foot in frustration.

"But someone is too stubborn to stop coming, so what could I do? Maybe I'm nearly as stubborn." Billi tried not to grin as he saw her little smile at that. He'd won. "Unless you want me to knock it down again? To make a point?"

"Don't be silly." Ellibeth looked back through the door again, then back at Billi's bed. Billi just smiled while Ellibeth worked through who was being silly about what. After that it was just a case of sitting there and being stubborn.

That became easier when Rubyn realised what they were arguing about. "This is my room? For me and Ma and Spots! Ma, our own room. Look at the fur Ma, it's hooooge. "Rubyn tugged on Ellibeth's arm. "Come and look. There's a big fur on the floor as well."

"I know, Rubyn, I'm just telling Billi that we can't…." Ellibeth stopped, because she couldn't break her littlun's smile. "Because. Since." She gave a big sigh. "That isn't playing fair, Billi, letting Rubyn see it."

"Is Edan being fair? Which unfair do you prefer?" Billi let his grin come now.

"Your sort, you silly man." She looked down at Rubyn. "I'll come and look in a minute." Ellibeth looked at Billi very steadily. "I'd better lock myself in then, and put that bar down. It'll make the dusting a bit awkward."

"You can leave it wide open when I'm not here. You can live in here, and sleep in there with the bar down, so nobody gets confused." Billi stood. "Now, can I get going?"

"Get you gone Billi, and thank ye." Ellibeth giggled as growling sounded behind her and she glanced back. "He's wearing the bed rug."

Billi wore a big smile as he headed into the green with Rabbit for three days. Two nights in that room and no matter what second thoughts Ellibeth might have, Rubyn wouldn't let her give it up.

* * *

When he returned the door between the two rooms stood open, the place was warm and dusted, and he could smell his dinner. "A bit of roast venison, taters and roots. It'll be ready in a while." Ellibeth glanced outside at the gathering dusk and smiled. "You'd best walk me home then, to stop all those wagging tongues."

"After you've barred the door from the other side and go out of your own door. I told you, I'm not going in there. If anyone visits, I'll make sure they try that door to make the point." Billi pulled out the three keys on a loop. "Here, you can lock the outside door on the way out."

Ellibeth stared. "That really is a waste of money. Iron locks are expensive, really expensive. There's not more than a score of doors with one on." Ellibeth was right. Iron locks really were expensive and possibly driving Billi's point home a bit harder than necessary.

Though Ellibeth had no answer when Billi told her why. "That's because there's very little worth protecting with an iron lock in this Village." Billi grinned. "Except reputations, and that lock should keep yours safe."

Ellibeth came over and bussed Billi gently on the cheek. "You are a very silly, but a very kind man, Billi." Then while Billi sat in shock she went into her room, barred the door, and Billi heard her close and lock the outside door. He recovered enough to put his coat on by the time Ellibeth came in his own door to pick up her parcel of meat. Rubyn carefully held his eggs, payment for chicken tending duties.

At her gate Ellibeth paused while Rubyn went ahead. "I'll be having a long talk with Da about all this." Da already knew all about it so Billi knew what answer she'd get.

So he grinned. "It isn't up to Viktor to tell a Hunter what to do in his own home."

Ellibeth shook her head. "You are a very stubborn man, Billi." Though she smiled as she went up the path.

Billi walked home with Rabbit's contented song in his head. He ate his dinner and hoped this time he'd finally knocked Edan back, or at least stopped the man picking on women.

* * *

The room accomplished both purposes. The rumours about Billi and Ellibeth stopped completely as Viktor confirmed ten-days later. Perry and Timath were bragging about how much the good reputation of their Sis was worth to a decent man. They were putting the emphasis firmly on the decent, and they were giving Edan's name as the opposite example. So were the others who knew exactly why the bedroom had been built. No hints or doubt this time, they gave Edan's name and were more or less daring him to object. When he didn't, and folk started thinking instead of just listening to rumours, that finally stopped most of the muck-spreading.

The reprieve wouldn't last because Edan wouldn't let it, and some would still see Billi's stump and believe the worst of him. Stopping any rumours about Ellibeth had been Billi's main intent and that worked, especially important as one of the farmers showed a bit of interest in the maid despite her littlun. Or perhaps partly because of Rubyn as he'd grown big enough to help out on a farm now and would only grow bigger. Rubyn kept insisting that he would be a Hunter, but so did almost every other littlun his age. Telling him he had the same chance as any other youth would have, about one in four, didn't deter the littlun one bit.

Rubyn really enjoyed his time in the hut. He had some space to run and took on total responsibility for the chickens. Billi made a point of giving him a few eggs as his pay every time, and Rubyn seemed just as delighted every time he chose his pay from the bowl. This winter Billi would ask Rubyn to tend a trap line in the winter fields to catch the little hunters in their winter coats.

The little varmints were encouraged in the summer to keep the rabbits, rats and mice down to a minimum so they wouldn't eat the crops. In winter the little hunting creatures themselves were tithed to keep their numbers reasonable and to keep them from the poultry, though perhaps the main reason for trapping them was because their winter coats were luxurious. Even if the Farmer caught Ellibeth, he wouldn't mind Rubyn learning that skill. Setting traplines would be an asset in either Farm or Forest.

The campaign continued against Billi personally but with less effect. There remained some lingering unrest about the fever, and the occasional mutter about cripples, but Billi didn't care and neither did Rabbit. They spent most of their time away in the Forest or at the lakes, or at home without going into the Village. As long as the people he liked still talked to him, the tradespeople would welcome him into their premises, and Hunters still dropped by for an ale and a gossip, Billi was satisfied. Not quite happy, the rumours still stung a bit, but happier than a one-legged man ever expected.

Billi went out to his valley a moon before the Village fish run and took a lot of fish, filling his pack with those he'd dried and salted and storing another pack full in the hut. Once again they sold or traded really well, as did the second pack full. When the Village fish run arrived he worked along with the rest. This year the run finished early on the third day, so the shares were smaller. Once again Billi salted his share to pack away in his store. Ellibeth told him he'd need to dig another soon so Billi traded more meat to the Traders in return for salt.

He asked, and Ellibeth thought the stored fish would be bought by the Village this year, because there wasn't as much about. Any Billi had left would sell best in the spring when the Traders arrived for winter meat. That wouldn't be the season for the fish and few would save some through winter, so Billi traded more meat to make sure he had space to keep the fish. Ellibeth admitted being impressed that Billi always had fresh fish in any season while the rest only had preserved. After that he paid her in fresh fish a few times, over her protests that they were expensive.

Billi took another bear just before they all disappeared for the winter, one that came after the blackberries festooning his bramble hedge, plump and ripe. The bear was plump as well, the meat rich and fatty and his fur thick and warm, and with a wry smile Billi wondered if a bear a year meant he'd started farming them. Billi salted a good bit of the bear meat and left it for the next trip, then brought the rest and a pack half-filled with blackberries back to the Village. Ellibeth made jam and some apple and blackberry pies when Billi traded berries and bear meat, some for apples. He also brought his bag of stones from the valley, and concealed them in the hut. The last Tinkerers of the season, the ones after the first snows just after Harvestfest, would buy the stones. He would also trade his best furs, the ones that weren't too beautiful to let go.

The Tinkerers meant he could also trade for Midwinter presents, because this year Billi wanted to give some. Billi hadn't really had friends before. Was he a good enough friend to give them a Midwinter gift? Were there rules about it, the same as chasing and gifts? This felt akin to traipsing through a swamp in the dark, backwards and being chased by a wounded boar. Gifts that Billi thought were cheap were expensive to others, and led to refusals, confusion and red faces. The rest of the youths learned as they started flirting and maybe chasing but Billi never expected to do that, and had never been at the dances to learn anyway.

Which meant he'd no idea what might be right. Billi wished he could let Ellibeth have a couple of stones or a pretty pelt for a midwinter present, because he really didn't have any idea what else to give her. Unfortunately, pretty stones and pelts were right there along with claws and fangs in the list of gifts with significance. Billi could let Bliss have a couple of stones or a pelt since she was already bonded, but what should he get for Ellibeth and her Bros, and Rubyn and Viktor?

At least the Harvestfest would be straightforward, and maybe he could ask some cautious questions.

Winter Storms

Viktor asked Billi to come to the Harvestfest with his family, which Billi did. He felt more comfortable arriving with people he knew rather than alone, especially as he had to leave Rabbit at the door. Edan attended with a small group who all glared at Billi so that had started again. He ignored them except for taking note that these were the ones to look for if trouble started again, more rumours and lies. Looking them over, Billi saw nobody among them whose bad opinion really mattered to him, and many more people in the hall were smiling and calling greetings.

Billi sat with the older men again and they started asking him what this year's excitement would be, in among the usual rumour mongering. They also pressed a bit about the fish farm, but Billi just laughed and said fish weren't easy to round up so he'd not got it right yet. Billi's Sibs came to say hello, with smiles, and Billi wondered if they were just relieved he'd been managing better. Though they all laughed about the extension and Edan getting pegged back, and that seemed genuine.

The first excitement turned out to be two bondings, both of them couples who were busy building Billi-huts. Those taken by the fever were remembered, and others had gone to the rock including a Hunter and a Hound. Two other Hunters and Hounds had been taken by the Wild, no worse than most years. The naming and welcoming of babes who had survived their first year cheered everyone up a bit after that. The elders followed with their usual summary of the harvest and how the hunting seemed to have gone, with a few comments about less fish coming into the Village this year.

Eventually the music struck up and the maids and youths started dancing and teasing each other. Billi relaxed and tried to spot why whatever the youths were doing meant they were chasing in some cases and teasing in others. Also why what the maids said and did might be encouragement or rejection, confusing because they sometimes used the same words. He could see a few maids had gifts, claws and teeth, but he already knew they weren't appropriate for a friend.

A couple of young men who had just become Hunters came over to ask if they could come on the next Winter Hunt. Billi said he didn't mind who went if another one became necessary, as long as the group didn't get too big. He didn't want to spoil the supply in case the Village needed more in a bad winter. The Hunters agreed to talk to the rest and seemed happy with that. Billi realised that the Winter Hunt might be here to stay and wondered just how crowded the Farm might be getting. He decided that the young Hunters might have the same problem Hektor had, not enough time to build up a winter surplus.

A bit of a joke went around that Billi should be asking for a payment when the newly bonded built a Billi-hut. The hut idea had spread quickly among those already bonded and living in crowded houses. The older men were pleased about that since the huts relieved the pressure in their homes, and meant less strife. Billi stumped over to get himself another cider and it came in a lull in the music, clear and loud enough to be heard by a good number of those present.

"It's disgusting what someone'll do for a bit of meat. Threw one maid at him and it didn't work so he threw the other and that seems to be working well enough. You'd think the cripple would do the decent thing but no, he builds an extra room so they can pack the littlun off out of sight. Let's hope he don't give her some other disease." By the time the words finished, the silence had spread and at least half the hall heard it.

Edan. Billi put his cider down and turned, and heard the music die out. He stumped across to where the group stood with Edan front and centre, wearing a smirk on his face. "It don't matter what ye say about me, Edan, cos ye don't matter to me, but ye've just dishonoured the maid for no reason. Now ye'll apologise to her." Billi cursed silently. His accent had gone back to Farmer. He'd thought that had gone.

"Why? It's not as if you can stop me. I mean you can't really fight me, man to man." The last part wasn't even said to Billi, Edan had turned to sneer it to the hall to rub it in. Something finally snapped inside Billi because this time Edan had finally done it right in front of him. Afterwards Billi thought he just wanted to shut the man up and he took the easiest way, since what Billi did was reach out with his right hand and grab Edan's throat.

One of the group with Edan spoke up. "You can't do that. There's no call for that sort of thing."

Billi turned on the small group. "No call? The man creeps around my house when I'm out. He breaks my gates and lets my stock out, and then hides. Then when I put someone in the house to keep it safe so I can hunt, as a Hunter should, he sneaks around spreading lies. The last time Hektor stopped him bad mouthing Bliss, so then he tried something else. I grieve for the littluns as anyone does but I'll not take the blame. Then he starts on Ellibeth who has no man as yet though ye all must be stupid, and if I had two legs you'd not get the chance. So I'm stepping up since his argument is with me, not her."

"You don't know it was him." Billi rounded on the speaker.

"Rabbit followed him home. Ask anyone with a Hound. I know 'twas him." There were mutters from the hall and at least one 'good enough' which probably came from a Hunter.

"Yes, well it doesn't give you the right to do that." One of the men came forward and reached out which worried Billi. He'd got a good grip on Edan that must have the man's attention as he could feel Edan's hands scrabbling, trying to break the grip. But now Billi didn't have a spare hand to deal with anyone else because he needed the crutch.

Before Billi could work out what to do, a low rumble from the door echoed through the hall. Almost everyone looked at the door, including Billi, and that wasn't a view of Rabbit he'd ever seen! Certainly not from this angle. The Hound's lips were up and back to expose his big canines and his ruff stuck up stiff and straight!

A voice came from the stunned crowd, very calm but clear in the silence. It sounded like Barimar, Hektor's Da. "Everyone stay still. Do nothing stupid. Edan asked for man on man in front of everyone and got it. Anyone else steps in the Hound'll kill 'em, so move back gentle like." There were startled looks, then realisation seeped in and the man reaching out to Billi went pale and carefully took a long step back. "Mind, you ought to put Edan down now Billi. I reckon he's done."

Billi finally looked back at Edan. The man had gone a bluish red colour and wasn't really trying to get free anymore, and the strain was only his weight as he slumped in Billi's grip. Billi let him go and Edan went down like a sack of taters and curled up coughing and spluttering, then thrashed feebly, fighting to drag in big gasps of air. Barimar spoke up again. "Well that settles that unless anyone else fancies insulting the maid, who be kin of my youth's lass." Everyone could hear a little bit of threat under that. Barimar wasn't happy, and Viktor looked fit to kill someone.

The crowd parted to let Canitre, Edan's Da, come through, and he had a face like thunder. "Not quite. I should have done this back aways." Canitre walked up to Ellibeth and gave a little formal bow to her and Viktor. "I apologise for not doing so and for any hurt ye've suffered." Canitre walked across to Billi next. "Ye're a good Hunter, generous with your luck and a good friend to Viktor and his family. I be sorry for the trouble." He lifted a hand as Billi went to speak. "No, 'twas my job."

Then Canitre finally turned to look down at Edan. The young man still lay on the floor and he'd got some breath back but not enough to stop panting. Enough breath to try and speak but Edan only managed a croak. Canitre ignored the attempt. "Ye were wrong in the Forest, ye weren't fit to take a Hound, and ye could no let it be. I told ye to let it drop, but ye've kept going until ye've caused a good man and two innocence maids harm. Well that's enough. Ye're no son o' mine. Ye can keep the land with the stockyard and make a living how ye wish."

Canitre gave the small group behind Edan a withering look. "Your friends can help ye find a bed or build a hut, I don't care, I'm done." The Hunter turned on his heel, followed by Autumn, his Hound, and stalked out. A storm of comment rose up. Edan disowned! No landshare!

Billi's head reeled. He saw all the faces looking his way and the scorn, the curled lips. Just as expected, the cripple was getting the blame. Billi couldn't stand that, all the accusations and shouting, so he headed for the door through the gap Rabbit had cleared. Ellibeth raised a hand but he kept going since he'd shown her up enough already. Billi stroked Rabbit's ears and headed home as fast as he could and all the way it went round and round in his head.

Sticking up for the maid had been her Da's job, Canitre had said so, or 'twas up to the Farmer who'd been showing interest, but Billi had stepped in instead. Then he'd nigh killed the man, and Rabbit had threatened to kill another. There again Billi felt proud of Rabbit because three legs or not he'd backed them all up. But what would they all think of him now, starting a fight at the Harvestfest? This was only the second he'd been to and he'd wrecked it. He'd be lucky if anyone spoke to him again, any of them. Billi replayed those looks, over and over in his head.

Worse still, it hurt, really hurt him deep inside. Billi had been resigned to being Stumpy Billi and escorting the wood gathering, and living quiet in his hut, then suddenly he had friends and life became so much better. Now one moment of madness and it was gone and he'd never be truly resigned to it again. Maybe he should just take Rabbit and go and live by the lakes. He'd been thinking of that, anyway. Though he'd expected to be able to come back now and then, to see his new friends.

The whole mess went round and round, and wouldn't straighten out no matter how many times Billi explained to the three bright eyes watching him. In the end Billi resorted to cider.

* * *

The mess in his head seemed no better in the morning. In fact, it felt worse since Billi had a raging headache and letting out the chickens and milking the goats were painful. Somehow the sun tried to burn out the back of his head from the inside or that's how it felt. More cider or ale was tempting, but Billi knew that would only be temporary and so he stuck to water. In despair he tried nettle tea, and then berry toddy, blackberry juice with honey and hot water. That seemed to have some effect or maybe the gallons of water he seemed to need finally had some effect. Billi really should have remembered why he'd not drunk too much for years.

The result had been worse last time. The rest of the drunken youths went staggering off home while Billi couldn't stagger. With only one leg, one that no longer seemed to work, he'd had to crawl home. Da had laughed at him and made him sleep in the shed since he'd got a good bit of lane and pasture in him by then. Ma woke him early to do chores, and stood over him as he hopped from job to job, half blind with a headache. Billi had sworn off too much ale or cider.

At least feeling sorry for himself kept Billi's mind partly off the real problem. He'd lost his temper for the first time in years, and ruined the Harvestfest. He'd damn near killed Edan and Rabbit had threatened a man, a villager. All the dogs and Hounds were expected to threaten a light fingered type from a caravan lurking around where he shouldn't be, but not villagers. That hadn't been a warning from Rabbit. It was a killing threat and everyone knew that, because Barimar made sure they understood.

Billi knew that it would have gone badly if Edan's friends had started on him so he couldn't be sorry Rabbit joined in. He really was proud of his Hound because Rabbit had backed down a whole hall, but between them they'd still ruined the Harvestfest. Under it all Billi already felt bitter about losing the bread and pies and warm welcome, because Ellibeth wouldn't come near the place again. Not after being shown up like that. Nor Viktor, so Billi had better learn to cure his own hides and pelts.

Billi cursed that temper of his, rearing up like that. Billi had tamed his temper eight years ago after smashing yet another crutch in pure rage and frustration. Billi sat among the pieces and realised he couldn't let life get to him like that, especially since it left him crawling around while he made another crutch, so Billi worked long and hard on taming his temper. Now he'd lost it again, in front of the whole Village. The day went slowly by as Billi churned it all over or berated himself again. Eventually Billi managed some dry bread with more toddy and finally hit his bed tired despite having done nothing much all day. At least his headache had subsided to a gentle thump.

The next morning Billi's head felt clear and he faced up to the dilemma. What did he do now? He'd obviously shown up Ellibeth in front of the Village, so her bros weren't likely to be keen on coming to look after the hut. Edan would be blazing mad once he'd recovered, and especially after being disowned, and he'd blame Billi for that. That bunch with Edan would help the stockman tear the fences down and trample this garden flat, or burn the hut, the first time Billi left it. But Billi couldn't be cooped up here all the time, not again, not now.

He'd come to love the freedom out there with just Rabbit, to crave the peace of the soft green light under the trees. Or the quiet calm amid the harsh lines of the branches and their shadows in the winter, and the thick snow drifting around the bushes and trunks. The place was dangerous because it was the Forest and the Wild always watched but that was part of why it pulled him. That danger kept Billi and Rabbit sharp and aware of everything, and spoke to something deep inside Billi and he couldn't give it up, not now.

Nor could he give up the glory of the song in his head when Rabbit went into the Forest, lifting to joy at a hunt, a new stream, or chasing flutterbyes in the sun. 'Twas a pity he'd grown to enjoy a bit of company, or he'd be off today and leave the hut to burn. But what about One-shut, and the chickens and goats? Billi now found it hard to just pack up and go, even when it looked as if that was the only way.

He'd had that idea in the back of his head, moving out to the valley and being shut of all the rumours, but could he really do it? Could he move everything to the valley if he bought a couple of ponies, maybe three, and loaded them? If he put the chickens in woven boxes and tied the goats together? That would take three days taking it steady and he'd not sleep much since they'd be a tasty target for the Wild. But better done now than later in winter when the snow drifted deeper and the Wild grew hungrier.

If Billi let Sis know, she could get someone in here if she wanted to keep the hut. If not perhaps suggest Ellibeth, then she could look after it until one of Sis's littluns grew old enough to want some room or found a lass. That would give Rubyn a bit more space to grow and he'd have his own room, luxury really. Best find out if that might happen so he could leave the rug and bed fur since the littlun had really taken to them.

Then again maybe he shouldn't mention Ellibeth to Sis or anyone. Billi had shown her up just as much as Edan did so perhaps he should just go. He could leave a message and the keys with the elders, and arrange to let his Bros and Sis sort out the reed bed. He'd let them know he'd not be back so they could deal with the hut and such. After all the hut would going to Sis in the end. Billi planned it out over the next couple of days but never actually got started on doing anything about it. Billi began to suspect the problem was that he really didn't want to go.

Billi thought the real reason he put off leaving could be his stubborn streak. It didn't like the idea of being forced out and all the reasons for not getting started might be just that, being awkward. There again maybe he plain didn't want to be all on his own again, not now. Rabbit wasn't pushing to go, not even hunting. He seemed mainly content, as if something had been settled instead of there being a big problem. Maybe Rabbit didn't want to leave, though Billi felt a troubled undercurrent in the song, a bit of worry. Anyway Billi had to wait to see the elders and then the Tinkerers to trade his furs and stones, unless he just wanted another excuse to stay.

The fifth day, in the afternoon, Billi was cleaning out the goats when Rubyn came up the path from the Village. It wasn't far since Billi could see the first cottages clear enough in daylight, but not a trip a littlun should be risking alone in winter when the Wild would be hungry. "Ye shouldn't really be out here alone, Rubyn, not in the winter."

Rubyn shuffled his feet a bit. "Sorry Billi. There's a Hunter with the sheep who can see me all the way, and I worried about the chickens."

"Worried about the chickens?"

"Yes, they've got used to me and I don't want them to get all fluttery again." Rubyn went into the coop and started stroking the chickens, crooning to them and looking for eggs. Sure enough they sat and let him. Which meant the chickens were contrary as well since when Billi looked for eggs they always objected and yes, they fluttered. Billi carried on with the goats and they both worked in silence for a bit, and then Rubyn took a big breath and stood real straight.

"I've been wondering, we all have, did we upset you?" The littlun looked downright nervous, which took Billi aback a bit.

"What? No! It's just, I thought, you know with the Harvestfest... Ah, it was after the littluns went home so you don't know. Look, I did something stupid and it's best I keep out the way for a bit." Billi certainly wasn't explaining that mess to a littlun, and wasn't surprised nobody else had.

"We all know, Perry told me that the b.., that, er, Edan insulted Ma. Did you really strangle him with one hand? Wish I'd seen that, serves 'im right!" It was like a spring flood, all pouring out of the lad with the words tripping over themselves and was that what it looked like to Perry? There again Perry was only a youth, hot blood and little thought.

Billi sighed and put up a hand to stop the littlun. "You wouldn't understand Rubyn, it's that grown up stuff. It wasn't my job. I shouldn't have stepped in like that and I lost my temper which is bad. Talk to your Ma instead of Perry. Go on. Ah, wait, you'd best have your pay." Rubyn went off looking determined, with a hundred questions dancing behind his eyes and three eggs held carefully.

Billi glanced at Rabbit and the Hound followed Rubyn until the little figure reached the first cottage, and then bounced back. Rabbit wasn't getting much of a run these last five days and the Hound loved it out there under the green as much as Billi did, maybe more. Rabbit's song showed that what just happened puzzled him, perhaps because they weren't going hunting as they usually did when Rubyn came? Billi made a firm decision, because he wasn't being fair to the Hound. After the last Tinkerers came through and he'd traded the good stones and furs to top up his nest egg again Billi would leave.

He'd leave a message for Sis asking if she wanted Ellibeth to look after the hut. He'd leave four chickens for Rubyn anyway, to give the lad a chance to start his own little nest egg, and One-shut to guard them. Or maybe One-shut would rather come. This time Billi refused to get side-tracked. If the Wild took Billi's chickens a few would survive here anyway. Then he could always come and trade for some chicks, and rear them with a stronger pen. Making a decision calmed Billi somehow.

It would be a ten-day at most before the Tinkerers came through but that was enough time to prepare properly. Billi slept a little better, but not much, because he still didn't really want to go and leave his new friends, if any of them were still friends. Though the other part of him still wanted to live in that beautiful valley if the Wild would let him. Billi refused to let his head run off round that circle again.

The next morning Billi worked round the garden, taking in the last of the carrots and a swede so he could make a stew to soften the last crusts of bread. Maybe 'twould be his own bread if the last of Ellibeth's was past saving. Billi didn't fancy that part, going back to his own bread, and foresaw a lot less bread in his diet and a lot more wild roots and grilled meat. He'd take a good few of the sprouts when he left and a couple of cabbages, and a couple of beets to tide him over until he'd found where the wild stuff grew.

* * *

Engrossed in the planning Billi's first warning came from Rabbit but not as a warning. The song lifted along with a soft whining to welcome someone, and a good friend from the little zing now in the hum. Then Billi heard Rubyn's voice, coming to tend the chickens again. Billi looked up to see Viktor's entire family coming up the track, including Bliss and Hektor and Viktor's two littluns who were, he thought a moment, seven summers and six? Cautiously he went to the gate, and they were all smiling and he could smell fresh bread? The whole crowd came in the gate and Dapple and Spots greeted Rabbit while all the rest said hello before they split up all over his little plot. Billi replied to the greetings cautiously, and definitely confused.

Bliss and Ellibeth took Hektor off into the hut and the smell went with them so maybe they'd been baking back home, while Rubyn headed for the chickens of course. The other four split up and started checking fences and the goats, clearing the bit of snow from around the well and generally tidying up this and that. The whole thing had the look of a planned exercise.

While he stood there, nonplussed, Viktor took him by the arm and drew Billi aside. "Now Rubyn came home with a lot of nonsense about you shaming my Ellibeth, or some such, so we've come to get the straight of it. And to find out why you're hiding out here and haven't been to the Village or hunting. What's up?"

"Well, I shouldn't have lost my temper, and I nigh on killed a man and ruined the Harvestfest. It wasn't my place when there was you and the Farmer there, and Rabbit threatened to kill another man. So I thought it were best if I kept my head down a bit. I'm really sorry Viktor, for butting in and showing your maid up." Billi had really hoped to avoid this bit, the confrontation. But why had Bliss come with Hektor?

Viktor laughed, then stared at Billi and cut it short. "Ah. I didn't realise that you meant that. Sorry? It was a blessing!" Viktor shook his head and his face hardened "I would have done something if you'd been slower, but I've not your heft, Billi. I would've used a blade and that could have gone two ways and might have meant a death. 'Twould have been much worse." Viktor snorted. "If the Farmer wanted to step in he seemed awful slow and he's not been near since, so maybe he wasn't that bothered anyway. As for Rabbit?" Viktor looked at the Hound and chuckled. "Most folk think he stopped the trouble. A couple of the Hunters say that the idiot reaching for you should count himself lucky. There's some Hounds wouldn't have warned him, according to them."

"But he threatened a man, a killing threat because I know Rabbit and that wasn't a caution. How was that stopping trouble? Mind, I'm glad he did, I've no spare hand and shouldn't get into that sort of trouble." Billi paused, trying to get his head around Viktor thinking of using a knife! That was as startling as anything so far. The mild mannered Tanner using a blade on a man? Then Billi caught the sense of the last bit. Some Hounds wouldn't have warned?

Viktor shook his head. "Ah, you didn't see. Perry had come up behind you and so had Hektor, and both your Bros were on the way as I was. The rest of Edan's crowd were getting set. It would have been a brawl, and who knows who would have been caught up in that? Hah, not after Rabbit said his piece. I've never heard a Hound growl and mean it! We see him so often with you, all daft and gentle, we forget that Rabbit is a true Hound and a big brawny lad." Viktor poked Billi in the bicep. "As you are, that's some grip!" Billi didn't know what to say, his Bros had been coming, and Hektor and Perry?

"But I saw them, everyone's faces. They were disgusted. And I showed up Ellibeth." He could still see those curled lips, the disgust.

"At the maggot on the floor, you lummox. You really thought everyone blamed you, after what you said? After what the maggot said?" Victor looked up at Billi with a little smile. "Ellibeth don't seem to mind you speaking up, and if she did that maid would say so. She reckons you shut up Edan better than any beating." A grim smile spread over Viktor's face now. "Well he'll mind his mouth now even after he can speak properly again. Disowned, and the elders have him shunned until he learns some manners. If he steps out of line again before then they'll banish him and that means the Forest or the caravans." Viktor gave a short laugh. "Since he's got no Hound it'll be the Trader caravans. They'll make him pay heavy until he can get somewhere that'll take him. Unless he joins that shifty lot, the Traders."

"Shunned?" The elders rarely took action because they didn't really rule the place, only guide, and the last shunning had been when Billi still had two legs.

Viktor slapped Billi on the shoulder. "So cheer up. You don't need hut guards any more since he's been warned that he's not to come anywhere near your hut. His own Bro warned him. Now come into your hut because those two will have got organised by now." He led Billi off to his own hut, which was sort of wrong, but Billi didn't care because a great weight came further off him with every step and off Rabbit as well from the happy lilt in the song. They could keep coming home and going out into the green and tending the lakes!

It wasn't until he'd sat in his chair with a piece of hot meat and tater pie and a drop of ale that the other bit struck Billi. "D'you mean none of you will be coming again, to look after the hut when I'm out?"

"Well there's no need now. Is there?" Hektor seemed to find that funny, as did Bliss.

"Well it's just. You know." Billi waved his hand around then stopped. "I was going to say look at the mess but it's all gone again." He sighed. "I've sort of got used to having the place tidied up, and a bit of nice bread, and I don't mind paying." Then he shrugged. "Too late now, with what I said, and Edan said. Ellibeth can't be staying here after that. Perry just isn't any good with a duster and I've never tasted his bread."

They all laughed, then Viktor stopped long enough to gasp out a few words. "I doubt many folk will say anything amiss about Ellibeth for a good while after that." He fought the laugh down. "No matter what she does."

Ellibeth came over, trying to stop her smile. "The Farmer had no understanding with me, none at all. He certainly has no say over who I see or where I go. As far as my reputation goes, Billi, you've always been very proper. Who else would have built that just to protect my name and have fresh bread?" She waved her hand towards the door to the extra room, behind Hektor who was sniggering at either her or Billi. Ellibeth glared at him, but without much force. "You can shut up young man. He's more careful of my name than you were with my sister's, even if you did put it right!" Hektor tried to look sorry but couldn't and Bliss whispering in his ear wasn't helping.

Ellibeth turned back to Billi. "Anyway, I wanted to say thank you for standing up for me. If you wish, I will be happy to come and dust and make bread. You really don't want to taste Perry's." She bent suddenly and bussed him firmly on the cheek. "There. That's safe enough with my Da and Sis in the same room. Mind you, if I come dusting you can't be taking any other liberties."

Billi blushed bright red. He knew he had and there were two pink spots on Ellibeth's cheeks as she turned away. He opened his mouth to point out he hadn't taken a liberty, but then he saw the smiles as everyone else enjoyed the joke and let his own smile join them. "I'll try to remember."

Even with her back to him Billi could hear the humour in Ellibeth's answer. "Good, now eat your pie or it'll be cold." So he ate his pie while Viktor confirmed that it did mean Billi wanted the youths and Ellibeth to keep looking out for the place. The Tanner told him he needn't give them so much pay but between bites Billi insisted. He'd got nobody to leave it to so he'd give what he wanted where he wanted, and for his own reasons.

That made Hektor laugh again, the young Hunter seemed in a funny mood today. Perry and Timath stuck their heads round the door to see what was going on, so they'd probably run out of jobs. The littluns were called out of Ellibeth's bedroom where Rubyn had been showing them the bearskin, and given berry juice. Despite protests Billi asked Timath to go into the cold store for butter, bacon and some cold cuts to go with the eggs just collected, and the fresh bread. Ellibeth and Bliss took over, quickly producing hot bacon and egg sandwiches and soon everyone sat eating and drinking. Even Rubyn had a bit of cider in his berry juice. Billi had no idea what the rest were celebrating. He just felt happy and the joyful song in his head made it perfect.

Hektor managed to quieten down eventually, enough to talk. "Could I take a few geese from the reeds, Billi? Bliss is making a jacket stuffed with feathers for seeing to the chickens and such in the cold weather?" Hektor shook his head in mock despair. "The jacket is needed because the furs I brought home for a warm winter coat are apparently too pretty to use in the chicken coop or the cowshed."

"I've got a few furs like that, too pretty to use." Billi stopped. "Cowshed?"

"Oh yes, Da has let me have a cow for milk and butter now, and cheese if you want to trade?" Hektor's eyes sharpened at the chance of a trade.

Billi smiled. "I only have cream cheese usually. When I don't use the goat's milk or trade it before it turns I drain the curds until it's fit to spread on bread. Something different would be nice."

Ellibeth jumped in before Hektor could trade. "I could make you some of the harder, tangy type of cheese with the goat's milk if you want."

For some reason that set Hektor off laughing again until Bliss jabbed him in the ribs.

Billi ignored the laughing. "Thank you, though I'll still trade with Hektor. I'll swap something, a stone for Bliss maybe, for some cheese right now, until Ellibeth makes some herself." Billi smiled at Ellibeth. "You'll want to take some home for the trouble, I should think?"

"That is kind. I'd appreciate it Billi." Hektor started laughing again. By the time everyone left Hektor had his humour under control though he still occasionally sniggered. Billi saw them all to the gate, paid Rubyn his eggs and watched them walk off to the Village, then came back inside still in a daze. A completely bewildered but happy Billi and a happy Rabbit sat in their spick and span home, until One-shut came in to claim his place by the fire and a few bits of bacon. They would be going out hunting for three days tomorrow which definitely had to be one reason for the big smile Billi went to sleep with. Another reason was the relief and contentment in Rabbit's song.

* * *

Life settled back down for Billi or rather he became busy again. His store became a really cold store again once the first snow had been scooped up and packed in the boxes down there. Now the room could be filled with meat for the winter instead of the dried, smoked or salted variety that would keep in summer. A good bit of that had been sold to the last Traders that came through and more would go to the last Tinkerers. A Hunter's stores were partly cleared out this time of year, only leaving enough to get through winter, and then properly cleared at the beginning of spring to leave room for a summer's hunting.

A good part of the frozen meat and fish left in the store when spring finally arrived would be sold to the first Tinkerers and Traders. They came early enough to keep the food cool until they reached a bigger settlement. That's why the first wagons braved the snow, to take the frozen spoils of a winter's hunting. The wild meat brought good prices if it could be kept frozen while it was taken to the right market.

That was strange to think of, deer or bear meat being expensive, but Billi had started to realise that expensive depended on the person not the goods. Expensive could be decided by what you were used to and what was rare a long way from Trail's End. The Traders and Tinkerers both agreed that little remained of the Wild in the edges of the Forest further sunwards so any Forest meat was exotic, and so were the skins and even horns.

Now was the best time to refill the cold store, while the animals were still plump and sweet with new fat, before the leaves fell and made it harder to hunt and the animals became leaner and tougher. All the Hunters were busy and Billi hunted in three or four day trips to get beyond the wary game remaining near to home. Out that far many game animals had still never seen a bow.

The villagers were definitely friendlier again. Somehow the argument, fight, whatever they thought it was had cleared the air and the rumours were gone like spring snow in the sunshine. After all that time, and all Billi had needed to do was lose his temper, which made life very strange and not at all predictable. When Kravitt the blacksmith insisted Billi joined him in the alehouse Billi was made welcome and included in the gossip. Not one person even mentioned Edan or the trouble at the Harvestfest.

Word eventually got back to Billi, through Perry who always seemed to know the gossip. Edan had taken to living with one of his friends, Aescon the Potter's youth, when he didn't sleep at the stockyard. He slept there alone since the yards were only used in summer, and the beasts were now safely penned in their home barns and pastures for winter. He might be building a small shelter there since Edan still had his big dogs and now four carthorses to start his new ventures.

What Edan didn't do was spread rumours, frequent the alehouse, or come into the Village even when his voice recovered. He didn't dare since the elders hadn't lifted the shunning. The maid he'd been flirting with had picked another target since she "wanted a proper man" so perhaps it was lucky he'd got the dogs for company. Billi didn't care much. He was out in the green even if it looked brown and a bit thin in a lot of places.

The last Tinkerers of the year finally turned up and set up their trading stalls and tents. Billi went round them and came away with a new spit for cooking in the cabin out at the lakes. He also bought a small potbellied stove he thought he could pack out there. The stoves were a new trade item that the Tinkerer claimed would throw out more heat than an open fire, and Billi could also boil a pot or kettle on it. Billi considered one for his hut near the Village but the ovens and hob built into the fireplace were more than enough so Billi settled for just the one, for the valley.

There were some lovely leather collars but Hounds were never collared. Firstly, it wasn't necessary and secondly no collar would hold a Hound. Well perhaps an iron one with a thick iron chain could but why would you? In the end Billi bought a new collar for Spot since he seemed to come with whoever looked after the place so the dog lived in the hut as much as Billi, just on different days.

This last caravan brought the right Tinkerer to trade the best stones to. Not only did this Tinkerer really seem to give the best prices, but Billi felt more comfortable dealing with this man and his beguilers. Billi knew these were all good stones as he'd used the five Tinkerer caravans visiting during the year to sort them. He had been putting a heap on the table, then only selling a third of what the Tinkerers wanted to buy, which had also given him a really good read on what they would bid up to. Refusing to sell the rest also meant that Billi had formed a real resistance to beguiling if he wished. The rejected lesser stones all went to the Traders for silver or salt. Billi had no use for them as he could find plenty of the better ones in his gravel bar.

In the evening Billi went to trade his stones. The beguiling ramped up as soon as he stepped in the tent and Billi laughed. They knew just who he was of course, and now they knew that he had good stones. One of the beguilers had a beautiful large sparkul on a chain around her neck that flashed in the lamplight every time she moved and Billi had to ask, how much are those sparkuls?

The Tinkerer promised to answer later. The beguiling increased if that was possible and continued while a selection of Billi's small stones were traded for little ingots and thick gold rings that weighed the same. Some settlements used them instead of ingots and coins, he learned. The beguilers put some on their fingers to show how the women of that place flaunted their wealth, but Billi would bet they weren't flaunting it showing as many tattoos as that!

After the small stones he'd brought today were all exchanged the Tinkerer sent a beguiler out. The remaining beguiler, wearing the big sparkul, moved to make it flash and burn in the lamplight and kept Billi amused until the other one came back with a strapping youth and six small bags. The Tinkerer carefully tipped each one out onto the soft cloth on the table and six fires burned in the centres of six stones in the lamplight. They were utterly entrancing. Billi found himself moving his head to watch the colours shift and joined in the laughter of those watching him. He pointed. "How much?"

The Tinkerer's eyes narrowed. "In exchange for what? Large stones, small ones, or gold?" Billi had sold a larger stone last time and the man knew there should be more but Billi hadn't brought them tonight. Though while trading for the smaller ones Billi had let him know there were more small stones if these prices were right.

This was the start of the bartering for tomorrow's stones. "Larger stones. Larger than even those larger sparkuls."

Billi gained a little knowledge, a hint about how sparkuls were made. "But yours are roughs, the small ones as well as any larger stones you have. Each of the sparkuls started as a larger rough stone, so maybe yours will become smaller as they become more beautiful?" The beguilers moved back in while Billi considered. His larger stones only became the size of these if they were big enough to start with. Then the Tinkerer would want his profit for making them burn inside like that, and that would be a big profit.

There were two coloured stones, a deep red and a dark green. The green looked very tempting given how Billi loved the green of the Forest but the other four, the clear ones, had captured him. Icicles along the eaves on a winter morning as the sun hit them, hoar frost on the grass on a still cold day, or the sparkling fire when a sunbeam caught a frosted spider's web. Billi could see them all in his mind when he looked at the glittering sparkuls.

One seemed almost square, two were rounded and the fourth made a teardrop and the Tinkerer explained they were all worth much more than the coloured ones. At least that told Billi that his clear stones should be worth more as well. As the Tinkerer talked, Billi also learned that shapes mattered, the shapes of his roughs as well as these. Billi knew he would do badly in the first trades, but that would be paying to learn. Even so, sparkuls might make a good addition to his nest egg.

The stones from the lakes were all the clear type, but Billi had one larger red stone, from an entirely different stream. He'd also found a few small red ones in that stream, and remembering that prompted his question. "Do red stones and green stones and clear ones come from different places? Or could a mixture come from one place?"

"Why do you ask?"

"I've only found one type in any one stream, and know which streams might yield each type." Billi looked from the coloured to the clear ones on the table. "I wondered if there might be different types further along those streams?"

The Tinkerers looked at his own stones and thought hard. "I've never given it much thought." This must be serious, because the beguilers had stopped flaunting and were listening intently. "The stones are very different, with very different values. The coloured ones are not the clear ones with colour. The coloured ones are softer, even for stones and the clear ones are very hard." He sighed. "You have more information about finding them than I do. As far as I can see, you might find two different stones in a stream, but I believe they will come from two different sources." The Tinkerer looked at the amount of a small stones Billi had brought, and must have thought about Billi promising more. "Have you found the source?"

"No. Just a place where they seem to have collected, as I said before. The source is somewhere inside the rocks, well beyond reach." Billi smiled. "Though I would prefer that to stay between us."

"Oh yes. A pity though. I would have loved to see a source, even if I had to pay a Hunter to take me. Even if I travelled blindfold." The Tinkerer sighed. "That would be a sight to see. There aren't even any legends about a source."

"You could blindfold me and take me as well? Just to make the trip interesting." The beguiler with the big sparkul laughed. Then she became more serious. "I could be very friendly to a man who took me to see the source or even where many had collected, especially if he let me choose one?"

"I'll remember, but I think travelling with you might lead to me being distracted. That is a very bad idea out in the green." Billi smiled. "Downright dangerous." Everyone laughed.

The Tinkerer and Billi danced around colours and the larger stones and value a little. They agreed Billi would bring his goods tomorrow evening and then the Tinkerer could be more specific on pricings. Billi went straight home, deep in thought. He didn't usually stay for the dancing or the after-dark beguiling, and definitely not tonight because he had a lot to think about. Deep thinking and Tinkerer dancing just didn't go together.

The Tinkerers were being mysterious about the dancing this year, promising something different and spectacular for the following night. That intrigued most of the youths and some men, considering the flamboyant and energetic dancing the tattooed maids usually produced. Billi could hear the music and the youths cheering and whistling as he headed for home, with Rabbit a dim shadow ahead. At least the usual dancing wasn't suffering.

Back home Billi tipped out his large stones on a bit of kidskin as he'd seen the Tinkerer do on his soft cloth, and looked through them. He also tipped out the small coloured and clear ones in little heaps. Billi knew that any of the red stones came from a small river that fed the one near the Village. Eventually he wanted to work up that one to see where they came from. That could be a very long trip since that waterway was larger than the stream he had followed to the valley. Billi felt a bit torn over whether he wanted to find another lake and valley because he had a full time job dealing with one.

Billi had only ever found one green stone, a small one which he'd kept because it did remind him of the Forest. Billi knew that all the ones the Tinkerers chose, but he didn't trade, had been clear or red because he'd scrubbed and inspected every one again afterwards. Billi had also learned not to bother offering the striped types and the black or clouded and white ones and sold those straight to the Traders.

Billi knew that these larger ones were all clear apart from one red one and some were bigger than the sparkuls that had been shown, much larger in two cases. They were all valuable, and Billi already knew that but if he traded them for the shiny ones, the sparkuls, could he then trade those to the caravans of ordinary Traders and make a profit? The Tinkerers forced the Traders to pay huge prices for the shining sparkuls. That was common knowledge because the Traders were always complaining, but never mentioned actual prices. If Billi could get the shining ones in exchange for the rough ones, then they might work out a better nest egg for his old age.

That still drove Billi, the thought of his leg failing and him being a burden to his Sibs, the cripple who couldn't earn his own food. He needed a big nest egg, the biggest he could manage and if he saved enough maybe he could hire a Hunter and pony to still visit the valley. Maybe if he had enough of a nest egg he could keep living there and pay a Hunter to bring what he needed? Neither of his two bright-eyed partners disagreed, but neither knew if the green or red ones were worth more. Billi slept and dreamed of glittering rainbows twisting in lamplight.

During the following day, Billi took the small soft pelts from the valley and riverbank and his thick furs to the tents and asked about the gold jewellery. He saw plenty, none of which had any stones in it because only one Tinkerer in each caravan dealt in sparkuls and they were always sold at night by the light of the lamps. Now Billi felt sure that was so the fire inside them leapt and flickered.

The gold became more expensive as it became more intricate and plain bands and bangles were little different to the price of the ingots they were made from. He traded furs for some fancy bangles and a necklace of interlocking sections that looked almost snakelike. Billi could trade for plainer gold items from the Trader caravans and they might even be a bit cheaper, but was the quality the same and how could he tell? Traders certainly watered the ale sometimes. The Traders also paid less for gold if they could, or gave less in return if he bought with it. Billi kept his gold nuggets for Tinkerers and used silver or copper for anything he wanted from Traders, if he had nothing they would trade for it.

The trading for gold led to Billi bringing out his little pouch of nuggets, some barely larger than grains, that he sometimes found while fishing. As he laid on the bank gently drifting his hand into position the gleam sometimes caught his eye, and after the fish was landed or escaped he would pluck it from among the pebbles. The Tinkerer wanted to know if he had dust. When Billi asked what sort of dust the man produced a little skin pouch with fine glittering dust inside, all of it pure gold. Dust could be found in the sand bars or mud banks where nuggets turned up and some might even gather downstream as dust carried further and dropped down where the current slackened. This was Billi's year for new discoveries.

A while later Billi came out of a tent clutching a large shallow dish and lighter by three small nuggets, but he knew how to find the dust in the sand if it was there. The Tinkerer had sprinkled gold dust in some ordinary river sand, in a bowl of water, and proceeded to swish and swirl. Then he'd shown Billi the thick yellow smear in the dish. The sand and bowl were how they taught the Tinkerer littluns, who searched every stream the Tinkerers crossed.

The nuggets were the cost of an intense lesson in how to do it and the shallow dish, allegedly the best implement, though Billi thought the pan for frying his bacon and eggs might do the job. Still, he quite liked the idea of sitting with his foot in a stream in the summer, swirling sand and generally just enjoying the moment. If he ended up with the little yellow curl, well it would be a bonus. Rabbit's song liked that idea though probably the sitting in the sun, not the yellow curl.

* * *

A definite air of anticipation gathered around the Tinkerer encampment as the sun began to sink, because the Tinkerers were teasing everyone a little about the dancing later. Billi would have a look this time, but first he could already feel the trickle of excitement that any truly serious bargaining session with Tinkerers engendered. The beguilers hovered, and Billi brought out a pouch. He bounced it in his hand. "Which are worth more? Red or green?"

The Tinkerer sat for a few moments looking at the small pouch, then the man laughed. "You have some in there?" Billi pulled out a small red one and his green chip. He wasn't parting with it and had no more but Billi needed to know relative values before they started. The actual value could take some time. Eventually the Tinkerer admitted that both were worth quite a bit less than clear stones, and the red was worth a little more than green. Billi put the green chip into the pouch on his belt and tipped the red stones out

"You are failing. Are you too old and wrinkled for beguiling now?" The Tinkerer pretended to be stricken by the trick, clutching his breast. "This man still has his wits!" That was all part of bargaining but well done and led to a distinct distraction to stop Billi keeping his wits. The tattooed beguiler with the large sparkul perched on his good knee with an arm around his neck! Serious beguiling indeed, usually they only perched on knees after already getting a reward.

She kept whispering just how much she wanted one of those red stones while Billi tried to think through the other offers, the ones for his stones. She didn't whisper during the actual intense bargaining over price, as that wasn't in the rules. There were rules to beguiling; the maids were there to rattle Billi's wits and disturb his concentration, but not actually interfere. Luckily Billi had spent the year practicing resistance to beguilers.

Three large green and three large red sparkuls were brought and Billi bargained for all six, singly and in sets, and the lot. Eventually he gained one larger green sparkul, and lost most of his small red roughs. Now Billi knew a larger sparkul cost more than twice the weight in small ones. "Would you like a little berry juice?" The Tinkerer smiled, "Or ale, or maybe wine?"

A new tactic, Billi hadn't been offered refreshments before. "Berry juice would help, please. My throat is dry, and it isn't the talking." Billi glanced at the beguilers and they laughed delightedly. "Could I see several different sizes of clear stones please? While they are coming, how much weight of small stones would equal a larger one?" Billi gestured. "That one cost more than double the weight."

"Much depends on the quality of what is offered, and the larger sparkul being traded, but yes you are right. Smaller sparkuls are not worth the same weight for weight as they get larger, and that is reflected when trading roughs into sparkuls." The Trader glanced at Billi's jacket. "Do you just have smaller roughs with you?"

"No, I have both." Billi wasn't worried about telling the Tinkerer, not least because they were notoriously honest and would not rob him. They might skin him alive in a trade if possible, but not physically rob anyone and in any case Rabbit laid just inside the tent. The beguiling intensified when the clear stones were brought out. Billi was immediately accused of cheating by checking elsewhere as he rejected the first bids outright. Checking wasn't cheating, but it allowed the Tinkerer to act stricken again.

"Of course I did." Billi laughed. "How do you think I built up some resistance to beguiling." The beguilers moved closer, "Though these two are prettier than the others." The two young women smiled happily.

"Naughty. You aren't supposed to beguile them. How did my prices compare?" The Tinkerer seemed confident, but then he always did.

"As you probably know, your prices are best but only just, so providing they stay like that I will bring my large roughs to you." Billi smiled at the beguilers again. "Since you have the prettiest beguilers." Billi really did enjoy flirting a little with the beguilers, especially since Tinkerer maids didn't seem to care about his stump. The rules for Tinkerer flirting were clearer than Village rules and he understood them. If he let one of them have a small rough stone, Billi would get to be cuddled properly with Tinkerer kisses. For a slightly larger rough stone or several smaller ones, he might be taken back to her caravan to follow the tattoos.

Billi sparred with the Tinkerer a little and sipped berry juice while they waited for the strapping youth and the big sparkuls. They came to a definite agreement, confirming that Billi would get a good price but would check now and then with others. The Tinkerer would pay a good price but only if Billi offered him most of the good stones. The beguilers were trying hard during the verbal sparring, especially one of them. The big sparkul on the chain would swing across Billi's eyesight and then back, pulling his eyes to the beguiling parts. Then she told him how much she wanted one of those stones, maybe that little one that had fallen away from the rest, for a closer look at this tattoo? Maybe that larger one to see where the tattoo went?

Billi finally asked about the stone. "How much would it cost to get a big sparkul put on a chain so it swings and flashes like that?" The beguiling backed off because the price trading had started. Though it didn't back off entirely as Billi had to take a good look at various sizes in different settings, usually with a background of tattoos.

"The mounting costs more if you want the setting to be more intricate and the best sparkuls demand the best settings." The Tinkerer beckoned to each beguiler, and each removed a sparkul. The Tinkerer turned them over. "As you can see, the reverse is different on each. Some will sell you a setting to take any stone of the right size." The curled lips on the Tinkerer and both beguilers were a clear comment on that idea. "Each sparkul needs the right backing, to hold it properly yet also allow the fire to shine through."

He twirled a finger at the beguilers, and they twisted and turned in the lamplight so that their sparkuls flashed and flamed. "And the right tattoos to show them off," Billi added.

"But even if the gold is very intricate, the sparkul is always the main value unless very tiny chips are used." One beguiler showed one of the gold rings usually used to pay with. This one had been covered in tiny chips and sparkled as if covered in a light frost.

Billi had finally realised that every sparkul on the beguilers had a different setting. "Are you wearing one of everything in stock, between you?"

"Yes, though if you want us to supply something else, something special?" The smiles refused to clarify if that meant beguiler or decoration so Billi moved on. Luckily the brawny youth had arrived. "Perhaps we can come back to gold settings once I see what the sparkuls might need. I can't afford a tattooed setting, certainly not to take home with me." The beguilers laughed as Billi gestured to the nine soft bags being placed on the table.

There was silence as nine large clear sparkuls were tipped out. They consisted of the teardrop and a pair of much smaller oval ones, two sizes of the square one, and four of the round ones all in different sizes. The remaining small red rough stones were still on Billi's side of the table and he tipped out one pouch of small clear roughs onto the cloth. Then he placed the small pouches from his pocket onto the table and Billi tipped out one of his larger roughs. He had done the same as the Tinkerer and put them in separate pouches so they could see he had more but not the sizes.

"Which of those stones would this one make?"

The beguilers hung back so this must be serious, and the Tinkerer looked, thought long and hard, and sighed. "You have brought too many so I must be honest, though the exact result will depend on the quality of your rough." He placed a finger on one of the sparkuls. "Please don't tell anyone or I will be ridiculed by other Tinkerers." Maybe so but that wouldn't stop the Tinkerer from bargaining hard. The Tinkerer began to examine all the large roughs as Billi brought them out. It wasn't easy to keep track because the beguilers worked as a team to distract him, and their laughter when he avoided the distraction was actually distracting!

The beguiling eased off and the one on his knee stood up, because now began a serious slow dance of words. Billi wanted some stones and some ingots and maybe a stone in a setting on a chain. More sparkuls came in, small ones, and they were added to the other side of the cloth. Those were to make up the differences, if Billi had more roughs to offer than the sparkul he wanted. Even the heap of small sparkuls looked entrancing as the light flickered.

Now there were two strapping youths by the entrance. Billi laughed, "I'll not run far." The Tinkerer nodded to them, and they stepped back outside. Billi felt sure they didn't go far, with good reason as the Traders would love to get near this table. Though most of the value sat across from Billi, tempting his roughs of all sizes to join them.

Eventually Billi had the green stone, and the teardrop, and the two small oval ones which he would decide on a setting for next year. The Tinkerer Billi would test the cost of settings through the year and promised a good price to bring Billi back. The second largest round stone would be Billi's as well once a twisted rope of gold and a delicate cradle of the same metal were holding it.

The value of that sat in a pouch kept separate from the meagre remains of his original hoard, and would be handed over when Billi collected the goods. Billi was content. He was almost certain he would get more from the Traders for these than for the roughs, and certainly not less considering how keen they were to get sparkuls. Billi looked forward to finding out what the mounted one was worth. The Tinkerer seemed happy so he had made a profit as well. It was the sign of a good bargain when both parties thought they had a good deal.

The beguilers gave a last little twirl. "We will not tell the other beguilers about those you have left. It wouldn't be fair. If you resisted us, they haven't got a chance."

Billi separated out two little red roughs and sighed. "But I didn't resist, not completely. There's one each as a reward for your hard work. You two will give me interesting dreams all winter so it's a fair exchange." They preened when the Tinkerer agreed that they'd had that effect ever since getting their first tattoos. Billi really didn't mind since he had thoroughly enjoyed the trading and the beguiling, and the stones were found goods anyway. The Tinkerer would be horrified at the last sentiment if Billi ever said it out loud.

The Tinkerer supplied a burly youth to lurk nearby until Billi came clear of the tents, an indication of the value that Billi was carrying, which was a bit startling. The beguilers though that giving him an escort was funny since Billi looked stronger and more frightening than either guard, according to them. Billi thought they were teasing the burly youth a bit. He wondered if they were flirting? Did Tinkerer maids flirt with Tinkerer youths as well as beguile?

The truly ferocious guard hopped along nearby, just content to be out of the tent and enjoying the scents of all those who'd visited the Tinkerers. Rabbit had laid quietly through the bargaining and the contented song in Billi's head helped a little when the beguiling grew intense.

* * *

The sparkuls went into a different hidey-hole in the hut. That was a loose rock in the wall and getting to it meant Billi holding the bed end up while sat on the floor. Not easy for anyone who didn't have muscles like Billi's, and even with the bed up the stone wasn't obviously loose. Billi had started hiding valuables because of Edan and now he also worried about Traders if they got wind of his stones. The gold work from this afternoon went in the slice that came free of the roof timber close to the wall. That wasn't as secure, but hard to see unless someone actually stood with their back to the wall with a decent light.

Billi decided to take all his sparkuls and gold out to the lakes and hide them well, but not tomorrow. The next day, since tomorrow he would be collecting the chain before the Tinkerers left to race against the snows of deeper winter. He had often wondered what happened if they lost because this string of fancy wagons had always been the last, every year. Perhaps their wagons were snug enough to survive while they dug themselves clear.

Right now though, he was intrigued by the promises of a different sort of Tinkerer dance.

Winter Dancing

Billi had a bite to eat and headed up the track again to see this dancing. The hints and teasing had worked. A few older men had even brought their lasses to see it although this was a very rare occurrence. That might be a bit embarrassing considering how uninhibited Tinkerer dancing could be, though only bonded lasses came and there were no maids. More or less all the youths and unbonded men in the Village had come.

At first the dancing seemed the same as usual. The tattooed maids flaunted and strutted with Tinkerer youths and men and their sparkuls flashed and glittered in the torchlight. The men left, leaving just the maids, and the music became faster and faster, wilder and wilder. A few discs of copper went onto the packed dirt to encourage the maids nearer, or to let a few bits of cloth flutter loose. Then silver glittered in the flames of the torches, and more clothing slipped free.

So far despite the amount of tattoos on show where the silver fell the thickest, this seemed normal, and Billi heard complaints that this was the same as last night. A rattle of the drum and a clash of bells and the music stopped, allowing the dancers to slip into the shadows. A single flute started, haunting, slow, and another maid stepped, glided almost, from the shadows.

A different sort of maid entirely and there were audible gasps from the crowd and a few appreciative whistles. Not a Tinkerer woman, not even a half-breed who were reputedly beautiful enough to drive men wild with a glance. This one looked like a spirit in the night. Her long white hair drifted, a fine mane that tumbled loosely around her shoulders and down her back, and her skin shone pure white in the flickering torchlight. That came as a shock after the usual swarthy Tinkerers and tanned villagers, especially as no villager ever looked that pale even when a shirt came off after a long winter. Her white skin looked even more startling because of the brightly coloured tracery of tattoos that ran riotously over every exposed inch, and over the rest of her as everyone could tell. The many strips of gauzy material blurred any real view, but allowed the eye to follow the stark bright lines.

The flute played a little faster and she danced, ethereal and light, skipping and twirling, floating across the pounded dirt and along the line of entranced men. Men who were suddenly looking into two chips of sparkling pale blue, something unique to anyone there. There were a few yellow blondes among the traders, with deep blue eyes, but not this almost colourless yet somehow intense version. Her face looked as different as the rest of her, fine, sharp featured with high cheekbones and brows so pale they were almost lost. Then her shockingly red full lips parted in a smile to reveal sharp, bright white canines, which contributed to her fierce, feral look. No raucous laughter and no crude suggestions came from the crowd, and no coins were thrown until the Dancer came to a halt. Then the cheering and whistling started and a shower of small copper and silver discs pattered on the dirt.

The Dancer held up her hands for silence, and when it almost arrived a deep, sensuous voice with a thick accent rang out. "I need parrtnerr, I dance wid, who iss ssrrongess?" A storm of noise answered as at least half the unattached men volunteered and were belittled by their friends. "Who iss ssrrongess heerr?"

"Billi, he throttled Edan with one hand." A chorus of agreement rose up, mixed with merriment as of course Billi couldn't dance. Edan sat among his friends, keeping quiet at the far side of the dancing area and though he scowled, he didn't deny it. The Dancer looked round and a few pointed, so Billi gestured at his peg and the crutch and smiled an apology. The woman looked around again.

"Iss de ssrrongess?" Billi braced himself for the laughter but she glided across and looked him over. The crowd fell silent except for occasional flurries of laughter. Billi didn't mind, this joke was on her since she had asked for the strongest. "Can dee liff a maid, ssrrong man?"

"He held up a grown man with one arm!" A storm of agreement rose to drown the negation from Billi and she leant in. He could almost feel sparks crackling in the air as the Dancer came closer.

"Sshow me, ssrrong man, sshow dee arrm." Billi's neighbours were gleefully pulling at him now, so he let them pull his coat back off his shoulders and arm and roll up the sleeve. Then he grinned up at her and flexed his bicep to a cheer. A few started to chant Bill-llee, Bill-llee. The ale and the joke were having their say now because they were all laughing at her. A glance showed that Billi one-leg was definitely the strongest here, and they really wanted to see how she would work around that.

"No Billee, dee iss Bearr, ssrrong Bearr. Will dee dance wid me, ssrrong Bearr?" Billi waved helplessly at his wooden peg, laughing himself now because this was so funny. The one she wanted to dance with was sat in a crowd of young men who'd kill for the chance and he couldn't. It was life's greatest joke so far. Her eyes suddenly fastened on Rabbit, sat with his tongue out, laughing along with the rest. "Bearr iss Hunnerr?" The Bill-llee, Bill-llee started up again with some Bear-rah, Bear-rah as she straightened and put out her hand, imperious. "Dance wid me Bearrr!"

Billi felt the joke starting to go wrong as hands pulled him to his foot and thrust his crutch into his hand. She was going to make a complete fool of him. His smile slipped and Billi felt the heat start in his face as she moved in closer. Those around were straining to hear now. "Big and ssrrong. No need forr move wid me. Need dee ssrrong, forr frrow, forr cach." Her voice dropped lower, almost a vibration against him, "dance wid me now, Bearr."

"May as well ride the joke to the end now." Billi stuck out his hand to take hers. She glanced around then led him, stumping after, to a big hitching post used to hold the bulls when they were being sold. "Wid back, dee brace on diss. Can liff me, can frrow?" The Dancer stroked Billi's chest and arms and though the crowd couldn't hear what she said there were plenty of suggestions flying now. Billi nodded, he couldn't speak because she was so close that she took his breath away. Taller than she seemed, though not quite his own height, she wouldn't be as light as she looked but even so he knew he could pick her up. "Pick me up, overr head, forr momenn."

She raised her arms and Billi rested his crutch against the post and put a hand each side of her waist. Then with a smooth surge he picked her up to the full stretch, holding her there as Billi concentrated on his balance. Billi barely heard the cheer. It wasn't easy to concentrate on anything but the woman in his hands, her skin warm under his palms. Moving skin as she pivoted forward to lie facing down in the air with arms wide before swinging back towards upright. Billi brought her slowly down to another cheer and she stood a moment and gave him the benefit of a big smile. Then the Dancer twisted out of his hands and plucked his crutch away, tossing it to the crowd. Billi noticed that Rabbit moved to stand over it, so at least he could find it again.

She turned and called out to the crowd. "Ssrrong enough. Rreally ssrrong Bearr." The emphasis on rreally sent a shiver up Billi's spine. A cheer greeted her because the crowd were loving this. "I dance wid bearr. You wan copperr dance, orr ssilverr dance?" Her voice dropped and became sultrier on the last two words. That probably sent the same shivers up other spines that Billi felt in his and it certainly produced a storm of glittering silver.

The Dancer twirled again and glided over, then started to unfasten Billi's shirt, smiling up into his face. "Forr ssilverr, muss ssee de musscle move. Sskin wid sskin." She started to push the shirt up and back, running her hands across Billi's chest. "Da was liff. I ssay frrow, frrow harrd away. If say hold, dee hold arrm out. Up, dee frrow iss up, harrd ass can. Sswing de ssame. Make ssure dee cach when I jump." Billi really did try to concentrate on what she said, but with her accent, that voice, and her hands on his chest and arms it wasn't easy. No matter how this ended, it was going to be memorable.

The Dancer held up a strip of gauze and gestured to numerous others hanging from her clothing. Her teeth gleamed white in a dazzling smile and she tugged lightly at a hanging strip. "You grrip dese, keep dese?" She ran her hands down Billi's arms, shucking the shirt off and scraped her fingers back up to his shoulders, "Mmm, maybe dee can keep all?" Her tongue came out and the tip ran over her canines as she lifted Billi's arms straight out to the sides.

"Diss be hold, now we dance!" The pale figure moved away and curtsied to everyone, the flute started up and the Dancer began to move. At first she danced around the post wide of Billi but this time the music started fast and then went faster as she closed in. Her eyes flashed down at the swirling strips and up at Billi so he grinned and snatched at one.

The Dancer gave a little shriek of alarm and Billi stared at the strip in his hand! Then she smiled at the crowd. "Is quick, diss Hunnerr." The pale shape danced past again, just out of range but Billi had the idea now. He was supposed to pull off enough of her coverings to give the crowd a show, but the inner ones would be tied tight. Billi was more than willing!

Cymbals joined in and the crowd were egging Billi on now, urging him to snatch another as she ran at him and called "frrow up!" He clamped his hands around her waist and did, expecting to catch her again though he remembered to keep hold of the strip of gauze.

No catching needed, the Dancer flew like a bird and from the cheer she landed well and a moment later Billi heard "hold" and stuck his arms out like a scarecrow. She swung under his arm, a littlun on a branch, but kept swinging around across his chest and her legs went across to the other arm. A surge and she slid across his chest, skin to skin for a moment, then came up. The Dancer sat for a moment on the bicep, not quite long enough for her full weight to settle.

Then she rolled off his arm and away, but not before Billi snagged another 'prize' and earned another shriek, and a cheer from the crowd. Billi thought the Dancer must had gauged his strength from the lift or something, but he still thought she took big chances. He wriggled himself against the post to make sure he was braced because he didn't want to fall now! Billi thought he might be strong enough, but balance was another thing.

Billi managed to keep his foot and peg on the floor and the seat of his pants off it as the music became faster and still wilder. The Dancer swung and flew and threw herself at and over him from every angle. She only gave Billi a quick clear call as a warning but Dancer knew her craft. Billi swung her out through the air and saw how she landed from his throws, and her agile rolls always ended in a graceful continuation of her moves. She did that again and again, around and over a truly impressed Billi. She couldn't be sure just how Billi would throw, he just made a best guess of where she wanted to be, but every time the Dancer made her landing look smooth and sure like a planned move. Billi knew this dance wasn't practised but felt sure it looked that way.

Somewhere along the way another flute, bells, a fiddle and drum joined in as Billi caught her high, twisting leaps and held her overhead as she gyrated, then flung her away. She swung up and over her dancing partner and the scattered scraps of cloth around him grew, as did the noise from the crowd. It had to end soon before she ran out of gauze, which wasn't helping Billi's concentration. Luckily the tattoos were coming at him too fast to get a really good look.

"Cach." This time she landed solidly, curled up so she almost tucked into the crook of one arm with her knees up. Billi brought his other arm across to hold her, and the music stopped completely. For a few moments Billi felt her breathing heavily against his chest and then her arm went up around Billi's head, just before her mouth came up and covered his.

With the wild music and excitement, and having just had her rub all over him and pulled off most of her coverings, Billi didn't hesitate. His arms tightened as he bussed her back for long moments. Then those sharp canines nipped his lip lightly, and the Dancer wriggled and slithered and danced away from him in long twirl and a roll that ended in a graceful bow. She also left Billi holding one more loose scrap, a long one. The crowd gave a collective gasp as she spun and spun and it unwound!

For a long moment everyone, including Billi, thought she'd lost the top half of her coverings! But no, she had a smaller strip still covering her breasts, more or less. A thick shower of silver rain glittered again. She'd played them perfectly, and Billi as well. Billi realised Dancer wasn't quite finished yet as she smiled at him, then them, and held up her hands. The crowd went more or less quiet, very impressive after that display.

"Ssrrong Hunnerr, and quick. Wach forr yourr maidss, he no chasse, nearrly cach me anyway!" A roar of laughter answered her. Her voice dropped lower, husky. "Lucky maidss, mmm, ssrrong arrms." The crowd laughed louder now, but some shouted for more and the Dancer swayed over towards Billi, teasing. She moved without music but the Dancer still danced, stepping to an unheard beat. Her eyes met his and glanced down, and he saw another bit of loose gauze!

Billi felt sure there were none a moment ago but she looked back up at him, her tongue flicked out to dab her lips for a moment and Billi knew his cue. A last one for the crowd. She twirled past, arms high and the bit of cloth blew out just far enough so Billi snatched it, laughing. Then he stood staring for long moments at the sharp nipples jutting from the snowy breasts with their swirling designs as she froze. Her arms came down to cover them with a shriek and the Dancer ran into the shadows leaving Billi with her breast-cloth!

The crowd went mad and more silver flew while Billi reran that in his head. Was he supposed to miss? No, he'd seen a curl of laughter on her lips before she shrieked and her eyes weren't shocked at all, and the Dancer definitely waited a long, long moment before her arms came down. So maybe that was his reward? Some reward, Billi would have interesting dreams for a year after tonight!

The Dancer came out to give a last curtsy with a shawl around her and wagged her finger at Billi, naughty boy. Another shower of copper and silver, in appreciation this time, glittered in the torchlight. Billi offered the cloth back but this time her finger went no, no, as did her headshake. The Dancer didn't dare get near the bearr again, her body language said. Instead of the crowd being disappointed at the dance ending the pale Dancer ran off to good-natured laughter. Billi reckoned she'd earned her silver, now being scooped up by the other dancers. They were still wearing the scraps they finished their acts in, to give the youths a final treat.

One Tinkerer maid sauntered over and collected the bits of gauze around the dancing bearr. Billi offered her the breast-cloth but she laughed at him. "She don't give that away before. Reckon ye get to keep that for catching her, your trophy." She leaned in. "If ye want another, ssrrong bearr, ye just might get one if ye can catch me as well." Then she laughed and twirled away. The Tinkerer maids were in a good mood tonight as well. Billi felt sure Dancer was no Tinkerer, not even some exotic type since her tattoos were painted on and those on Tinkerer maids were stained into their skin.

Billi knew her tattoos were different because he'd been close to both sorts, close enough to Dancer to see the blurring from her sweat and the smudges, though nobody else would have noticed in the torchlight and the speed of the dance. Those smudges were going to be in Billi's dreams as well since he'd made them and a few were places he hadn't expected to touch any maid in public! Hektor came over with Billi's crutch and a laughing Bliss, and Billi wondered what she was doing here?

"Hello ssrrong bearr, are the maids going to have to watch out now? After all, we know you can catch them, but none are here to get the warning." Bliss obviously found the whole thing hilarious. So did Hektor, the bit about the maids being warned had him sniggering nicely. Then Bliss turned serious for a minute. "So do the tattoos go all over?"

Billi sighed and confessed. "Yes, that wasn't a trick and I was as surprised as anyone."

"But not as disappointed as the rest since she kept her back to them." Hektor grinned and Billi realised that was true, now he actually thought about it. Definitely his reward then. Hektor kept up the teasing. "That's a new one, do you want to see my tattoos? Or was it can I see your tattoos? Nobody could hear what you pair were saying!"

"I didn't ask!"

"Good job. They're leaving in the morning or she might have decided to make a run, to capture a permanent dancing partner." Hektor tried to mimic the Dancer's voice. "Mmm, ssrrong bearr."

"I don't think so. Anyway, I'm tired. I'm going home because in case you didn't notice, that maid was bigger than she seemed and I've been chucking her around the place." Billi found it hard to be serious because he wanted to laugh. Billi had been a dancing bear. Though his leg hurt now, he'd put it through a lot of punishment tonight even if Billi hadn't noticed at the time.

"Well you'd know how big she was." Hektor found that hilarious as well and Bliss giggled.

"Have you two been at the cider?"

"No Billi, well not a lot. It's just that you're so proper around the maids. Then she'd got your shirt off and rubbed herself all over you, and you stripped her clothes off in front of the whole Village. Better yet, they were all cheering you on!" They both collapsed against each other and Billi had to join in with the laughter because put like that? He looked round and Rabbit stood over his jacket, though he'd let Hektor take the crutch. Billi donned the jacket but stuffed his shirt through his belt because he was hot and sweaty enough.

He thumped through the crowd and collected his congratulations and slaps on the back until only the track to his hut lay ahead. Billi bid goodnight to Hektor and Bliss, who went off still laughing. Not much cider? A bit too much maybe but then again they were bonded and going home with Dapple, so it didn't matter.

Rabbit seemed to be triumphant and Billi caught a definite sense of humour, and wondered again just how much the Hound picked up.

He didn't waste time getting to bed when they arrived home because he really did feel shattered, just taking off his coat and putting the shirt over his chair. Billi found the breast-cloth in his coat pocket where he must have stuffed it and threw it on the chest that held his bedding and spare sleeping furs. Just what was he supposed to do with that? Billi laid down and had his first instalment of interesting dreams.

* * *

In the morning Billi called in to see the Tinkerer, and the sparkul had been fasted on its chain. As promised the stone flashed with an inner fire when he took it to the window to catch the sun. The Tinkerer's two maids were dressed in long embroidered robes and not beguiling this morning. They were a bit taken aback to find that the sparkul wasn't for a maid and more so to find that Billi hadn't got one. The maids advised him to hang the sparkul in the window to catch the sun and then sort through the offers for a maid he liked. Both thought they should come and give a bit of opposition to encourage the local maids to try harder. Billi told them that he might hold them to it if he couldn't find one and they parted laughing.

Billi spent rest of the day preparing for his trip to the valley, and that evening before bed he took all the sparkuls and fancy gold and tucked them in his pack. He hadn't much else in there because he'd be taking the pot-bellied stove. When Perry turned up in the morning Billi and Rabbit were ready to go which disappointed Perry. He wanted to know all about the dancing and the maid, and did Billi really see all her tattoos, and did they really go all over?

That would be the code, apparently. Billi would be confirming how far tattoos went all winter. The answer would probably lead to more of the curious going to check if the other Tinkerer maids had the same coverage. The whole affair made wonderful advertising for them and Billi wondered if he should have insisted on a share of the silver. That kept him amused as he clumped through the snow and out along the stream to the valley. Being out in the green made Rabbit happy anyway of course, so they had a really enjoyable trip even in the snow.

As well as his musing about Dancer and tattoos, Billi spent the time clumping through the woods in planning for next summer. He would check some sandbanks for dust, ones where he had found nuggets in the past. Billi wondered if he could follow gold dust back to a source? Did all the gold in a stream come from one bank of gravel or a heap of nuggets somewhere? Billi built up some snow to stop the wind as the light faded. With plenty of dead branches to make a fire and Rabbit tucked up against his back, Billi slept warm enough in his furs through the night.

Another hard day's travel brought them close, but dusk fell so once again Billi built up snow and lit a good fire. Early afternoon the next day Billi arrived in the valley, and used some of his dry wood to light the fire and warm the hut up. He hid most of his gold and stones in little bits here and there, ate, and collapsed into the bed in his lovely warm hut. The following day Billi set into fitting his new stove.

That took all day, because he had to pull out part of his old fireplace while the stones were still a bit too hot for comfort. Though when he'd eventually jammed the new iron chimney pipe into place and sealed round it with mud, Billi found that the Tinkerer had been right. The stove threw out a tremendous amount of heat once the metal body heated up and soon warmed his hut. He ate a late meal of fresh fish, then decided to have an early night. Snow had started to fall and if that continued tomorrow he'd best head home.

Billi lay in his bed considering if there was anything else useful that needed doing on this trip when Rabbit came onto his feet and looked at the door with his head on one side. Billi caught an air of expectation in the song, muted excitement, something new, and then someone knocked at the door! It had to be a Hunter but why hadn't the Hounds spoken to each other? Billi laid in the dark, ready for sleep, so now he stood and opened the door on the stove for light. He picked up his crutch, and spear because after all he'd just brought those sparkuls out here, and carefully opened the hut door a bit. Then Billi stood with his mouth open, stunned into silence as the shaft of firelight fell on the figure standing in the falling snow.

"Is cold heerr, Hunnerr." The Dancer and, yes, it would be cold because she appeared to be stark naked without even the tattoos! In a daze Billi moved back and opened the door wide and she stepped lightly through and moved to the stove. In the same moment Rabbit slipped out of the door and into the snow. Billi barely noticed him go as she stood in front of the stove, holding her hands out to the open door. As the firelight gleamed on her pale skin Billi became even more aware that this time she didn't even have paint on.

The Dancer rubbed her hands on her arms and Billi shut the outside door, put the spear aside and wordlessly picked the fur off the bed to offer. She turned and took it without any sign of embarrassment which was more than Billi could say. "Mmm, warrm. Kind and ssrrong. Many would no coverr me. Dee no like?"

"Er no, yes, er, I mean I like, well, you're lovely but why? No clothes in the snow? What happened, are the others all right?" It had suddenly occurred to Billi that there should be a line of fancy painted wagons and a lot of other folk with her, Tinkerers. Surely Rabbit would have bayed if there were? Why weren't they at the door as well? He had no idea what disaster might bring them here and leave her naked in the snow but it couldn't be good.

"Drream of dee ssrrong arrms. Everry darrk sso iss now forr me. I come an' find, uderrs dey bide, maybe, orr I find. Laderr, now iss for ssrrong arrmss." It was hard work listening, and for her to speak as well and Billi wasn't sure why. Didn't she usually speak? Was it a problem with her mouth or just a foreign tongue maybe? He'd heard there were other ways to speak, or maybe her being in his hut and naked wasn't helping him understand.

"Do you want food or a drink?" Billi finally remembered his manners, or perhaps just didn't know how to answer her words.

"Juss warrm an furr, good. Dee need bed, iss cold." Yes, it was, even with the stove. Billi realised that was because he'd put his wet trews to dry and his short pants didn't cover his stump. A wave of embarrassment swept over him and Billi grabbed the fur from the chair and laid on the bed to get covered. The Dancer had now folded gracefully down onto the floor next to the stove. The door on the stove closed and the light dimmed, then he felt the fur lifted! The Dancer slid into the narrow bed and pushed the warmer fur across, under the cold one from the chair.

"Warrmer wid uss. Now, ssrrong man, big bearr, dee dance wid me?" Dance? Billi realised she'd warmed up fast for supposedly being cold and there really wasn't room in here. Then there was just enough room as Billi realised what sort of dance she had in mind. By now Billi really didn't care why.

When he woke in the morning Billi thought it had been a particularly vivid dream, right up until he heard the stove door and then a warm someone slipped back under the furs. He opened his eyes and the morning light through the small, thick pane of glass in the door timbers showed a mane of pale hair on his chest. "Mmm, bederr dan drream." Yes, Billi had to agree even if he had no idea why this was happening or where Rabbit had got to.

He could still hear Rabbit's happy song, now spiked with excitement, a happy excitement with no alarm at all. Billi should be wondering what the Hound was up to since Rabbit never went off on his own, but that happiness in the song soothed any worries away. Anyway, Billi was distracted, and suddenly even more so. The Dancer slithered around under the furs, wriggling across him and Billi remembered just how limber that pale body had been in the torchlight, flying and twisting and dancing. Then Billi realised just why she'd started wriggling. Again, in the morning? Though that suddenly seemed a wonderful idea. His arms came up and round and she almost purred into his chest, "ssrrong."

* * *

Afterwards Billi thought he'd 'lost' about six or maybe seven days, perhaps only four or five. He occasionally tried to work it out, but it didn't worry him as lost days should. The whole period felt like a dream afterwards. The Dancer never gave her name, she wouldn't. She refused to call him Billi, only bearr or hunnerr, and the way she said ssrrong sounded downright seductive and put a shiver up his spine. Beguiling paled beside it. Billi tried asking how she got here, or where the others were, but every time she would wriggle all over him and her lips would close his mouth.

Billi had trouble concentrating even out of the bed because the Dancer refused to wear a stitch even when she came outside. She did that several times to watch Billi take in his trap lines or fish, and she helped him clean the catch. Somehow, standing in that setting with the snow and the ice of the lakes she looked natural, as if being naked in the snow was as she should be. Maybe because of her colouring, all pale hair and white skin and teeth, and those ice blue eyes. Though it couldn't really be normal and natural for her as Dancer always had to warm up afterwards. Well she said so anyway, though she never seemed that cold to Billi. Not when the Dancer insisted on only one possible way to get warm. Watching him working in the snow seemed to set her on fire somehow.

Billi found that Dancer didn't have any tattoos at all. The only small marks on her pale skin formed a birthmark which at the right angle made a stylised running wolf. Just a few curving lines from an angle and in a place nobody else was likely to see it, though Dancer deliberately showed ssrrong bearr. She'd had precious little on after the dancing but Billi realised the birthmark had been safely hidden. For the only time she seemed almost shy, while making sure Billi saw that clearly, odd considering her disregard for coverings. The Dancer insisted Billi didn't need much on either with the door shut and eventually Billi learned to ignore his stump as she did.

Then she slid out of the bed one morning, kissed him gently, and said "go now." She wouldn't take clothing or food, or a gift, insisting that she had all she'd come for. She had something to remember his ssrrong arrmss and was content, but had to go. Yes, now and he couldn't come, mustn't follow and no, he'd never see her again except maybe once. A beguiled and bewildered Billi really had no answer. In the end she agreed to take a pale blue stone he'd kept because of the different colour.

Just a small one and he could never be sure where he'd found or traded for it but as Billi told her, it matched her eyes. That Dancer finally accepted and held it as she slipped out of the door after raising a cautionary finger, do not follow. As she did, Rabbit slipped in! The song sounded happy, and quietly and contentedly triumphant. Billi hadn't seen a sign of the Hound all the time Dancer remained, though the happy song in Billi's head showed he hadn't gone far.

Billi ruffled Rabbit's ears and went to the door, but when he opened it, a pale wolf stood there! Not threatening but a clear message, don't follow. No wonder Dancer felt safe out there with a companion such as that! Billi shut the door and concentrated on saying hello to Rabbit, and soon afterwards crawled into the warm bed as exhaustion crashed in. Part of his uncertainty about time came because he had no idea how long he slept. The stove only held cold ashes when Billi woke but it might have been burning low when she went, and he'd not topped it up.

However long she'd been here, Billi spent a day getting his head in some sort of order and checking his gear for the trip back to the Village.

He had come out here to clear his head, and now felt more confused than ever! How did the Dancer find him here in his valley? Billi hadn't even considered that before. Nobody should to know where it was, but she'd come straight to his door even in a snowstorm.

* * *

The snow had frozen hard which would help him travel. When he threw the remains of his fish into the bushes Billi could see that the Great Hunter had been clawing the edges of the pool to get a drink. The beast probably didn't fancy leaving cover to go and drink at the outfall or where the current kept a patch of the lake clear, or maybe he wanted fish. Billi smashed the ice with a rock and pulled the chunks out to slow down the refreezing. He preferred losing a few fish to encouraging the beast to wander around the valley. The familiar work around the valley helped to pull him out of his daze.

The freezing definitely came as a blessing for travelling, because it had snowed hard during the last few days and when Billi looked out past the dam the woods were choked with drifts. He looked around but found no sign of anyone leaving, just animal tracks and few wolf ones. It could have snowed after she went, he wouldn't have known, and Rabbit wasn't interested in looking. His song sounded downright smug, as near as Billi could describe the tone of it, and Billi thought of that wolf. Had Rabbit been beguiled? Billi thought of the chip of blue stone and smiled to himself as he'd insisted on being beguiled in a way. Though the Tinkerer maids would be a bit tame after this and his bargaining would be much fiercer in future.

Billi slept in his bed one last warm night, then emptied the stove and swung his pack on his back. He closed the door, put the big timber across it and took a last look around. Then they were on their way, Rabbit leading the way out over the valley edge. This time Billi didn't hunt or fish. He carried enough fish in his pack with the night furs to get them home and the store at home had plenty of food. Billi concentrated on travelling, a chore for him all with the big drifts. The woods were quiet after such a heavy fall, every sound muffled and even the birds seemed reluctant to be their usual raucous selves.

Billi heard a howl far away in the night, and a coughing roar a little nearer, but there weren't even many tracks since the grazers must be staying put. All but the largest, as the deep trough ploughed through the drifts down to the water showed in a couple of places. If he'd tripped over one of those animals Billi would have to let it go. He couldn't pack that much meat out in this weather even with a travois and taking it slow, he'd break the crust with his boot every time he heaved. He already had enough difficulty travelling as the crutch and peg still went through occasionally despite the wider end.

Billi talked quietly to Rabbit as he went. Rabbit still sounded in a tremendous mood despite the snow being heavy going for him as well. When the Hound came onto his single foot it sometimes broke through with all his weight behind it. Billi talked about the Dancer, and asked the Hound what he'd been up to out in the snow to be in such a good mood. Was he chasing a pretty white wolf and did he catch her? Because although he couldn't actually tell from his angle Billi had a distinct impression that the wolf was female, and Rabbit had raised absolutely no alarm at her walking up to his front door.

Then again Rabbit hadn't made much fuss about the Dancer arriving either. Not that she was dangerous in the accepted sense. Just to his sanity as Billi still couldn't make sense of most of his time with Dancer. It all blurred, pale hair and white skin and her moving and stroking and speaking in that purring or grrowling way. Billi was grateful the woods were so beautiful and that the snow made him concentrate on where to step next, it kept his mind on something else.

For two and a half days the two of them struggled on, Billi lost in a mixture of memories and the sheer glory of the winter wood. Perhaps that explained why it took a moment for Billi to register the change in Rabbit's song. A hopeful, hunting note but Billi wasn't so sure, not in all this snow? Until now Rabbit had ignored all potential prey so Billi strung his bow, more or less as a reflex. Maybe Rabbit thought the Farm near enough, and the whatever small enough for Billi to stagger home with?

The pair moved forward, not exactly stealthy but the snow muffled their clumsy progress. When he saw the deer Billi thought stealth made no difference. They were too far to risk only wounding as these were smaller and faster than the sort making troughs in the snow. There were seven deer, digging with their hooves where they had found some grass or hay that wasn't buried too deep.

Billi could hit one, but not to be sure of a killing hit. At this angle he couldn't even be sure of hitting a lung to stop the prey from running far. If Billi wounded one they might end up taking a couple of days hunting it down, then a couple more days to get back this far, and Billi didn't fancy that. Sure enough the deer scattered as soon as one saw him, bounding outwards from the patch of rough grass they'd scratched at. Big leaps, swift and agile on the thinner snow.

Billi relaxed but the song spiked suddenly, and Rabbit's attention fastened on the two deer that had faltered. Billi could see they'd gone through the crust into deep drifts and both were floundering, fighting to get enough purchase to scramble clear of snow deeper than they were. But Rabbit watched just one, and the song urged Billi on.

The deer stood, or struggled, side-on. Rabbit bounded forward and scrabbled out through the drifts. The Hound wanted to get across the deer's line of flight if it fought clear of the snow after being hit. Billi propped his crutch up against his side and pulled the bow, swiftly and smoothly. It dropped onto the target and he loosed the shaft. Billi fitted another shaft but then removed it as Rabbit bayed triumphantly.

The Hound bounced through a shallower patch to plunge into the snowdrift directly ahead of the deer then the Hound waited, poised to seize the throat if it tried to turn or get past him. A reddening of the snow close to the thrashing deer confirmed Rabbit's assessment, the shaft had gone true. Billi stumped forward as fast as possible, then swung off the pack to get at his spear. There were no horns but that head or those sharp hooves could still do serious damage.

Once Billi arrived Rabbit hesitated, chose the right moment and fastened onto the deer's muzzle, the spear went in hard and fast and they had a meal. Several meals, the meat would still be plump and juicy and Billi worked quickly while Rabbit stood guard. He threw a few chunks to Rabbit and popped a slice of fresh liver into his own mouth, still warm, then rolled the meat up in the skin and tied it into a bundle on top of his pack. That sorted out a good part of the pay for hut guarding very nicely.

The deer made the pack heavy but Billi had carried heavier, and it wouldn't be for long. On an impulse Billi took the two sharp teeth that jutted from the vegetarian's mouth, for Rubyn. The males used them to fight but they looked incongruous on a non-predator and were sometimes used on necklaces because of that. Then he waved to the gathering crows and ravens and called Rabbit to finish his meal. They set off at as good a pace as Billi could manage, to let the smaller scavengers get a meal before their larger cousins moved in.

In this sort of weather everyone needed a bit of help. Though if it lasted there would be plenty to scavenge as animals caught in drifts weakened and died, or were found and finished by predators. Billi thought of what the bard said. 'Buzzard and Raven, Fox and the Crow, waited, impatient for death in the snow' or something close. The man had got that right. The bards often did although they didn't actually hunt.

When the caravans with bards had gone, the villagers sometimes wondered about that. About if a bard had to go out and try lots of different ways of making a living first, because they were so good at catching the heart of it. The bards always had a new one to go with the old favourites as well. The alehouse customers wondered did they make them up or did someone sit in a hut somewhere doing nothing else? Billi wondered what a bard would make of the woods right now? It was a shame that none of them would ever see it.

* * *

Sure enough, whether it was just that Billi pushed hard or the way became a little easier nearer home, before dusk Billi came out of the Forest and onto the barren fields. At this time of year there were no guards as every animal and crop had been tucked up safely for the winter, in barn or storehouse. Even the stockyards were empty and deserted and Billi wondered briefly where Edan and his animals were. Maybe a friend had given them shelter. Edan's four big dogs would be costing him a fortune to feed in this weather, especially with the early snow. That cost might be the ruin of Edan's schemes.

Two straight lines of smoke climbed into the dull grey sky as pink began to tinge the clouds, a sure sign of Ellibeth. Billi felt a little lift at the thought of fresh bread, though she may not have baked as she wouldn't know he'd be home. Billi heard Spots and as he came through the gate his door opened and Ellibeth looked out and smiled. She looked relieved and Billi wondered who she might be expecting? He must be very late so maybe there'd been bother from Edan.

Then Billi remembered that all the Edan nonsense was over, so perhaps she'd been worried about him. Then he wondered why would Ellibeth worry about him? There again she was a friend. Billi still wasn't used to the idea of friends and the thought left a little warm spot inside. Billi swung off his pack and banged off the snow so he didn't trek it in since he knew the hut would be spick and span again inside. He didn't want Ellibeth to think he didn't appreciate her work. Billi couldn't stamp his boot but he banged the crutch a couple of times and came in. He dumped the pack on the floor and took a deep appreciative breath of fresh bread. As Billi opened his mouth to say something about it, he saw his chair.

The Dancer's breast cloth hung over the back and looked as if someone had cleaned and ironed it. Worse still that meant Ellibeth since the youths might have looked at it but they wouldn't have done that! Billi felt the heat in his cheeks and he stood here with his mouth open. Sure enough as the door thunked behind him Ellibeth looked at him, then the chair, and back. A tiny smile, maybe, showed at the corner of her mouth, possibly because of how Billi looked so he shut his mouth.

"I didn't know what you wanted to do with it, big bearr?" The definite amusement in Ellibeth's voice blended with the beginnings of a smile and genuine curiosity as well.

"I've no idea!" That maybe came out as a bit of a complaint, but Billi really didn't know.

"You could nail it up above your bed?"

Billi wondered, was Ellibeth teasing him? "No, why would I? And she's not been in the bed!" Well not this one Billi mentally added, while his sense of humour pointed out she wasn't wearing a breast cloth either but he'd best not mention that. "Though the Tinkerer maid told me to keep it as a trophy." Billi's sense of humour prodded. "Maybe I should put it in the alehouse with the boar's head?"

Ellibeth laughed, so she obviously had the same sense of humour. "That would be popular with the youths! Mind, it would be fair warning to the maids because what did that Dancer say, the maids should beware those ssrrong arrms? Though the maids have been warned now since a lot of youths have mentioned that part, among the rest."

The two accented words brought back some interesting memories, and actually sounded rather nice from Ellibeth and Billi flushed at the thought. He chose the safe route and kept his thoughts firmly off how Ellibeth sounded. "I'm not going to catch many like this." Billi gestured at his leg. "The Dancer gave her warning while stood safely clear of me." He shrugged.

Ellibeth stepped forward and her hand came up, then a finger tapped his chest. "It isn't how fast the man chases, it's how fast the maid runs away." She turned away and he heard the humour as she continued, "and what if the maid does the chasing? Silly Billi." Billi stared after her, was Ellibeth teasing? He hadn't heard silly Billi since he'd finished school. Ellibeth would be the right age to have heard him called that though he doubted she'd have been one of the taunting voices. So that might even be flirting given the light tone and the words seemed different like that, from an adult voice.

Should Billi tease back, or chase her? He'd been very careful not to let such thoughts about any maid take root as that might lead to him doing something foolish. Did Billi want to chase Ellibeth? He had to admit the thought of chasing Ellibeth appealed but if she was joking he'd ruin any friendship. Billi would have to do or say something because the silence went on too long and then a ferocious growl came from Ellibeth's room!

Well ferocious for a very young bear in a very big skin. Rubyn had the floor fur with the bear's head over him and wore bear feet. On him they were oversized boots with claws! Viktor had given Billi the feet back and now Billi wasn't even sure where he'd put them, but Rubyn had found them.

Billi burst out laughing and a moment later Ellibeth must have looked because she started laughing too, and a delighted young face popped out of the fur. "I've just the thing here. A big bear like that should have big teeth." Billi ignored the snort from behind at the big bear and dug in his pocket for the little package, then threw it to the bear in the doorway. A bit of intense unfastening later and Rubyn brandished the deer fangs, then looked at his Ma.

"Ma? Can I? Please?" He held them up in front of the defanged bear's head. "Please?"

"Yes, but after they've been properly cleaned. You'll be having a fine collection if Billi keeps this up." For some reason Ellibeth found that funny. As Billi shrugged off his coat and jacket she looked at the breast cloth again and Ellibeth smiled properly this time. "So what will you do with this if it's not going on the wall or in the alehouse?"

"Well it's really thin?" Billi ignored the snort and continued. "So I thought, maybe it could be used for cheese making, to drain the curds and I was..." Billi managed to stop because his brain had caught up with his mouth and remembered that he didn't make his cheese now, Ellibeth did. Billi felt stone certain that on the list of significant gifts a breast cloth went above claws, teeth, fancy furs and probably that big sparkul on a chain!

Though his humour did point out she wouldn't flaunt it. Billi's sense of humour was getting a good workout today. Inspiration struck, helped by the bear in the doorway. "I was going to give it to Rubyn so you could teach him how to make cheese." Billi had to smile at the giggle when the laughter that had been building in Ellibeth's eyes broke free. It was fairly obvious he'd been going to say something else.

"So you are giving your trophy." Ellibeth giggled again. "An exotic dancer's finest quality breast cloth, to a lad of nine summers to make cheese?" Her eyes were dancing and Billi could only hope Ellibeth limited who she told about this. "Are you trying to corrupt my boy?" Billi opened his mouth to protest and her laughter came properly. "Oh Billi, if you could only see your own face!" Ellibeth got herself under control and sort of straightened her face. "Rubyn, would you like to learn to make cheese?" The glee still showed in her eyes and some was in her voice.

"Oh yes, can I? Please? Goat's cheese?" The fur dropped, because this was important. Real work but even better, new work.

"Yes, because Billi's found you a suitable bit of cloth." Her voice wavered a bit over 'suitable' and then carried on. "It's on the back of the chair, so fold it up and look after it."

"Thanks, Billi." A furless and barefoot bear gave Billi a quick hug and scooped the cloth up. Rubyn folded it neatly and tucked it in his belt before looking up with his eyes shining. "I'll make you some really special cheese."

Billi daren't look at Ellibeth. He knew she'd be a glance away from laughing or another comment and then her voice came, definitely humorous, "I'm sure Billi will love it. Now pick up your clutter and put everything back where it belongs, though I've no idea where the feet go."

"Stick them under your bed, Rubyn, for if you want something to keep your feet warm." Another bright smile and Rubyn dashed off.

"Well, you'd better sit down, since you must be tired. I'll pack the meat away. There's fresh bread here and a bit of butter in the cold house. Rubyn will get that." Ellibeth kept smiling but seemed back on balance, her fit of giggles stifled. Billi wondered who might to be asking him about special goat's cheese in the future because there was no chance she wouldn't share it. He would if it had been someone else. Billi sat and stretched his leg gratefully then he suddenly realised.

"I'll get the butter later. It's dusk now so I'd better get you home."

"When you've eaten and had some rest. You've been pushing to get home I'd wager, so now you bide a while. Did you want a bit of cider warmed?" Billi opened his mouth to point out Ellibeth would be here after dark but it wasn't bothering her so why mention it? Ellibeth continued, so she must have been thinking of the same thing. "I'll be safe enough going home in the dark, with a Hound and a ssrrong bearr to watch over me." A growl answered from the doorway but the gleam in her eye wasn't aimed at Rubyn. Billi remembered what he'd meant to ask when he came in and quickly steered the conversation to normal matters.

"How did you know I'd be home tonight, or was the fresh bread just a bit of good luck for me?"

"Ah, well, I make a bit any night you might be home. Rubyn and I eat it if you don't come so there's no waste." Ellibeth had stopped laughing all right. Her reply sounded shy if anything and she had two spots of colour on her cheeks.

Billi wondered if Ellibeth worried about the flour and such being used? "Oh. Well thank you. 'Tis something I miss out in the green. Don't worry if there's a bit wasted. The chickens will eat it and it's worth it for the welcome."

"Then I'll make sure there's always a welcome waiting." Her voice sounded better now, and happy again. "Why do you call it the green?

Everyone else says Forest. Even the Hunters are wary when they talk about it but you can't wait to be out there, which is a puzzle with all the danger."

"I love the beauty. It's lovely out there, so beautiful and alive and the danger just makes you more alive and it all seem more beautiful." For the first time, as he ate and drank his bit of warm cider, Billi told someone of his love of the green. "There's nothing like the dappled green light as a sunbeam strikes through the leaves, then bursts into colour as it strikes a blossom or a bird. A turn in the track, or coming round a bush, will suddenly reveal a wall of bright forest blooms. When I brush against them, the scent follows and lingers. There are hidden clearings where the short grass is starred with tiny flowers, where the chattering streams wind through the bushes and trees to the sound of the birds. And there's the birds, so many birds, chattering and cheeping and singing and scolding, or flitting from tree to tree shining like sparkuls, or hopping brown and shy under the bushes."

Ellibeth nodded, and frowned just a little. "But that is summer, and the leaves and flowers are all gone now."

Billi sighed. "But it isn't just colour and sounds. The whole forest is silent right now. The snow has blown and frozen between the trees into big curves and swirls, caves and spires. Some trees have snow built up the sides to coat them, where others stand out stark and clear. Branches are heavy with snow, groaning and creaking with any breath of wind. Some have even snapped off under the weight, or bent down to where the ends are now frozen to the ground. Others are glittering as if dusted with tiny sparkuls, all afire in the sun. The ice on the streams lines the banks, and goes right across in places. Then I can watch the water racing by, out of reach even if I can see it. There are even fish in there, silver streaks that are safe from any fisher, Man or Wild."

"Where the water can be reached, the marks of the animals and even birds are clear when they come to drink. Tiny feet, mice, and the small furred hunters like those pelts in my pack. Then hooves and pads and eventually, sometimes, a big cat, a true hunter. They are why even in the beauty and the quiet, the Wild is watching." Billi smiled at Rubyn. "No bears in winter because they all go away someplace, but even the danger is beautiful, look at these."

Billi stood up and pulled two of his treasures off the shelf above his bed. He unrolled the two spotted furs from the first Winter Hunt. "These are so beautiful that I can't bear to trade them yet, but these cats would catch me in an instant if Rabbit and I let our guard down. That is a part of what I love, the sheer beauty mixed with the danger. That is why I go back," Billi looked at Rabbit, "we go back, again and again because Rabbit loves the green as well. It's in his song." Ellibeth seemed to understand, sitting smiling as Billi talked and talked. Rubyn sat entranced and Billi had to warn him, it was only beautiful if the Hunter had a Hound to watch and listen. Rabbit's tail thumped agreement from where he lay next to the littlun with Spots on Rubyn's other side.

"Your clearing, your place with fish, must be very beautiful from the amount of time you spend there? Is it dangerous as well?" Ellibeth had no idea what sort of danger or beauty!

"Yes, very dangerous but also very beautiful and very peaceful."

"Some of the Hunters were talking, wondering if it is worth a trip since 'tis Forest, not claimed." Ellibeth saw Billi's bolt of alarm. "Why haven't you claimed it? Is it too much part of the Wild?"

Billi sighed. "Not now. I've been cropping to make the valley into Farm but didn't expect anyone else to bother."

"When you keep turning up with such beautiful, plush pelts?" Ellibeth stroked the thick white bundles that had been strapped to the back of his pack. "Somebody is bound to go and look, and they've been looking out for reed beds as well, and pools with fish. Oh, Fellip is waiting for you to come back and so are Perry and Timath because 'tis reed time. I think Perry is hoping to manage a bit of chasing with a feather pillow if he can persuade either Sis to sew it."

"I'll bear it in mind while sorting out their pay. Maybe Rubyn would like his own feather pillow if the right fowl wander in front of the bow?" Rubyn's enthusiastic nod settled that. "Thank you for the warning about the Hunters." Billi sighed again. "I'll see the Eldest tomorrow and make it official." He would, first thing because if anyone realised how many stones were there they'd all be digging! Billi realised it was all the people in 'his' quiet spot that bothered him more than the digging, fishing or hunting.

"Thank you for the thought, because Rubyn does like the pillow. Did you want a second?" Her humour flashed. "Just in case you manage to catch a slow one?"

"I would love one, so we need feathers for two or Rubyn will be out here using mine." Billi let his humour show, the lad could use it while he was away, in fact... Billi quickly didn't offer his pillow for a maid's room and bed. "You'd better get used to swan."

A flash of alarm showed on Ellibeth's face and Billi remembered that a swan was too much. Once again he wondered if someone had a list of these rules? "Swans because I'll also need to pay you for the sewing, and also plucking and cleaning. Anyway swan will make a better pillow according to the Tinkerers."

"Thank ye kind sir." Ellibeth mimed a curtsy from where she sat. "Now unless I'm to make more pillows quickly you'd best get me home. In spite of that big bar on the door, 'twould not be right for a maid to stay with the Hunter home." Ellibeth sounded teasing again, but gently as the maids sometimes did just for fun, a new situation for Billi.

Well, he'd try some. "But you'll be safe, since you've got a big bear to guard you."

"Ah, but look what happened to the last maid that stayed too near, too long." Ellibeth kept smiling, but she might not if she knew what really happened to Dancer. Billi braced his hands on the chair arms.

"We'd best get you safe then, because I wouldn't want your littlun shocked." Her laughter sounded like music, and Billi felt very pleased with himself because he hadn't stuttered or retreated into silence. Maybe building his resistance to beguiling had another result? Perhaps he could talk to a maid he liked as if she was a person?

Ellibeth stopped and stared. "That is a fresh skin and the meat's not frozen! When did you catch that, or where?"

"This side of the old Wood Hunt place. A small herd ran and one ended up stuck in the snow so I thought it would do as your wages, or most anyway."

Instead of arguing Ellibeth looked almost awed. "Nobody has brought meat in since this snow started, yet you come hopping along and a deer gets stuck in front of you. No wonder there's folk say the Wild likes you." She looked alarmed. "Not in a bad way, the Hunters especially just seem to think your luck goes beyond just that, somehow." Ellibeth gave a short, uncertain laugh. "I must be tired, going on like this." And with that she went into her room to put her coat on.

They made their way to the Village and Ellibeth thanked him and went in. Rubyn had run ahead as they came near, balancing the need to keep his eggs safe against the need to show off his deer teeth. Then as Billi stumped away, Perry came out to let him know the Thatcher had been looking for him. Also to ask very privately if he could have a couple of fowl with good feathers for a pillow this time please? Billi told him no problem, and on the way back he wondered if he might need to make a bit of noise coming home when Perry looked after the place. The smell of bread still filled his hut as Billi drifted off to sleep and his dreams were both interesting and confused.

Being home seemed to have cleared up Billi's bemusement with regard to the Dancer and her visit, though he never would sort out the days. She became a warm, private and precious memory. In an odd way Dancer left him less worried about his stump, or rather of its effect on others. Billi still didn't let anyone else see the stump but he began to realise that folk looked at him and not, as he'd always thought, at the shortened leg of his trews. Maybe they didn't all think cripple whenever he came in sight? A really new idea to wrestle with.

Hunting and Chasing

The day after his talk with Ellibeth, some talk that, Billi went to see the Eldest and explained what he'd done, and that he wished to lay landclaim. A proper landclaim so if he had anyone to leave it to they could trade it as their landshare, to a Hunter if they'd no Hound of their own. Several elders were called, and Kina brought out ale and juice. Billi soon realised as more arrived that the elders had been getting really curious about the fish farm. From the looks of it, none wanted to miss out on the description.

Billi had to describe just how to find the valley, and they laughed at "just follow the stream." The description of his valley became much more detailed than he'd expected as they kept asking questions about the size of the clear land in the valley, and the valley sides. The elders also asked about some being fertile enough for a crop, and all the dead timber, and even about the open woodland just in front of the dam. For a start Billi had never paced any of it, even stumpy paces, which everyone seemed to think he should have done.

Billi confirmed the open land up on the hillsides and further back had no trees, no Forest. Billi thought that the grazing would support sheep but outside of the little valley had seen no water, except a trickle over the waterfall that dried in midsummer and froze in winter. There might be a stream or pool up on top of the hill but Billi pointed out that if so it wasn't supporting heavy growth. There were no treetops visible even when looking at the upland from a distance. After Billi estimated the area of land, he explained the amount of water in the middle.

The elders all started laughing. Kina, the Eldest, pointed at him and shook her head. "You called it a fish farm. All this land you never even a mentioned, and the fish farm is just a lake in the middle." She glanced at her parchment. "Two lakes. Have you no idea how many are trying to work out how to trap fish in open Forest?"

Billi grinned. "I never mentioned open Forest. There's only Forest at the front, one side of the dam, though it comes awful close in one spot. That's where I leave the tithe."

"Why a tithe if it's Farm?"

"Why not? 'Tis a small piece of Farm, and a big Forest, and this way I'm making a boundary." Billi watched the elders, because he wasn't sure on this himself.

They were looking from one to another. "Ye could be right Billi." Devved spoke slowly, thoughtfully. "How does the first bit of Farm happen? There is no record of how Trail's End began, no hint of how the first hut was raised and why the Forest and the Wild accepted it."

"I've put up a hut." They all stared at him and Billi shrugged. "For the winter. That's why I can stay out a week in the snow."

"How did ye manage that? No offence, Billi, but is it a few bits of wood and hide, or a real dwelling? 'Tis important." Guthra seemed intent and the rest were leaning forward now. Billi explained about using whole trees and boulders, and then reeds from a bed by the lake. He told them about his stone table and big rocks making a cold room, and the crude bed and pot-bellied stove.

A long silence followed when he finished, and then Kina sighed. "Ye may have already done it, Billi. Ye may have already made it Farm." She shook her head. "Maybe this is how we started, with the broken rock that must have been laid around Skull rock. The first hut may even have leaned against it." All the elders were looking a little awed now.

Billi was puzzled. "Why is that so important to the landclaim?"

"Not the landclaim, Billi, though that will bring food into Trail's End for many long years. 'Tis the area around. If there is enough to split, eventually, then there'll be a Farmer there as well as a Hunter. Then maybe a Shepherd, if flocks can be grazed above." Starr was looking inward, a quiet smile on her lips. "I can see it, a little community nestled in the valley bottom, all because a Hunter had one itchy foot. We must record this, so it isn't lost."

"We must, because this landclaim must never be let back to the Forest." Kina sounded determined. "We are always short of land as families grow, bit by bit. The Forest does not give ground easily and families grow faster than the Farm."

"I can keep an eye open for another bit like this or maybe without the lakes? Someplace with water and a bit of open ground." Despite what had been said here and there, Billi had never truly realised the food shortage came down to lack of land. The worry about the size of Bliss's brideshare suddenly made more sense. "If a Hunter can claim it, 'twill leave land free on the Farm."

Guthra laughed. "There are already Hunters looking for reed beds or a similar piece of land to claim, but there is nothing within a day's hunting, or even two." He smiled. "Or nothing big enough to be worth the effort though a few have mentioned a line of youths with hoes." Billi smiled as he heard his own joke come round.

"There is no big timber, but one Hunter seemed to find some when he needed a tree's worth for something important." Starr seemed very satisfied with that idea. "There might be more land a bit further out. Some of the younger Hunters are talking of going further as you do, Billi. They reckon that if you can stay out two or three nights then so can they. 'Tis the lure of a whole new landshare beckoning."

"Not just that. Those are chasing and maybe close to catching a maid. Others are attracted by whole trees and fancy stones for either chasing Village maids or tempting Tinkerer beguilers. Word is out that Wandering Billi finds more stones than others, since he is looking where nobody else has?" They all waited so Billi answered Devved's question.

"I do, and part of it is because I don't always hunt. Sometimes I just like travelling fast, sort of." Billi gestured to his peg. "I like to see new country and then I find a stream, and a likely spot. I catch a few fish, have my bite to eat, and we search a bit." Billi sniggered. "If the other Hounds are as smart as Rabbit that will help, since Rabbit finds stones all by himself." Billi hoped the rumour came from the Traders, not the Tinkerer, and thought so as nobody mentioned sparkuls.

The Eldest, Kina, sounded a note of caution. "Everyone has always said that you are a cautious Hunter, Billi. Some meant it as a slur, but not anymore, not given how many nights you spend out in the Forest and what you come back with. But we must make sure the young Hunters understand that you really are cautious, or they'll take too many chances. Some things they might get away with and still stagger home from a half-day away, but the same injury two days out will leave their bones out there."

"We lose two or three Hunters and Hounds every winter, and maybe one in the summer, and no insult meant but they have two legs or four. Even your luck may run out some day, Billi, or maybe Rabbit's." As an elder, Guthra understood a Hunter wouldn't leave a wounded Hound to face the Wild alone. "With all this land, ye can't leave it all hanging. Ye must decide, properly, who is to get the reed bed and landclaim if ye don't come home one day." Guthra grinned. "Else half the Hunters on the Farm will get trampled in the rush."

A fair question since not coming home came as a part of the Hunter's job, though from the alert looks he'd best not give them any grounds for gossiping. Billi realised that, back in his head somewhere, he and Rabbit had sorted it out. They knew who they wanted on their little patches of wilderness, or in the valley at least. "The profit from the reed bed is to be split as I said before, among my sibs. They can hire a Hunter or trade for land on the Farm and split that." Billi took a deep breath. "The valley landclaim is to go to Rubyn, Ellibeth's littlun, but nobody must be told unless I don't come home for at least a twenty-day past when I'm due." Billi smiled. "I can get held up and have to take my time."

"But why say nothing?" At least three wanted to say something else and all had mischievous smiles, which was why Billi had a reason that didn't include Ellibeth.

"Rubyn is almost nine summers, but his Ma is still young and his Ganda is still here. Rubyn will have to wait out his Ganda, for his Ma to get her share, then wait for her to go to the rock before he can have a home. This is a way for him to break free and set up home earlier if he finds a maid." Billi waited, and sure enough some smiles broke into laughter.

"Just how young d'you reckon a maid might catch him with a landclaim like that?" Starr said it but others were nodding.

"Which is why he's not to know until he's bonded, then he won't be caught by a maid just after the land. Until then it is to be rented to a Hunter and the silver given to his Ma, to help raise him." Billi leant back with a big smile, because that also meant there'd be no loose tongues about the why either. Both Billi and Rabbit liked the idea of Rubyn in that valley. His sheer wonder at the descriptions of the Wild, and eagerness to help and learn, meant Billi had taken to the littlun.

Kina frowned. “How do you think that’s to be explained. To his Ma, let alone everyone else?”

Billi laughed at them. “I’ll be gone to the rock, or they’ll never find our bones, so that will be a problem for the elders.” Billi also knew that meant ‘twould be too late for Ellibeth to say ‘too much’ and refuse.

“That’s, that’s.” Kina scowled. “Time for me to go to the rock I reckon. I’ve just been outsmarted by a youngster still wet behind the ears. Scat, before I spank you for insolence.” Though she kept smiling as she started writing on the parchment while the rest had their heads together scandal-mongering, but ‘twould only be between them.

* * *

The landclaim could wait a bit now, because the reed would be ready for harvesting. A calf in the larder is worth a bull still in the Forest so Billi called by to see Fellip on the way home. Twice while going through the Village a voice warned a maid to watch out or the bear might catch her. The shrieks and laughter were in jest, not mockery; clearly the story had spread.

The Thatcher could start reed cutting any time Billi liked but a day or so didn’t matter, as long as the snow didn’t get any worse or thaw into mud. They arranged the trip for two days’ time and Billi went home. He found Rubyn with the chickens when he arrived back, on his own which he shouldn’t be. “Rubyn, you shouldn’t come out here without someone looking out for you.” Billi tried hard to be stern when faced by a smiling littlun with straw in his hair.

“But the chickens need checking, and er, I’m sure someone could see me?” Rubyn tried to look penitent but it wasn’t working.

“Where does your Ma think you are?”

That brought some foot shuffling and downward glances. “Playing with Eddwyn, maybe. I didn’t say, quite.”

“Come on, we’d best let her know the truth.” Billi hesitated, then gave up. “I suppose you’d better have your pay.” Then Billi took Rubyn home, but only clutching one egg and starting to actually get apprehensive.

* * *

He looked even more worried when Ma took him by the ear and

led him off for a quick lecture, though Ellibeth soon came back with a chastened Rubyn following. Rubyn hung back by the doorway, looking a little embarrassed. "I'm sorry Billi. He gets used to racing about out where your hut is, and the yard isn't big enough. Though he'll be only coming out there with someone else in the future." She sighed. "He'll no doubt talk Timath into it." A bit of mischief sounded in the next bit. "Perry might not want company all the time."

"Well Rubyn will get five days out there soon. It's reed cutting time." Billi remembered what he'd intended doing when the snows came and lowered his voice. "There is something I wanted show him, something Rubyn shouldn't hear unless you say yes."

Ellibeth moved closer and lowered her voice, though mischief sparkled in her eyes. "Have you found another cheesecloth?"

Billi laughed, but kept his voice down. "No. But if you can spare Rubyn for a while, he can help me set out a trapline in the fields. It's time to take the tithe there and collect some winter pelts."

Ellibeth glanced back and moved even closer, speaking very quietly though as yet Rubyn still wasn't paying attention to them. "Are you sure? He'll be running all over and not a lot of help."

Billi answered just as quietly. "He'll be really quiet and well behaved, because I'm going to teach him how to do it properly. Then if he gets the idea, he can tend them while I'm cutting reed." Billi winked. "He might even earn a couple of furs."

Ellibeth opened her mouth and Billi waited for the objection and then she hesitated, and smiled. "That would be kind, and be useful to him in the future. I thank ye, Billi."

"No need, since I'm supposed to trap the fields anyway for my Sis. Rubyn will be doing my chores, and he will pay a share to the Farmer if he catches anything. I'll bring him back at dusk, and the same tomorrow?"

"You'll bring him back well before then so I can scrape the fields off him before he eats and goes to bed." Ellibeth smirked. "Tomorrow ye can stay and eat my food for a change."

That startled Billi. "But what about Viktor? 'Tis his house and table."

"This will come out of my meat, my wages, and I'm cooking it, so Da won't mind at all." Ellibeth turned to Rubyn and raised her voice. "Ye don't really deserve it, not after running off like that, but Billi is going to take you out to the fields." Rubyn's eyes lit up. "Not to play, there'll be no messing about. You've to behave because he's going to teach you to lay a trapline, like a real Hunter.

Rubyn looked from one to the other, unsure, until Billi nodded and then a big smile broke over his face. "Can I tell Ganda? Please?"

"Yes, but be quick." Ellibeth barely got the words out before Rubyn raced away.

"Ganda, Ganda. I'm to go and learn to hunt with Billi. I'll be a real Hunter. Ganda!" Ellibeth and Billi smiled at each other and shrugged.

Timath looked in to see what the noise was about. Once he knew, he laughed. "He'll be safe enough with a bearr, a Hunter and a Hound."

Billi sighed. "How long will that keep up?"

"Oh, a long while yet." Timath grinned. "The Village youths are proper proud of our ssrrong bearr. They're bragging about how you actually caught her at the end though they're all bit jealous of the cuddle and the bussing, and some want to know how far those tattoos went?" Timath waited hopefully, so he was one wanting to know.

"Yes, how far do they go?" Ellibeth had a wicked smile, and Billi decided to get out before cheese cloths were introduced to the discussion.

Luckily Rubyn arrived back. "Not something to discuss with Rubyn present." Billi saw it in Ellibeth's eyes; she was going to mention cheese. "Rubyn, are you ready?" The sheer volume of chatter one littlun produced stopped any other discussions, but conversations around Ellibeth were going to be fraught for a while. Rubyn kept it going all the way back to the fields, and in the hut while Billi sorted out some extra traps and gloves.

What Billi would teach Rubyn didn't need a Hound or a Hunter because the fields were Farm, though trapping could provide useful winter income even for a Farmer or Tanner. They laid a dozen traps and this time Billi did it all, explaining everything he did and why while an impatient littlun watched carefully. Tomorrow morning after either Billi collected him or someone brought Rubyn out to the hut, Rubyn could learn how to empty and reset any with prey. Tomorrow evening, if he could repeat the lessons back to Billi, Rubyn could set a couple.

Perry brought out the apprentice Hunter the next morning, "So I can get some peace. He's been rattling on since his eyes opened."

"Thank you, Perry. You can go back home now and get some sleep." Perry rolled his eyes and set off home, though Billi doubted that Viktor would let the youth go back to bed. Billi and Rubyn checked the traps, took out the catch in three, and reset them. Billi explained, again, that they had to take the traps in tomorrow evening as Billi wouldn't be here to empty them the next day, he'd be away to cut reed at first light.

Rubyn stood there hesitating, then took a big breath and it all came out in a rush. "Could I take Ma round to help me empty them since I'll be here right over the fence and so will she and your hut isn't big and doesn't need a lot of cleaning every day?" Then Rubyn stood there, barely breathing, and waited for the reply. Billi thought the littlun must have been churning it all over all night.

Maybe it just made Billi a soft touch, but this would also bring in a bit to start the littlun's nest egg. After all, Rubyn had no Da to teach him or find him jobs to start him off. With a little smile Billi realised this skill would also come in handy if Rubyn ended up with the valley landclaim. "Yes, if your Ma agrees but you've got to let me talk to her alone, to work it out. No pestering while we decide, all right?" Billi didn't fancy trying that with Rubyn butting in every few seconds. Actually, Billi expected Ellibeth to say no.

Billi started by giving Rubyn a lesson on the Laws. The littlun had the words from school, where he'd be going today as soon as the traps were all checked, but until now they wouldn't seem real to him. Being told not go near the Forest or wander about on his own in case the Wild snatched him made sense without the Laws. Now Billi made it clear, Rubyn had to act like a Hunter. The littlun had to obey the Law of the Wild and Billi tried to remember when they'd really impacted him. When he had reason to notice no doubt, when it suddenly mattered because he started hunting.

The lessons continued after school, about using a skin that had no Man or Hound smell on it to carry the traps in, and about boiling them to get all the smells off. "Take care with the bait, just tight enough so that the prey has to tug, not loose enough to grab and run or big enough to take a piece from the edge." The man and other scents didn't matter so much here in the fields where man and dog and Hound were all over the place, but 'twas best to learn the lesson from the off. Even if Rubyn never had a Hound he might be living in that valley one day, and while ever there were fish in those lakes there'd be winter pelts to trap. On the Farm there were other problems that wouldn't come up in the Forest, such as Spots marking the traps. "Spots will try to mark every one because the trap is yours and he wants to tell everyone to stay off."

"There's a lot of traps, Billi. Will they all catch something?"

"No, not every time and some will only catch rats or mice, though Spots will enjoy those. Take care, make sure everything is dead before you try and take it out because even a mouse can bite." Billi wouldn't say so but knew Rubyn might mess up and maybe catch little or nothing. If it was nothing Billi would have a look with a lantern after the littlun went home and put it right, then set Rubyn right in the next lesson

Taking Rubyn home that evening felt really strange, because Billi cleaned himself up first. Then when he delivered Rubyn, instead of going home as usual Billi came inside for his meal. He couldn't remember the last time he'd eaten in someone else's house, if ever. Billi thought about that and he'd never sat around a table with others to eat since his Ma and Da went to the rock. Apparently Viktor really didn't mind who his maid invited to dinner, and acted as if Billi usually ate with them. At least Billi didn't have to make conversation because Rubyn entertained them all, expounding on the lessons he had learned, and the importance of the Laws. Then Billi found himself discussing what they'd done with Ellibeth in greater detail.

Ellibeth seemed impressed by the extent of Rubyn's lessons. She understood well enough that this would be a useful skill even if Rubyn never had a Hound, and told Billi that having a Hunter teach Rubyn was a gift in itself. Ellibeth had no problem with killing whatever Rubyn caught, or gutting and skinning, when Billi mentioned Rubyn's idea. As a tanner's littlun she sometimes helped her Da scrape hides. What she'd never had to think about was the tithe for the Wild. Most farmers didn't bother because the Law of Man ruled on the Farm and anyway the dogs or cats often ate any vermin caught whole.

Billi tried to explain. "This is my luck. I'm a Hunter, so I prefer to act like one even on the Farm." Billi smiled. "I even do it out where the valley is, put the tithe from the fish and anything I trap or hunt at the edge of the Forest. I do the same with the reed bed, I clean any birds in the trees, not in the reeds, and even put the weeds into the Forest." Billi chuckled. "Us Hunters are a funny lot. Leave the tithe from the traps for me to take, since going to the edge of the Forest without a Hound is risky."

Ellibeth didn't find him or his habits funny. "I do understand, Billi, sort of, and if it's your luck that's good enough for me anyway. I told you, a good few Hunters reckon the Forest likes you, Billi, and didn't your luck rub off on the whole Village after the Wood Hunt?"

"That really was blind luck, Ellibeth, and some of the luck came from having everyone along." The importance attached to the Wood Hunt still made Billi uncomfortable. "I still can't work out what I'd have done with a whole Great-Boar all alone in the Forest. With just me and Rabbit there, we'd have had to live in the Forest eating boar rather than waste any. Eventually we'd have eaten enough so I could carry the rest. It's the Law."

Ellibeth burst out laughing. "Sorry Billi. 'Tis the thought of the two of you living next to a big frozen pig, with a little fire so you could cook it a bit at a time. Though you'd have had plenty of firewood from what Bliss said." She sobered a bit. "Though that means it was our luck, yours and everyone there because I have fond memories of roast pork that winter." Billi gave up, because there really had been a lot of luck involved one way or another.

* * *

This morning Rubyn turned up early, towing his Ma up the track. The trainee mighty Hunter arrived keen, noisy, and had trouble with the slow and careful part. Since he didn't need to sneak up on anything that wasn't too bad. With his small hands Rubyn found the little scraps of bait easy to fix though his wrists weren't quite strong enough yet to put the full tension on some of the traps. Billi took up the strongest traps as an accident with those might have cost the lad a finger, and the rest were good enough for the little furred hunters.

Rubyn promised to work on his wrists and grip so even if he couldn't manage this year, he could set the other traps another winter. Billi told him that would come with the years as he grew, and growth would deal with the herb-boiled gloves being too big but that could take years. Ellibeth came round with them to see what Billi wanted doing, and now she had a good look at the gloves. "I'll ask Da if he's any scraps of leather and make some small ones for now."

"If not, take a bit from one of those he's curing for me, because these big gloves really will make him clumsy." Billi shrugged. "Take a piece from the end of a leg since the quality of the leather won't matter for this."

"Will I get lessons in skinning if I have proper gloves, Billi?"

Billi smiled at Ellibeth's startled look. "I told him he'd cut himself using a knife with these. I didn't expect someone to make him a small pair."

Ellibeth smiled back. "I'll skin the ones from the traps for now, and I'll keep an eye open for something Rubyn can learn on. Perhaps you could leave the hide on my wages for him to start with?" They both laughed because Billi paying for goods with meat still bearing hide or fur was a Village joke, even if he rarely did.

"You could start him on rats? I had to teach myself to skin prey without spoiling the hide or pelt and used rats, and if he learns to skin rats anything with a thicker skin will be easy." Billi frowned as a thought struck him. "He could learn to cure them as well."

"Rat skins?" Ellibeth laughed. "I doubt there's much point. There's no real use for rat skin, is there?"

"Rat skins actually make a decent thin leather, it's just that most people don't like the idea. Not only that but 'tis finicky work. I had a go to teach myself to cure my hides, then gave up and came to your Da." Billi looked over at Rubyn, busy explaining to Spots why he couldn't lift a leg on the traps. "Maybe he'll start a new fashion and in any case he'll learn to cure skins. Then if he ends up a Tanner?"

"I doubt rat skin will catch on but Da will probably enjoy teaching him and it'll keep Rubyn's hands busy instead of finding mischief." Ellibeth laughed. "If you get a rat skin purse or gloves, you'll know he's got it right. Now I'm going home to set into the sweeping. Do you want me to take Rubyn? There's no school today."

"Leave him. We'll spend the day working on this and that and going over his trapping lessons, and he can earn a couple of eggs." They both smiled at that. With all day to fill Billi ended up helping Rubyn with a snowman, something he'd not done for much too long. Rubyn couldn't manage a one-legged version but did insist the Snow-Billi had a crutch. He also insisted there had to be a Snow-Hound sitting alongside.

Well before dusk the littlun bounced off home with eight pelts for Viktor to deal with, his eggs, Spots, and Rabbit to watch over him to Victor's gate. Meanwhile Billi tidied up and waited for the Hound so he could take the scraps to the Forest. Billi debated if he did worry overmuch about tithing these bits? Rabbit would barely taste them, and there would only be a couple of mouthfuls for Spots, but Billi had decided long ago that he would keep to his idea of the Law at all times. The Forest really had been good to him, perhaps because he didn't cheat the Wild.

* * *

A crowd gathered outside Billi's gate in the morning as the reed party and the hut sitters arrived together. Ellibeth brought a piece of leather and Billi confirmed Rubyn could have it for gloves, and the Thatcher's party set off for the reeds. It took a bit longer to get there this year because of the deeper snow but the three youths went ahead, towing the boats, and trampled a path for the 'olduns' to follow. They were in high spirits since this break from their normal life also paid well.

Even wading in the icy water didn't slow them up and the youths built a bonfire to warm up while they had their dinner. The first bonfire used the broken wreckage of reeds where something large had wanted a drink and took the direct route through the reed bed. Because Fellip had been out three times since spring little weed had grown, and the bundles of cut reed were soon piling up. The harvest would still take five days according to the Thatcher because Fellip had been right and the reeds were taller and thicker in the parts that had been mostly overgrown last year. The rest of the reed also grew stronger and without rotten stalks mixed in. Billi used the standing reed to stalk the birds for everyone's pay, then went looking for Ellibeth's.

He went to the bend again and waited as disturbed bits of weed floated downstream. When he came back there were a few comments, but Billi explained he wanted a pillow so the maid wouldn't get the whole swan. While he'd been out of hearing there must have been some intense discussion about Rubyn's trapping lessons because both Perry and Timath let Billi know they were interested in a bit of tuition. They had both laid snares for rabbits in the communal rough grazing with varying success. "I've promised to teach Rubyn first but then I'll show you." Billi grinned. "Unless you can persuade Rubyn to pass his lessons on?"

Neither seemed keen on a littlun teaching youths to hunt, but then Timath suddenly smiled. "Rubyn will come out to your hut while you're hunting, so I can go round the traps with him and learn as fast as he does." Timath glanced at Perry. "Since I'll not mind big eyes and a big mouth seeing who calls by."

Perry looked really torn, then he smiled. "If I spend a few days learning I'll catch a few pelts, then I can cure them to get more business. Better still, I can make a really fancy present out of a couple for someone." His smile faltered. "Would you mind looking if my traps aren't working Billi, just to check?" The same question appeared in Timath's eyes. Billi agreed, and had a quiet smile at the thought of Rubyn lecturing two youths on the Laws, since Perry was twice the age of the littlun.

While everyone ate their midday meal the bros confirmed that the whole Village already knew about Billi's landclaim and speculation had started over the actual size. Could a man actually live there full time with his lass? Billi refused to confirm or deny that, though after the talk with the elders he wondered himself. Timath wondered if, with a proper landclaim, some maid might hang about near enough to see if "ssrrong bearr" wanted to catch one?

On the other four days' day Billi took the party into the nearby Forest when they arrived, to collect wood to build their bonfire. Billi made sure everyone had geese on at least three days so that anyone wanting pillows could collect enough feathers. That wasn't difficult as a flock were feeding in the shallow water each morning when he sneaked in ahead of the reed cutters. The snow had covered most of the grazing on the banks, so the cleared portions of the reed bed attracted plenty of fowl. Fellip traded for geese once he heard about the pillows as his lass would probably appreciate fresh feathers.

More comments greeted the second swan for Ellibeth but once again Billi explained the sewing and plucking fee for his new pillows. Everyone agreed her stitching would be better than any man would manage, and now Billi found that it would be better than most maids could achieve as well. Ellibeth apparently sold bits of embroidered leather portraying small creatures, good enough that some maids sewed them on their coats for a bit of fancy. Her Bros both claimed she would put something fancy on the pillows since she didn't seem able to manage plain sewing.

Billi took three yearling swans altogether, and two geese on the last two days to leave the original parent swans and one yearling. He told Ellibeth that Viktor should sell what fowl he wished, as the youths also had geese so that Perry could have his pillow. Ellibeth told Billi he was a soft touch, but smiled and this time took the birds without making a fuss.

Each night Billi came home to fresh bread and then sat while Rubyn showed him the take from the traps and explained where each one came from. Rubyn dragged his Ma out to the hut early every morning so Billi could go out with him, before leaving, to look at the traps that were taking nothing. Sometimes that was the way he'd set the trap, sometimes they just found a different place.

A couple of days after the reed cutting finished, a fine new pillow arrived in the hut, one with a spray of embroidered leaves in the corner "because you like the green, the Forest, so much." When Billi threw it at Rubyn because it would stop him stealing the one from the bed Ellibeth blushed and confessed. She'd made an extra one, for her bed through there, so the big new one wouldn't really fit. They compromised and Rubyn ended up with the smaller one Billi normally used, the one Bliss made so it was a good pillow.

Billi only needed the new one, since Ellibeth pointed out if someone ended up sharing his bed they probably wouldn't mind squeezing up a bit. She still teased him a little bit now and then about how the cheese lessons were coming along and also about ssrrong bearr. The maids in the Village didn't let it drop and Billi still received the occasional shriek as some maid would claim the bearr had made a grab for her. A couple might have been testing, since some started wondering if Billi had a cabin out on his landclaim for the winter trips, and might need a maid. A lot of speculation started up about the landclaim generally, and according to some stories there would be room for a whole new Village.

* * *

Winter closed in and the heavy snow and sharp early freeze threatened this would be a long cold one, the second in three years. A few villagers asked if Billi had a Great-Boar lined up just in case. More snow and more freezing meant Billi only went to his lakes twice before midwinter. Both times he broke open the ice and moved the lumps so that the Great Hunter could get at the fresh water and fish from near the trees. Billi took a good crop of thick winter fur from the small hunters and the second time a young lion who wanted the contents of the traps.

Billi salted some fish and left them in the cold store, filling his pack with lion meat and the pelt. The stripped bones and offal probably made a welcome easy meal for the Great Hunter. The tracks the following morning said that the big cat had taken the lot from the Forest edge where Billi left his tithe. Rabbit kept marking any sign of the huge cat anywhere around the lakes so the marking war was still on.

The other war still continued in the Village, though not fiercely enough for Billi to let it worry him. Despite the shunning, now lifted, Edan still managed to spread tales and rumours or Billi assumed Edan did so. The young man did nothing open, but occasionally Billi would get some unfriendly looks from folk he had never upset. Unpleasant though the looks were, he no longer assumed that his lack of a leg was to blame. There were a small number of people who refused to talk to him and avoided contact but most seemed to be the small group that Billi associated with Edan. Some of Edan's friends and his Ma glared, but said nothing to Billi's face and nothing would alter their opinion, so Billi didn't try.

He now had more friendly nods and greetings than Billi had ever expected to see, and a welcome in the alehouse and the stores. The maids didn't seem to be put off, and were occasionally emitting shrieks of panic when the bear came near. Edan's continued campaign stayed annoying, or rather the thought of Edan still out there plotting and stirring rumours annoyed Billi sometimes. The muttering and stories no longer caused Billi any actual trouble in the Village, nor any real distress.

Meanwhile Billi continued going hunting when he wanted, and coming back to fresh bread and a thoroughly dusted home. He continued the trapper training and Rubyn started building a little stack of the plush pelts from his share of the take. Both of his Unks were taking 'lessons' by coming with him and both had spoken to Farmers and negotiated fields for their own trap lines. The three of them had a Tanner at home who helped them with the pelts, and Perry used his to perfect his own skills.

Viktor's skills, or experience, led to another something new or at least different. The young lion's skin had a half-grown mane because of the cat's age, which Ellibeth and Rubyn hadn't seen before. Nor had most people, even Hunters, and a good few called round to see Viktor and take a look. The lions within the normal hunting range of the Village were older, wilier beasts presumably driven out by younger males as were the occasional old, scarred wolves. Though driven out from where puzzled the Hunters since few females had ever been seen.

The old discussion came up, why Wolves and Lions, Boar and Stags had names but many others were simply striped hunter, dappled hunter or straight-horned deer. As usual nobody could decide since the reason lay somewhere back beyond legend and memory. This beast looked like a lion, and the pelt seemed right, but nobody could remember a male without the full shaggy mane. Viktor told Billi the half-grown mane would make a warm but unusual fur hood so he asked about getting one made. Ellibeth sewed it as a thank you for her Da's pillow but Billi wasn't to mention the pillow to Viktor. Ellibeth explained that with the number of swans and the geese, and some feathers from Timath, Ellibeth had enough spare to make a pillow for her Da, for a Midwinter present.

She even lined the lion-mane hood with some of the soft fur from the traps near Billi's huts and looking at it he thought the result much too good to wear out in the Forest. Ellibeth's neat stitching in the thin leather included a bit of fancy along the edging and the hood looked more like a maid's luxury item than something to keep a Hunter's head warm. Billi arranged for Ellibeth to stitch a pair of soft fur mitts for his Sis once he'd seen her work. She put on a bit of embroidered ribbon and some fancy stitching so her Bros were right about her never doing any plain sewing. Billi had plenty of the small soft furs since the vermin were determined this year and One-shut ate well while defending the chickens and their feed.

The only real cloud on Billi's horizon wasn't a big one but became more urgent as Midwinter approached. With all the fuss at Harvestfest Billi never did sort out the gift problem, what might be suitable. Now time started running out and there'd be no Tinkerers to buy from. Billi finally plucked up courage to corner Barimar at the alehouse for a quiet word. "What exactly is the right and wrong thing to give a maid as a present if she is a friend? A gift that won't embarrass her by suggesting more than friend?"

Billi didn't expect the strangled laughter, only strangled since Billi had asked Barimar to keep this private. "Forest and Farm, Billi. Half the Village are wondering if you are chasing Ellibeth because of what you've already put on her table and bed." Barimar sniggered. "A good few are wondering when she'll stop running. Then there's one or two maids thinking that if she keeps running, you might prefer an easier target."

Barimar paused to get his breath back and have a drink of his ale. Billi tried again. "I'm serious, what are the rules if I'm not chasing?"

Barimar kept to just smiling this time. "There are no set rules about gifts. A lot depends on how the gift is given." Barimar shrugged. "After all, if too much is given without any hint of chasing, there might be rumours of a different arrangement."

Billi sat a while, puzzled, and then blushed scarlet. "No! I'd never do that! Ellibeth is a respectable maid, not a Tinkerer."

"Nobody thinks any different after your building spree, Billi, and if they do they'll never dare say so." Barimar laughed again. "Ooh, I haven't had so much fun for ages. This is better than trying to steer my littluns through it all since you're a grown man, Billi. How did you get to what, twenty-five summers, without knowing any of this?"

"I've never had any real friends since I lost my leg. This is all new, Midwinter gifts and folk who invite me into their homes and I don't want to spoil it." Billi sighed. "I still don't expect to ever have a lass all proper like, but this is better than I had hoped for at one time." Billi looked up at the head of the Great-Boar. "I owe that beast a lot."

Barimar sobered up. "Ah, right. Never thought of that. You were out there in that hut, and you rarely came into town. We more or less forgot you were there I suppose. Hide and Hair, but you've fixed that now! Just the Billi-huts will keep your memory alive long after you go to the rock, Billi." Barimar took a pull of his ale. "Right, gifts. Friend not chasing, though I reckon you should consider that with the right maid at another time. You might be surprised, Billi."

"Friends, Barimar. I've got all on dealing with that right now."

"Friends." Barimar smiled. "Those spotted skins, if you've still got them, and Tinkerer sparkuls, if you ever get any, are not on the friend list. They are at the top of the chasing list or more probably the catching list. You know that stones, claws and teeth aren't for a maid, not as a friend anyway?" Billi nodded. "Furs are acceptable, from a Hunter at least, providing they aren't too much. A long fur coat would be more than friendly."

"What about mitts or a hat, maybe boots?" Billi still couldn't work out how this was scaled.

"Yes, mitts or a hat, or maybe a pair of winter boots from a Hunter wouldn't be too much. The fur doesn't matter quite as much if it comes with lunch rather than bought specially. Though a full set would be a definite statement of interest. Some would think four swans was." Barimar laughed as Billi blushed again. He tried to explain about the sewing and the older Hunter cut him short.

"I know Billi. We all do since Ellibeth made a point of it to a couple that asked questions. I just couldn't resist teasing you." Barimar finished his ale. "Have you got the idea now, or do I get some more fun?"

"No thanks. Barimar. I think I've got the idea or near enough not to offend." Billi finished his own ale and went home to plot with Rabbit.

Billi still felt a bit confused but he had an idea now and just before Midwinter spoke to Viktor. Billi carefully explained that he valued Ellibeth too much as a friend to embarrass her but wanted to give her a Midwinter gift. Viktor promised to make sure that Ellibeth knew the gift wasn't meant to embarrass and needn't say where it came from if she preferred. Billi had gifts for the rest of Viktor's family because that wasn't such a problem, but didn't mention them or the man would try to get something in return. Billi knew the Tanner didn't have much to spare, and didn't want to put him in that position.

Billi went into the Village to the seamstress with the hood, which already seemed suitable for a maid but now he wanted some real fancy work on it. They discussed just what sort of fancy sewing would look best. Like many others, the seamstress seemed to be over her previous antagonism and she suggested some bits of ribbon for a maid's gift. Especially if it was for a special maid? Billi explained maid but just a friend and she smiled and agreed to find something suitable.

* * *

Viktor probably had a bit of a shock Midwinter morn when his family opened their presents. Billi had never had someone to buy gifts for before. He had planned what the youths were getting back in autumn, while he had plenty of meat and hides to sell. Billi decided on belt knives for Perry and Timath. He also traded for a knife for Rubyn. Just a small blade in a soft sheath with a bit of fancy on it, enough for nine summers and yet useful for skinning small prey. All of the knives were good blades from the Tinkerers, even if the grips were plain. Held up to the light, they all had that wavy pattern in the metal though every pattern seemed different. Billi had looked and they were both a mystery and pretty.

Viktor received some pans and a new kettle because Ellibeth had mentioned the kettle getting thin and it had been mended twice. Billi already knew Viktor had few pans since the man had said so himself. Bliss and Hektor received a young cat, allegedly one of One-shut's offspring and definitely the same charcoal black. The kit had already become a fierce mouser so if he grew to the size of his sire Bliss's hens would be safe. A good mouser at that age cost him some fierce bargaining but Billi wanted a decent cat for them because the house cat at Hektor's home farm hadn't produced this year.

What Billi didn't expect when he delivered the kitten was the little bundle Bliss gave him to take home. Nor did he expect the wrapped presents from Viktor's family when he left his own little surprises. Presents made Midwinter's morn completely different in the little hut this year.

* * *

Midwinter morn Billi ended up sat in his chair with his small mug of warm cider and the opened bundles on the table in front of him. He was a little bemused by the soft furry ear muffs, fancy carved horn tips for his bow, a complete set of new sheaths with fancy stitching for his set of hunting knives, and a small pillow from the two youngest, to use in the Forest. A pair of thin leather gloves with fancy stitching were 'for dancing' according to Bliss.

Rabbit had a big bone, One-shut a couple of thin lean slices of cold roast, and they were all sat contentedly when the Hound came to his feet. The small noise and lift in the song turned into a little whine of welcome and he hopped to the door. Billi looked out to find a repeat of the visit after Harvestfest, which seemed a year ago and wasn't.

Viktor waved as they all trooped in through his gate, smiling and muffled up in winter clothes though Perry, Timath and Rubyn all had their knives on their belts in plain view. The two littluns had small folding knives since a youth or even a littlun needed a knife to learn with, to Billi's way of thinking anyway. He knew he'd loved his first real knife. The little folding ones weren't cheap but were less likely to end up stuck in a leg while the youngest got used to them.

He knew that Ellibeth wasn't embarrassed because she wore the lion mane hood with a big smile and stroked the outside to make sure he noticed. Ha, everyone would notice and Billi hadn't realised just how distinctive that would be. Billi had settled on the hood because Ellibeth had helped make it so it wasn't such a big gift. Not significant, just friendly. Now he wasn't sure if maybe he'd been wrong. Maybe he'd overdone the extras? All the fancy coloured stitching had definitely made it a maid's hood, a pretty one. The blue ribbons to tie it, threaded back around the edge to draw it tight around her face, sort of drove pretty and maid home. The hood was warm though, as Ellibeth told him on the way in. Just as Billi started wondering where they would all sit he found out nowhere.

Ellibeth started banking the fire and took the pot of water off to cool, the youths were getting Billi's coat and Rubyn brought one big furry bearskin boot. Viktor clapped Billi on the shoulder. "I've enough pans to cook for a visitor now, and we've picked on you. We need another to make sure all the pans get used, according to Ellibeth."

The family escorted him and Rabbit back and Billi spent the day in the middle of a happy family. It was the busiest and happiest Midwinter for Billi in many years, and he ate much better than he expected. Rabbit also had a Midwinter feast, and laid by the fire with the two dogs. The song said Rabbit felt happy, contented, and had maybe eaten just a bit too much, which was how Billi felt as well.

Ellibeth wore her hood to the evening dance and pointed out to those who asked that Billi had given her a hood because he didn't trust her with a knife. That wasn't true as she often helped him to cut and trim his catch into handier joints after bringing it home, but her answer took some of the speculation out of the questions. The fancy fur hood with the luxurious lining now looked to be well past borderline as a friend gift but Billi didn't care because that wasn't bothering Ellibeth. He thought she might really like it because the hood had been improved. It now bore some bright red ribbons with a little bit of embroidery on instead of the plainer dark blue the seamstress had provided. It certainly looked a lot prettier like that, and ensured that everyone noticed what she wore.

The bearr jokes were in full flight and in the end, of course, Billi had to stand and brace himself against the big centre post. A succession of maids swung around him by grabbing his arm and then pretended relief at escaping. Several waved little bits of cloth and carefully tucked them safely away else he might grab them, and they all had a lot of fun. Billi danced with more maids than in his entire life up to now. Not hard to do but still he had a great time. Ellibeth put her hood on and made a great play of the hanging ribbons when she danced past, so he caught one and the hood. After the cheers and laughter, a lot of loud speculation started over what the forfeit would be to get her hood back. Ellibeth moved closer and grinned at Billi, then turned to the others.

"Billi is too good a man to ask for more than the usual forfeit, the chance to buss the maid." Ellibeth put a bit of apprehension in her voice. "I'm lucky it was Billi caught me, and not the bearr." She turned back, smiling, and Billi bussed her firmly. The Village youths cheered while others laughed or called out tips on how to hold a maid properly for bussing.

Viktor came over to them. "Here Billi, I've brought a cider to ransom my maid since she's been careless enough to be caught." He grinned. "I thought she'd got more sense." A blushing Billi sat back down with the older men and spent the rest of the dance there. Several of the other youths stood by the post with their arms out for maids to swing on. There were definite attempts to catch some of the maids and some made sure they were caught, so the youths and maids had a new game they could claim was just dancing.

The older men were more interested in the landclaim and several of the younger men and youths dropped by to ask questions. The questions weren't general, they were about the area and the land nearby. Could Billi be sure about there being no water on top of the hill? A lot wanted to know if there might be room for another hut and landclaim inside the valley. Billi told them the place wasn't fit for anyone to live there just yet. Once he'd got it squared away, he told them, he'd take someone out to have a look. It wasn't a "no," and all they really wanted to hear. At the end of the dance Billi and Rabbit went as far as Viktor's gate with the family before heading home followed by good wishes. After this dance Billi slept well without any cider to help.

* * *

Winter ground slowly on and gave no hint of relenting and eventually the river actually froze over. The ice stayed thin in places and holes were smashed to water the stock but the freezing came as a startling indication this year was much colder than usual. Only Kina and one other elder remembered the river freezing before, when they were littluns. That boded ill for the Village as both remembered the winter being very bad, lasting long enough for the farmers to kill breeding stock for food. Families inspected their stores and some started to tighten belts to ensure that there would be enough to last through until spring.

Anyone going outside muffled themselves up in thick furs, and came back indoors as fast as possible. Ellibeth had good use out of her hood, and the soft fur mitts her Bros had made her from their trapline victims. She also had a pair of soft furry ear muffs from Rubyn, the whole family had them and they were handy for quick trips into the cold for firewood or suchlike. Billi wore them inside his hood when out in the Forest to deal with the draughts even if they muffled sound. Rabbit's ears were better than his anyway.

The water fowl deserted the reed bed because that froze over as well. That came as a blow because Billi had told Hektor and some of the other Hunters they could take a few birds when the hunting became harder. He didn't even get out along the banks to set his traps as much because of the heavy snow. After the big freeze Billi stopped trapping along the river bank as they were emptied by the Wild before he got to them. Many of the small streams also froze so the chances of fish from them dropped away.

Even Billi's usual extra sources weren't helping this winter.

At least the freeze meant a snow crust firm enough for him to walk on so Billi could visit the lakes and he collected more pelts and a pack full of fish. He also cleared the ice dam on the gravel so the spring thaw would be less destructive, though spring seemed a long way away. The morning he packed to leave Billi opened the door and stopped dead, because the Great Hunter crouched by the trees! The beast had several fish on the snow, taken from where Billi had smashed the ice yet again.

The big cat had been drinking but now he froze, staring back with big fierce yellow eyes and they stood out because the beast was black! Billi had found black hairs and thought they would be from the stripes but the stripes were only an impression in the gleaming expanse of pelt. Definitely a Great Hunter, and even with Rabbit stood beside Billi the huge cat wasn't even slightly frightened. The Great Hunter watched carefully, but after some endless period his head dipped and the startlingly white fangs reached to delicately scoop up the fish. He stood with heads and tails hanging from his jaws and looked at Billi again. Then the great length turned smoothly and shouldered the bushes aside. A thick black whip waved goodbye and Billi could breathe again.

Everyone talked of the Great Hunter but to see one like that, clearly, the full size and length, was so much more than imagination. Though the sight settled one item. Billi would be sharing his paradise because that beast wouldn't shift unless and until he wished, regardless of what Rabbit marked. Replaying those few moments kept Billi occupied for a good part of the trip home, and he knew they would stay with him forever.

Fresh bread smell greeted him and by now Billi knew it would. If he stayed away overnight then regardless of who had started looking after the hut as Billi left, Ellibeth would be there with fresh bread when he arrived back. Just "as he'd asked" she told him and he might have, Billi couldn't remember the wording when they talked about bread. He told Ellibeth about the Great Hunter, quietly while Rubyn played with Rabbit, and asked her not to repeat it. Some idiot would try for that beautiful midnight pelt, and then the Great Hunter would kill the Hunter and Hound. That would be the end of the valley because once attacked the beast wouldn't allow men near again.

* * *

The good hunting over the summer and a good harvest meant nobody actually felt hungry yet but more belts were being tightened. The local game had almost gone not much over a moon after midwinter, the few animals left too thin or too wary to provide meals for anyone. Everyone in the Village now lived off their stores apart from that one pack of fish Billi brought home. The Hunters were staying home now, and only going out with the wood gathering parties. Even those were going further as the wood gatherers dug in the snow to strip the Forest of even the small dead wood to keep the cold at bay.

The elders broke tradition and agreed that the villagers could use the wood gathered for the fish run. Billi took a group of Hunters and Hounds with ponies and youths on a double overnight, to collect firewood from a place with a small fallen tree and plenty of deadfalls. Soon afterwards a small deputation came to see Billi, led by Barimar and Canitre, to talk about these valleys with game. They had spoken to the youths and young Hunters from last time but now they needed a seasoned Hunter's assessment. Would there still be game in the other valleys even in this weather?

Billi was startled at being referred to as a seasoned Hunter. "Yes, I'm sure there'll be game. There are clearings, and large trees with only a little undergrowth to provide some almost unburied grazing. The rest has thick bushes for browsing and cover, and the faster streams should have a stretch still clear of thick ice to provide water." Billi gestured. "You saw it, Eddmune."

Eddmune shrugged. "I only saw one valley for one hunt, Billi, whereas you'd seen them all before we ever went near. We want you to lead the hunt."

"I'll be really slow in this weather so it'll be quicker without me." Billi wouldn't mind since he had enough in his store to go through to spring, or he could go and smash the ice again to get more fish.

"We can't Billi. The young Hunters won't go without you and neither will Cynel or Eddmune." Barimar shrugged. "They all swear they aren't confident of the direction with all this snow and without you along."

Billi smiled. "I can remind them of the directions if you like. You should remember, Eddmune."

Eddmune grinned and shook his head. "With all this snow the whole Forest is different this year. We need a Winter Hunt so we need our guide."

Canitre snorted. "The real reason is straight enough. Ye're a lucky Hunter Billi, and the Wild has taken to ye. The younger Hunters just won't go without ye, and I'd feel better if ye came along."

Eddmune laughed. "If Billi had more feet one of the younger Hunters would have stolen one as a charm."

"As long as it wasn't given to a maid. Would a Stumpy Wanderer foot mean the same as a stoat's foot?" Hektor sniggered at that.

"A ssrrong bearr's foot might be the same as a stoat tail." That brought a round of laughter. An interested youth might give a stoat's tail to a maid as a cheeky gift. If accepted it would be made into a wristband after the bonding, because that gift meant much more than chasing. Anise had a row of them across the back of her winter coat to advertise her profession.

Once the hilarity died back Eddmune picked up the discussion. "We already have the solution. Billi rides a pony again. We'll be taking ponies anyway and on the way out Billi can ride and even switch if one gets tired. If the hunt is as successful as hoped the ponies will break a trail for everyone and be moving slowly on the way back. Very slowly since we all intend to be towing travois full of meat."

Billi still felt a bit embarrassed. "So I ride again while everyone walks?"

Eddmune laughed. "No, we'll use the same pony. Then the pony will show us where the game is so you may as well get a lift since you're going the same way?" Billi had to laugh with the rest at that and he stopped objecting. Nobody seemed bothered about him riding now or the last time, and it was a practical solution. Though he still thought some other Hunter with a family should go instead because they'd need the meat more.

Though the older Hunters should have enough to last the winter, and yet they wanted to come. "How come so many older Hunters are coming? I would have thought your stores were full?"

"Probably full enough, but we want a good few older heads on this trip Billi." Raban sounded dead serious. "This is a hard winter, the second such winter in three years. The more of the experienced Hunters know how to find these valleys the better, because there are no certainties in the Forest. The Wild might snap up any Hunter, even the Wanderer." Billi could see the hard logic in that argument, so he nodded and the talk moved on to practicalities.

This would be a much more organised expedition, as there were families who would be tightening belts and waiting hopefully until these Hunters arrived back. This time the Hunters would take eight ponies. With them and the eighteen Hunters and six youths pulling or carrying all they could, the trip should be enough to feed every family getting short until the weather broke.

"The families closest to trouble should send someone round and I'll let them have enough to get by." Billi shrugged. "I live on my own so my store is still well stocked. Anyway, I can always head off to the landclaim and eat fish until spring." Billi intended doing that while he still had some food in his store - enough to keep Viktor's family going if things got that bad.

That sparked a quick discussion and an agreement that Billi would take a couple of the older Hunters to see the landclaim when the weather broke. Just so the place could be found and maintained if Billi went missing. If there were still fish there in a bad winter, such a place must be kept for other bad times and not lost if Billi made a misstep on his travels. It felt a bit strange speaking of making real plans in case the Wild caught him out. Billi had sort of agreed to show people but the harsh urgency in the requests now emphasised a hard logic.

Billi had lived until now on the assumption that the worst would happen one day or night and his nest egg was to cover if it happened in the Village. If either he or Rabbit broke a leg out there they were both done, because neither had a spare, and neither would leave the other. Billi had always assumed that apart from the hut going to Sis, him not coming home would make no difference in the Village. But now he had made definite arrangements about the valley and reeds, so Billi had to ensure that the Hunters could find his valley and know how he'd made it into Farm. Purely by accident he had created something the Village wished to keep, and now Billi wanted someone to benefit from that.

He'd started by wanting a bit of peace, a private place to go and relax. As he slowly made the valley his, Billi didn't want to let the place disappear if the Wild took him. First he wanted someone, then a certain someone, to benefit, and possibly to move in as he intended to himself. If he never lived there, properly, Billi felt content with the idea of Rubyn running about in there one day, scaring fish and staring wide-eyed at everything. Now Billi realised he wanted more, he wanted the valley to be a real home, maybe even a place with a neighbour or two. More, he actually found that providing an extra food source for the Village against times like this mattered to him, and Rabbit's song chimed agreement.

The older Hunters hammered that part home now. "It isn't just what you happen to see on your wandering Billi. Now 'tis knowledge that will keep folk alive." Canitre leaned in, his voice grave. "Your memory could mean life or death for some families. Not just your valley, but your other wanderings."

Eddmune added his weight to the discussion. "There's a grain of truth in what I said about the Winter Hunt valleys. I went once, without deep snow on the ground, and might have trouble hitting them again." The Hunter shrugged. "Going astray in this weather could kill us all. You know the way regardless of the weather because you know the area out there beyond the hunting grounds."

"Your valley, with fish and therefore probably game will be an even greater prize in future years, and I for one don't fancy following written directions." Raban shook his head. "Nor do I want to break whatever way you farm the valley, however you persuaded the Wild to let it go. Right now the valley could be lost by a twig turning underfoot and you or Rabbit breaking a leg."

"But first we choose Hunters for this Winter hunt, a mixture of experience and eager youth. The Wild might object to such a large expedition even though we will be almost all Hunters so we'll stay well inside the Laws. We must bear that in mind when inviting hunters and youths." Others nodded at Canitre's words but he puzzled Billi.

"I thought we had plenty of volunteers?"

"We do but the Wild is fickle at all times, and just now the Wild will also be hungry. I will go because there's another Hunter in my house." Canitre looked round. "Every family with two Hunters should send one of them, so that fewer families with only one have to risk it."

"Aye." Cynel sighed. "If the Wild does close in and none of us come back that'll mean there are both experienced and young Hunters left to keep the Village going."

That finished any hesitation Billi had about going. "Then I will definitely come, since nobody will starve if I don't come back."

Raban nodded. "True. Young Hektor will come and his Da, Barimar, will take care of Bliss if aught happens."

Eddmune nodded. "Mikkel and Ewward, with Tempert on a spear because he's blooded and will be steady."

"Grantel's not blooded, but we must leave some blooded youths here as they might get Hounds if we fall." Cynel shrugged. "We can't be sure of him, but that's better than taking all the blooded youths." Eventually the group had a rough idea of who would be asked, though in some families 'twould be a choice between the two and left to them. Others may not come because they had enough and didn't want to risk the trip, or their families might object.

* * *

The following day four men with families and sparse storerooms turned up at his hut. Billi wouldn't be short of chicken feed, flour or goat fodder next winter, since all were Farmers except the Potter. That had to be hard for the Potter after how he'd treated Billi, but the man swallowed his pride for his family which made him a good enough man for Billi to let it go. Billi told the Potter he'd take some crockery for the valley whenever he had fuel to fire the kiln. Right now any remaining wood or charcoal had to be kept for heating homes.

Even though Billi would have given them the meat and fish, all would be terribly shamed if he even offered. Everyone paid the Hunter because everyone knew that despite every youth hoping to be a Hunter, despite so many maids finding the Hunters a better catch, the Hunter and Hound risked their lives on every hunt. Hunters died every year, their skulls or tokens the truth behind every mouthful of meat and scrap of pelt that came from the Forest. This time the Hunters would push their luck further than usual, and maybe that explained why some wanted 'Lucky Billi' along.

Two more days of gathering supplies and making plans for the worst, and then they were all lined up outside Billi's hut. This time almost the whole Village turned out to watch them go, but without the party atmosphere, without laughing and joking even from the youths. Instead there were some intense goodbyes and the good wishes were heartfelt.

Billi gave Ellibeth a folded reed parchment. "This has the instructions on how to get to the valley, better instructions that I gave the elders." Billi smiled at her worried face. "I expect to come back, but if I don't there's a list in there of the rules, what I do to make the valley Farm." Billi didn't tell her that the paper also gave Viktor's family everything left in his food store if he didn't come home. Billi knew his Bros and Sis would have enough because he'd checked, but knew his friends would run short. Ellibeth took the paper, tucked it in her coat, then gave him a fierce hug before stepping back pink-faced.

"I'll look after it but 'twill not be needed. You bring yourself and Rabbit back, you hear. I don't want the bread to go to waste." She smiled, just a little one. "Or the cheese."

"Well in that case I'll be here ahead of the rest." Rubyn gave Billi's leg a hug and then the pony came up with a rough pad strapped to its back. "That's supposing I don't fall off this." A couple of youths steadied Billi until he had a firm grip on the rope around the pony's neck and off they went with a bedlam of good wishes and goodbyes. The Village dogs kept with them up to the edge of the Forest, then the trees closed around them and everyone put their heads down and pushed on.

* * *

Rabbit could keep up well enough with men and ponies, though the Hound appreciated the system of using a couple of ponies to break trail. That saved him periodically breaking into deep snow and having to struggle out. The party rotated the ponies and those leading them so that none became too tired to maintain the pace. The Hound's song had a playful, joyful note as he raced about with the other Hounds, because hunting with others made this an unusual treat for Rabbit. The rest of the Hounds also followed the broken trail except for a couple out to each side keeping an ear, an eye and a nose on what lurked.

Even with the trail breaking arrangement and so many fit, experienced

Hunters, it still took two nights in the Forest before Billi led them to the small rise, the one that gave them a view of the ridges jutting clear of the trees ahead. The younger Hunters and youths climbed trees again while the older Hunters gathered to look through the gap. The Hunters agreed with the tactics used last time, but amended them because this time they must take as much game as possible. The flanking Hunters and Hounds would set out earlier to properly seal the escape route, and there would be six bows on the hillsides.

Canitre pointed out the biggest problem. "You can't lead eight ponies into that, Billi." He smiled. "Or lead seven and ride one. Even if ye could pull that bow of yours like that, the ponies will panic when wounded animals start running at them."

"We can't tether them for later." Baran gave a harsh laugh. "In this weather we'd come back to bones. We're not the only hungry Hunters." That was true enough. They'd seen sign each morning that some Wild hunters were lurking, hoping for a stray from this strange, dangerous pack moving through their territory.

"But we need every bow." Billi wasn't being left someplace while the rest went hunting. It was a matter of pride, for both him and Rabbit. "We can't leave a youth, since the Wild will just treat him as extra meat." The youths all nodded in agreement. They knew full well they only survived out here courtesy of the Hunters and Hounds around them.

"True Billi, we need that big stave of yours at the back again." Eddmune looked round the group. "Billi followed to stop the big ones that ran with an arrow in them." Most of them nodded understanding but a few took a proper look and reassessed the size of the bow-shaft across Billi's back. Billi pulled a huge stave, possibly the biggest on the Farm, and would knock down many of the smaller prey as they came past at close range.

Canitre nodded. "So you don't follow, Billi, but ye can still seal the valley entrance. We'll tether all the ponies somewhere with a good view, right across if possible. If we leave Billi and Rabbit, and a youth, that'll cut off any escape for wounded prey."

Tempert stepped right up. "I'll stand with Billi. I was blooded last time and picked up a scar so I'll be careful, and I know what that bow does." He looked round the other youths. "I'll wager I finish the biggest beast of the hunt."

"Not a chance. I'll wager a copper or two." Billi had opened his mouth to object but the youths had accepted. At least with Rabbit and a Hunter with a bow there, the Wild hunters would either go after wounded animals or get clear of the killing.

"Take down many as possible Billi, but if something really big comes past without an arrow in it I'd rather you let it go. Even with one of your shafts in it, we can't spare the time to run it down."

"Don't worry, Raban, I'm never over-keen on hopping around the Forest after wounded prey." They all laughed at that. "We'd best send a couple of young Hunters ahead to find a good spot to tether the ponies. It'll decide which valley to hunt."

"I'll go." Nortan nodded to Billi. "I'll find you a good spot, one where you get a clear shot across the width if possible."

He looked round and another young Hunter came forward to join him, Ewward. "I know which valley we hunted before." He smiled. "Even if last time I had no Hound."

"If we take help, a youth, we can remove dead branches and grass to clear a field of fire if need be. If we don't hunt or go into the valley, that won't disturb anything before the rest arrive." Youths raised hands, eager to be at it, and the Hunters chose one.

Mikkel sighed in mock resignation. "We'll need to set off early as well, so we can get up the ridges before the rest arrive." Canitre and the other Hunters nodded agreement and smiled with no sympathy at all.

"We'd best push on to get close and settle down for the night. Then those three and the ridge Hunters can be off at the crack of dawn." Several other Hunters agreed with Billi and the whole party moved off as fast as possible. The whole group kept going until full dark to get within about a candle-mark, then made camp.

Billi heard the advance parties move off the next morning. While it might have been the crack of dawn, it must have been a very small crack and Hektor or someone must have looked hard to spot it. Billi didn't have much longer in his furs, and neither did any of the rest because despite the grim necessity of the hunt everyone felt excited. There had never been a hunt like this, not from Trail's End.

* * *

The tracks of the three men led the rest of them to a glade, just inside the mouth of the fourth valley. A huge oak, slightly off-centre in the valley bottom, created a wide open space by stifling competition with its spread of branches and roots. There were another four large spreading trees nearby which extended the clear area, and the three young men were busy clearing old creepers and long dead grass as the party arrived. They couldn't cut trees of course, but threw all the dead wood to the sides to steer running prey back to the centre.

The ponies were securely tethered behind the oak, with both hobbles and a rope to the tree. The wide swathe of open grass would be an extra deterrent for the Wild hunters. "We could rope ye to the tree, Billi?" Eddmune nodded at the oak. "We brought plenty for making travois and strapping down the loads. Put a rope right round the trunk and it'll be easier for you to turn."

Afterwards Billi realised, probably for the first time ever, he didn't even wonder if it was some sort of a slur on his lack of a leg. Eddmune had a practical solution, because Billi really did have trouble turning quickly. A rope around his waist, and loosely around the tree, would help keep his balance. "Good idea, Eddmune."

"You could have done with one at the bearr dancing Billi." Nortan started grinning.

"To rope the Dancer?" Tempert started laughing now. "She seemed to be a bit slippery, Billi?"

Nortan joined the laughter. "Maybe you should have asked Rabbit to catch hold of her nose."

"Wrong prey today, you pair. Come on." Canitre rescued Billi though everyone had big smiles now and the tension that had been creeping in had gone.

"Just remember to come back and untie me?" That kept the smiles going, because Billi had his knives of course.

"Just remember that any plump rumps wearing trews aren't prey, Billi." Canitre pointed at Eddmune, and the Hunter waggled the rump in question.

"Smoke!" Everyone stopped joking when Cynel called out. The ridge Hunters had lit a fire to say they were in position. The Hounds were already strung across the valley entrance, eager and alert, and the Hunters and youths spread out to join them.

"Tempert?" The youth came closer to Billi. "I'm pleased it's you, because we'll need a cool head here. Not someone looking to be blooded." Tempert smiled. "I mean it, because you've got to know when to hold back." Billi gestured to Rabbit. "You take your cues from Rabbit, because he's done this before. He'll know if something needs another shaft." Billi tapped his head. "Rabbit will let me know, so don't get between me and a wounded animal. Stay just back from me to leave my view clear, and let Rabbit grab them. Then finish them quickly."

"Will Rabbit catch hold of them all?"

"No, but you'll know if the animal is too badly wounded to be a problem. He'll be busy slowing up something more lively, either for you or me." Billi smiled. "He might even finish a couple himself, the smaller ones."

"All right Billi." Tempert grinned. "I don't fancy one of your arrows in my rump either." He hefted the spear and moved out to one side and back a little, with Rabbit in close attendance.

Canitre spoke to them all. "Now we've seen the place, and can see what Billi meant about the open spaces under the big trees. That means with eleven bows we can take almost everything as we move up the valley."

"Not mothers with young." Raban fixed a stern gaze on the young Hunters. "Then the young would die, slowly of starvation or because they hadn't the knowledge to survive alone. That would break the Law." The younger Hunters nodded agreement, this wasn't the time to be careless.

"But we take the rest." Eddmune looked over the youths with spears. "You'll have to be quick and finish anything that drops because we'll be busy sticking an arrow in something else. The Hounds will help, but they'll also be watching their Hunter and flushing game from cover." He gestured at Billi. "Remember, if anything looks too big and isn't wounded badly enough, leave it for Billi."

"Spread out into a line, and get set." Canitre watched both ways until everyone lined up, then the Hunters and Hounds set off as one with the youths only a moment behind. Everyone including the Hounds struck up a cacophony of shouts and whistles, howls and barking, and the line swept off up the valley.

The hunt turned into sheer bedlam again, but even louder than last time and Billi actually appreciated being stood back. That played to his strengths, a succession of clean targets he could hit in the side of the ribcage as they tried to run past. He soon found himself busy, using the rope to swing quickly from side to side. Some unwounded animals still made it, finding a route that didn't give Billi a clean chance or dashing through as he aimed at another. Any animals trailing blood or limping were his priority even if something bigger escaped. The sharp call in the song telling Billi when Rabbit spotted the wounded made that easier.

The smaller deer and sows, smaller hunters and wolves, and the younger animals of all breeds didn't give much trouble. Those were already dying if a shaft had struck true, or only needed one shaft from Billi if they weren't already mortally wounded. Rabbit could even finish a few of them unaided, as could Tempert. The problems were the Stags or the old Boars, a big male lion, and adult moose, buffalo and elk, because even with a shaft in their lungs they would run. Such animals could run for hours, sometimes, especially the Boars; they always clung to life with a fierce, stubborn tenacity. Even with two or sometimes three shafts in those, Billi would try for another to avoid the hours of tracking.

Billi's extra shafts didn't drop them all, but then Rabbit leap forward, snarling and threatening. As the prey lunged and feinted to get round him their life drained into the snow, then when they went down Tempert would move in with the spear. Where possible Billi put extra shafts into the largest as they hesitated, to make sure they went down quicker. Only three struggled on past, avoiding Hound and spear, and all of those left a thick blood trail.

Ahead a confused mixture of calls of either encouragement or warning drew away as the Hunters pushed forwards. Though the number and urgency of the shouts didn't die away at the end as some game that had been driven before them finally made a break for freedom. No clear howl to signal the end this time, because the ponies could carry everything they killed. Instead the sounds became less urgent, then began to come back down the valley towards Billi. The occasional exclamation now would be where some wounded creature turned out livelier than expected. Some of the larger animals took this chance to make their break.

"Back Tempert, no!" Too late, the Stag had gone down, but from a stumble not an arrow and Tempert leapt in with the spear poised. "Earth, help, Billi!" The animal rolled and twisted and as Tempert leapt back from the thrashing antlers a kick put the youth down. Billi put a shaft into the Stag's ribs that slowed it up.

Rabbit dashed in, snarling and lunging. "Crawl clear, quick!" Tempert scrambled away one-legged, but kept his spear. "How are you?" Billi put another arrow in the Stag's ribs as Rabbit darted in and out to keep the beast occupied

Tempert stood, pale-faced and favouring his leg. "It hurts, but I can stand." He straightened. "I can still use the spear, Billi." Billi put another arrow through the Stag's ribs as it staggered to its feet, head down but still full of fight.

"Rabbit will watch. When 'tis weak enough he'll lunge and hold, so be ready." Billi turned away to take down a Boar already carrying three arrows, then a smaller deer hobbling on three legs. A snarl and a quick thrashing and when Billi glanced over Tempert and Rabbit had made sure this time. A last unwounded monster Buffalo bull smashed a way through the bushes and ran for his life and Billi paused, listening. The sound of dying animals faded as the line of spears swept back down the valley and stilled them one by one.

Billi freed himself and went to help Tempert make sure of those definitely down but perhaps hanging on to a last breath. The youth gestured at his leg. "My own fault, Billi. I was too keen." Tempert couldn't keep his smile back, even through the pain of his leg. "I didn't want a Great-Stag to get away. I reckon I might have a hoof-mark on there for life, but better than an antler."

Billi looked over at the animal in question. "I think you're right about that being a Great-Stag." He glanced at Tempert's leg. "You're lucky that's not broken."

"Hunter's luck? I hope." Because Tempert wasn't a Hunter yet but he'd been on a Winter Hunt twice now so maybe the Wild would notice and would send a Hound.

Four of the Hunters and their Hounds, and two youths leading ponies, went off to follow the wounded animals. "Come on everyone. Take a pony and a rope, and pull everything to the clearing up here by the stream. Quickly before we all stiffen up." Canitre limped into view. "A few of us won't be much good for that, though I can skin and joint without moving about."

"Nortan can stand guard with a bow if we find him something to sit on." Cynel pointed back into the valley. "He said his leg is broken, and Eddmune is staying with him because his arm is badly hurt."

"Did everyone make it?" Tempert looked around those he could see.

"Yes, but Streak will be on three legs going home because he pulled the bull back. 'Twas wounded but Eddmune slipped on the ice going to finish it. The first strike got a horn into his arm and the second attempt near broke Streak's leg I reckon, but then Grantel got a spear into it." Cynel grimaced. "If Eddmune and Streak had been Hunting alone, the Wild might have taken them."

All those who could manage took ponies to drag the prey to the water's edge, where Canitre for one set into skinning. Billi and Tempert used a pony to drag the Great-Stag to join him and Tempert looked at the game animals already collected. "These are all in good condition Billi. Nothing sick or weak."

Billi grinned at Tempert and gestured to a dappled hunter being towed out of the undergrowth. "Not prime condition because it is winter but you are right, they've got plenty of meat on them. Those, predators and scavengers, really are in prime condition. They've been pulling down anything that faltered."

"The boars are in lovely condition." Canitre gestured towards one. "They've probably been feeding from the remains of kills."

"What about horns and fangs, claws, the usual trophies?"

"We take trophies for the youths that have been blooded, and anything truly exceptional, but leave the rest." Farimer grinned at the young Hunters. "Fill your pockets with claws and teeth, because the travois are for meat and the best hides and pelts."

"I'll carry my antlers." Tempert laughed. "I might wish I'd killed something smaller." He took the rope off the Stag and they went back for more victims. Already a few birds circled up high, and other scavengers would be taking note. As the collection grew, the first victims and Hunters from the hillside began to arrive and there had been lucky escapes up there as well.

Some were very near escapes. Billi saw a very pale and shaken Hektor staggering down the slope carrying his spear and a broken bow, with Dapple limping close behind. Then he saw why as the young man moved and his heavy clothing gaped open, almost from one shoulder to the opposite hip. Four big claws had cut through the leather and had marked his skin here and there enough to bleed, but not heavily. Dapple sported a long gash down one flank and across his haunch, a deep one, still weeping blood.

Behind them a youth with a pony dragged the cause down to the stream for skinning and butchering. A striped hunter, a big male! A pale-faced Hektor sat and cleaned up Dapple's wound with icy water, then he told Billi about it while he tried to rough-sew his gear together with trembling hands. The result wasn't pretty but Hektor wouldn't freeze. Billi listened while he skinned and butchered, because every hand had to keep at that to get done before dark.

"I did it right Billi, dead right. The striped hunter came out of the trees and straight at me." Hektor paused, obviously re-running that sight. "I've never seen anything like it. My first shaft went right under his head, in the base of his throat and into his chest. He should have dropped, or swerved at least." Hektor made a shaky attempt at a laugh. "He felt it, his head whipped sideways at the pain, but came straight back to me and he never missed a step. I tried to get another shaft in the bow, I really tried Billi, but the speed of it!" Hektor stopped for a moment.

"They are fast, all the hunting cats. A big one like that covers a huge distance every bound." Billi thought of the Great Hunter, and how few bounds such a beast would have needed that morning to close on Billi and Rabbit.

"Yes, I know now! It gathered itself and leapt and," Hektor shook his head briefly. "I should have died right there Billi, but a shaft hit him in the ribs and he twisted in mid-air, snapping at the feathers." Hektor's hand reached out to ruffle Dapple's ears. "Then Dapple hit him, hard, and it was just enough."

Billi looked at the striped hunter, now hung up in a tree and losing his beautiful pelt. "Either on their own might not have been enough to stop that."

"Both weren't. The beast still flung out a paw that smashed my bow and did this." Hektor indicated the torn leather clothing he'd tried to fasten back together. "The striped hunter landed on his side, but started to get up again. A paw knocked Dapple aside because the beast still wanted me. I could see it in his eyes." Hektor shuddered briefly. "I'd stuck my spear upright in the snow beside me, handy like, so I grabbed it and jumped in." Hektor sighed. "Got it right first time, which is a really good thing. Even then he knocked the spear out of my hands."

"You always were steady with a spear." Billi's comment brought a little smile to Hektor's lips, as Billi intended. "Your Bliss will have a really pretty rug, or a bed fur looking at its size."

"Which is really good because there'll be three under it. Oh. Ah well, never mind. I'm supposed to keep it quiet for some reason, until she tells everyone or the bump shows." Hektor glanced round. "Don't let on I told you, will you Billi?"

Billi grinned as he realised what Hektor meant. "A bairn, a babe? That's wonderful Hektor." Billi glanced at the skinned cat. "That really does make you lucky. 'Twould have been a terrible thing if you'd not come back."

"Or Dapple. I'm starting to realise why Hunters are like they are when they lose a Hound. The feeling in your head sort of gets to you, doesn't it." He chuckled. "Dapple seems pleased about the babe, his buzz is happy in my head. Bliss has been making a little feather pillow and a feather mattress and quilt from the fowl you told me I could take." Hektor glanced round. "You don't think anyone else heard, about the babe?"

"No. They're all busy, and the youths are already arguing if the Great-Stag antlers or your striped hunter fangs are the better trophy." Billi looked at the state of Hektor's leathers. "You'd best put a pelt inside that, fur in, to keep out the draughts. Are you all right now?"

"Yes, I think so. Da will be terrible upset. He knows about the babe and wanted to come instead of me, but he's limping from a bad fall so I said no." Hektor stood and wavered a little. "I'm steady enough now to go and find Mikkel and thank him for that arrow." Hektor moved off, still a little unsteady, and Dapple limped after him.

By the time the last carcase had been skinned and jointed, night had fallen and everyone felt exhausted. Others had lesser injuries, and there were once again two broken fingers. Some reckoned the fingers were a tradition now. The Hunters had collected the usual selection of strains and bruises and maybe sprung ribs and sprains, and sore muscles from pulling the bows again and again. Even the worst injured agreed the result, the sheer amount of meat, made the pain worthwhile. That included the youth who'd keep the three scars up his forearm for life, and memories of a dead cat that wasn't.

Fires were lit and the worst wounded sat near them with heaps of dead wood to keep the blaze going. Nortan's leg now had a splint, while Eddmune's arm had been strapped and padded and he'd been teased about how his plump rump had saved him from more injuries. Youths smashed the ice lining the small swift river to help the fires in keeping the scavengers at bay, and the Hounds ringed the campsite. From the noises, scavengers were already tearing into the piles of offal on the hillsides and in the trees.

The travois were started overnight by the guards, to save time in the morning. Nobody wanted to linger because the number of watching eyes shining in the firelight grew throughout the night. By morning shapes could be seen moving in the trees and the branches were thick with birds, some of which were already darting in to snatch a meal. The party had to move, but where had been the question that kept all the night guards arguing through the night.

They'd taken a magnificent haul of meat but with so many men and ponies, more could be carried. The Hunters knew about Billi's idea, moving up two valleys each hunt so the game weren't too alarmed and the valleys each side would help restock those hunted. He'd meant each year but that would still work for a double hunt, especially as they wouldn't take as many from the second one. The prey two valleys up shouldn't be unduly alarmed by today. By the time everyone had slept and dawn arrived everyone agreed.

The whole party including the loaded ponies moved past the next valley and across the end of the chosen one. They ate a quick meal, and talked it through. "We can't repeat that, we haven't the room for the meat."

"No Canitre, but that means we can take the prime prey this time." Raban looked around the party. "We couldn't do it again because we haven't enough bows now."

"True, and I'm one that won't be much help." Canitre carefully straightened his leg. "I'll stay with Billi if he don't mind an old man stealing a few targets." He smiled. "I'll have to rope myself to a tree as well."

Billi smiled. "Having two bows will be easier, if you take one side of the valley. This one doesn't give us such a good position anyway so we'll be taking more time over the shots."

Eddmune waved his spear. "I can use this and I'll back up the youths at the entrance, because neither me nor Streak are up to running about."

"I'll sit on a pack and watch the rear because the ponies and meat might tempt something." Nortan looked pale but determined. "We won't have anyone on the ridges this time so that will speed up the butchering."

"We'd best get to it then." Mikkel nudged Hektor. "Remember to duck this time."

"I'm pointing to you if another one turns up." Hektor grinned because if another striped hunter lurked it would break for the ridges and not come near the bows and Hounds. Then his grin wavered. "We'll want to be clear before that Great-Wolf or his friend turn up."

"Hide and Hair, I hope so!" Raban waved everyone who could still walk and hunt forward. "Listen for the Hounds, then stop immediately." This hunt might have been quieter, but not much though 'twas much shorter. Billi wasn't as busy, because he and Canitre concentrated on dropping the wounded or hitting prey who would be killed by a single arrow. Not a single injured animal made it through the limping Hounds and injured Hunters. Long before the line of Hunters and Hounds reached the head of the valley everyone heard the warning howl. Farimer called enough and the line worked back to the valley entrance finishing the wounded.

* * *

Mikkel came back to fetch Canitre, because Raban and he were old friends. Billi followed the pair to where Raban and Fleet lay. The story was plain even if Raban hadn't been conscious enough to tell them. "It was yon boar." A big, scarred veteran, the Boar showed the marks of tooth and spear but no arrows. "He waited in the bushes, and then charged at the last moment and put me down." Raban took a pull on the cider someone had given him. "Fleet pulled him off but the beast gored him." Raban paused again to stroke Fleet's head where he'd been laid across Raban's legs. The Hound opened his eyes and then closed them again. "I got my spear into him and Fleet came back for more, but you know boars. He died hard, and did for us both by the time he quit."

The pony dragged the boar off to butcher it, and Canitre spoke quietly to the others. "Raban might make it, though he'll be badly crippled. I have to offer." He went back to the badly wounded Hunter. "We can put ye on a pony or travois, if ye wish?"

Five Hunters and their Hounds, including Billi and Rabbit, heard the reply. "I thank ye, but I'll not be coming. Fleet won't make it back, and I'll not leave him to face the Wild alone." Raban sighed. "I don't fancy going out crippled and alone when it gets too much for me, so I'll bide here."

"We'll see that Treese get her share, your share. I'll stay back a moment if ye have a message for her." Canitre, an old friend of Raban's, stayed while the rest went back to skinning and butchering. When Canitre came out of the bushes, the Hunters and youths went in one at a time to say farewell.

"I'm sorry, Raban."

"Nay Billi. We all knew the risk. My luck ran out, or the Wild wanted a price." Raban stroked Fleet and the Hound's ears twitched. "If we'd been hunting separately Eddmune and Nortan wouldn't have made it either, and maybe some of the others with injured Hounds." Raban managed a smile. "You stop worriting so much, catch yourself a fine maid, and drag her out to that valley." Raban sighed and winced. "I would have liked to see that. What is it like?"

Billi spent a little time telling him, and then put a horn from a bull next to Raban. "A trophy."

Raban tried for a smile. "I thank ye. Now get gone or the rest will wonder if you've keeled over as well." They clasped and Billi left, though he had to take a moment or two before he could see clear enough to use a knife safely.

Grantel came back with the Hunter's knives. "Raban says they're for when my Hound arrives." The blood lines for Grantel's first kill were streaked with tears and he wasn't the only one.

The Hunters went to say farewell, one by one with their Hounds. Each left a trophy tusk or horn so that the Wild would know what it had got, a true Hunter and Hound. Hektor came back with Raban's bow and quiver to replace his wrecked bow. He came to sit and carry on the butchering next to Billi. "I told him. About the babe. Since he'll not be there."

"I told him about the valley, since he'll not see that." They worked in silence, as did the rest, though everyone still hurried because the feast two valleys up wasn't keeping all the scavengers occupied.

Canitre went back last, and by the time he came out the rest were lined up and ready to go. "Raban says he'll make them pay for the meal. We've to look for the skulls next year and if we can't find Fleet's we've to let Raban's bide here. Raban says it'll be a comfort for Treese if they're both on Skull Rock, but he don't want to be on there alone." Canitre had trouble getting it out so nobody asked anymore, and the ponies were urged into motion.

* * *

Despite all the meat 'twas a sombre trek home. Everyone knew that if they'd been told at the start that one Hunter and Hound would die for this bounty they'd still have come. They'd even planned for if nobody came back, but a Hunter always hoped to beat the Wild or why be a Hunter? Raban's lass, Treese, would be broken-hearted. Raban's heirs were both bonded so only the young man and his lass were still in the family home with her and the house would seem empty without both Hunter and Hound. Raban had a big enough farm for the family to live well enough, but they'd miss the Hunter's catch next winter. Not this winter, as they'd still get Raban's share of course.

Everyone ignored the sound of the scavengers gathering. From the sounds many were capable of catching their own but would welcome a free meal. Raban hadn't asked for the mercy stroke, but if Fleet passed on before the Wild closed in Raban might do it himself. If Hunter and Hound were still conscious, the meal might not be free. There was no way of knowing as the party drew further away from the fighting and feasting.

As they sat around their fires the first night of the trek home a deep echoing roar announced a Great-Hunter arriving for his share. "That really is a Great-Hunter this time, isn't it?" Hektor looked over at Billi, since last time he'd drawn the pug mark.

"That's a Great-Hunter, but not the one I've heard before."

"You've heard a Great-Hunter often enough to recognise the roar?" Eddmune shook his head. "Now I'm glad I've never been tempted to look for those fish of yours."

"Is the Great-Hunter near your fish Billi?" Others moved closer, waiting for the answer to Eddmune's question.

"Why do you think I'm so careful about putting the tithe well away from the landclaim?" Billi smiled. He would let them have a bit of information because that would take all their minds off who they'd left behind. "From the stride I don't want to tangle, not ever."

Billi had to draw the pug mark in the snow again, and Hektor placed a paw from the striped hunter inside it. That sobered them all. "The same as the other Great-beasts then, maybe double the size?"

"I reckon. It picked up a bear carcass I left, after I'd stripped the meat of course, and carried the lot off into the night." Billi didn't want anyone getting ambitious.

"You youngsters pay heed. Yon striped Hunter was still getting up to finish the job after shrugging off two shafts and Dapple. If ye see a track like this, let it go." Despite being pale-faced with pain Nortan wanted to make a very serious point, and one after the other the young Hunters and youths nodded agreement. The paw sat inside Billi's pug mark didn't need much more explaining.

They tried to sleep but the night echoed again as both the Great-Wolf and then the smaller Great-Cat turned up again. There were no sounds of strife between the large carnivores so they'd found enough to share. In the morning the black cloud of wheeling birds made it clear the scavengers hadn't finished, and that cloud stayed visible until late afternoon. The group weren't making great progress and it wasn't Billi slowing them up this time.

Canitre had a lightened pack and a branch to help him walk, and he limped along with Billi so he could get lessons from the expert. Nortan's leg might be broken in several places and even with a splint he couldn't manage on a crutch. The Hunter sat on a pony, clinging to it white-faced at every bump and jar. Cider might have been helping but not enough as he had the same problem as most men on a pony. The sturdy little beasts were so low a man had to hold his legs up and forward to ride them. At least Nortan could use the loops of rope fixed up to help Billi on the way out, but the rope wasn't gentle on his leg. Nortan would have looked comical with the big splint jutting out one side if it wasn't for the suppressed exclamations now and then.

The rest of the wounded limped, hobbled and winced their way with a travois if they could, or lugging the biggest pack they were capable of. Several had slings for sprained elbows and shoulders, and one for a broken forearm. Three more had made crutches to help them walk. Oddly enough there were still only the two broken fingers though one youth had three broken toes which had been stamped on by a Bull.

The walking wounded included several Hounds since it had been fast and bloody in there a few times. Rabbit wasn't the only one operating three-legged, though the others should get back to four in time even if one had a splint. A good few Hounds would have scars, and two would be impressive. Dapple had a long line down his flank and Farimer's Midnight had four gashes across his shoulder and down his ribcage from a dappled hunter. Both were bound up after the wounds were cleaned but couldn't move any faster than the injured men. At least nobody would need to hunt again for a while.

The group slept out three more nights, in a circle of fires each time while bright, hungry eyes peered from the gloom. Hunger or greed added two tawny skins and a bit of extra meat to the loads when a pair of lionesses became too eager. They knew these pair were lions because the Hunters glimpsed the male roared from the shadows, too wary to come into the light. Now everyone knew that lions came from towards the highlands or maybe on them, which at any other time would have meant excited discussion. Twice the relatively fit split off to hunt for meat to feed Hunters and Hounds so that the full loads would get back. The last night they ate some of the catch since they were near enough to home for there to be no game.

* * *

By the time the first pony left the Forest, some of the minor bruising and aches had eased but the deeper ones were biting harder. Billi's left arm felt sore and had stiffened, and he'd torn the callouses from his fingers pulling his bow again and again. His one knee really felt the weight of the big pack now, as did the shoulder with the crutch. Rabbit had lost his bounce, and his weariness threaded through his song.

Some Hounds ran ahead and the fittest young Hunters dumped their travois and packs and dashed off, the Hounds baying joyfully to let everyone know they were back. Hounds never grieved for long except for their own Hunter, but then they died of it. As with most of the Wild, death was the way of life to Hounds. The party gathered in a loose group as, one by one, they stepped out onto the Farm and could relax a little. All of them felt relieved that they'd made it without spending another night out, though only just, as the shadows were lengthening.

Before long ponies, men and youths with spare packs trotted across the snow-covered fields to relieve the Hunters and their ponies of their burdens. The runners had told the villagers about Raban and Fleet which muted the celebration but couldn't stop it entirely. The mound after mound of fresh meat following the men and ponies out of the trees or humped above the shoulders of the men would ensure a good wake for the Hunter. In that at least the Winter Hunt had succeeded. There would be no slaughtering of stock beasts this winter, and no littluns with hungry, pinched faces. Not a bad legacy for a Hunter and Hound.

Treese, Raban's lass, came with tear-stained face and listened while Canitre spoke to her quietly. Then she turned to the group busy with repackaging meat and skins. "I'll miss them both, but 'tis how they would want it." She gestured out at the Forest. "Together, out in the Forest and facing the Wild at the last. I will be obliged if the Hunters look for their skulls next year as 'twould be a comfort to me. To know we'll be together on the Rock when my time comes." Treese left quickly, which allowed the others be welcomed properly and the villagers to celebrate and gloat at the bounty.

The Hunters sorted out Treese's share. "I'll take my lass and we'll deliver the meat and skins, Raban's share. We'll get it all dressed out and stored properly." Canitre looked drawn and pale and some might be grief and not just his leg from the look of his face.

"I'll come to help." Farimer sighed. "I've known them both a while. We'll let Raban's family know the full story."

"Thank ye, Farimer. 'Tis hard on a Hunter's lass, knowing how it is betwixt Hunter and Hound, yet never being part of it. Knowing of the call of the Forest and the Wild, yet never hearing it." Canitre sighed as well. "Knowing that if the Hound dies, her man will likely walk out one day with a spear and never come home."

"Aye." Farimer's smile had little humour in it. "'Tis a wonder to me that my lass ever agreed to a bonding." The two turned to organising the packing of Raban's share as well as their own.

Ellibeth met Billi at the gate and for a moment he thought he'd be getting another hug. Ellibeth stopped her half-move, glanced round, and went to the growing pile of fur and meat. "I thought it must be you when so many Hounds started, Billi. They sounded so happy. I've got bread in the oven, since I've kept dough ready these last two days." She smiled happily. "Since you like my bread."

"I do indeed, and I've missed it." Billi tousled Rubyn's head. "I hope you've been tending the traps?"

"I have Billi, and..."

"You can stand guard on this if you've done strangling Billi's leg. You can tell him in the warm, in peace, when this lot is safe inside." Ellibeth cut off Rubyn's recital before it got started. "Keep Spots off it since he's taken to raw meat these last few days."

Guarding the meat, dealing with Spots, and helping to move skins and furs indoors slowed but didn't stop Rubyn's tale. He replayed every single trap laid and every single skin taken and how brilliant his knife was and how well he was doing with the skinning and how many rats One-shut had taken and how many of them Spots had eaten and how many eggs the chickens laid and….

The constant torrent of excitement continued as Perry also arrived and helped bring Billi's share inside. Then Perry ran off to help Timath with Hektor's share. Billi got his coat and jacket and then his boot off, and the weight off his leg at last. By then there a drop of warm cider sat on the table, waiting.

"I'll start with this." Ellibeth gestured to the haunches and legs and cuts of meat roughly wrapped in raw hides. "At least it was cold enough to keep it all fresh. Some is nigh on frozen." Ellibeth sharpened a couple of Billi's cooking knives and put the first haunch on the table for jointing.

"Here Ellibeth. I'll give you a hand in a moment, but meanwhile these are better for the job." Billi took off his belt with his hunting and skinning knives and passed it over.

Ellibeth pulled out a knife to give it an appraising look, and her eyes widened. "This is pretty, and I know that means a good blade though I've never seen a big one before." She glanced at the rest of the sheaths for the different sizes and widths. "Are they all the same, like those that you gave my bros at Midwinter?"

Billi laughed. "They are so now you know my secret, what I spoil myself with. A few might want a bit of an edge put on them since we were in a hurry to get away after the butchering."

"If you sharpen them, I'll get started. Then you can tell me about it while I work." She chuckled. "It will be a real pleasure with knives like this. Rubyn you stay clear of these or they'll have a finger off. Sit down with Spots and give Rabbit some fuss. He's been out in the cold and he'll be tired as well." Rabbit was tired and Billi could feel the Hound's appreciation of the fire, and Rubyn stroking him and playing with his ears.

Billi tried to help but Ellibeth insisted that he needed to rest, especially when she caught him favouring his left arm. Soon enough she took the fresh bread out of the oven and smiled as Billi breathed in the smell. "Just give it a minute to cool, enough so it doesn't collapse when it's cut. I'll just grill a few bits to go with it. A bit of liver, some kidney, and some thin slices of venison."

"Only if you sit two minutes and eat as well, else I'll feel guilty." Billi did feel a bit guilty though this really felt sort of homely with Ellibeth fussing around like this. He quickly steered his mind away from maids and homely and Midwinter bussing.

"Just for a minute. Rubyn, scrub your hands first if you've been rummaging through those pockets full of teeth." Ellibeth poured water for hand scrubbing and by then the butter had warmed and the meat grilled.

"Now if I could just pack a stove with me, this sort of meal would make camping in the Forest much better. Though I'd need a bread baker as well." Billi waved his bit of buttered bread to make the point, then finished it. They set into the raw meat again, with Rubyn taking some of the smaller pieces down into the store with Rabbit and Spots as escorts.

Ellibeth peered inside as they finished emptying Billi's pack. "I'd not fit in your pack or else I might be tempted to go out to look at this landclaim of yours." Ellibeth giggled. "You'd better check your pack before you leave next time, since there's a couple of maids considering hiding in there."

"It's a bit too rough for them out there. Dirt floor and tree trunks and rocks for walls, and a bit of bracken and dry grass to sleep on." Billi laughed. "The maids will be too busy chasing trophies to hide in anyone's pack. The youths argued all the way back about which would get most attention. 'Tis between the fangs from a striped hunter, and the antlers from a Great-Stag." He sniggered. "The youths say it will be decided by which get the most attention from maids."

"You could get some attention yourself with that lot." Ellibeth waved at the fangs, tusks, claws and a pair of long, straight horns with a spiral pattern running up them. Rubyn had untied the horns from Billi's pack, and tipped out the bag with the rest. "Those horns are pretty."

Billi bit back an impulse to offer them to Ellibeth, since pretty trophy horns definitely meant more than friend. "The rest have as much, or the Hunter's do anyway. We left much of the horn but all the youths have something special. Tempert has the Great-Stag antlers to make up for it nearly breaking his leg. Mikkel has the striped hunter's fangs as a fair trade for Hektor's life."

"What!"

"Oh, sorry." Billi hadn't thought about Ellibeth knowing Hektor through Bliss, or that Ellibeth wouldn't know about the incident. Now he explained quickly, trying not to dwell on how close Hektor's escape had been. "He's fine, though Dapple will have a long scar to remember it by. Bliss will be doing some serious stitching on Hektor's leathers. Her first job will be to unstitch what Hektor did to keep the wind out on the way back."

"That would have been terrible for Bliss."

"I know. The close call really shook Hektor and he sort of let slip her bit of news but just to me." Billi glanced at Rubyn and Ellibeth shook her head slightly. Rubyn didn't know about the babe.

"It'll be obvious soon anyway. 'Tis only her winter coat that stops some noticing now." Ellibeth looked at all the trophies again. "I'm not sure which trophy will get most attention, because there's some that think Mikkel isn't running. Though he's being very shy who he's not running from, and whoever it is, she's being coy about either running, chasing, or being caught. Tempert isn't chasing or being chased, not yet."

"Mikkel might not be caught. He seemed very interested in how much attention the fangs would bring." Billi shook his head. "The whole thing is a mystery to me. I can never work out who's doing which, and if they're serious or not."

"A few of us have noticed that, Billi." Ellibeth giggled. "We're waiting to see if you ever get it straight." Ellibeth sobered. "Maybe you'll get a better idea at the wake for Raban." Those unloading the meat at the gate had told Ellibeth about Raban. "Seeing Bliss will be a bit of joy for those who notice, a new life for an old." She still avoided telling Rubyn, probably because he'd shout it down the Village street.

"Aye, Raban and Fleet, and then seeing Treese when we came back, made me wonder. You know, why a maid would choose a Hunter? Knowing that one day he might not come back, or might walk off one day with just a spear." Billi sighed. "I understand that part. I couldn't stand living without Rabbit's song."

"Rabbit's song? The mystery of Hounds, that none but Hunters can ever know. Hektor calls it a buzz without words, but you call it a song." Ellibeth really sounded curious, it was in her look as well as her voice.

"Because it is a song to me. A constant tune that warns, and comforts, and laughs and sometimes hurts. I open my eyes in the morning and it's there, and 'tis the last thing I hear at night. 'Twould be a cold, lonely life without it." Billi sighed. "There, you see, Rabbit's song is telling me not to worry. He'll be with me at the end, whenever it is."

Ellibeth's eyes were soft, with maybe the hint of a gleam of moisture. "Maybe I understand better now. I've never heard it put like that." She sighed. "A maid can't compete with that, though maybe they can in their own way." Her little smile came back at that.

"I don't see why they try. The Hunters always get a maid and there's actually competition, which seems strange." Billi caught her growing smile. "Whole Hunters do, not the hoppity sort."

"You might want to test that out one day, Billi." Ellibeth smiled properly now. "As to the why, maybe it's the bit of Wild in every Hunter that calls to the maids. You say you feel the Wild call to you, well maybe maids do and the nearest they can get is a Hunter. Any Hunter."

"I'll watch out at the wake to see if the Hunters really do get chased more." Billi steered off the last part, because Ellibeth had said a couple of times that Billi made a good catch for a maid if he'd stop worriting about his leg. Billi couldn't believe it or was too frightened of the consequences if he did and didn't want to work out which.

"You'll be busy at the wake, ssrrong bearr." Now real mischief sparkled in Ellibeth's eyes.

"They dance at a wake?" Billi hadn't really thought of that.

"Oh yes, and you'd better wear your dancing gloves this time." Ellibeth was a hair away from laughing now.

"Dancing gloves?" She'd completely baffled Billi now.

Ellibeth giggled. "We expected the joke to break at the Springfest. What did you think Bliss sewed you a pair of thin gloves for, with that fancy stitching?"

"I'd no idea. I thought the bit about dancing was just a joke. They're too thin for work, and when else would I wear gloves?" Billi frowned, and thought, but in the end he had to ask. "Why are they dancing gloves?"

Ellibeth finally gave in and a delighted laugh broke out. "They're for the dancing bearr, so that the maids don't slip through his hands. After all, he let the Dancer get away."

Billi's blush became worse soon after because Ellibeth mentioned, sort of casually, that Rubyn was making his first cheese though unfortunately it wouldn't be ready by the wake, or possibly by Springfest. Rubyn picked up on that and confirmed it enthusiastically. At least he didn't race off to bring the proof.

It was full dark before they'd done with the first rough jointing of the meat but Ellibeth said her Da knew where she was and that she'd be safe. They put the hides in his pack and Billi put his coat on while Ellibeth closed up her room, and her and Rubyn muffled up as well. He'd bring the pack tomorrow rather than risk the icy track in the dark. Ellibeth promised to come back with him in the morning, to finish sorting out the meat since Billi's arm needed to rest for the dancing.

Stood at her gate after Rubyn ran inside, Ellibeth put her arms round Billi and hugged him firmly. "I'm proper glad you came home safe Billi, you and Rabbit." Then she stepped away quickly with a little smile and murmured "nearly." As he watched her going indoors Billi realised he'd lifted his free arm to hug her as well. Which wouldn't have been a strictly friendly hug, he realised.

If he could really persuade himself to chase a maid, Billi thought it might be Ellibeth, but she was a bonnie maid and well out of his reach. Those were definitely not comfortable thoughts on his slow and weary way back to his hut. It didn't help that the pillow smelled slightly of some sort of herb or flower. That was very nice, but Ellibeth smelled the same so it was probably whatever she washed clothes in. Thinking of clothes and cloths didn't help either, but eventually Billi slept.

* * *

Since Raban's body wasn't waiting to be burned, an eight-day went by before the wake. That gave Treese time to get past the first shock before she had to sit through it all. It was also plenty of time for some serious meat and fruit pie baking, much meatier baking than would have been possible without the Winter Hunt. A couple of people mentioned that seeing the difference the hunt made to the Village helped Treese accept what it cost.

Billi contributed a steak and kidney pie, a proper one with a pastry bottom so a novelty from him. Billi's pastry made good sealant for round the chimney but Ellibeth baked this. He'd never have believed his oven could manage a proper pie with a pastry sides and bottom, though both Bliss and Ellibeth had made dishes with a pastry top. When he mentioned it Ellibeth promised a proper pie now and then.

Billi presented his pie to admiring and some quizzical looks. Billi had been known for raw meat, sometimes still in its skin or feathers, for so long that the change still came as a shock to most. Treese met everyone going in, and thanked them for coming and for the food or drink they brought. Billi told Treese the truth of the hunt. Raban had done well and been a good Hunter, and Fleet was with him at the end. "But I really am sorry the hunt ended that way."

Treese smiled a little sadly. "Too many Hunters end up that way, and this time Raban's luck ran out. He followed you out there by choice, Billi, because the Village needed the meat. We had enough good years to make it all worthwhile." She pressed Billi's hand. "That's all a maid asks for when she chases a youth, especially a Hunter. Enough good years to leave happy memories, and hopefully time to raise the littluns." Billi thought about that as he headed to Mandy's food table and then a chair.

The first villagers set into the food and the ale and cider joined the fruit juice and water and some hot berry toddy, a favoured winter drink. Billi stuck to the latter as the Eldest said goodbye to Raban and told the tale for anyone not knowing. Treese thanked them all for the food and drink and told them to enjoy themselves, since Raban would want that. After that the music started.

Perry had called round before Billi left for the hall to carry the pie and remind him he'd need his gloves. Word had spread about them which meant Billi had been set up properly by Bliss and Hektor. Perry confirmed that the ssrrong bearr would be called on to make an appearance, so Billi should go steady with the cider and ale. Which was cheeky from a youth, but cheeky almost defined most youths anyway.

The dancing started as usual but the occasional glances and smiles said that everyone must be in on this joke or plot. The men next to Billi confirmed that when they began to speculate on how easily a bearr might catch a maid. Especially a bearr with a landclaim out there in the Wild maybe waiting for some home comforts. Everyone had a wonderful time tweaking Billi, but he worried a little about this being a wake. Then Treese paused while coming past to point out she'd been looking forward to seeing a bearr dance, had anyone seen one about? Billi relaxed and went with it. He could stand there in gloves for a while. It wasn't an unpleasant job after all.

Eventually someone started chanting 'Ssrrong Bearr' and soon most of the youths and maids were joining in. Even Ellibeth and Perry, though Billi thought they might be leading the chant at times. Hektor and a Bliss with a definite belly-bump were definitely leading the chanting and laughing. A good few of the adults were laughing by now and the older men were helping him up so Billi heaved himself onto his foot. He stumped over to the post and stood with his back to it.

"Dancing gloves. Where are your catching gloves?" Several voices called out so Billi shook his head and pulled them from his belt. They were a good fit, and once they were on Billi made some pretend grabs at thin air. The maids started to act worried, while the youths were now pushing them forward. A lively little tune struck up and the maids started dancing and within a few minutes Billi saw a difference. Several had put on scarves and were waving the tasselled ends.

Billi wondered briefly, was this a game or did they really want him to catch hold? Billi made an attempt at catching some scarves, being careful to miss, then realised from the pouts he wasn't supposed to miss. Two of them danced by really close and jumped away squealing but laughing, and several maids were definitely coming into range of his arms. The next one moved a bit slower and her scarf end flew out his way so Billi caught it.

She shrieked but her eyes weren't worried at all, and of course she asked Billi about her forfeit? Billi knew his lines for that and as the shawls and scarves fluttered past he found he'd bussed more maids than in his entire life, and none were horrified. The next shawl fluttered and Billi caught it, and the maid caught hold of his hand in turn and neatly curled it round her as she twirled in. Suddenly they were face to face and he'd caught Ellibeth!

The problem now was Billi really fancied bussing Ellibeth good and proper, especially tucked into his arm like that, but they were in the middle of the dance floor. Ellibeth shrieked and beat feebly on his chest but her eyes were laughing. Her struggles were very feeble, even when Billi tightened his arm a little. "Da, Da, help me! I've been caught by the bearr. Ransom me Da, quickly, because he's got me caught proper."

Viktor didn't seem at all worried that the bearr had caught his eldest and laughed. "It you keep dancing with bears, you have to expect one to catch you. Sorry Ellibeth, but you'll just have to pay up."

There were a lot of suggestions coming in about appropriate forfeits. Billi grinned. "What is it to be then, Ellibeth?" He spoke very quiet, and with all the laughter and calling out, no-one would hear.

Ellibeth smiled, "Maybe I should pay forfeit for the scarf first?" The bussing felt definitely firm and didn't worry her enough. Billi was lost again. Was Ellibeth running or not, or was he chasing, or was this teasing? Billi also realised that Ellibeth expected him to demand a forfeit for catching the maid, not just the scarf. He hadn't expected that and the suggestions from the youths and maids, although not too clear, were shading towards dangerous territory.

Billi raised his voice. "The bear has never caught such a fine maid before, so the forfeit will need some thought." He hadn't thought that through, until several voices complimented Ellibeth since she must be a better catch than the Dancer.

Instead of Ellibeth dancing off to let Billi think she gave a little shriek of horror, and turned to her Da again. "The bear won't let me go until he's decided. I've to sit with him until he's made up his mind!" Billi liked that solution because Ellibeth did feel sort of comfortable tucked in there. "Just remember, bearr, I'm a respectable maid and you can't keep me after dark. I have to go home with my Da, all proper-like." Da still didn't seem worried while her Bro had nearly doubled up laughing.

"I'll remember, but I think better sitting down." Billi headed for the seats and Ellibeth sat next to him. She held on tight to Billi's finger, so his arm stayed round her but just around her shoulders and there were a couple of comments from the group of youths and maids about who had caught who. More made suggestions about who would be paying a forfeit to ransom what back, and what the forfeit might be.

Billi knew he'd started blushing a little bit. He'd been enjoying himself but had strayed onto dangerous ground, and Ellibeth had just reminded him she was an honourable maid. He hadn't a clue what the forfeit should be, and hoped he might get to buss her again. Maybe his indecision showed since Ellibeth stopped him wondering. She leaned in closer. "Billi, will you show me the landclaim, please. In the spring, when the snow has gone?" Ellibeth spoke quietly so Billi answered the same way.

"Yes. Of course." Billi could take a couple of Hunters to show them the place so there'd be plenty of people. That would keep it respectable as Ellibeth could use his hut and the rest could sleep outside.

Ellibeth raised her voice. "Ooh, naughty bearr!" Billi wondered what he was going to be accused of now, since Ellibeth obviously had something in mind. "He says he wants a Tinkerer bussing, on his knee! Da?"

"You got caught, you pay the forfeit because I'm not sitting on his knee." Viktor waved a casual hand and Perry ended up sat on the floor, holding the wall to stay upright. Billi wondered if maybe he'd been at the cider, though Hektor and Bliss were nearly as bad and so were some of others.

"What should I do?" Ellibeth had appealed to the other maids? Billi had lost the script entirely, again.

"Buss the bearr, buss the bearr." A line of laughing maids were chanting now and some were looking speculative as well, wondering if Ellibeth would? Billi knew she would, it was her idea!

Ellibeth stood up and perched decorously on Billi's knee and then lurched in a bit so he tightened his arm to catch her. Then Billi saw the laughter in her eyes, so Ellibeth had known he would. Had Ellibeth been at the cider? "Ooh, definitely ssrrong!" He realised it looked as if he'd grabbed her. Then Billi lost the rest of the thought because she bent her head and whispered, "This is all you get."

Ellibeth's lips went firmly onto his and Billi forgot the world, except for the bright, joyful spark from Rabbit. Ellibeth didn't give him a

Tinkerer bussing but this one seemed a lot firmer and somehow softer than any of the others tonight. In fact, Billi might have carried on a bit longer, or never stopped but Ellibeth let go of his finger and danced off to her Da, giving a twirl to wave her scarf as the maids and youths cheered. "I was worried for a moment that the bearr might check for tattoos."

Billi blushed bright red now and knew he'd been set up but for what? He didn't actually care since he really liked the result. But when there were calls for more bearr dancing and he saw the looks at least three maids were giving him Billi backed off. "That's tired me out. I'm not used to dancing." There was some laughter at that because it was true enough.

"You should practice. Some of the maids might not mind even if it isn't at the dance." Tempert ducked away from the raised hands but some of the maids laughed.

"I promise to practice, so I can dance longer next time." Billi could have danced some more right now, but didn't dare. If those three maids all sat on his knee and bussed him the same Billi might enjoy it too much. He might forget to keep his guard up and break one of those rules, those rules he really didn't understand. He'd been reminded a few times tonight that a Hunter with a new landclaim might be a good catch for some maids.

Billi didn't want a maid who wanted his landclaim. Which was awful picky for a man who hadn't expected any maid to look twice, let alone want to sit on his knee and give him Tinkerer bussings. Some of the youths were chasing the maids now, growling, and a couple of the maids were 'caught' and sat on a knee to pay the forfeit. If ssrrong bearr never danced again he'd given the maids and youths another way to flirt and chase right out in public. The youths who stood by the post each caught one or two scarves, and one caught the same scarf three times.

Nortan, Canitre and Eddmune sat with the older men this time. They weren't really up to dancing or even standing with their families all night. "This arm still hurts too much for peaceful sleep, or for hopping about." Eddmune smiled. "I didn't enjoy that thorough cleaning in ice cold water but it seems to have kept the rot from it."

"But it is healing?" Nortan looked down at his leg. "This is, or so I'm told but it don't feel like it. I might need lessons Billi so I can stump along with a crutch." The Hunter's smile took any sting from that. "You'll have to wait up for me on a hunt."

"Aye, my arm is healing but might never be quite right." Eddmune smiled. "I might need to get a bit nearer for the bow work but I'll be out hunting again eventually." Billi could see the longing in his eyes, so it wasn't just Billi who loved being out there. Maybe that love for the green was what brought the Hounds? Perhaps they could sense those who would truly want to be out there? No matter how many legs they had. Billi noticed that the worst injured Hounds were taking full advantage of the sympathy by the door to scrounge extra scraps.

Some men wanted a really serious talk about this landclaim now. Eddmune pointed out he'd got a youth at home chasing, the maid ran slower every day, and Eddmune already had a house full. "Do you need a Farmer out there Billi, or maybe someone with a few sheep on the hillsides? Then there'd be someone to keep an eye on the place while ye went hunting." He had a little smile when he said it, as that would mean Billi could keep a few chickens or a goat in the valley. If someone with a dog lived there, Billi could make a proper home out of the place.

Eddmune obviously knew Billi would work that out, and that it would be a big incentive for Billi to arrange the additional space. Two more men mentioned they had a lad or a maid who might fancy trying a bit of fresh country if Billi found more land nearby. With a Hunter living there they could make a run into the Village now and then to visit relatives or trade, or catch the Trader caravans and Tinkerers. More Hunters and some villagers came to join the discussion for a while before drifting off, adding advice or suggesting who might want a place out there.

Perry mentioned that with a Hunter living there, it might be worth a Tanner coming out and stopping over for a ten-day to deal with the pelts and hides. Would there be somewhere he could stay? Someone else pointed out that the valley should have at least two Hunters. The idea that the hillsides might support sheep or goats seemed to have really livened up the debate. Billi couldn't confirm a water supply up on the hillside so there really might be room for more than one family. Billi thought they'd have a Village out there by the time they'd done! Many people thought the fish, as a reserve for bad times, would make homes for at least a couple of families possible. It all made a better subject for conversation than the loss of Raban.

The wake wound down and everyone said goodbye to Treese and headed home. She gave Billi a quick hug and told him to stop worriting. He was to cheer up and get on with dancing and chasing the maids as any young man should. Young man? Billi was twenty-six summers. He considered the young men to be those such as Hektor, all of seventeen or eighteen summers.

Then Billi realised that he thought of Ellibeth as a young maid and she must be twenty-four summers, or not much more. She must have bonded young because Ellibeth had been at school the same time as Billi. Billi stumped back through the Village in the dark with several families. The three maids with them, including Ellibeth, were all making a point of hiding the other side of their Da because of the bearr. The joke would be running for a while yet.

Billi had something new to think about on the way home. Did tonight mean Ellibeth really might be chasing, and if so would he run? Or maybe he'd started chasing a bit by mistake, with Ellibeth just flirting as the other maids did. Though some of the flirting seemed to be beyond what he'd thought, but then he'd no idea really. So perhaps Billi had finally been flirting with a maid? Billi had never gone through chasing a maid round the haystack to buss one. He was a bit old to learn at his age, as any maid waiting to be caught might be serious and not flirting at all. She also might be offended if it wasn't supposed to be serious. No, safe would be best, so Billi put thoughts of chasing back out of his mind, almost.

On the way home Billi finally put Raban's death straight in his mind, because he'd felt just a bit guilty for leading the hunters out there. Treese had managed to settle that tiny lingering doubt. Raban had taken the chance, knowing what might happen, and it could just as easily have been Hektor or any of the others or Billi himself. It nearly had been Hektor, Eddmune, Nortan and possibly Canitre. The Village all seemed to feel the same way, except for a few who would think the worst of anything Billi did.

* * *

Billi went out to his valley once more before the thaw. He broke the ice dam again and the ice by the trees. There were plenty of big pug marks this time and they were spread over a wide area. There would be another chore in future summers, as Billi would be keeping the dam repaired. The Great-Hunter had broken open the beaver lodge, the claw marks on the timbers that were pulled aside made it clear who did it. The ice had finally been thick enough to support the Great Hunter, though the beast hadn't caught the beaver in there.

He'd caught them breaking out of the edge of the ice to escape after swimming clear of the lodge. Billi read the tracks and the broken reeds and other evidence. The Great-Hunter had thrown one beaver well clear of the water, presumably to stop it hiding in the lake, before killing the other. The thrown one had tried to run but he had gone after it, killed it, and then eaten both. Both would have been heavy with winter fat and a real prize for the beast.

That also removed the last hold the Wild had in the valley, the last creature of the Wild actually living there. The rest only came at risk from Billi's bow which matched the Law of the Farm. Billi felt sure that although that might have not been the intention, the Great-Hunter had confirmed his landclaim. That made cropping his bit of Farm even more important. After taking a few fish for his 'crop' Billi collected more small soft pelts with his traps, maybe another crop.

Deer were still coming to drink and scratch for grass underneath the thinner snow on the hillside. One deer made a mistake when, warned by Rabbit, Billi came out of the hut with his bow ready. It ran across the ice and slipped, which gave Billi all the time in the world to make sure his arrow flew true. Two days later a second deer turned to run when it saw Billi and realised that a steep hillside and the line of brambles lay ahead. The deer hesitated too long.

Each time the bones and remains were gone from the Forest edge the following morning. The pug marks showed the beast must be close by though Billi didn't see it again. Billi salted some of the deer meat and left it in the meat safe. With all this meat a pony would have been handy and Billi realised that, if another family lived here, the grazing would support one. Gradually he began to accept he would have a neighbour here if he finally did move.

Broken reeds in the morning showed the path a family of wild boar used to come looking for water plant roots so Billi waited for them. He took a youngster, nearly a yearling, as much to dissuade the rest from breaking his reeds as for the meat. Billi took a small one because he didn't have room in his pack to take any more meat out and in addition, the youngster would be sweet and tender. Billi salted more deer meat to make room in his pack for tender pork.

* * *

The pork tasted both sweet and tender. Ellibeth slow roasted a leg with some roots and cloves, and salt to make the scored skin crunchy and tasty. It had been a long while since Billi had eaten pork that way as he was a boil or grill man usually, unless he spit-roasted his meat. She also made sure to leave a tidy bit for cold cuts another day or for a sandwich when Billi went hunting, to save him stopping to cook.

The sandwiches were a new idea because Billi's bread could never have been used for those. Billi had become quite domesticated and thought more and more about the benefits of a housekeeper. Even privately Billi still daren't say lass, not even silently in his head. That became almost superstitious now, the idea that even thinking lass might destroy any faint chance of getting one. Though when he'd left a laughing Ellibeth at home after more jokes about cheese and dancers and bearrs, the thought would sneak back in.

* * *

Springfest arrived at last, with Billi properly involved for the first time. The celebrations with the eggs and lambs in the morning were for the littluns to celebrate being able to race about a bit and let off steam. The very little were supervised as they searched along the hedgerows for the brightly coloured eggs, hard boiled so that little hands didn't break them. Then they traded their prizes for honeyed fruit or the hard sweet drops of boiled and set pine sap.

Those a little older chased around the flocks to find the lambs with ribbons tied around their necks. They had to have a little patience as well, since the ewes soon taught them to be gentle when approaching lambs. Those ribbons could also be traded, sometimes for little honey cakes or tiny buns with berry preserves inside, baked for the occasion.

Hektor, Mikkel, Eddmune and several other Hunters had descended on Billi's hut to insist he come to help this year, "Instead of lazing about in your hut." So Billi and Rabbit joined the rest of those with Hounds, standing watch to make sure that the Wild didn't take advantage of a careless littlun. The littluns still insisted on the racing about and searching for hidden prizes even if this year the snow and some ice still lingered. That meant that by the time the dance started, as usual the younger littluns were tired and ready to sleep.

The dance in the evening wasn't for littluns so Billi had never been until last year. This year he would attend a Springfest, and also dance. The new confidence Billi had gained, that people weren't always looking at his stump, would get another proper test. He would be in full view of more or less the entire Village again. This time Billi had been told by several maids that even with his gloves he wasn't going to catch them at the Springfest. Even Billi realised that was more or less an instruction to be there, and a hint he might catch them.

"I'm worried about this bearr dancing, Barimar. It's sort of getting out of hand and I'm worried about putting a foot wrong." Billi gave a faint smile. "Worse for me with only one to start with." Billi sighed. "It's a bit past a joke about that Dancer now."

"Ah, well, that would be down to me, and Canitre, Cynel and a couple of others." Barimar looked a little bit embarrassed.

"I thought it was the youths?"

"The youths and maids started the jokes after the Tinkerer Dancer, and had made a bit of a game about the bearr catching. Then we thought that making a bit more of it would help Treese through the wake. Give her something to smile about." Barimar chuckled. "That worked better than expected."

"But Perry says it's not going to drop now. I've got maids telling me I can't catch them even with gloves, and more or less telling me I've got to try."

Barimar laughed. "Billi, you've got to be the only young man or youth in the Village that would worry about it. Don't fret. The ones you catch will want to be caught, so you buss them and turn them loose." He shook his head. "It'll not stop now even if the elders stepped in. The youths and maids have a new way to flirt, in plain view." The Hunter suddenly looked more intent. "Or is there a maid ye'd like to catch?"

"Not you as well. Look at this, Barimar. One peg, and a leg that's taking twice the punishment because I'm a Hunter, so I work it too hard. Rabbit's got the same problem, and ye know what'll happen if another of his legs gives way." Billi shook his head. "That's not so much of a catch, not for a bonnie maid."

"Some will think it is. You could take it easy if there's all those fish, give your leg and Rabbit a rest." Barimar sighed. "But you won't, because ye want to be out there, same as the rest of us. So buss the maids, then get off to your valley and dream about it." Barimar chuckled. "And if one chases you out there, grab her because she means it."

Barimar went off chuckling and shaking his head. Put like that, Billi realised he might be a bit of a real silly Billi. He should buss the maids and enjoy himself while he could. Though a little bit of him wondered if he should enjoy catching one maid quite so much.

* * *

Billi knew the rules had been changed again as soon as he braced his back against the post. Perry brought a chair across and put it nearby. There were chants of "bearr chair, bearr chair" from the youths and some maids, so that wasn't just Perry's idea.

"A bearr chair?"

"In case." Perry tried again because he nearly choked with laughter. "In case the bearr catches a maid."

Billi looked at the chair with dawning realisation and the music struck up. When the maids started dancing, they'd all got a scarf hanging loose. The whole hall started laughing or joking about it but Billi began to worry. Surely every maid in the Village didn't want to be caught by a bearr?

Though he soon realised they didn't. A good few, especially the younger ones at their first dance, were careful not to let their scarves get close enough to be caught. Billi pretended to try anyway, and they shrieked and ran before joining the dance again. The older maids joined in and suddenly Billi had scarves that dangled or fluttered well within reach, so he caught one. "Help, help, the bearr has my scarf. How do I get it back?"

Billi had to laugh because the maid kept smiling even as the chant struck up. "Buss the bearr, buss the bearr." He bussed the maid, and she took her scarf before re-joining the dancing to a round of cheering. Billi had no time to wonder when all this had been worked out, because another scarf fluttered invitingly close. As the music continued, Billi once more bussed several maids, including Ellibeth. She bussed him firmly for her forfeit, and so did enough of the others for Billi to wonder if any of them were flirting.

Then Billi caught a scarf, one still attached to the maid, but not Ellibeth! Eweyna, older sis of Rubyn's friend Eddwyn, beat feebly on Billi's chest. "Help, help, the bearr has me. Oh no, not Tinkerer bussing!" She shrieked, but wasn't convincing because of her big smile.

"Bearr chair, bearr chair." Billi found out exactly why Perry put the chair by the bearr. Ellibeth had sat on his knee to give him a Tinkerer bussing when she'd been caught, and now Eweyna expected the same! Barimar had been right though, Eweyna had meant to be caught because she'd pinned her scarf around her neck so it couldn't come free.

"Well Eweyna, it looks as if I get to sit on the bearr chair?" Billi left the question in it, to be sure if he'd got it right.

"Oh no, oh no, he insists. I've to sit on his knee!"

That seemed clear enough, so Billi sat and received Eweyna's version of a Tinkerer bussing. Nothing like the real thing, but a lot firmer than the bussing to forfeit scarves. Billi took his hand from round her waist to let her free, and she giggled. "How many buttons need to be undone to check for tattoos, Billi?" She glanced down and yes, she'd got an extra button undone!

Billi replied just as quietly. "I'm not checking anyone for tattoos in public, Eweyna." Billi wasn't checking for tattoos, or even pretending to, here in the hall. Or anywhere since he felt certain that counted as catching, not chasing.

Eweyna bounced to her feet. "Ooh, the bearr tried to check for tattoos!" She twirled off, waving to her friends and Billi stood against the post again.

Three more times Billi found that he caught the scarf still firmly attached to the maid, so he caught her as well. Ellibeth and the other two all shrieked and beat his chest, and all three of them sat on his knee for a 'Tinkerer bussing' and claimed he'd been trying to check for tattoos. Billi had a lot of fun dancing and now felt sure a couple of the maids really were trying to find out if Billi might chase. Maybe just in case this landclaim turned out as good as rumoured and he needed a lass to settle it.

The bussing from all those he caught felt decidedly firm, and Billi reminded himself not to buss them back too hard. Ellibeth came twirling by. He'd already caught her scarf once and her once, and her bussings were decidedly firm. Two of the others with loose scarves had already ransomed theirs twice, so Billi caught the scarf tugged.

He caught the Ellibeth as well this time, a second time. "Oh no, not again. Help, help."

Billi tightened his arm a little bit and spoke quietly. "Well now Ellibeth. This is twice." Ellibeth beat on his chest, and shrieked again, but Billi could see the laughter in her eyes. "So just what do you think the forfeit should be this time?"

Billi felt certain Ellibeth had already decided, and that her ideas might be safer than trying to guess. Definitely safer than a few that flitted briefly across Billi's mind. Ellibeth turned to the crowd, scandalised. "He says this is twice, he might keep me until after dark!"

A lot of folk agreed that he should, and Billi really would have liked to but Ellibeth was a respectable maid. "If that's what I want, what are you actually going to agree to?"

Ellibeth laughed and turned her head away. Then she spoke up, in suitably shocked tones. "He can't do that, not until after dark! My Da is here! Help me Da, rescue me."

A few voices told Viktor to leave so the bearr could keep her, and a few told the bearr to catch Ellibeth when her Da wasn't about. "I can't rescue ye, not from a ssrrong bearr." Viktor laughed at her. "If ye keep dancing with the bearr, ye'll have to persuade him to let ye free." Perry curled up laughing again, and Hektor and Bliss were holding each other up as they laughed.

"I'm very tempted to keep this one." A lot of maids and youths thought he should, but Billi couldn't. Not after dark, or the end of the dance. "So she'll have to persuade me to let her go. I'm tired now, and I won't be catching any other maids, so persuading me won't be easy." Ellibeth had a question in her eyes now, and Billi answered it.

"I think she should sit on my knee and try some beguiling." There were shrieks of laughter at that. Some of the looks from the maids were definitely speculative, since maids only had rumours of how beguiling was done. "It will come in handy if she's going to be Tinkerer bussing in the future." Billi hoped she might, since Ellibeth seemed to be a bit easier to catch than some others. Unless that was wishful thinking. Billi had to watch out for that.

Billi kept hold of her hand, and Ellibeth headed for the bearr chair. "Oh no. Some other bearrs might want to dance." Billi had suddenly realised that if he stopped, so did the bearr dance and everyone enjoyed that. This way they could keep going. "So I'll be going back to my seat now." Billi saw the surprise in Ellibeth's eyes, and then the humour.

A chair was cleared at the front of the older men, and Billi sat down. Ellibeth perched decorously on his one knee, and stroked his hair and gazed soulfully into his eyes. "Is that right, Billi?"

"That's a really good start Ellibeth. I'm not sure what Village beguiling is, so we'll just have to work it out." Billi wasn't sure if this came under teasing or flirting, but he had a bonnie maid on his knee and nobody glaring at him.

A cheer went up as the first substitute bearr took his position at the post, on one leg with arms outspread. The maids started dancing again and there were still scarves a'fluttering so the chair might still be needed. It was, and a few of the bussings for forfeits, and the Tinkerer bussings, raised eyebrows.

Billi kept trying to work out where the bussing turned from teasing or bearr dancing into scandalous. There were lots of hints because the older men around him were gossiping about every catch. He realised that some serious chasing went on under cover of the dancing. No wonder the youths and maids wanted it to continue.

One maid declared, in scandalised tones, that the bearr had actually tried to check for tattoos. Then she looked really worried, and wondered aloud if he'd insist if he caught her alone. Ellibeth fluttered her eyelashes to beguile and leant close to murmur. “That’s settled then. ‘Tis an invitation to find her on her own, and he looks keen enough.” Billi glanced at her startled. “Oh yes. It might take a bit of time, but they’ll be looking for a Billi-hut by Harvestfest at the latest.”

Occasionally someone would ask why Ellibeth wasn’t beguiling. Then Ellibeth would stroke Billi’s hair and flutter her eyelashes a bit. Meanwhile she whispered that she needed lessons and did he know any dancers who gave them, and similar cheeky comments. She also whispered scandalous comments about some of the dancers and Billi’s laughter kept some of those watching intrigued.

Eventually Ellibeth smiled happily and raised her voice. “He says ‘tis enough, as long as he gets his Tinkerer bussing.” Then Billi received a bussing that wasn’t Tinkerer, but much too nice for his peace of mind. Ellibeth jumped up off his knee suddenly. “Ooh, naughty bearr! If I’ve got any tattoos they’re none of your business.” Then she twirled off back to her Da with a big smile, to cheers from the maids.

Billi looked at the curious faces, smiled and shrugged and they smiled back. The conversation around him turned to asking him about the valley, and if he really would take some Hunters there. The dancing wound down, the last bearr chased a maid and caught her, and the Springfest ended. Once again Billi stumped back through the Village in a happy crowd, a habit now, a really nice one and Rabbit seemed to agree.

The End of the Forest

Billi had been looking forward with mixed feelings to letting a couple of Hunters and two Farmers have a look at the lakes. One Farmer ran sheep and the other raised crops so the place could be properly assessed for both. Part of his reluctance stemmed from how keen they were for someone to actually move there if it proved suitable. He still hadn't settled in his mind that the valley should have more than him and Rabbit there, not until after he went to the rock.

The Hunters were coming to see some new country and calculate if the place might support a second Hunter, if Billi would permit it? They were all dancing around this permission thing. Billi couldn't see how he could stop someone just building a hut nearby and starting up, so he went to see Kina. "They're asking about permission, Kina. I haven't even drawn it out properly, and how could I stop them moving in anyway?" Billi sighed. "I could end up with no room left myself."

Kina laughed. "No Billi. You've got the landclaim so the lakes and at least some land, the valley bottom, will always be yours. Though it should be measured properly so others can look for space nearby. They're asking because you are the Eldest, out there."

"That's silly. I'm not old, let alone Eldest." Billi smiled. "You are, which is why I'm pestering you again."

"Not if it becomes a settlement. Then you are Eldest." Kina laughed again. "It's nothing to do with age. You have built a hut, so you are the first settler. Any who follow must respect that, according to the old lore. The first is responsible for keeping order, and for agreeing where anyone else can put up their houses." She leaned forward and took Billi's hand in hers. "Ye've started something Billi, so ye take the responsibility."

"I just wanted to find a few stones, and to see where a stream led. Then there were the fish, and it is so peaceful out there." Billi smiled. "I might take off and find another if it gets crowded."

"But before that, make sure the place is set properly Billi. Ye owe that to the young couples who'll come out there, given a chance. Set it up right, and none will begrudge ye any peace and quiet ye want." She inspected Billi carefully. "I reckon I can see the first few whiskers for your beard sprouting already. If they don't come through white, catch yourself a maid. She'll put white in it fast enough."

"Ha, there'll be a few white hairs on my head if there really are folk moving out there. It's not like here, we're awful near the Wild and they'll have to be very careful." Billi waved his arm to include all the Farm. "Most are a long way from the edge of the Forest here."

"So make a proper set of rules Billi. Tell them straight." She patted his hand and sat back. "We, the Village, need the space if ye'll let us, Billi. 'Tis getting very tight here, which is why the bad winters bite so hard. Too many folk living on too little land."

"But the Forest will give a little more, surely? There'll be a fire, and the land will join the Farm." That was how it always happened, though Billi couldn't remember the last time.

"It's not as likely now. We've reached a river both ways, even if the other one is more rocks than water. To sunward the Farm has run into rough land with mainly evergreen bushes, which will not burn so well without some leaf litter. The other way, Skull Rock and the shattered land around it will support little but goats. Even if there is a fire the other side of the rivers or the broken ground, 'tis much harder to keep it safe from the Wild since it'll be cut off from the rest." Kina sighed. "It's a worry that the elders have chewed on a few times, and a new settlement could be the answer."

Things were a lot worse that he'd realised, and Billi gave up on objecting. "So how many make the place a settlement? When am I supposed to insist on rules? After all a Hunter could just set up anywhere on that hillside."

"I don't know, but maybe you tell the first one the important parts so 'tis all set straight to start with. Maybe three or four huts or houses will make it a definite settlement and not a camp. Maybe when the first non-Hunter moves in?" Kina shrugged. "Even three or four couples moving out of the Farm will make a difference, make life a little easier. Even if it never becomes a settlement, just stays an outlying part of the Village."

"Put like that, Kina, I'll do my best. We will, because if Rabbit don't like it, I'll not go through with it." Billi ruffled Rabbit's ears. "He's never been wrong."

"Aye, I know as much about Hounds as a woman can, I suppose. I bonded to a Hunter, and consider it a blessing that both skulls are on the Rock, waiting." Kina sighed. "I hope ye find Raban's and Fleet's since they'll be a big comfort to Treese."

"We'll try, I promise." Billi realised he'd just agreed to a Winter Hunt next year, things kept creeping up on him these days.

* * *

When the small party collected for the valley trip Billi found Eddmune among those coming to assess the place. "My arm's still out of action but Streak still thinks I'm a hunter. If ye stick an arrow in something I can get a spear into it sharpish so it should work out well. The two of us together make up a full Hunter but one with two Hounds. A different sort of Hunter, since not many have three legs and three arms." Eddmune seemed really happy to find an excuse to go Hunting even with one working arm, and Billi could sympathise.

"I'm coming because following you around is always interesting." Mikkel smiled happily. "Not only that, but since Bettram and Patre are both old men you'll need someone younger to run about after you all."

The group were ready to go, just waiting for Billi's hut guards to turn up. Billi looked over at his goats and chickens. "I'd not bother with guards now, except Rubyn does enjoy earning an egg, and does keep the chickens laying well. The bread's welcome when I come back, even if I suppose I could trade for some."

The four others looked at each other and Bettram spoke up. "Ye might want to keep an eye on your hut, Billi, since Edan's all fired up again." Bettram hesitated. "He still reckons he should have got Dapple, and now he's blaming ye for Raban."

"That's a nonsense, and I was there." Eddmune gestured to his arm. "It could have been me, Nortan or a few others just as easy."

"The tale is you hung back, safe. Another Hunter in the line would have saved Raban and Fleet." Bettram shrugged. "I wouldn't be here if I believed it, but a few will."

"Not Treese, Billi, and no Hunter. After all, Canitre stood back with ye, and there were others behind ye like me that couldn't even pull a bow." Eddmune scowled. "I thought he'd quit that."

"It's the winter. Edan earned enough meat for the dogs and some fodder for his horses, and then winter bit deep and it wasn't enough after all." Patre sighed. "He had to trade one of those big horses he intends to breed for more fodder, and silver for meat. He was lucky someone took that horse. Arikk reckons it might be better for ploughing that clay soil of his."

"Those beasts are too big for this place." Bettram shook his head. "A pony does well enough and don't eat as much."

"But why is that my fault?" Billi really was getting sick of Edan, but there was little he could do. He'd just relaxed and now the youth had started again.

"Canitre said that he was asked, and told Edan he couldn't have meat for those dogs because they were a waste. There were some words about how much silver Edan spent on ale instead of keeping it for his livestock." Eddmune grimaced. "Bad blood 'twixt kin is the worst."

"Not just bad blood, with the cold winter nobody had meat to trade, or not in return for guarding stock. That's why Edan needed silver and had to let a horse go. Then he had to spend the silver on the only meat available, meat from the Winter Hunt. The hunt you led, Billi." Bettram shrugged. "Everyone kept saying they were lucky to have any meat to trade, that only you knew where to get it. That must have rubbed him the wrong way."

"Him and those four who are always round him. Two are from Trader caravans and a rough pair they are. Ye'd best keep your guards Billi." Patre looked along the track. "Though that seems a couple too many." Ellibeth, Perry, Timath and Rubyn were coming from the Village.

Billi laughed, pleased for the change of subject, sort of. "Perry wanted to come and I said yes, so Timath probably wants to come as well." Though as they came nearer Ellibeth had a pack, and Timath didn't.

Billi looked at the pack, and then Ellibeth's face and she smiled. "I've come to pay the rest of the forfeit Billi. You said I'd to come out and look at that valley of yours so here I am." She glanced at Rubyn. "Timath will mind Rubyn, he'll mind the chickens, and Perry will come along to mind me." She chuckled. "Since I'll be out in the Forest with the bearr." The rest laughed and Billi couldn't argue.

After all, Perry would be along to keep it respectable. Billi felt sure he hadn't asked about Ellibeth coming, though the thought brightened up his day considerably. He waved his crutch. "You'll have no trouble keeping up."

Mikkel waved Ellibeth forward. "We'd best be off then." The waiting men were all smiling and chuckling, so it had cheered them up as well.

The group took it steady as the non-Hunters were used to hard work but not trekking, and that made time for a bit of hunting on the way. The walk came as a novelty for the Hunters in one way because the other four were really excited about being out in the Forest, so far away from the Farm. They were soon well past where any wood gatherers would ever go. Perry had been out on trips with Billi and ponies to bring charcoal and trees and a Winter Hunt, but not like this, just walking. The four chattered almost continually and the Hunters enjoyed airing their knowledge. Though camping out in the Forest stopped all the chatter. The villagers spoke in whispers, sat in the middle of three big fires with Hunters and Hounds in the gaps. By the third night they had started to enjoy the idea, because as promised the Wild left them alone.

The Hunters became more excited as they approached the valley. Both exclaimed over the amount of game, and Billi confirmed that he never had any problem hunting here. The area would easily support another Hunter without ruining the supply. Billi hadn't taken meat from the usual areas near the Village for a year now, and the game here still weren't really wary. It took a different type of hunting because of the open woodland, but a Hound could scent and follow the game until something made a decent target.

Billi felt decidedly nervous when they finally approached since although he loved the place it was a bit rough and ready compared to the Village. Then the others were all exclaiming at the big fish swimming lazily in the lake and pools, and the big tree forming the dam, and all the wide- open space. Perry stuck a bit of mud over a little leak in the dam, just looking after his supper he said. Perry wasn't a Hunter so he thought the fish were a tremendous asset for anyone settling here. It would be hunting without going out or even a Hunter.

The party split up. Eddmune took Patre all around the valley bottom and sides to see what would be fertile enough for crops. The Farmer would also assess the state of the vegetation along both sides of the water to see if any could be replaced with something more useful. He'd already eyed up the reeds with a smile, and pointed out that some of the plants already there were edible.

Meanwhile Bettram set off up the hillside with Mikkel to check for both hunting and grazing, and to see if they could see any water up there. That left Perry and Ellibeth, who stayed together because that stilled any tongues where Ellibeth was concerned. Billi gave them a tour of the valley. Perry couldn't get over the amount of fish, right outside Billi's door, and Billi mentioned his idea of digging a channel from a river and creating a big pool to do the same elsewhere. They agreed that would be a huge amount of work.

Billi had never shown his valley to anyone and he enjoyed doing so right up until he opened the rough door on his hut. He could see Ellibeth mentally dusting and sweeping and inwardly cringed because the place looked pure bachelor Hunter. All rock and rough wood, even the bed and seat, except for the very modern potbellied stove. Ellibeth asked about that, inspected the gap behind it and Billi's stonework, and started laying a fire in the iron belly.

She asked if there were any of those fish handy, since if they were staying everyone might as well eat properly. Perry and Billi took the hint. They brought her fish and firewood and got out of the way. By the time Bettram and Mikkel came down the hill the gentle aroma of fish wafted across the lakes. A hint of what turned out to be wild herbs and roots wafted with it, a new smell for hut, stove and valley.

Over the meal the group discussed first impressions. Patre led off because he had a puzzle. "The size of this valley is a lot bigger than you've been saying, Billi. I would have thought you'd estimate closer."

"In what way?"

"The valley bottom, the part useful for crops, goes a lot further from the lakes than I'd expected. Are the lakes low?" Patre really seemed puzzled. "Why did you plant brambles across the middle of the pasture land?"

“I didn’t. I planted them where the flat land ended, at the edge of the valley bottom.” Billi thought about it. “The grass beyond that isn’t as good so I thought that would do for sheep. It also trapped a deer really neatly and I thought the brambles made a good hedge.”

“They’ll split the pasture, and that will mean keeping them trimmed back into a hedge. The good soil goes a lot further than that, at least as far again.” Patre’s face cleared. “Did you do the same the other side? Take the first slope as the edge of the valley bottom?”

“Yes. Since I thought it would be the rock causing the slope.” Billi grappled with the pasture being twice as big. That settled it, he would end up with one neighbour at least.

“No, there’s at least twice that in fertile soil that side. The soil with a slight slope won’t be quite as deep, but then it won’t get as waterlogged so that works better for some crops. There’s a good farm each side of these lakes, Billi.” Patre did some mental juggling. “I reckon two big enough to split for three decent landshares. So two families.” He frowned. “They might have to take hay from the Forest, but it’s open out the front so that isn’t a problem.”

“There’s plenty of bedding up the top, for as much stock as we can raise. There’s heathen, bracken and rough grass as far as the eye could see.” Bettram sounded awed by his next words. “This could be the end of the Forest. There’s not a tree in sight.”

A long silence followed as they all looked at each other. “Are you sure? There’s not some in the distance somewhere?” Eddmune sounded almost tentative.

“There are stunted ones here and there, but no. There’s something in the distance, big hills maybe, but too far for detail. I can see for leagues.” Bettram sighed. “Though precious little sign of water. Otherwise this would be a stretch of Farm bigger than all of Trail’s End.”

“No water? I thought there might be pools.” Billi had assumed so, as no water came down the hills except that thin trickle.

“No, I’ll get to it in a while, but I’d like to hear Patre out first since I’ve an idea or two.” Bettram waved to Patre.

“In that case, one stock farm this side, because the grazing could be split up and stock could drink from the smaller pools. There's more of a muddy edge yon side and anyway the soil is better." Patre gestured off towards the cleft. "That water supply is unlikely to ever dry up. Nearby the soil is rich and I reckon deep enough to take some fruit trees. Add a few fruit bushes and maybe a couple of hazels and that gives an orchard to go with the stock."

Patre waved the other way. "If there's cattle and maybe a pony or two, they'll need a dog of course for warning. This place would support more stock if they browse out past the dam, in the edge of the Forest."

"Stock in the Forest? That's asking for trouble." Billi shook his head. "We'd lose them."

"No, not if there's a Hound about. That's very open out there because it's been browsed very heavily. I'd guess the permanent water attracts grazers, especially in winter or drought." As Patre continued Billi remembered the approach and how the Forest opened up. "The hay will definitely want cutting every year to encourage new grass to grow."

"But that can only be done when a Hunter is home." Billi wanted to make that clear. No taking liberties.

"Of course Billi, for now at least. If a few goats get at that stretch they'll finish the few bushes and stop any more rooting. It'll be Farm one day." Bettram chuckled. "Though we'll not see it."

"Aye, if no new trees grow, the old ones will die eventually." Patre looked at Billi, Mikkel, Perry and Ellibeth. "Ye four might even see it, though more likely your littles will. One day the remaining trees will be too few, and the plough will move in. 'Tis good land when that happens."

The four of them looked back, mouths open, until Ellibeth managed an answer. "Truly. Forest into Farm without even a fire?"

"It's not common, but some rough ground near the sunward end of the Farm came because the goats stripped the bushes and the few trees died in a drought." Patre literally rubbed his hands. "But that's not rough ground. There's another two good farms out there one day, maybe three. This will be a Village one day."

"Forest's End?" Mikkel still looked shocked and wide-eyed.

Perry soon made them chuckle. "We can call it Billi's Fishpond."

"Done Wandering, Billi?" Ellibeth smiled as she asked, because she knew Billi loved being out here.

"We'd best get a settlement before starting on that, I reckon." They'd definitely thrown Billi now. "I'd just thought the open ground would stop the Wild coming for my chickens."

"Aye, it'll do that as well. Well the rest is straightforward enough. Ye've got a reed bed, which will get round the shortage of straw for thatching and make a better job anyway. There are some other water loving plants, lotus and watercress for a start. You'll want some mint to add a bit of extra taste to the meat." Patre saluted Ellibeth with his next mouthful of fish before eating it. "Or fish."

Billi wasn't sure what would survive among the plants already there. "There's a lot of weed in the shallows over there."

Patre nodded. "Which makes that side the ideal place for duck and goose runs, since they'll love the weed. Just put a fence into the water, build a coop and clip the wing feathers so they don't fly off. If the wildfowl stop coming the eggs and increase of the domestic flock each year will be a steady supply of feathers and food anyway.

"How fertile is the water's edge? I was thinking, would it grow rice?" Bettram looked intent. "That's a good crop along a muddy bank, especially protected like this. There's a shallow pool on the Farm and the farmer grows some there when the birds let him."

"If the pool overflow is blocked to allow it to fill to the brim just once, the flood line can be established. Then we can pick the parts that flood but are shallow." Patre nodded to himself, thinking. "Rice will increase the grain crop and the straw. The rest of the valley will raise a good crop of corn and roots. There will never be a drought here unless rain stops for long enough to leave dead trees from here to the Village because if need be the crops can be irrigated from the lakes." Patre sat back. "That's my bit finished."

"I need to know if that water supply really is reliable, Billi. Has that flow ever slowed up?" Bettram looked intent again.

"There's always a good flow, though it gets stronger around now with the melt, and if there's a lot of rain." Billi smiled. "I know because I use it instead of the lakes. Too many dead fish, or living, in that water to be drinking it.

"The houses on the other side can come and collect water until they dig a well. The soil will filter what seeps through and it'll be fresh and sweet. But more importantly, if you'll allow it, that water will mean a real Village here." Bettram wore a huge smile now. "I'd need a second or third opinion, but the land up on the top really does look more Farm than Forest. The problem would be water, from the looks of it, but the water is right here. It might mean bringing the stock to water, but that is done back at Trail's End."

"I looked Billi and there's no large bushes, nothing higher than tall reeds or grasses." Mikkel still looked a little dazed at that.

"How often does that little stream dry up, Billi, the one over the end of the valley? If the valley doesn't need it, a bit of a wall would create a shallow pool up there." Bettram smiled. "That would save bringing stock down here."

"What about winter? There's a good bit of snow." Billi already felt crowded.

"Sheep could use the valley sides. They'd scratch away the snow and get at what's left there. Cut some of that rough grass up there for fodder to go with the Forest hay, and bracken and heather for bedding. Cutting the bracken and heather will improve the grazing with new shoots."

"There'll be plenty of berries as well, from the Forest nearby since nobody else is after them." Ellibeth smiled. "Not like near the Farm, where there's two people after every berry."

"No, but there'll be bears." Eddmune's face split in a grin. "Which means thick furs for the beds."

"So it'll support as many sheep and goats as can winter down here in the valley. A good percentage will become joints for winter, so the summer flock can be grown to match the grazing." Bettram looked over at Patre and they reached some unspoken agreement since both nodded.

"This is a proper chance Billi, a balanced piece of Farm if ye give the word." Bettram looked round. "Ye might want to spruce your hut up a bit before bringing a maid." Then he looked at Ellibeth. "Though this one ain't run off screaming."

"I've seen the state of Billi's other hut before it met a duster a few times." Ellibeth giggled, "Though I will admit this would take more work."

* * *

The men all slept around a fire outside, rolled in their furs, which left Ellibeth in the hut. Billi had a little smile in the morning because everything looked definitely more organised in there. He was sure the hut had been dusted and swept even if he had no dusters or brooms. Maybe Ellibeth had charmed the piskies into doing the work, even without milk to leave out for them? If there truly were piskies, the magical little folk of childhood tales, this would be the place to find them.

Ellibeth dragged out Billi's sleeping fur and hung it over a dead branch, then set into giving it a good beating with a length of firewood. Billi took the men to the Forest, to where he considered it began with those few trees that crested the rise into his little paradise. He showed them the big pug marks and explained that he left the small pool for the beast to drink. All five stared at the pug marks.

Eddmune looked back at the valley. "That's awful close, Billi."

"But he's never bothered me. I break the ice for him to drink and fish here, and he leaves the rest alone."

Patre thought about that. "The fields at the edge of the Farm are as close to the Forest, which is why we never leave stock there overnight. Though here you might want a fence to mark the beginning of the Farm? It'll prevent stock and littluns from wandering too close to the trees."

"It won't stop a Great Hunter or any of the larger cats but that would mark where the Law of the Farm began. Have you ever heard it come and go?" Mikkel stared at the pug marks. "I thought you were adding a bit when you drew that mark." He glanced back up the valley. "That hut isn't far for something this size. Are you sure it doesn't mind you being here?"

Billi pointed at his hut. "There's big timber under those reeds, but even so it could get in. Look at the beaver lodge." They did. "That was only done this last winter, and the marks said 'twas this beast."

"It's a good job you've got a Hound." Eddmune also sounded a little subdued.

"That beast isn't frightened of Hunter or Hound, and I reckon I'd be lucky to get a shaft fitted and loosed in time. It just doesn't seem to care about the rest if it gets its fish and a drink." Billi indicated the pool.

"Surely it's wary of a bow?"

"No. If anyone comes here, they don't ever raise a bow to it. I stood there with Rabbit and the beast gave us a good look over and left, but in no hurry and he picked up his fish first." Billi realised what he'd said as everyone's eyes widened.

"You saw it? What is it like?"

Billi sighed. "Huge, Mikkel, and I mean really big, and black from nose to tail."

"Black?" Eddmune frowned. "There's sometimes tales of a black cat, but always from three villages away and never a pelt. I'm asking you all to keep quiet about this as otherwise some stupid young Hunter will go for this pelt."

Mikkel looked annoyed about Eddmune's glance. "Not me. I'm young but not that stupid."

"Fair enough. It's just that both Hunter and Hound would probably die, and if the beast takes an arrow it might hunt the easier prey on the valley. The easiest are the people, and if that happens we'd have to hunt it down. Killing that big cat would take a dozen Hunters and Hounds or preferably more, and some would die. If that beast is annoyed it might be cheaper to abandon the valley, cheaper in Hunter's and Hound's lives." That sobered everyone, but not for long. The rest seemed to believe the Great-Hunter would be an acceptable neighbour, maybe because Billi seemed to live in peace with it.

The group discussed the best route for a path for stock up the hillside, one supported by the jutting rocks so it stayed firm in winter. By that time Ellibeth had re-joined them. Ellibeth pointed out a gentle slope would let a maid with a littlun get up there to help with gathering hay or bedding. It would also allow Billi to get up there to stand guard with Rabbit but nobody mentioned that bit. He appreciated how they were accommodating him for perfectly good other reasons, again.

"What are the valley slopes like in the winter?"

"How deep is the snow?"

"Are there any other big hunters here, or does the Great Hunter keep them clear?"

"Have you looked around the local area for berries and wild fruit?"

"Does that water running over the gravel get deeper? Does it freeze in winter?"

"The fish in there, are the small ones younguns or a different type?"

The questions went on but eventually stopped, and became suggestions and propositions. "The homes can be cut into the valley sides to preserve fertile land and help provide stone for the rest."

"A spring flood must be allowed to let some of the small fish escape, to grow and come back for another fish run."

"You will need ponies to pack hides at least to meet the Traders and Tinkerers."

"Once you agree on others coming here, they will come out to cut all the hay and put it in stacks. Useless this year, but it will bring the most new growth in spring."

"You will need Syman the stonecutter to live here at least a year, maybe more."

"That back cliff will make a good Skull Rock." The suggestions rolled in about plot sizes, gardens, fishing rights, heather for fuel, wintering stock, and renting his land so he could hunt.

Billi started off resentful, reluctant, because although he'd sort of accepted that others would move here, he'd not expected this. Everyone wanted to go so fast, they'd took one look and suddenly had plans for six or seven huts. As they kept going the idea took hold, maybe helped by the bright excitement in Rabbit's song. Eventually Billi sat there stunned, fascinated and also grateful. These people were perfectly happy to give him all the benefit of their experience or ideas on the off chance one of theirs might benefit, even if it was only by a larger landshare back in the Village when a sib moved here. Now all he had to do was remember some of it.

"Of course, if the Wild decide this is still Forest, that will be the end of everything." Billi still wasn't sure how the Wild stood on that. A row of cottages might be too much, or a flock of sheep too tempting.

"That's always a delicate negotiation since neither party actually speaks to the other." Eddmune wore a little smile as he spoke because many hours were spent over an ale trying to work out how the Laws were agreed. "Though the Wild does seem to be staying clear." Evening had fallen again and they were all sat around outside Billi's hut, eating a small deer that Mikkel had surprised while looking along the base of the escarpment towards the sunrise. Once more Ellibeth had found some herbs and a few roots to give it a bit of extra taste.

"Did you do something different here, different to what we do on the Farm? That may be important." Patre looked at the tongue of woodland on the valley edge. "Something has persuaded yon beast to let you be."

"Billi always give the Wild a tithe, even when he catches small animals in his traps on land that is Farm." Ellibeth sounded curious now. "I've not heard of anyone else doing it, but I don't see too many folk."

"That's a very close interpretation of the Laws, and Farmers don't usually do that. We give the guts to dogs and cats, or to the pigs." Bettram also looked at the bit of woodland. "But most farms have a bit of water at least betwixt them and the Forest."

Eddmune nodded. "Maybe that's a difference that needs to stay. You'll be putting that in the Laws of the Farm for here, I would think, Billi?"

"Er, right." Billi was sure he could feel his white Eldest beard already sprouting.

"If nothing else it'll stop the smaller scavengers coming into the valley, and maybe leading the way for something bigger." Billi nodded because Mikkel could be right.

Bettram hesitated, then came out with it. "If ye decide on how the valley land might be split or rented, and agree to it, I'd like ye to consider my Gerant. Him and his lass Lilith would love this and it would save me building a Billi-hut." Bertram smiled. "They'd have plenty of privacy and space out here. I could save some lambs to grow on this year, and a few calves and kids to set him up, then throw in a decent ram and a couple of good ewes to keep the lines strong."

"Wool would help for clothing, and a bit of milk from the goats will come in for making cheese." Ellibeth looked at Billi but nobody else noticed the mischief in her eyes as she said that.

"I'd throw in some silver for a stove and such if he'll take that and the stock as his landshare, and that would help his sibs by making theirs bigger. They could come out for six or seven days now and then to help set it up." Bettram looked at Billi. "If you'll allow it?"

"I promise I'll sit down and work it through as soon as I'm back and get my head straight. It's all a bit much right now." Billi chuckled. "I'll never remember half of it. Then when its straight in my head Gerant and Lilith can come out and see, and make their minds up." He raised his hands in mock surrender. "In time to start barns and cottages and such this year, honest."

"You'll need a Hunter, Billi, and he don't need to have a lass. Then he could live with one of the first families. A good night guard, extra meat for them, and when his home is finally built the maid part might not be a problem." Mikkel's smile meant he fancied the place.

"I reckon he'd need his Hound to keep the maids off at the dance after his hut went up." Perry grinned. "I'm wondering how soon you'd need a Tanner and lake repairer, since I reckon anyone out here might find a few maids chasing." They all laughed at Perry's hopeful expression.

"When the sheep, goats, and maybe cattle start being slaughtered, that might work." Mikkel nudged Perry. "Keep working on him. Billi might want a hut guard this end."

Though Bettram wanted something more immediate if Billi would go for it. Next year, because this year the cottage, barn and paths would need planning and a start made on building. Once again Ellibeth slept in a definitely cleaner and tidier hut, while the men slept round a big fire.

* * *

At dawn Mikkel, who had risen early for that reason, took a deer that came for the fresh grass just outside the valley and a drink. He quickly butchered and packed his catch and the group had a good breakfast of fish after Billi explained cropping them. Then Mikkel set off with the non-Hunters while Eddmune and Billi waited in hiding. Billi expected more game to come when the party left, and he was right. They took a small deer, and then a young Moose that came for the water weed. He'd already put some weight on and this would be where it had come from.

Both were quickly butchered and the Hunters threw everything they weren't taking down by the trees for the Wild. Both Hounds gorged on the remains. They probably wouldn't eat tomorrow but would have no trouble keeping up with men. Both men were loaded down with good meat and pleased that the party had slowed to make catching up easier. The two of them spread the load out a bit, and it would lighten again after supper.

The weather had warmed, and today might be the last time Billi could take meat in the valley and get it all the way home without smoking or salting it first. The Hunters took two more deer on the way back since they had additional people to carry the meat and hides. The nice bonus for all three Hunters affirmed just how much prey the local woodland supported, and how easy it was to hunt. Patre thought the ponies in the valley could even transport meat to the Village.

Especially in spring before the hunting grounds near the Village picked up. Spring had definitely arrived, at last. The first flush of green showed on the early trees, the forerunners of the deep emerald blanket that would turn the pathways into gloomy tunnels all summer. Blossom burst from the bare branches on other trees and bushes, bright in the pale sunlight, stark against the dark trunks and branches. Some flowers dangled in the breeze, shedding pollen to dust the world with gold or smear thickly on careless travellers.

The fresh flush of new grass had already thrust through remaining snow, or sprouted from the bare ground. Soon the creepers would burst from their winter prison to clamber exuberantly over the fallen branches and old hay of last year, burying it all in blossom and leaf. A scattered, fallen rainbow of tiny wildflowers starred the thin grass, desperate to claim their share of sunshine. All of them trying to lure bee or flutterbye before the rougher growth swamped them. Right now was the turn of the small, swift and bright, the transients and in days they would all be gone for another year.

There wasn't enough browse or grazing for grazers to be tempted back nearer the Village, but out here the woods were alive with game. A lot were still lean from winter, but packing the meat back on as fast as possible. The air seemed alive with fluttering and buzzing, and biting now and then of course. At least alongside a running stream there were few pests. By the stagnant pools that sometimes lingered in Forest glades the biters gathered in thick clouds. Billi looked for different flowers and brought them for Ellibeth to see and she put some in her hair. Then both stopped and blushed after comments about putting flowers in a maid's hair.

The trip back slept out three nights, still a novelty for the non-Hunters and Ellibeth agreed the stars out here were bigger and brighter somehow. A steady and lively discussion continued all the way about changing hunting methods, about perhaps starting out that way in the valley. Also about Hunters deliberately hunting two days away, to preserve local hunting for winter. That would keep the area well stocked and the game less wary, and the party agreed that Billi should add it to the local Law of the Farm. There were other snippets about developing and organising the valley, and Billi tried to remember it all.

Not that easy when as he walked in the green with Ellibeth, who wanted to know about every bush, tree, flower, insect and bird. The lack of thick leaf helped her, since every splash of colour or flicker of movement caught her eye. Later many of them would be hidden in the Forest, but now they were all on show. Many didn't really have a proper name as they were only seen in the Forest so Ellibeth started naming them and the others joined in. Instead of bringing flowers, Billi showed Ellibeth and she gathered a few to take home.

Billi hoped someone else remembered some of those names, because his head was bursting with all this information. It was bursting with the song as well because Rabbit truly enjoyed being out in the green with other Hounds again. It was almost becoming a habit.

* * *

A riot of discussion exploded in the Village when the group arrived back. That went on for a whole half-moon while Billi tried to sort it all out in his head or with scratched maps in the dirt. His preferred solution rather depended on one thing, or one person. After his second four-day trip to the Forest to think, Billi arrived home a little bit early to ask her. After all, how many could live there depended on her answer.

"Your bread will be a little while Billi. You're early." Ellibeth smiled.

"It's usually dusk before you can bear to leave the Forest."

"Ah, well, I've been thinking."

Ellibeth laughed. "I know, and so do the Village. They keep asking me what you've come up with. I tell them all I can see is the smoke coming from your ears, but I've no idea what it means."

"Well now you'll know."

"I will?" Ellibeth sniggered. "They all will if you're off to the elders because one will talk."

"But I need some advice about part of the answer, so we need a quiet talk without someone getting excited and the wrong ideas." Ellibeth understood that.

"Rubyn, take Spots and check the chickens and goats again will you? Just in case there's rats about since One-shut is still asleep by the fire." Ellibeth had barely finished before Rubyn was on his way out, and Rabbit followed. It wasn't that far off dusk so it was best to be safe. "Now, what do you want to talk about?"

"I'll be taking the side of the valley with the pastures and my hut as a landclaim, and letting the other half go. After what Patre said the whole valley floor is too much for one landclaim." Billi took a deep breath. "Would you take most of the other half, Ellibeth?"

"Me? Just me? That's a lot of land for a maid, Billi, more than a lot of landshares here in the Village and Farm." Ellibeth hesitated. "Why me?"

"So that Rubyn has a landshare before you go to the Rock, if he needs one. In time you'll get a share from your man's family, and another from your Da. That could be some years and meanwhile this will give you a living." Billi paused but Ellibeth stayed silent, waiting for the rest. "Then when you have your shares, you can give Rubyn the valley land, or your shares here in Trail's End." Billi smiled. "He'll not need a Billi-hut."

"So this is for Rubyn?" Ellibeth seemed insistent on that and Billi knew why. If it was for her, then she would say too much. Billi nodded and Ellibeth sighed. "Which means I can't say no, because he'll love that valley." She smiled. "And you knew that, you sneaky man. He might get a Hound?"

"Then he'll be able to rent the land out and will have a good base for hunting." Exactly what Billi had arranged for if he didn't come back from a hunt one day, though he didn't mention that.

Ellibeth still wasn't totally convinced. "That's a bit close for a maid to live to a man. We'll be neighbours out there in the middle of nowhere, with only the gravel bar betwixt our cottages."

Billi shook his head because he knew just what would keep her reputation safe. He'd let in more people, in return for getting Ellibeth to live out there. "No. I've decided, and if there's room for six more cottages as Bettram and Patre seemed to think, then I'll let them come. It'll be a proper Village, so perfectly decent." He grinned. "You'll just have to be careful where you wander at night so a bear doesn't catch you."

That made Ellibeth laugh, but then she sobered. "I can only come if it really will support both of us. I'll not be a burden on anyone." She smiled. "Though it'll be handy for if you want more cheese."

Billi took out the thin flat rock he'd been drawing on with chalk, out in the Forest. "It'll be plenty. Look, this is the valley, and I've sort of marked you up for two thirds of that side. Patre said that side was enough to split into three for littluns eventually, so this part will support two of you."

"What about that gravel bar? You've not put it into any share."

"I'll be keeping the gravel though everyone will use it to cross the valley for fresh water." Billi hesitated and then told her. "There's a lot of stones in there, the good ones for Tinkerers."

"In that case." Ellibeth took the chalk and drew a line to put the gravel in Billi's landclaim, then added a little bit onto hers to block off the other end of the gravel. "Now nobody has any reason to do other than walk across it. If there's gravel needed for paths it'll need searching first." She put the chalk down. "I'll help with that to make sure you get all the stones." That came as a surprise for Billi that he was careful not to let show. Ellibeth would search the gravel bar for his pretty stones, not for herself?

Then Ellibeth pointed at the rough drawing. "Are these the other cottages, along the valley edge?"

"Yes, I'll let them take a small claim on the valley floor for a garden."

Billi indicated the lines around each cottage.

"That's generous, Billi."

"Not really. We're all going to be neighbours, and it's all found land." Billi grinned and Ellibeth smiled back.

"Everything is found and so it's free as far as you're concerned." Ellibeth sniggered, "Free land. You'd give some of the farmers' seizures if they heard that. Don't say it to the elders." They were forced to stop talking and joking about seizures in the end as Rubyn came back so Billi took Ellibeth home.

The following day Billi took Ellibeth to see the Eldest and she registered her landclaim, and Billi confirmed it. Then they had to explain again because it made no sense to the Eldest for some reason. Then one said there could be more and they all nodded and got on with it. Soon the elders were asking exactly how much other landclaims would take on the valley floor and how they'd have water access for stock?

The numbers and positions of other plots went on another piece of that reed parchment that came in so handy for such as this. The Elders and Billi were both uncertain about limits to the landclaim up on the moors. It seemed open land but the Wild would put in limits as would the lack of water. As Kina wrote it all down Billi could feel everything becoming more solid, more real, no longer just talk around a campfire. The written words had a power all of their own.

Billi mentioned that even Farmers would give the tithe in the valley, and where it must go, and that went onto the parchment as part of the Law of the Farm. "It really is Law?" Ellibeth had heard Billi say it, but still didn't quite believe it.

"We've be talking and looking and as far as we can see, the Law of the Farm is what the founder says." Kina smiled. "Though the elders might alter it once he's gone." She looked at the drawing. "News of this will go up and down the trails. A new Village of eight houses, taken straight from the Forest all at once. I've never heard of that!" Kina looked at Billi, her old eyes bright with excitement. "What will ye call it?" Ellibeth laughed when Billi said he'd think on it, since she'd heard a few suggestions.

* * *

The Village came alive with discussion and rumour, and speculation ran riot. At least that partly counter-balanced the rumours about Billi standing back from the Winter Hunt and letting Raban go to his death. Part of the trouble with that rumour was that Billi really had stood at the back and some non-Hunters didn't understand or believe the Hunters who explained why. At least the Hunters had no qualms, and nor did Treese, though the continued nasty undertone in the Village left Billi even keener to be out on the green.

A half-moon later Billi took Ellibeth again, with Rubyn. This time Gerant and Lilith came to look over the possible landclaim, with Hektor as the second Hunter on the trip so that one of them could manage some hunting. Lilith in particular seemed very excited. They weren't quite bonded yet but only because they had nowhere to live, and had been nudging both parents about a Billi-hut. This would be much better all round.

This trip out meant another three nights under the stars, and Rubyn, Gerant and Lilith were all very quiet the first night. Once again that slowly became excitement especially on the last day when the Hunters took an opportunity to collect meat for when they arrived. Hektor and Dapple worked around a small herd of deer so when they took one the rest ran towards where the group waited, hidden. There Billi took a second. Rubyn in particular looked utterly awestruck by being at the hunt, and then wanted to help with the skinning using his little knife. In the end he had to be content with the promise of a trapline overnight on the moors for birds.

He'd never caught game birds. There were none near the Village now but the chances were good, and he'd want to start practicing. There should always be some near the valley as the moors would remain the roughest of pastures, and Rubyn could gain a steady little income that way. Billi stressed that there must always be a Hunter up there to watch over him. This place wasn't as tame as the fields near Billi's hut.

The courting plumage on these birds would be a lovely surprise for Rubyn as they had been for Billi. He had seen a few from below, strutting on the upper slopes and had no idea what they were. Maybe the Tinkerers would have a name for them? Billi couldn't get up there to snare any so he was looking forward to seeing the feathers close up. The rich, almost orange browns and flecks were no doubt wonderful camouflage in the dried heather and bracken. The longer tail feathers of the males, strutting with their glistening emerald throats distended and crooning softly, should be a good sale item with the Tinkerers.

From the comments around him a lot of the small wildlife down below would be a welcome surprise for those brought up in the Village. Billi had never fully realised how the birds changed as he came nearer to the fields except they were quieter. The larger birds raided crops of course as did flocks of some of the smaller ones, relying on numbers to keep them safe. It was the small flocks and solitaries that dropped away, and often the solitaries were the most colourful and sang loudest. The trip was accompanied by exclamations as bursts of colour and song assaulted them from the spring courting season now in full flight.

Rubyn and Gerant were both delighted to catch some unwary fish in the stream on the way with lines borrowed from Billi and Hektor. They were warned, the fish would become warier as more people trapped them. There should still be some though, if everyone took care not to overfish. That might be the reason for the poor fishing near the Village. Another line went onto the new Village's Law of the Farm.

Rubyn finally managed to find a use for his knife, as he cleaned his own fish under close supervision. The littlun carefully put the tithe for the Wild under a bush before they moved off. He kept a fishtail though Ellibeth wasn't sure how well it would last as a trophy. The group arrived at dusk, tired from the trip so after lighting the stove and cooking and eating a meal they went to sleep. Though not before Rubyn persuaded Hektor to go up onto the moors so the littlun could set a few snares. Rubyn had no traps with him but Hektor helped him to improvise.

The maids slept in Billi's hut with Rubyn. The men slept nearby with two Hounds and a fire that burned bright and hot with heather, then died down to provide a bed of embers round a thick log. The next day Billi's bed had a makeover with a load of heather being brought down the hillside to replace the dried grass, leaves and reeds. Rubyn went up with the heather collectors to check his snares, and brought back a mottled brown bird with a plump breast.

Hektor and Gerant went off to properly assess the moors, so that Gerant could choose which cottage he preferred. The two would overnight up there, heading out in a wide arc to really explore the moor and water supplies. Gerant and Lilith already wanted a claim, any claim but since they had a choice Gerant wanted to get it right. Apart from that both wanted to move out to the valley yesterday please. Billi and Rabbit remained to guard the maids and Rubyn.

Billi took the opportunity to weave his brambles into a better barrier and clean out the sediment between the smaller ponds, enthusiastically helped by Rubyn. They were both scolded by his Ma when Rubyn returned to her scratched, muddy and dripping. Though Rabbit should have got the blame since he loved finding someone who would race around in the shallow water and mud with him, and had made the most of it.

Billi slept outside alone but he'd done that with Rabbit many times in much wilder places, and had a pile of heather to lie on this time. Though it felt strange to sleep in the valley with others in his hut, smoke coming from the chimney, and a faint light from the tiny window in the door. Billi watched that smoke and light for a little while, and drifted off to sleep.

* * *

Rabbit roused him, just enough to wake and the song sounded happy, not a warning. When Billi looked carefully around someone had come out of the hut. Ellibeth? His alarm died at the slow, careful way she picked a path and turned to humour. Was Ellibeth trying to sneak up on a Hunter with a Hound?

As she arrived Billi half sat up and opened his mouth to ask, but the maid bent and put a finger on his lips. She kept it there as she pulled the furs back with the other hand, tugged his arm aside and slipped in next to him. Ellibeth put her mouth up near his ear and whispered "no gloves, you must hold me very tight Billi bear" and then replaced her finger with her lips!

Later, they cuddled together under the fur and watched the stars. "That one is the Lodestar, and tells the Hunter where North lies, the same as a Lodestone. The four stars there, with the last one turned in towards us, that one points at Trail's End and we call it The Way Home. In the winter it points at the Stooping Hawk, and Trail's End lies betwixt them." Billi found out that Ellibeth couldn't see the Hawk, or the Hawkfly, or the Broken Arrow, and spent a while showing her each one until Ellibeth could recognise them. By then the wheel had turned, the stars spinning around them as they did at night, Billi explained how that told Hunter when dawn would come. "Now I must learn exactly where the stars should be in the sky to get me here, for when I roam away from the stream or the edge of the uplands."

"To find your new home?"

"And yours. Maybe?"

"I will like that, and Rubyn will love every minute." Ellibeth sighed. "It hasn't been easy for him, since he had to stay close to home with no Da to take him out here and there." She chuckled. "He'll be following Gerant all over the place."

"That will give you a bit of freedom as well."

"To wander about? In the dark?" Ellibeth kissed him. "But there are bears out in the dark." Ellibeth hugged Billi. "You must think me a terrible careless maid, to be caught so easily." Her finger went over Billi's lips before he could speak. "Shush, and listen. I was bonded for five years, and now I've been alone for nearly the same, and sometimes I miss strong arms in the night." Ellibeth giggled. "This might not look like it, but I've been very careful of my reputation. And you, you silly sweet man, have done your share with that. I've never found someone I liked enough, and trusted enough, to risk my name."

Billi hugged her tight. "I swear, Ellibeth, I'll never let anyone know." Which was a shame, he'd have liked to let everyone know but having him stumping alongside would be embarrassing for a bonnie maid.

"I know, silly Billi." Ellibeth hugged him just as tight. "Is this why you wanted me to live out here? In case I wandered at night?"

"No! I swear, it was to give Rubyn a landclaim in the end, instead of waiting." Billi felt horrified that Ellibeth even thought that!

Ellibeth giggled. "So you won't be sleeping outside all the time, just in case I sleepwalk, or wander a little?"

Billi chuckled. "Tempting. After all, if a maid wanders about in the dark she should expect to get caught by a bear now and then."

Billi saw her teeth show white in the moonlight as she smiled, then

Ellibeth murmured "That's all I need, Billi." She bussed him, gently, slipped out of the furs and crept back into the hut.

Billi waited for the voices as someone roused but nobody raised an alarm. Then he laid thinking about what had just happened. Ellibeth didn't want to be bonded, to be a lass, she just wanted strong arms in the night now and then. Billi could live with that, because 'twas a lot better than he'd ever imagined or hoped for. If Billi could have that with Ellibeth the other maids could flirt as they liked, because 'twould be enough for him as well. It did cross Billi's mind that this valley had a strange effect on maids, though not one he would ever complain about.

* * *

The next day Ellibeth and Lilith greeted him cheerfully and hoped he'd slept well, and by mid-morning the two came back from the moors. Hektor had to go straight back up with Rubyn to check the snares and this time they brought back a bigger bird, not as mottled, and two of the snares were broken. Hektor thought that might be the really big, fast, long eared rabbits he'd seen during the day. Billi told him they were called hares. He'd described them to the Tinkerers when he saw the first ones up on the slope but he hadn't seen this bird before.

Billi ended up describing the two types he had seen, in pretty plumage so probably the males. The birds had been strutting about on top of the cliff and Gerant and Hektor confirmed that they'd seen some strutting on wide flat stretches of rock. The birds flew off but not far or high, and everyone agreed both were some sort of ground living bird that must live in the heather, or the sinkholes. Whatever they were, snares caught them and the meat turned out to be stronger than chicken or duck, different and tasty once Ellibeth and Lilith got to work. Better yet, they were extra food that could be caught by those tending the sheep.

The sinkholes were in clumps and Gerant thought that with other men herding up there some low walls could be built with the loose rocks, high enough to deter the sheep or the daft creatures would fall down the holes. There were bones in some holes and Hektor thought from the remains of their fleece some sort of browser or grazer came through. Perhaps a different sort of goat or sheep, a wild one, though none were in sight. If there were grazers, there'd be predators, so the sheep would need extra guarding until a bit of culling made the predators wary of Hounds and bows.

The five of them squatted around the valley plan on the parchment and scratched it into the mud so the parchment could be put away safe, in the hut. Gerant and Hektor paced it out and Billi, Ellibeth and Lilith marked the landclaim boundaries with sticks driven into the soil with Billi's hammer and the back of his axe. Gerant chose the hut at the front of the valley so he could graze a few cattle in the open woodland and also take his sheep up the hillside to the moor.

Billi had to keep stopping to add extras to the provisional Law of the Farm, this Farm, as the group came up with suggestions on how to make sure the new settlement didn't ruin the fishing, the hunting, and the grazing. He swore he could feel the beard growing every time he did. The rest laughed at him, bright-eyed with excitement because this wasn't a dream any more. There really would be a new Village, and suggestions came thick and fast for names.

Lilith's excitement wasn't just that she and Gerant would be bonded and out of the family home before their parents passed, she absolutely loved the whole idea of living out here. "Look at the trees and bushes on the hillside, and flowers. Even that hillside is so different from the flat land of the Farm around the Village." Lilith waved her hands around. "It's, it's, magical, like the tales about piskies and fey."

She didn't care about trekking for water, being isolated, or living rough to start with. Farmers with big ponds in the middle of the Farm considered frogs a treat, and Lilith loved having them and fish on her doorstep. She also wanted flowers from the Wild planted in her garden, and a window to look out on the Forest every morning. Lilith's main concern lived on the other side of the lakes, in that piece of Forest. "I'm pleased the water is betwixt us and that Great Hunter. 'Tis best the Forest borders your landclaim, Billi, and not someone else's, because everyone knows the Wild likes you."

"True. This valley would be too dangerous without you, Billi, and your way with the Wild." Gerant sounded totally serious.

"I haven't got a way. The Wild will scoop me up if a I make a mistake." Billi felt certain of that. He'd already had a few close calls with a Wild hunter, or wounded game.

"Everyone thinks the same Billi. Not that the Wild won't take you, but that it maybe gives you a little more leeway." Ellibeth sounded serious as well. "I've seen you when you've been out here and can sort of feel the Wild on you, and in the way you speak of the Forest."

"Well I'll feel better with strong stone walls rather than relying on the Wild being friendly, so we'd best finish this job." They'd made Billi feel a bit uncomfortable, talking of him and the Wild like that. Though Billi did love the green, and the Wild did seem to be letting have this valley.

Even as they marked the plots with the pale coloured stones or sticks Rubyn found for them, Lilith carried on talking about her new home. She wanted to bring two young cats, ones trained as mousers. "Though out here I reckon I'll lose one to the Wild before they work out which bit is safe."

"Maybe not. After all, everyone says a cat is part Wild anyway?" Ellibeth paused. "One-shut certainly is and I reckon he'll fit in fine." She sniggered. "A few of the smaller Wild hunters round here could get a shock when that one eye shows up in the night."

"I can't make my mind up about One-shut. Maybe he'd be happier left in the hut?" Billi wasn't sure One-shut would take to moving house. Cats weren't keen on moving once they were grown and if One-shut tried to go home from here, the Wild would snap him up.

"Bring the chicken coop. One-shut will sleep in there and stuff himself with rats, and never notice the move." Hektor laughed. "As long as there's a warm spot by the fire."

"I'd best bring two females then. A litter off a big tom like One-shut, growing up here, will sort out the rats and mice." Lilith seemed happier with that sorted, but then rats and mice were the bane of a Farmer's life. "What about you, Hektor. Don't you fancy moving in?"

Hektor stopped pacing a measurement and looked round. "I would love to. Look at all that Forest, barely hunted, barely explored. Then there's the moors on top, who knows what a Hunter might find there?" Hektor looked round again. "We can't, not with Bliss having a babe. By the time the babe is old enough to come out here, another Hunter will have taken up the place."

"I think we can find room for another Hunter, Hektor, especially if you'll be content with a small plot like mine at the Village? That would ease the pressure on the two Hunters here as they will be spending a lot of time guarding sheep. On top of that I don't want Ellibeth bending my ears over seeing her Sis and the babe." Billi grinned at Ellibeth and she grinned back. "How long will it be before you would want to come?"

"I don't know until I talk to Bliss. She might not want to come."

Ellibeth laughed. "Bring her out here to visit. She'll be moving as soon as possible after that."

"That would be a comfort, another new Ma when I have my first." Ellibeth blushed a little. "After all, I'll be having my first out here, once Gerant and me are bonded proper-like. You'll be a comfort as well, Ellibeth. A Ma who's already raised a fine littlun."

"And a handy babysitter?"

"I wouldn't say no."

"Helping me babysit will tire Rubyn out." Ellibeth looked over at Rubyn, now sat watching them. "Though his eyelids are drooping right now."

"No surprise at that. He's been finding marker stones and thin sticks to mark boundaries nearly non-stop." Billi looked over at the littlun. "We'd best eat before he's asleep."

Rubyn did go to sleep as soon as he finished eating, and his Unk Hektor carried him into the hut. Then the rest sat around the fire for a while and beat some more details to death, in between watching falling stars and listening to Billi and Hektor explain the night sounds. Billi had heard these calls all his adult life, ever since he started hunting, and understood what they meant. But as the three non-Hunters asked more and more questions the calls were becoming more real, not just a noise that meant the way was clear or that danger lurked. The men slept in a close group around the fire again and the party headed out first thing in the morning, with a good load of fresh fish.

* * *

The trip back kept everyone entertained. Ellibeth had remembered some of the names for birds and flowers from the last trip and invented more, and now Rubyn tried to memorise them. So did Billi because most hadn't been named before, and Lilith joined in to name even more. "We wondered about that a time or two Billi, out on the Winter Hunt. If everything had a name once?" Hektor nodded towards the maids and Rubyn, exclaiming at each new blossom or creature and trying to name them all.

Billi had often wondered. "Maybe this is how the named ones became that way? Perhaps we should do that instead of sticking to dappled hunter and suchlike."

"Shade-cat?" Hektor smiled. "It'll be up to Hunters because the maids won't see them, and I'm realising that's a pity." He'd picked a flower and now realised he couldn't give it to a maid.

"There. That has to be a Dancing Maid" Billi looked at where Ellibeth pointed, and so did the rest. "If you squint a little bit, you can see her scarf."

"Ooh yes. All the coloured and embroidered scarves and ribbons when the maids dance with the Bearr." Lilith laughed, and Billi realised she meant the long trailing courtship feathers, dangling and twisting as the bird posed.

"That one is the Bramble Bee, I remember from last time. If you go close to the bramble blossoms so they fly near, the wings make a soft buzz." Lilith, Rubyn and Gerant all went nearer the brambles to check, and agreed. Ellibeth named the Beguiler after the riot of colour on the breast of the otherwise innocuous little blue-grey bird. She also tried hard to find a Careless Button for Eddwyn's sis, because she kept leaving one on her blouse undone while dancing. In the end Billi showed her a small button mushroom. If a Hunter put one of them in his stew he'd get interesting dreams and be very careless.

"Peek, peek." Rubyn kept pointing when he saw one because the Peeker did just that, sticking its white capped head out from behind a bush or tree with quick, furtive movements. The day passed quickly as the two Farmers were also caught up in the naming. Though even Ellibeth and Rubyn had to give up on naming the different Flutterbyes. The myriad patterns and colours overwhelmed them though Billi had to agree that the Sparkul, named by Hektor, fitted since 'twas a rainbow on the wing when it flitted through a sunbeam.

All three from the Village were startled by the different colours of the Hawkflies, and at first thought they were something different. "No, look." Hektor had relaxed, getting into the swing of this naming as well now. "The crimson and sky blue ones chasing flies are flying backwards as well as darting forward. That's just the same as the usual black and brown ones do near the Village."

"I'll never manage to name all those." Ellibeth laughed because even with Rubyn and Lilith helping, there were just too many new things to remember.

"I'll catch one, a pretty one." Rubyn darted forward.

"You'll come away from the stream." Ellibeth glared at him. "You'll end up in the water and it's too cold to walk home dripping wet." Rubyn continued trying to catch any that came his way and Billi wondered if that might be why there were no pretty ones around the Village. Had the littles caught them all? Was that perhaps the reason there were no Bramble Bees in the Village berry patch, or Dancing Maids in the orchards? They'd all been caught for the pretty feathers?

The tiny multi-coloured flowers of early spring were gone, buried by the eager grass and the sprouting leaves and creepers. Already the first big blousy blooms shouted for their turn, beckoning to bird and bug, calling them to pillage their treasures. They were all calling to Ellibeth as well, apparently, demanding names. Billi pointed. "You see the long trail of pale blue funnels hanging from the tree?"

"Yes?"

Billi pulled one blossom loose, carefully. "Now suck the bottom there, where it came free. That is what the bees are after."

"That is sweet, really sweet." Ellibeth reached out and carefully pulled another. "Rubyn, try this."

"Can we try as well?" Lilith and Garten were reaching as well.

"Honeypot. That has to be the Honeypot." Ellibeth reached again and then stopped. "No, we must leave them for the bees, and then Billi might find us some honey later in the year."

"Wild honey?" Hektor's big smile echoed everyone else's.

"That one, the clump deep in shadow, is shy. The pale pink ones."

Lilith pointed into the shadows. "They are blushing. Shy Maid! That one has to be Shy Maid."

Billi wished he could have taken Ellibeth along the tunnels in the green, so that she could have seen the beauty that waited in clearings and hollows. But this was the Forest, and despite the beauty the Wild still lurked in all its guises, as proved when Rubyn caught the wrong pretty flier and had a red, stinging bump on his thumb! Both of the maids wanted to know if some of the flowers could be moved to the edges of the valley, or maybe the Hunters could collect some seeds?

The first two days of the return trip consisted of laughing and naming, then trying hard to remember some of them. By then both maids had a bunch of flowers, ones they'd picked themselves or with Gerant helping Lilith. The third afternoon and the following morning the new and the named dropped off rapidly as the party approached the Farm, and this trip really drove it home. There would have to be a line in the new Laws of the Farm to try and avoid that, to stop the new villagers driving the Wild deeper into the green where it couldn't be seen

* * *

On their return, Fellip the Thatcher produced another two sheets of reed parchment when Billi asked, pointing out that he'd made it out of Billi's reed so 'twas cheap. Billi drew the final plan after a dozen trial runs in the dirt and on a flat rock with chalk to see how it looked. He put in all the measurements they'd paced and tried to get the proportions right. Drawing the final version turned into a busy and exciting day with Hektor, Bliss and Dapple there so Hektor could help, as well as Gerant and Lilith. Then Patre, and Eddmune and Mikkel came with their Hounds, to help with the proportions and where boundaries should run. The boundaries in the valley and where claims ran onto the moors were clear but their outer boundary wasn't marked. Then after rain or if someone found a pool sufficient to water stock, the grazing could be extended.

Ellibeth and Rubyn helped, and Rubyn entertained them all with a blow by blow account of his trip and his trapping and fishing. Gerant's and Lilith's name went onto their claim, to their great excitement. When everyone agreed the dirt version looked right, Billi carefully copied it twice onto reed-paper. Kina the Eldest would keep one as the Village record and the elders would show the second to those interested in applying for a landclaim. Applying, because the Eldest, Billi, must approve the landclaims. With that in mind, Ellibeth insisted that Billi made a third copy to keep so he could check who had which plots when folk asked.

The meeting with the elders seemed strange, because they kept deferring to whatever Billi suggested. Not only that, but Lilith, Ellibeth, Patre, Bettram and Mikkel came along as well to give their opinions on the possibilities there. The extra lines to the new Law of the Farm were added, with a comment from Kina that if anyone disagreed they shouldn't apply for a claim.

* * *

Billi went out hunting again and when he came home dealt with a succession of people, both parents and potential settlers, wanting to ask about this detail or that. Because of that Billi only went overnight at the most. He didn't want to go out for too long just now in any case, since he didn't want to miss the next Trader caravan. Though now he started to bring back a few flowers because after the trip Ellibeth had put some in a mug in his hut, so he had a little of the Forest there. Billi also brought back any pretty feathers he found and left them lying about. Sure enough Rubyn would claim them, and twice they'd reappeared on Ellibeth's coat.

When the caravan arrived Billi took his reject stones, the one's the Tinkerers didn't want. He had cleaned and polished them to be sure what the stones were and among them were, once again, some that were the type that made sparkuls but had been rejected by Tinkerers. As usual, the Traders were eager to take them all. Billi tried to work out afterwards if he'd got a little bit more by cleaning them.

The following day he took his silver to buy salt, and traded some hides for more. Billi asked Hektor to come along, though didn't say why, and the young Hunter joked it must be to help with carrying the salt. Once the salt had been safely loaded onto a hired pony Billi told him the real reason. "I don't trust the Traders."

Hektor laughed. "Nobody does."

"But I'm going to the stone trader with a real sparkul, a very small one. I know they're keen to get them, and I want to know how keen. I'd as soon have another Hunter and Hound handy if the man gets greedy." Billi showed the tiny sparkul, but didn't tell even Hektor about the larger one he carried. Not because he didn't trust Hektor, but he'd seen both Hektor and Bliss after a bit too much cider at the dancing and something might slip.

Hektor suddenly became very serious. "Don't worry, Billi. Rabbit will let Dapple know, and we'll be straight inside."

Billi went in with Rabbit and sat at the table. "Did you want ale or wine, or maybe cider?" The Trader waved at a table full of bottles and flasks.

"No thank ye." The Traders used those instead of beguilers, and ale worked well enough with some. "I've got another stone to show you."

"One? Let's see it then." Billi put the little package of kidskin on the table and unwrapped it, leaving the sparkul in solitary splendour right in the middle. He put it in a sunbeam, and the tiny stone blazed with inner fire. "A sparkul! How did you get that?" The man put his hand out and Rabbit grumbled just a little, but enough to stop him. "I was just going to check what it was."

Billi laughed. "You know what it is. Does anything else look like that?" Billi leant forward and gave the man a hard look. "I traded for it with the Tinkerers. A sparkul isn't cheap, and I want to know if I've been cheated. I'll know by what you'll give me for it."

The Trader blew out a long breath and nodded. "You're right. I know what it is and no, nothing looks the same. What are you asking?"

"Gold. A good bit. How much you part with tells me if I'm to trade for another when I've put the price together." Billi looked down at the bright spark between them. "If we reach agreement you can handle it all ye like."

"I can find a better price if I'm the only one you sell to?" Billi almost smiled, because that meant the Trader really wanted the little stone. "Can I look at it closer?"

"You can pick it up with an open hand under the hide. If you close your hand, Rabbit will get the sparkul back even if your hand is in the way." Billi had seen the Traders doing tricks with cards and stones, making them disappear and appear again.

"Don't you trust me?" Before Billi answered the Trader smiled. "I wouldn't trust the rest of them round a sparkul so fair enough."

He carefully picked up the hide with both hands and slid one right underneath, then brought the stone nearer to his eye and produced a magnifying glass on a handle. Billi had seen those, they were like a lens out of a far-seer with a frame round them, though he'd not seen one with a handle. "That's a very small sparkul."

"It's a sparkul and worth a lot more than the usual stones, even bigger ones." Billi knew that for sure, but wasn't sure how much the Tinkerers charged the Traders.

The serious bargaining began with Billi putting one of the one-gold rings on the table. "That's to check yours against. 'Tis how some trade, and the value is exactly one gold, so if someone has passed ye a gold ingot that's got the wrong metal in it'll show on the scales." Which was a polite way of telling the Trader not to pass Billi forgeries.

"I've seen those before. Now, how much gold is the question." They went back and forth and round a bit, and eventually Billi had enough gold and some silver in front of him. More than enough for a decent trade, so the Tinkerers really did make the Traders pay well. Billi had no intention of trading his other sparkuls, because they were easier to store than gold. Not only that, but if word got back to the Tinkerers, the prices would go up.

"That's a trade." Billi scooped up the price, and the Trader wrapped the sparkul. "Ye'd best not mention that, or the Tinkerers might not trade another."

"I'll not be telling the rest of the caravan, never mind the Tinkerers. Did you get any hints how they do it?" The Trader didn't seem hopeful, but they always asked anyone with stones.

"No, but now I want you to consider carefully. I've another here and I want your best price again." Billi reached into his coat.

"You should have traded for both and maybe got a better price."

"Different sizes." Billi unwrapped the kidskin and the smallest of the larger sparkuls blazed into life on the table.

The Trader didn't move. He sat for a long time, staring, and then wet his lips before speaking in barely a whisper. "Blood and gold man, how did you get that?"

"I found a pocket of good stones, the sort the Tinkerers like, then I bargained hard. Now I want to know if I made a good trade." Billi paused. "How much gold will ye give me for that?"

"More than I've got." The Trader thought hard. "I might be able to borrow enough from others here in the caravan?" He hesitated. "Perhaps. If we come to a price. Can I?" He made the barest move towards the sparkul.

"Very, very carefully and flat again. If ye take hold, ye'll not have chance to let go and I'll keep the hand." Rabbit muttered to himself. "There's another Hunter and Hound outside so there'll be no help and I don't even need to speak to warn him."

"Aye, Hounds. We know enough to be sure of that. I'd like to keep my hand, but I'd also like to hold it for a moment." The Trader picked up the hide and sparkul on his flat hand and held it in the sun to move it a little this way and that and Billi watched the fire sparkle and the rainbows dance inside the stone. Then the Trader sighed. "I've never held one that size." Billi suddenly became even more cautious but the Trader put the sparkul back down.

"So can we try to come to a price? That cost me a lot of stones."

"I'll wager!" The Trader pulled his eyes from the sparkul and sat back. "In gold? You won't take other stones, or other trade goods?"

"Straight gold, tested right here." The negotiation started agreeably high for Billi. In the end Billi sat silent for a long time, as if in thought. Then he sighed. "Close, but not enough because of what I paid, but you gave me my best offer for the sparkul." Billi just wanted to get clear and leave the man hopeful. "I'll bury it back in the Forest, and think long and hard. I'd hoped for a bit more but maybe that'll be enough." He smiled and waved at his peg leg. "Maybe enough to get a maid to overlook this."

"Enough to get a Tinkerer maid to move in for a while, I'd wager." The Trader looked at the sparkul. "I would prefer not to borrow from some of the others since they'd wonder why, or I would go a little higher. If you keep it I'll come prepared next year, and I'll think long and hard about that price. We can find a way. Keep any little ones you get as well."

"I will, as long as I don't hear tales going to the Tinkerers or anyone else." Billi worried more about tales going to the Traders and others here in the Village because he'd been offered a lot of gold, maybe enough to set up his valley home properly! "I don't want anyone trying to steal it."

"Thcy'll not try from someplace in the Forest. That'll need a Hunter and Hound, and you lot stick together." The Trader nodded to Billi. "Very clever. Not only that, but I'll wager there's no sign of where its buried."

"Ye'd be right." Billi wrapped the sparkul and stood. "I'd best get it back out there as soon as possible. I thank you for the offer, and I will think on it." He'd make sure all the sparkuls were in the valley, and probably just outside it in the Forest nearby. The Tinkerers might not sell many, but they really made the Traders pay well judging by that offer and now Billi wished he'd not brought the larger one.

Hektor leant against the outside of the wagon, with Dapple laid at his feet. "Did you get a price?"

"I did, and the Tinkerers get a really good price for them. Now I'd best get this salt home, and my profit tucked away." Billi laughed. "I'll be able to spruce up the hut in the valley at this rate."

"Oh yes, I saw Ellibeth raising dust when she went there. You'll need a broom for starters if she goes again." Hektor followed Billi home and then went off to his own Billi-hut.

Billi unloaded his salt, put the big sparkul in the hidey hole under the bed, and took the pony back. When he returned, there were marks on the door of his hut where someone had tried to lever out the lock! It hadn't worked, but Billi would make sure never to leave it unguarded when Traders were here. Showing the sparkul really had been a mistake. At least he'd not taken a larger one, or one set in gold as he'd intended. Now Billi could only hope that greed kept the man's mouth shut.

Billi made sure to go out for three days straight after the Traders left, in case the man had spoken to anyone here. Anyone watching would presume the sparkul buried over a day away in the Forest. On his return Ellibeth greeted him with fresh bread and a pie, and messages. Viktor wanted to talk to Billi when he had time, and so did Mikkel.

Ellibeth laughed and told Billi that as an Eldest he had to get used to folk wanting to talk, and to Rubyn's questions. Rubyn had plenty about the Forest, valley and moor, mixed with recitals of egg-collecting and trap-emptying. He also asked about feathers now, and any different flowers, so Billi had an excuse to bring both. The traps had taken few little hunters, and Rubyn looked downhearted. Billi explained that it was time to switch to snaring rabbits, and anything else that wanted the crops that were beginning to show green in the fields.

* * *

Viktor wanted to talk about how to set up his eldest maid's home out in the valley because the cost of the hut alone worried him. Billi eased his mind. All the cottages would be built cheaply because they'd all help each other. He'd trade Ellibeth a stove against cleaning and pies and bread, and maybe a bit of grain and straw from her crops for the chickens and goats. She wouldn't need so much meat with the fish and the birds from Rubyn's traps. Others would trade their help against future flour, grain and straw, and Billi would be paying Rubyn to look after the chickens and Billi's waterfowl. Viktor made that easier by offering to give Spots to Rubyn, to be the valley guard dog.

Dealing with Mikkel turned easier in a way, but unexpectedly so. "I'd like to take the second Hunter's cottage, please, Billi."

"You're the first Hunter to come straight out and ask, and I know ye well enough Mikkel so it's done. Who's the lucky maid?" Billi assumed that whoever had been chasing or running was caught.

Mikkel looked a little bit shy. "Nobody, Billi. There's a few chasing but I'm still running hard. I'll only need a roof and someplace to leave gear I'm not carrying, and store pelts and meat." Mikkel shrugged. "If I've got a storeroom for that, I can live with another family there for a while. My cottage can go up last."

"I'm sure someone will be pleased of the extra meat, and a store wouldn't take much to build." Billi chuckled. "I'm going to sort it all out with Syman, but I'm hoping to arrange for him to cut me a cold store into the rock face. The stone can go into buildings. You could do the same?"

"I will, thank you. I can grow a few vegetables, and build up some fowl if there's someone to look out for them. I can pay the minder with meat or furs." Mikkel smiled. "If I can find someone not too busy."

"Rubyn and Spots will be looking after mine, so yours won't be much more work?"

"He'll be a good catch himself at that rate." Both laughed because if Rubyn started earning now he really might find a lot of interest when he came of age. "I'm not ready to be caught just yet." Mikkel gave that half-shy smile again. "I'd like to get a home set up, proper-like. Then when I happen on a maid whose family expect her to get more than a Billi-hut, I'll be set."

If Mikkel had a cottage and a real landclaim, that would be enough to keep them until the young Hunter inherited his landclaim in the Village. It also spoke well of Mikkel that he would wait for the right maid and the young Hunter certainly seemed sure the maid would be there, whoever she was. That sounded like family, not the maid, being the problem. Billi wondered which maid's family thought being a Hunter on top of whatever landclaim Mikkel would get wasn't enough. Though one point needed driving in, with Mikkel being young. "The Great Hunter could be right there one morning, at the Forest edge, taking a drink. You won't be tempted, will you?"

"I'll nod politely, and step back indoors, and Pointer will come with me. I've still got a paw from the striped hunter, and after seeing those pug marks I got it out to look at. It looks like a kitty-paw in comparison." Mikkel sighed. "I still remember how big that striped hunter was, and how hard to kill, and I've no intention of tangling with its big bro."

"Good enough. We'd best get to Kina and get your name down."

"Thank ye Billi. I can't wait to look at all that new Forest and that moorland. The birds up there are new, so who knows what else a Hunter might find?" He grinned. "I could become a Wanderer as well. I've been asking around and some of the Traders are also wondering if you've reached the end of the Forest."

Kina seemed more than pleased to add Mikkel, she sounded enthusiastic. "That's what you needed, Billi. With a second Hunter in place, the rest will fill up fast. Bettram has already left stock to mature to start Gerant off, and there's others doing the same just in case." She sighed. "I'd love to come on that trip, driving all the stock out there. Still, there'll be plenty of Hunters up for it, and the sibs of those going will help as well if only so they get their extra landshare here."

"I'd not thought of that. When will the stock be old enough?" Billi suddenly envisioned a flock of lambs in the Forest, and the carnage that would follow.

"Next spring, after any adults have weaned their young so they can leave them. Most of the stock will be yearlings, and breed the first year there. Those who can't give the younguns stock will be sending stoves and cooking pots, crockery and bedding. You'll need all the ponies on the Farm I reckon." She reached out to stroke Billi's chin. "You're leaving it late to start that beard."

* * *

Billi made trips out to hunt for meat, and for wood, and sometimes to the valley. Summer peeked, liked the view and moved in. The Forest and the Wild relented after the winter and game increased as animals moved onto the unused grazing and fresh young browse. Crops sprouted and the young farm animals took a firm hold on life and packed on size and weight. The Hunters were out and busy, or were kept occupied guarding the young stock and new crops.

Though Billi found time for his talk with Syman the stonecutter, because Syman had to start before anyone else. "I wondered how much time you could spare for the valley, Syman, and what it would cost?" Because this would cost, and probably more than anything else. Only one man could cut and true the stone blocks to anchor the walls properly, and build a wall that would stay strong and true. "We've got plenty of stone there."

"I've been listening, Billi, and I've a question. Is there room for one extra small cottage? One with a bit of garden and a space on the shore for a few ducks?" Syman smiled. "A Billi-hut." The Stonemason waited while Billi thought about it.

"If there's no need to have a landclaim with it, I could find a spot tucked in close to the cliff at the back. There's probably space the other side of the fresh water inlet." Billi chuckled. "Depending on the size of the cottage." That part belonged on Billi's side, and by rights on his pasture, but cut off from the rest by the flow from the cleft.

"I could cut the hut into the cliff in that case. Since it's for me that would be right, a Stonemason in a cave." Syman smiled.

"You?" Billi looked around at Syman's house. "What about this place?"

"My lass is long gone to the rock. I've got one youngun living here with his lass, and the other with her man's family in their home. If I had a Billi-hut, out in the valley, then they could have their brideshare and landshare. The lass and her man could put a Billi-hut on her brideshare if she wanted, and the other pair could have this house. Or the other way round, 'twill be up to them how they sort it out." Syman sighed. "I just need somewhere to keep me going until I go to Skull Rock, then it'll come in for someone else once I'm gone. Maybe another Hunter?"

"But will you have enough work? Once the cottages and sheds are up, there'll not be much stone-cutting?" Billi would love having Syman out there full time until then, but eight homes wouldn't need him afterwards.

"Stonecutting is only a part time job anyway. Mostly cutting more niches and ledges for skulls in the Great Rock these days." Syman smiled again. "The one ye all call Skull Rock now. The boulders around it are more or less gone now, and little new rock has been needed for a good few years. There's been a flurry of Billi-huts but there's still enough loose rock in the shattered ground, the rough grazing, for those."

Billi and everyone else knew the shattered ground. The Great Rock, now called Skull Rock, looked as if a giant bird had dropped it from the sky in the middle of the flat ground. Big boulders had flaked off leaving the solid pillar standing up stark and clearly visible from at least half the Farm. The ground for a large area around it really seemed shattered, with rocks sticking up and little growing. Every house and barn in the Village had been built of rocks from the lumps that had broken away or been dug up.

"There'll be a lot more stone cutting in the new Village, but I'm still not sure how you'll manage after." Billi grinned. "No offence, Syman, but I'm worrying about how to pay you for that, let alone find work to keep you."

"Ah, but if I come out to live there, the stonecutting will be much cheaper. In return for a home until I go on, I'll cut into the valley sides and ends and shape the stones to build all the cottages and barns. I'll even cut ledges and niches for skulls and steps up the valley sides and help to build the walls around the sinkholes so they are solid." Syman chuckled at the expression on Billi's face. "I told ye I'd thought on it and asked about."

"But after that?"

"For all the stonework I'll want a place to live for as long as I need one. I should take an apprentice as well, but not just for stonecutting. I'll need shelter, firewood and enough to eat while the building work is finished. I'll waive the food if I can run a few sheep with the flock, and a few geese and ducks that are watched over with the others, and have a few fish. My apprentice will want the same deal but will earn it." Syman waited for Billi to think it through.

"A share of fish and a place for waterfowl come with a cottage out there. What other work?" Because Billi realised that an apprentice stonecutter really would be needed in time, either in the valley or here in the Village.

"I can make charcoal, and throw pots if you find some clay even if they won't be as fine as the Potter's." Syman gestured round his home. "I can carve wood or horn of course. That's my other source of income to eke out the landshare. Hah, sometimes my main source. I'm a better carver than stonecutter because that used to be my trade. I'll make sure my apprentice learns them all so your valley has the skills when I'm gone."

Put like that, Billi didn't need to think hard at all. "Deal, Syman. There's enough dead wood and loose rock to build temporary huts like mine for three or four couples so you can have one to start with. The first settlers will move out when their proper cottages are built, then the timber and stone can be reclaimed and used for more cottages." Billi held out his arm. "You can build your own cottage however ye wish, once I've shown you the space. It'll be yours and the apprentice's as long as you want it, and the apprentice's after."

"I thank ye, Billi. Give me a moon to get organised and find an apprentice, and I'll be ready to go." Syman reached out his own arm and they clasped to seal the agreement.

Billi took four young Hunters and four youths with six ponies to bring back a huge load of firewood from two days into the Forest, because there was little left nearby after the bad winter. They also built three charcoal kilns while there, and left them to burn out. The result kept the Village supplied for a while and made a tidy profit for everyone involved, and that encouraged the young Hunters to branch out.

The young Hunters now began exploring in groups, out beyond the usual boundaries, looking for more wood or stones, or perhaps their own valley. Two asked Billi if he minded them supplying the Blacksmith with charcoal in future since Billi would be supplying the valley? By an unspoken agreement none explored towards Billi's valley, leaving any extras there for the new settlement. The preparations at Billi's valley now had to wait until the summer bounty had been harvested, from the ground or taken with bow and snare.

Law-Breaking and Tithes

There were no more attempts on Billi's door, so he assumed whoever the Trader had sent left with the caravan. He had worried about it being Edan and his friends, but Edan must be too busy now. The young man had managed to work off his debts and would be trying get ahead for the next winter. The stockyards were busy because the young stock needed to be inside fences at night. At the moment the smaller hunting creatures could sneak up and snatch one, so they couldn't sleep in the fields with the herd and just one Hound and a Hunter.

Arikk, the farmer who'd taken a horse for fodder and silver in the winter found that it did well ploughing the heavy clay soil. Unfortunately, the beast ate heavily as well so nobody could decide if the idea would be viable once the clay was broken, since a pony might do the job in future. Edan kept trying to push the benefits, hoping to sell the colt now prancing behind one of his mares. Several people mentioned how much such a horse might drag out to the new Village, or back for trading, but Edan never approached Billi as a possible customer. His small group made periodic attempts to rouse resentment over Raban's death, Hektor's Hound, the fever, and any slight misfortune that could be blamed on Billi.

Edan also hoped to sell some of the pups his bitch had produced. The dogs were certainly big enough to guard stock on the Farm, but despite Edan's claims nobody thought even four would stop one of the larger Wild hunters or a pack. Edan pushed hard, trying to trade pups for silver or the promise of fodder and meat over winter. One or two were considering that, those with farms nearer the Wild, since the pups would be nigh on full-grown by next winter.

* * *

The traded horse wasn't really fully occupied once the ploughing finished and the Farmer's youngest, Kelli, had taken to the big, gentle steed. She enjoyed riding the horse down to the river for water each day with a pad of fur for a saddle. Sometimes Kelli would ride out to the fields to tease the youths tending the flocks and herds, since she would soon be old enough for her first Harvestfest and her first bearr dancing. Then one morning the horse came home, wide-eyed and lathered, without Kelli.

Billi was home when the Hounds' call went up and he and Rabbit answered as fast as they could. Rabbit and almost every Hound on the Farm took the scent from Kelli's bedclothes before they all spread out back along the way the horse had come. The Hunters had backtracked the horse part of the way but too much stock moved around the Farm in summer and the tracks had been obscured. That only left searching for her scent and the Hounds spread out in a fan.

'Twas past midday when the call went up, the baying of a Hound followed by a distinct urge in Rabbit's song to go and see. Billi and Rabbit were working along the river bank and it took them a long time to get to the right place. By that time Arikk, Kelli's Da, and most of the Village were there. Nortan's Hound, Sunrise, stood looking steadily at the edge of the Forest and Nortan looked sad, but certain. "The Wild took Kelli." He sounded as if he'd said it more than once already.

Billi realised why, her Da wouldn't accept it. "No, how can that happen? The horse came home unmarked. Why would the Wild be here now? It isn't winter and there's plenty of game in the Forest." Arikk shook his head in denial. Then he rounded on the Hunter. "Why didn't you or the Hounds see what happened?"

"There's no flocks or herds out here, Arikk. Just empty pasture and the sign says the horse was galloping." Canitre pointed, but Arikk didn't looking at the sign. "Kelli might have come out here to run the horse for fun, out where there's no crops to harm or rocks in the soil."

"But you could be wrong."

Nortan had kept everyone back and now he raised his voice. "Four really good trackers, the best please." That wasn't Billi because he rarely tracked game, so he stayed back while other Hunters carefully worked over the ground. Eventually all four had done.

Nortan already knew but he asked anyway, for Arikk. "What happened, best ye can tell?"

"The sign says the horse galloped along here, then reared for some reason." They all four pointed where, and Farimer carried on. "The horse bolted across here, but we think 'twas lighter by then. We're more or less certain, but Kelli wouldn't have weighed much so there's little difference especially as it changed gait."

Two Hounds, Midnight and Autumn, worked over the area where the horse reared. Both hit her scent at the right place, near enough for a fall, and followed it towards the nearest big tree. Then both stopped and looked into the Forest, exactly where Sunrise had been looking. "That settles it." Nortan took Arikk's arm. "The Wild took her, but we'll do our best." Six Hunters and Hounds set off including Farimer, Midnight, Canitre and Autumn because those two Hounds were known to be some of the best on a trail.

"But why would the horse rear? 'Twas a gentle creature, but big enough to stand it's ground." Arikk still wouldn't let it go.

"We've no idea, Arikk. It could have been spooked by the predator's scent, a rabbit, or a bit of grass on the wind. The horse certainly took off at an angle, away from the trees, but that might be because the predator struck." Nortan kept talking quietly, trying to get Arikk to understand.

"But there's no paw marks, are there?"

"No Arikk, and no sign of a struggle so 'twas big and fast. The creature, probably a big cat, waited in that tree and dropped without warning. She'll never have felt a thing." Nortan carefully avoided what all the Hunters knew. There would have been nobody near enough to hear Kelli's cries even if she stayed conscious. She might have been carried off screaming but her Da wouldn't want to know that.

"But why did she go towards the Forest? Kelli knew better."

"After a fall she'd be stunned, hurt or confused. Perhaps Kelli went to the tree for support if she hurt her leg?" Nortan had an arm round the old Farmer now, and three of his friends were doing their best to get him to come away and leave the Hunters to work.

The six Hunters already in the Forest were followed by another half dozen once they'd collected packs so they could keep going. The first set were hoping the cat had stopped to feed and might still not have finished Kelli, a very slim hope. At the least they might bring her body back for her Da to have a proper pyre and wake.

That became no hope when the second six returned after dark to report that the trail went into a tangle of bushes and trees and didn't come out. They'd even beaten the bushes, a very dangerous occupation if the cat had been trapped in there. Now the Hunters believed the cat had gone up into the trees and moved off because the scent trail stopped. Perhaps it had heard the pursuit, or perhaps the beast obscured any trail back to cubs or a den. Kelli had been taken by the Wild.

The following day was a sombre one in the Village, and all over the Farm. Arikk took it badly which wasn't unexpected, with everyone else hoping he would come to terms with what had happened. He refused to even consider a wake as Kelli might not be gone, just lost in the Forest. Arikk kept asking Hunters to go and find her. Billi wasn't really involved beyond the initial search because he couldn't keep up so the next day he took a wood gathering party out. Arikk came up as they set out and asked him to keep an eye out for Kelli. Billi agreed and waited as the man asked each member of the wood gatherers to do the same. Then Billi shouldered his pack and set out.

Billi had been affected by the general air of hopelessness around the place as everyone wondered how to get Arikk past this. He decided to have a few days at the valley and hope the man felt better by then. Billi didn't know Arikk so he couldn't help the man, and in any case Billi was hopeless at that sort of thing, personal emotions, and knew it. Going to the valley wouldn't help Arikk but nothing Billi did would help the man.

Maybe Arikk wouldn't get over it. Billi remembered as a littlun he'd seen one man who walked around with the weight of the whole Farm on his shoulders. He searched all the time, wandering around unkempt and uncaring. His littlun had fallen in the river and drowned and the man kept saying the littlun could swim, he'd be fine in a while. One day he'd been found in the river. Billi hadn't thought of that for a long time and he really hoped that Arikk didn't end up the same.

Billi made his best pace and the villagers collected wood quickly and quietly with no banter at all, and everyone headed back. When they reached the fields and the first Hunter guards with their Hounds, Billi waved and turned back. As he stepped into the green again Billi began to feel better. He had to stop doing this, using any reason to come out here, but there again next year they could come and live out here. Despite the circumstances, a happy something joined its song to Rabbit's.

* * *

Billi pushed on until dusk, ate a beef sandwich and made camp for the night. He ate his last sandwich in the morning and set straight off. Billi travelled steadily, wanting to get to the lakes and relax. He didn't intend stopping for anything, even hunting if he could manage with a bit of fishing, and could feel himself already relaxing. Then suddenly, late morning, Rabbit's song gained a different note and seemed uneasy. Billi couldn't understand because the song said warning but not prey. Rabbit didn't sound the ambush warning, nor anything Billi could make sense of.

Rabbit's song was never specific, but usually easy to understand when combined with body language and any signs Billi picked up. No other Hunter understood their Hound any better, which Billi knew because occasionally Hunters discussed it. They compared how it felt sometimes, and tried to work out if the song, voice or hum of Hounds had once been more, or could be more. Billi thought Rabbit's might be clearer than many, easier to understand, from what others said.

Often Rabbit's song seemed more companionship than anything, especially when travelling like this and the Hound's joy in the green always gave a lift to Billi's step. Now the song sounded worried and confused, and Rabbit kept looking back. Billi slowed a little, and debated going to see, but couldn't detect an urgent need to do so in the song. Eventually, just after midday, Billi heard a strange baying. Not a Hound, more of a howl, and not any creature Billi had heard before. Not wolf or Hound, Billi decided, but maybe a big dog or more than one, which meant Edan. The only big dogs in the Village were Edan's, but Billi couldn't work out why they would be in the Forest?

A Hunter and Hound must have brought them, but Billi couldn't understand why those dogs were along. Sounding off like that, the beasts were challenging the Wild to react, and that would go badly. Stranger still, Rabbit wasn't answering and a Hound would always answer a friend. Did that mean the Hunter and Hound weren't friends? That really set Billi worrying about something else. If Edan had followed Billi into the Forest did that mean the stockman finally persuaded a Hunter to bring his mischief out here?

Billi glanced around for the right place, then carried on to the next bend in the stream. He moved off the grass strip alongside the water, behind a big tree where he had a good view of the bank back to the last bend. Billi settled in to wait because if this group were following him, he should find out why. That would be better done here than letting them follow him all the way to the valley. Billi didn't want Edan there. That would spoil the place somehow, and Billi would never feel truly relaxed again.

Billi removed his pack, had a stretch and made himself comfortable, then sat on the pack with Rabbit laid by his foot. The Forest sounded peaceful and he amused himself by watching the squirrels and other small life that came out once they thought he had gone. A Zigga ran down from a tree for a drink, and Billi smiled as he remembered Ellibeth naming them. During the trips since then he'd reminded himself of all the names for flowers and birds and little animals, as many as he could remember. He heard the sounds again, nearer, and those were definitely big dogs. Worse, from the direction the dogs really were coming up the stream.

Suddenly, in a flicker of fur, the Zigga shot away and Rabbit stirred. The song peaked a little so the followers had come near enough for Rabbit to feel unsure about what to do. "Hush." Billi stood up behind the big tree trunk so he could get a look before they saw him. He could hear some voices and the sound of people breaking twigs as they walked, though they were speaking in hushed tones. Not hushed enough when tramping about in the Forest like that, so what were they doing?

* * *

A group came around the previous bend and the four big dogs on leads were on a scent. That had to be either Billi's or Rabbit's trail but why? Billi looked carefully at the group and they had no Hunter! What were the idiots playing at? At a low rumble from Rabbit the dogs stopped, barking furiously at the noise. Billi rolled his shoulder around the tree trunk and into sight.

"There he is!"

"Where is she?"

"Animal."

"Give her back!"

The shouts weren't easing off so Billi held a hand up and most quietened. "What's the problem?"

"Give her back. Where is she?" Billi recognised Arikk and tried to be gentle, but he had to raise his voice to be heard above the dogs. "I don't know where Kelli is Arikk. The Wild took her. I wish I could help."

"Liar, you've taken her for your new village!" Edan came to the front, with his dogs fastened to his waist and his group of friends clustered round him. Billi recognised some of the others in the party but had no idea why they were here in the Forest. They all looked to be angry at Billi, which really confused him.

"Don't be silly. There's nobody there yet, not until spring and it's not my village." Claiming to be the Eldest didn't seem to be a good idea right now.

"Not anymore." More mystery, from one of Edan's group. The one who'd been about to set into Billi at the dance. Aescon, a youth who didn't want to be a Potter like his Da, or a Farmer, or anything else it seemed.

Billi tried to be reasonable and ignored the mystery statements for now. Getting them safe was more important. "What are you doing out here without a Hunter? The Wild won't allow it."

"Don't give me that nonsense. We've got proper dogs now and don't need a Hound or a Hunter. We've got bows and these dogs will kill any Hound or creature foolish enough to take them on." Billi had heard about Edan spouting this sort of nonsense, about Hounds not really being necessary since a crippled one seemed good enough, but didn't think the idiot really believed it. Edan's friends were nodding, but Billi could feel the amusement in Rabbit's song so he certainly didn't believe Edan.

"I doubt it and the Wild won't care what you say. The Wild will kill you, can't you understand?" Billi shook his head. "Arikk, Kelli isn't here. Go home and grieve before the Wild takes you and the rest as well."

Arikk shook his head violently. "No! You've got her. He found the signs and the dogs followed the scent."

That made no sense to Billi because Hunters and Hounds had looked and found nothing. "What sign?"

"Your stick, the marks under the leaves right where she went, then going off onto the trees and the dogs followed it." Arikk seemed totally certain about that, but then the Farmer wasn't thinking clearly just now.

Billi shook his head, gently. "Possibly followed my scent but not from there. I never stood there because that would have messed up the sign."

"We saw it. He showed us." Another one of the villagers, not one of Edan's little gang so why had he come out here?

"He's just going to lie. Take him to his village and we'll find her. Then we'll finish the cripple and it'll be our village." That Aescon again. Did they intend taking over the lakes? The Great Hunter would kill the dogs at least and the Wild would take everyone else. Then the Forest would move back. Rubyn's future, all gone because of a fool and a grieving old man.

Billi straightened. "Not a chance. First I'm not taking you, and second if I did, the Wild would destroy the place so you can't have it." That was the Law of the Wild. Billi wondered if Edan somehow infected all of them with his daft ideas? The tall stockman seemed to have told himself them often enough to believe.

Edan turned to the group. "See, I told you. The same old story about only the Hunters being allowed to have the benefits. One look and anyone can tell the Wild and Forest would never respect a cripple and his crippled dog if it really is dangerous out here." Edan turned back to Billi. "Well you Hunters are all finished. When we prove we can make our own Village with my dogs, without any precious Hounds, we'll have our own rules and the first is no Hunters. After all, that place is at the end of the Forest." Edan really believed it, the utter conviction in his voice said so.

"Too late, because the landclaims are in. Ellibeth and Gerant have already started work on theirs." Only a bit of bush clearing, but near enough.

"Ellibeth, another maid led astray! Well she's welcome to come. I'm sure we can make some arrangement for a fine maid wanting some company and help with a landclaim." Several laughed and they were all Edan's group. "Especially when we've got your sparkuls to offer." A worm of anger started in Billi. They had no need to talk about Ellibeth like that, again.

"Hey, leave the maid and the landclaims out of it." One of the other villagers spoke up and Billi felt relieved, since it meant they weren't all here for his valley. Those at least might listen to reason and hopefully soon because of the patch of silence over there in the trees where the little creatures were frightened. Then birds started scolding deep in the trees across the stream. At least two Wild hunters had come to look, and Billi hoped they weren't a pack.

"What about my Kelli?" Arikk sounded impatient, he didn't want to talk about other maids or villages.

They were starting to argue but Edan wasn't having that. "I told you, he's got Kelli and he'll tell us where he put her. Then we take the valley and sparkuls and have our own village."

"No, we find Kelli and take her back home." Hurwald, one of those with Arikk, wasn't interested in anything else. Billi hoped they'd argue among themselves and eventually calm down though he had to get them moving back towards the Village soon. Billi briefly wondered if the valley might be nearer but no, Edan wasn't getting anywhere near there!

"He's killed her you fool. That's why he has to die." Rabbit rumbled, a definite threat this time and the dogs lunged on their leads, snarling. Edan's bow came up. "The crippled mutt first."

Billi's bow came up. He barely remembered putting the arrow in but it centred on Edan. "You loose at Rabbit, and you die."

"I don't need an arrow, and you won't hide behind the Hound this time." Edan fumbled with his belt where the leashes were clipped. "Kill it!" Billi hesitated as the four dogs leapt forward, wondering if he should risk ignoring Edan to put a shaft in one? But Rabbit's song surged with confidence and a savage glee so Billi held the half-draw still pointed Edan's way.

The dogs closed rapidly and then Rabbit gave one rumbling snarl and shot forward. As they recoiled from the volume and pure menace of it the Hound struck. One dog hurled into the air, blood jetting as it bounced once and laid threshing and squealing briefly before going still. Another yelped and then the three survivors were gone into the trees. That left just Rabbit, stood there with blood on his jaws and his hackles up.

"No!" Pure shock and disbelief sounded in Edan's voice, and everyone else finally shut up. A good few of them had a bow part raised and Billi tried to watch them all. At least some of the others were either terrified or frozen in shock.

"That's why the Wild allows Hounds and not dogs. Now go home before you all die." Billi wasn't arguing anymore, because Edan had just tried to kill Rabbit!

"No!" That came more as a scream and Edan's bow came up and swung towards Rabbit, now hopping back to Billi. Billi finished his draw and loosed without any conscious decision. The man couldn't be allowed to kill Rabbit. Billi had a big bow even for a Hunter and a man made a big target well inside Billi's usual hunting distance. Edan went over backwards and sprawled with the shaft jutting from his chest.

His legs kicked briefly, he shuddered then he lay still. Nobody saw where the Edan's arrow went because all eyes went to the body, and back to Billi, and a few bows started to lift. Billi already had another shaft ready and Rabbit whirled, all his ruff upright now. A continuous low rumble came from the Hound's throat, and everyone froze like that for a long moment.

When the yelp came Billi almost loosed, but he hadn't picked a target since none of the bows were full drawn. The yelp came from the Forest on the other side of the stream where one of the dogs had gone. Moments later the other two came out of the trees this side and dived into the middle of the men where they cowered, whining. "What was that?" Hurwald stared across the stream, his face drawn and pale.

"The Wild." Billi thought the something must be big, since that wasn't a small dog but it hadn't had the chance to fight. The one yelp had been cut off short.

"Something bit her leg off!" Billi looked and yes, half of one dog's foreleg had been cleanly removed and blood poured out.

"Hopefully Rabbit or it'll follow the blood trail. Bind that or the dog will die, and binding will stop it leaving a trail for the Wild." The youth bent and worked on the dog with another helping to hold the injured animal. The rest were looking from the dead dog to the dead man to the injured dog and back to Billi and Rabbit. That had certainly stopped all the shouting and such but Billi had a sick feeling in his gut. This wasn't holding a man's neck. Billi had killed a man sure as he'd killed every deer he'd loosed at.

"Why did you do that?" Aescon finally spoke, and with a stupid question really. Billi sighed, then clenched his muscles a moment as his gut rebelled.

"Edan's dogs tried to kill Rabbit so my Hound killed one. Then Edan tried to kill Rabbit and I stopped him. He'd threatened to kill me; what did you think I'd do?"

"But how could you? You're. Your dog. I mean look at it. A cripple." The man sort of gestured at Rabbit and he seemed really confused but Billi had no time for this, had the idiots forgotten?

"I'd worry more about what killed the other dog. Something big." All eyes swung to the other side of the stream and bows came up. "Don't be stupid. If you hit it with those you've got to follow it and finish it. You all know the Law of the Wild. Do you want to follow something wounded and big through the Forest? I don't and if you hit it, I won't. The Wild can have you." Billi had started to get angry as well as sick and he felt angry because these idiots had followed a bigger one. Now the bigger one had Billi's arrow in him and shunning wouldn't fix this.

A deep, blood-curdling snarl sounded from the other side of the stream and the bushes moved. Billi caught sight of a patch of black gleaming pelt as something massive pushed through almost in sight and then disappeared. People were exclaiming, and some were looking back down the stream the way they came. If any of them ran the beast would chase, because it wouldn't be able to help it. "Stand still!"

The bows, spears and dogs wouldn't even slow this beast up because they'd attracted the Great Hunter! Billi really hoped it didn't attack, because he didn't want to die. His guts churned again. Not now when life had been going so well. If the Great Hunter attacked the party Billi wouldn't be able to stand and let it kill them, but even if he got a shaft into its ribs that killed it eventually, the beast was too close. The Great Hunter would kill him and Rabbit before it died.

Though the beast had stopped all the threats aimed at Billi since everyone now stared at the bushes. "What was that?" Well at least the stupid idiot had some respect in his voice now. Billi wasn't feeling tolerant since they'd just ruined his lovely new life.

"That is the Wild, Aescon, because some stupid idiot thought he could come into the Forest with dogs and a bunch of other idiots came with him." Billi gave a short laugh. "He's my neighbour. Since finding the valley I've worked out an agreement with him, and you lot have just trampled right through it."

"That's your neighbour? You're insane." Aescon stared, horrified.

"No. I didn't wander into the Forest with four dogs and an idiot in charge. That's insane." Billi really had lost any patience with this fool, and the churning kept getting worse, and he daren't let the bow slacken. "That beast doesn't lie about me, or try to steal my landclaim, or spread rumours about the innocent. That makes him a better neighbour than some." Billi knew the bitterness showed, and didn't care anymore.

"What about my Kelli?" Arikk's quiet voice sounded plaintive, and confused.

"The Wild took her." Billi gentled his tone. "I am truly sorry." He was. Billi wasn't angry with Arikk. Edan and his stupid friends had led the poor man out here where he might easily die.

"But he said." Arikk looked round, wide-eyed. "The Wild took her? That took her?" Real shock stopped him, and a dawning horror showed in his eyes as Arikk looked round the group hoping for a different answer. Billi realised that in common with most villagers Arikk had never seen a live Wild predator.

"Not that one. He lives further away and those dogs probably attracted him. But yes Arikk, something like that took her." Billi saw the man's face crumple.

"The Wild took her." Arikk burst into tears. Not the loud sobbing sort, but a steady, silent flood of despair as his shoulders shook. Hurwald put a hand on his shoulder and others moved closer.

"What do we do?" At last someone had realised they were in trouble, Seifort, the youth who'd fixed the dog. "We were wrong and I'm sorry Billi. Edan showed us proof and well, Arikk seemed so sure as well." He shrugged unhappily. "It all made sense at the time, but he said nothing about killing or taking villages. I'm sorry."

Billi didn't even answer the reasoning or apology. "Put all your bows on the floor, arrows as well, and stand back off them. Take Edan with you."

Aescon gestured at the dead dog. "What about the dog?"

"Tithe for the Wild. Hope that it's enough." Billi was either going to be sick or lose his temper soon. They were still arguing with a Great Hunter at the most two bounds away!

"What about the bows? We'll be defenceless." Billi didn't even have to answer Aescon since Seifort did it for him.

"The Law of the Wild, only a Hunter with a Hound can carry a bow in the Forest. Worse still, that thing won't notice our bows. Look at what the Hunter's pulling and he doesn't think that'll stop it. These are toys but he doesn't want them pointing at his back." The youth threw his bow down. "I'm betting my life Billi is the best bet for getting me home because he's a Hunter. That's if he'll take us since some of us just threatened to kill the man, and tried to kill his Hound."

The bitterness in that wasn't aimed at Billi. More bows followed, and quivers and a pitchfork. Two spears followed, and another pitchfork. The youth stepped back and someone eased Arikk that way, and slowly most of the group dropped their bows or spears and moved back. Those left were Edan's group and they weren't convinced. The two surviving dogs were. They'd gone back with the other villagers but they were frightened of Rabbit, not the Wild.

"Why should we give up our bows? What are you going to do with us, you or that animal?" Aescon again, and Billi's patience snapped completely.

"I'm going to take those people home, because they're worth saving. Keep the damn bows and stay. If the Wild eats you at least I'll be shut of you all. But if you want to live, PUT THE DAMN BOWS DOWN!" Billi shouted the last bit, and Rabbit had picked up his anger of course and gave a blood-curdling snarl. The Hound had put up with enough as well.

Billi wasn't surprised by the anger in the song, or the eagerness to do something about it. What did surprise him was the rumbling growl from the bushes on the other side of the stream! A clear threat but against Billi and Rabbit or the others? Billi didn't know if the growl came in reply to his and Rabbit's anger, or the beast had realised the other group had no Hunter.

The group, even Edan's friends, had no doubt at all. Bows and quivers and two spears hit the floor and the first ones encouraged anyone a bit slow. They didn't even look at the Billi's bow and the Hound because everyone's attention stayed on the bushes, still mercifully undisturbed. The last couple of bows and the quivers hit the floor, four of them picked up Edan, and the six of them moved back to join the rest.

Rabbit followed until he stood over the weapons and Billi felt the savage edge go off the song. Rabbit's ruff went down a bit, and Billi relaxed a little as well. He finally eased right off his bow, and removed the shaft. Billi picked up his crutch and turned to get his pack but came over dizzy and put a hand on the tree. Then Billi was thoroughly and violently sick. He heaved until he had nothing left, and then coughed and spluttered and spat some more. Billi turned and glared at the group, daring someone to make a smart remark. They were all still staring at the bushes and Billi wasn't even sure they'd noticed. Well in that case they could wait a moment.

* * *

Billi rinsed his mouth out a couple of times and had a long drink of the cold water, which settled him a bit. Then he shouldered his pack and put the bow over his shoulder, still strung. Billi picked up his spear in his free hand, set his crutch right, and headed over to the rest. The churning had gone, replaced by a heaviness in Billi's heart. He'd be going back to the Village now and could already feel the accusing eyes because he'd just killed a man. There'd be no doubt where the looks were aimed this time, and Billi could already feel the eyes on his back.

The crowd watched him approach and then one pointed, and another, and several were muttering. "What's that?" One of the older men with Arikk, another Farmer Billi thought, spoke up. "What's that, on your crutch, and on your peg?"

"What? Nothing." Billi watched them closely, wondering what they were going to come up with now. He could feel Rabbit, poised, on edge again. He waved the end of his crutch and put it back down.

"That round bit on the end. How long's that been there?" At least half the others were looking now.

Billi wondered why the little wooden foot seemed so interesting? They were all looking at it now, even Edan's idiots. "Months. I can't remember. Ask Syman because he carved it for out here where the ground is softer. I don't use it around the Village because the track is gravelled." Billi just wanted to get going away from the dead dog and blood, away from the gathering Wild, and especially away from the big black beast in the bushes.

The man wasn't looking at Billi now, he looked at Edan's body. "The stinking rotten little swine! If he wasn't dead, I'd kill him myself!" He half moved to kick out at the body, then stopped.

Billi didn't want to think about Edan. This man was too late because Billi had already done it, killed Edan and in spite of everything Billi wished he'd missed for once and wounded the man. "Too late, now can we move away from the blood and body before something else gets hungry?" That stopped all talk of crutches and got them moving!

The group headed away, muttering among themselves and glancing at Rabbit and Billi but keeping ahead of both. Billi looked at the bushes before he left and waved at the body of the dog, and the half leg he could now see. "Tithe." He really hoped the beast accepted the gesture even if the words meant nothing to it.

* * *

They trekked steadily, stopping occasionally for a breather and drink before pushing on. Billi started getting worried again and not just about the Wild this time. Edan's group seemed to have recovered from their scare and their glares were making Billi nervous, since all six still had their belt knives. He couldn't leave them with nothing if the Wild did decide that one Hunter and Hound wasn't enough of an escort. Then Edan's friends started murmuring in a group and looking at Billi, especially when they thought he was looking elsewhere.

Billi took a firm hold on the spear. He had the feeling that once the party came near enough to safety for the bunch of them to feel secure those six would have a go. Despite his spear they might swamp him and get a knife into him. Then even if Rabbit fought them off the Hound would just lay down with his Hunter and die as well, which would be the final injustice since the Hound had done nothing except defend himself against the dogs.

Before that Billi had a more immediate worry. This group wouldn't be out of the Forest by dark because Billi would hold them up. He couldn't tell them to make a run for it, because from the absolute lack of game or even small animals at least one something still stalked them. Billi didn't think the Great Hunter had followed. Hopefully that had been satisfied with another dog though the spiked collar might have slowed it briefly. Which briefly took Billi's mind off the worry about tonight, and churning over Edan's death. He realised that Rabbit must have seen the collars and understood, since he'd torn out one dog's belly and bit the leg off the other. Billi had always thought Rabbit a wonder, but even he'd not expected the speed with which the Hound had scattered the dogs. Now Billi realised Rabbit had thought it through as well.

Then Billi went back to worrying about the coming night with over a score of unhappy men and one Hound and a Hunter, all in a circle of fires. If Billi dozed or something distracted Rabbit either the Wild or the men might strike. Billi could have been seriously tempted to put them in a circle of fires and then camp away from the lot. At least then only the Wild would threaten him and Billi could handle that overnight but no, he just couldn't leave them to it. Arikk at least couldn't be blamed. The bereaved Da plodded along being steered by one of the others, and every so often the man's eyes would stream tears again. He hadn't said a word since they started back. Billi thought that at least some of those with him only came to look after Arikk. Billi sighed, so he couldn't let the Wild take them either. Why couldn't anything be straightforward?

The afternoon wore on and became evening. Now and then Billi would stop and take a drink and have a breather. No point in rushing because he wouldn't get near enough home by dark. Eventually Billi judged it late enough. "That's it for tonight. You must all gather firewood now. A lot, as much as you possibly can, big or small, to keep the fires going all night."

"Why can't we keep going through the night?" Aescon just never gave up.

Billi didn't even argue. "Off you go. I'm stopping here, and I reckon those two dogs have got the sense to do the same." Billi turned to the rest. "There are at least two Wild predators stalking us now. This group is too large for just one Hunter and Hound to escort and the Wild is gathering. I can't stop them in the dark, but fire should."

"Good enough for me." Hurwald looked around. "If someone keeps an eye on Arikk so he don't wander off, I'll get started gathering wood."

"I'll give you a hand." Seifort moved off towards a fallen branch. One man stayed with Arikk, and the rest started picking up branches and sticks, even Aescon and his cronies after a brief hesitation.

"Keep where I can see you, and if I tell you to back away from somewhere, just do it." Billi had an arrow in his bow and Rabbit went on full alert, sifting the Forest noises and scents. At least one something kept trying to creep closer according to Rabbit's song. Billi faced that way but kept glancing round.

It didn't make Billi feel better when some of Edan's lot hefted the branches they picked up, and they weren't thinking of firewood. Rabbit noticed that as well and Billi could feel the tense watchfulness in the song. He knew his own uneasiness would only feed Rabbit's tension but couldn't help that. There were more than a few hairs on Rabbit's ruff up all the time now and not just because of the men, because more predators had gathered in the growing shadows. Billi pointed at the wide swathe of grass bank next to the water. "Build a ring of fires, close together. Small and close is better than one big one. Don't light them yet. Put one here, right on the bank."

"That leaves a gap by the stream." Seifort sounded worried rather than causing trouble so Billi gave him the reason.

"We've not enough wood to keep a complete ring going all night. I'll be stood here with Rabbit, next to the single fire and the stream and the Wild will be less keen to come past us." Billi looked around, assessing. "The fires are big enough now. Put the rest of the wood just inside the fires, where it can be used to feed them. Don't use it up too fast."

They sat and anyone with some food ate it. The rest would sleep hungry because Billi hadn't hunted. He had a sudden insane vision of himself trying to tickle fish for supper while Rabbit kept that lot off him. Anyway, Billi's stomach didn't fancy food just now. They sat until Billi thought it too dark for safety. "That'll do." Billi lit the small fire on the bank. "Collect a brand from here and light them all."

As they closed in to get the lit brands, Billi thought the moment had come. Edan's lot were tensed, their makeshift clubs in their hands as they came for their fire. Then from behind them Hurwald spoke up. "Don't be so damn stupid. I'm not sleeping in the Forest without a Hunter and Hound, so ye back off." It was enough, since Edan's gang didn't seem confident the rest were going to stay out of it. The clubs went onto the firewood heaps, for now.

Everyone settled in, more or less because now the whole group except Arikk were frightened. Billi could understand the cries of fear and anxiety when the fires lit up eyes watching from the darkness, but only one pair really worried him. Billi brought up his bow and that pair backed off. Billi just knew this would be a long night.

The time dragged because although he sat on his pack Billi daren't sit on the floor and rest, let alone lie down. He'd never get up fast enough to defend himself or anyone else. Edan's friends sat in a tight group muttering away to themselves, while the rest made another, slightly looser group around Arikk. Billi and Rabbit sat on their own and Billi churned it over and over. He'd killed a man, a man who wasn't even aiming the bow at him.

At least the edge in the song helped Billi keep awake. Rabbit's spike of anxiety each time he heard or sensed something brought Billi alert every time. Sometime just before dawn the sheer brightness of the alert brought Billi to his feet. At least the threat wasn't Aescon's men, not yet. Billi half-drew the arrow in his bow and faced the right direction, and questions came from both groups. "Shut up. I need to hear."

Rabbit's song faltered, and seemed puzzled, and then Rabbit raised his head and bayed, loud and clear! There were shouts from some of the men, and some cringed away. The two dogs whined and crouched low but Billi felt his spirits soar. The song rose clear and bright and joyful! Whoever was out there, Rabbit knew them as a friend. Billi listened carefully but couldn't hear anything, so the whoever were a long way away.

Then Billi noticed the group around Edan's body. Poised. He wasn't going to let them know he had friends coming. "All of you shut up and sit down. I need a clear view since I'd rather not stick an arrow in someone now but I'll not hesitate to try and aim past you if some beast comes out of the Forest." There were some startled glances and mutters, but at least that got them all sat again.

Better still, the alert gave Billi a reason to be up on his foot with an arrow in his bow with nobody wondering why. For a little longer Billi stood, listening, and then he heard something faint. Rabbit bayed again, full-throated, his call ringing out across the Forest. The replies were the same, even if faint, and there were a lot of them! Hounds, and presumably Hunters. Billi wondered what so many were doing out here and if they believed the same nonsense as Edan did?

Then sense prevailed. No, or they would have been in this group. The Hunters had probably come to try and save this group when someone found out they'd gone without Hounds. But now Billi worried about what the Hunters would say about the body. He stood there with an arrow in the bow as Rabbit periodically bayed and the replies grew closer. The others could hear the Hounds coming now and obviously the Hunters and Hounds knew where this group were. Billi watched the tension leave the group around the body.

His own tension grew as the sounds came clearer. Rabbit's tail started wagging now so he knew some of the Hounds and Billi felt a bit more hopeful, right up until they came into the firelight. He recognised one of the lead Hounds as Autumn, Canitre's golden brown Hound so Canitre, Edan's Da, would be right behind. Edan's body lay plain enough on the ground with Edan's friends grouped around it and then Billi could see Canitre. The Hunter looked at the group and the body with puzzlement and growing concern, moving forward to see better.

The rest of the Hunters were a mixture of puzzled and angry though as yet their anger seemed to be directed at the group. Billi relaxed and unstrung his bow, and put the arrow back into the quiver. This wouldn't be that sort of struggle. He sat on his pack as exhaustion swept in. "What happened?" Billi looked up at Nortan, Barimar and Cynel.

But Aescon spoke up before Billi could answer. "He killed Edan!" Canitre moved forward far enough and the group stepped aside. The shaft still stuck out of Edan's chest, clearly visible in the firelight and Canitre swung back, disbelief and grief warring for control.

"He threatened to kill me, then he tried to kill Rabbit." Billi felt sorry he'd killed the man, but not of the reason.

"It's true, and I'm not proud to be part of it. We came to get Kelli and take back the Hunter to answer for it, but she isn't here and Edan set the dogs on Rabbit. Then when Rabbit killed one and scattered the others, Edan tried to kill the Hound, so Billi put an arrow in him." There were several glances at Rabbit, checking for damage Billi thought, and Canitre swung on the speaker, Seifort.

"Kelli? Why would she be here? The Wild took her." Then he seemed to notice Arikk for the first time. "Arikk, what are you doing out here?"

"He said my Kelli was here. But I saw it, I saw the Wild. It took my Kelli." The tears started again but Hurwald, the one with his arm around Arikk, took it up. Billi also got part of the full story at last.

"We were told Billi had taken Kelli, because he wanted a maid for his new village and no proper maid would touch him. Edan showed us the marks of Billi's stick, and then his dogs followed the scent. He said the Hounds wouldn't follow a Hunter or a Hound, but his dogs would and he'd get Kelli back. I wasn't sure but the stick marks were there." The man glanced at the body and spat on the ground. "Except they weren't Billi's crutch. It's got something on the end and the other's not just a peg, which means that rat did it on purpose with a branch or something. Sorry Canitre, but if Billi hadn't done it I might've killed the little shite for doing that to Arikk, once I knew."

The Hunters were looking properly at the group now, and Cynel pointed. "You came out with knives and four dogs?"

"What did he mean, he saw the Wild?"

"Are you all stupid or drunk?"

"Where's the other dogs?"

Barimar snorted. "Why would Billi need to steal a maid? He's beating them off with a stick."

"What are you doing here?" The last Hunter stared at the youth, Seifort.

Seifort shuffled a bit before answering. "Sorry Da, it all made sense at the time and the dogs were hot on the scent and I was there with my bow so I came along." The youth really did sound apologetic. He must have been chewing it over and obviously expected to be in a lot of trouble.

Robbin looked around. "Where's the bow now?"

"He made us all give them up so we had no defence again his beast." Aescon had started again. Eyes swung to Rabbit. "Not that crippled thing, the big black one out there. It took the dog. It's his neighbour. The cripple is in league with the Wild and he probably gave them Kelli." The man went down, staring up in shock and putting a hand to his bloody mouth as Hurwald stood over him.

"You ever let your lying mouth say her name again and I'll cut your tongue out. Whatever that was, if Billi hadn't been here it would have taken us all and he surely didn't call it. That shite's dogs did." The farmer went back to Arikk.

"Neighbour? The Great Hunter is here?" Eddmune's bow came half up but he relaxed again and glanced at his Hound. "No, something is but not a Great Hunter." Some of the other Hunters were looking at Eddmune. "Sorry Billi, they all need to know now." He turned to the rest. "Billi really does have a Great Hunter as a neighbour and I've seen the pug marks. It leaves Billi's hut and the inside of the valley alone, and it tolerated us so the Wild has made a decision. The valley is Farm, not Forest."

The Hunters were full of questions now but weren't asking Billi because they had Eddmune and Mikkel right in among them. Arikk spoke quietly to another Hunter, Nortan had his head together with another villager and the Seifort kept talking fast to his Da. Canitre went on one knee by Edan, head bowed. Nobody even looked at Billi anymore.

Billi picked up his pack with his free hand, stumped over to a small tree, propped his pack against it and sat down with a sigh. Billi leaned back against the pack, and Rabbit laid next to him and sighed as well. That wasn't quite enough for a smile but it helped Billi. Farimer came across and gestured to the ground and Billi waved 'go ahead' so the Hunter sat.

"Bit of a mess."

Billi sighed again. "Just a bit. I didn't have a choice."

Farimer nodded. "From the sounds of some of that, I might have been tempted to leave the lot out here."

Billi shrugged. "I couldn't run fast enough."

Farimer snorted. "And it never crossed your mind."

Billi put a hand on Rabbit's head. "For a moment when they tried to kill Rabbit."

Farimer reached out to ruffle Midnight's ears. "I might have done the same, if someone went for Midnight. Did the dogs really go for Rabbit, because even the Traders' dogs won't usually tackle a Hound?"

"I thought about it a bit on the way back. Edan had to have trained them and maybe he kept them away from Hounds, so they never met one." They both looked over to where the two big dogs were trying to be invisible, crouched down looking nervously from one to another of the Hounds walking around. "I think they've learned respect now."

"Aye. Those collars aren't usual, and would protect them from a dog and maybe help against some of the Wild hunters. No use against a Hound though." Farimer stroked Midnight. "The Eldest will want to talk to you when we get back. Are you coming with us?"

Billi stared, surprised. "I have a choice?"

"Well yes. This is outside the Farm and partway to your valley, where I've heard you're the Eldest, so right here is as much your place as the Village's. You don't have to come and anyway there are enough others to tell the tale." Farimer glanced over. "I think young Seifort is going to tell it just as it happened because Robbin isn't happy." Robbin had a face like thunder, and kept asking Seifort more questions.

"Seifort isn't too bad. He reminded them all of the Law and told them to chuck away the bows, and was the first to do it. That youth just got caught up in whatever this lot thought they were doing." Billi thought about it. "I've just killed a man, and it doesn't sit well. I'd rather have a bit of time in the green before all the eyes are watching, enough time so everyone knows the full story before I have to tramp through the Village." Billi sighed. "There's going to be a lot of talk before it's all sorted, and folk will be suspecting this and that. I'll come in, and I'll be in the valley if you want me first, but if it's going to be allowed I'd rather have a bit of peace first."

"Aye, we all feel that sometimes, Hunters that is. It's the call of the Forest, the green you call it? That's as good a name as any and we all go on a hunt when we don't really need to, looking for peace when we want to sort out a bit of a problem without a lot of folk nattering." Farimer got up, "I'll tell them. The Hunters will understand, and I don't care much about

Billi went over it all again and again and again for the next three days and he still couldn't see a way round it. He couldn't have run because he couldn't move fast enough and anyway the dogs would track him. Billi definitely couldn't lead Edan's group here and destroy everyone's dreams of new landclaims. Then when Edan went to kill Rabbit only an arrow could stop him. That made Billi a murderer. He'd killed a man who wasn't actually threatening to kill him, not right then. Though Billi couldn't have let the man kill Rabbit. Then Billi's mind went off round the whole circle again.

* * *

On the sixth morning, following another restless night attempting to find a way out of the mental maze, a zing in the song woke Billi. Enthusiastic tail wagging by Rabbit, then a cheery hail, told him Hektor had arrived with the dawn. Billi threw on a coat and trews and came out, heading for the entrance to the valley and wondering why Hektor hadn't come straight in. Then he stopped, mouth opened to greet the young Hunter. Hektor stood there, but with Cynel, Mikkel and Canitre! Edan's Da? Billi braced, because this wouldn't be good. "Welcome. Come in, please." Billi gestured to the valley. As the four came over rise beside the dam and walked nearer Canitre stepped ahead.

"'Tis time to come back Billi. For Arikk and for Kelli's wake if nothing else. Arikk has accepted she's gone and it would be better if you were there. After all," Canitre managed a faint smile but it took an effort, "you'd be missed from the dancing."

"Look, Canitre, I'm sorry, I really am but…"

The Hunter raised his hand to stop Billi. "But there was no other way. I've run it around myself and I've heard everything everyone's got to say and if anyone's to blame it's me." Canitre looked round at the disagreements from the other three Hunters. "I should have slapped him down harder after the Wood Hunt, and maybe before to take some of the arrogance out of him. But that just seemed a part of him, that belief that he could do anything, and seemed to be just overconfidence." Canitre shrugged. "That's not unusual in a youth. Then Edan just couldn't accept he didn't get a Hound, and now maybe we know why he didn't. It could be something in him, or what he said out in the Forest, or both, but it wasn't you." Canitre sighed. "After all, who suggested Hektor for the spear?"

"Mandy. I asked for the steadiest and she said Hektor. Then he really was steady. I kept checking and he was always looking back, always watching with the spear ready." Billi shrugged. "That's why he got the chance."

"And you not wanting to show your stump with everyone there. We all know Billi. I've asked Mandy and others, at the time and now again." Canitre sighed. "But you've said it, Hektor earned his chance."

Mikkel slapped the Hektor on the back. "Wish I'd seen that." Billi opened his mouth but Canitre raised a hand again. Edan's Da had something to get off his chest so Billi held his peace.

"Let me finish now. His Ma encouraged the foolishness and I let her, and you seemed to have settled the business about your stock and gates well enough. I set him up in the stockyard so Edan would be occupied but didn't have to work in the fields. He was out with the Hounds on guard and might still have got one. Then he didn't and he found friends who would sit with him over a few ales so I let his Ma slip him the silver for the ale, and for the dogs and the horses after Hektor gave him a beating."

Canitre looked back. "Sorry about that Hektor; please tell your lass, Bliss. I should've done it but I just couldn't believe he'd said some of those things." Hektor waved him off and the Hunter turned back. "Then there was all the trouble with those men and your store, but it wasn't actually Edan and you seemed to have sorted that out. I thought Edan had settled, and 'twas his friends causing the trouble. Right up to the Harvestfest and from what he said then, well it was obvious he'd been a lot worse than I'd thought he could be. You did well, Billi, and so did Rabbit, there was a brawl coming and you stopped it. So I did what I should have done before." The man looked stricken. This was tearing him up but he was determined to get it out.

"Even after the shunning his Ma slipped Edan silver but not where I'd catch her and for a bit he seemed to be quiet, even if he had daft ideas about the dogs and horses. Those kept him occupied after the maids turned away. That hit him hard, the maids, they'd always liked him before." Canitre sighed, a long, sad sound. He looked around the valley. "I'd no idea he'd been plotting this nonsense about setting up without a Hunter but 'twas planned for a while, maybe since the first talk of the lakes. Those fools really did intend to start up a place without Hunters because the dogs would protect it. Edan should have known better."

"He planned to bring all those folk into the Wild?" Billi spoke without thought, because that horrified him. To risk so many lives!

"No, not so many. From what they've said, Edan just took the chance when it came along, to get rid of you and take over. Edan persuaded Arikk you'd took his maid and enough came along to support the poor man." The Hunter sighed. "Enough to give them a strong party, though Edan and Aescon didn't mention the killing or village."

"But to come without a Hunter?" Billi couldn't get past that bit.

Canitre scowled. "Edan's friends really believed that those dogs and all the bows were enough. Rabbit came as a terrible shock to them." The Hunter put his hand down to stroke the strong back leaning against him in a show of support. "We always forget that part, how strong and fierce they are, because they are our friends, but some of those men will never go near a Hound again."

Billi scowled. "They didn't before, but caused plenty of trouble. I don't reckon that Aescon has learned much."

"More than ye think, maybe. Edan's cronies were badly shaken and we had it all out of them afore they recovered. My littlun or not, my kin or not, if Edan had threatened to kill me and then drawn his bow on Autumn I might have done the same. So I might avoid ye a bit, because of the memory, but it's not blame." Canitre put out his arm and they clasped arms briefly, then he turned and went back out of the valley. Billi started after him but Cynel caught his arm.

"He needs the Forest, Billi. 'Tis a hard thing to face and harder to admit and he'll need to walk a bit." Well that's what Billi came here for, so he could understand that well enough.

"I hope Canitre has better luck sorting it out." Billi really meant that because he still didn't feel right about killing.

"Ellibeth said that." Billi stared at Hektor. "She said you'd be sat by the water or on the hillside, staring into the sky or the lake and going round and round it all. You'd be trying to find a way out of it and there wasn't one, Billi. The Eldest and the elders agree." Hektor's voice had some grim satisfaction in it. "It don't matter if Aescon learned any lessons, since the six of them are banished. They're sat waiting for a caravan since none have a Hound."

Mikkel spoke up. "Canitre didn't give you the rest. Those fools, especially Aescon, believed that you and Rabbit were cripples and useless. If the Wild could accept you two out here then big dogs and a lot of bows were better, especially out here at the end of the Forest. They were sure the dogs could take Rabbit, and what he did has seriously frightened some of them." Mikkel also had some satisfaction in his voice at that. "Edan simply couldn't stand you having a Hound, even what he considered to be a crippled, useless one. Not when he didn't get one. It ate him up and so he used every chance to cause you trouble."

Hektor gestured around him. "Then you had a whole new valley, and were going to be an Elder, and the idiots thought they'd just take the lot." He sighed. "Those with Arikk did just follow a last hope for Kelli because Edan did some fast talking. Arikk and his friends were tricked, very deliberately. Some of Arikk's kin might kill another of that bunch if they get the chance for feeding Arikk's hopes and bringing him out here." Hektor gestured at the crutch. "One of them, Edan they claim, used a branch to make crutch marks off into the forest from the tree."

"Good job they'd never really looked at the end you've got now. Edan and probably Aescon persuaded Arikk you'd taken Kelli alive." Cynel's lip lifted in scorn. "They're a sorry bunch now, sat in the hall because the elders have warned them. If they go out into the Village they might not come back."

Hektor shrugged. "I suppose we'll stick them in a shed for the wake if they haven't left." The young man's face cleared, and he smiled. "Anyway, I'm here under threat because my lass has word from her Sis. Ellibeth is going to dance round the post in the hall at the wake and there'll be trouble if there isn't a bearr to catch her." He laughed at the expression on Billi's face.

Then Billi felt himself blush, and Cynel laughed as well. "Don't blame Hektor, he's not alone. I've been told twice since we decided to come that I'd better bring a bear back for the dance. You'd better practice running ssrrong bearr, because word of this place is spreading and it wasn't the same maid telling me each time."

"Three maids told me, which is embarrassing since I'm not caught myself and apparently not a suitable dancing bearr." Mikkel didn't seem upset, not from his grin.

"But I killed a man." Billi began to hope, but a killing was a big thing, bigger than bear dancing.

"His own Da just said he might have done the same. Don't make him go through that for no reason, Billi. You won't forget, but nobody's going to lie awake worrying you'll murder them in their beds. We had a dozen volunteers to come and get you. A few villagers might look a bit sideways but nary a Hunter will." Cynel shrugged his shoulders. "Ye can't threaten a Hound or the Hunter will step in, ye can't threaten a Hunter or the Hound will. If ye threaten both? The Hounds are content, the Wild is content, the Hunters are content, the Eldest is content." Cynel slapped Billi on the back. "Let it lie."

"Anyway, if we hurry back by tomorrow night there'll be fresh bread and steak and kidney pie, I've heard." Hektor grinned. "I was told if you wavered, to mention it." Billi heaved a big sigh of relief. They all meant it.

"I'd best get my pack then, unless you want breakfast?" Because Billi didn't think they'd make it by then, despite that pie sounding very tempting.

Hektor shook his head. "Oh no, if you ever catch a maid you'll know it's best to do what you're told, and I've been told by tomorrow night." Cynel agreed, once a maid became a lass she also became a tyrant but neither seemed sorry to be under the heel.

Billi smiled a little in spite of himself. He went in to get his pack and the cold meat left from the previous night, and Hektor waved eight fresh fish as he came out. "For later, to save time, come on!"

They did indeed make good time because the three Hunters made sure Billi didn't need to stop, except briefly to eat. They hunted in turns to feed the Hounds and the group, and divided the contents of Billi's pack between them for speed. As darkness came on Mikkel pushed ahead and by the time Billi and the other two arrived had a cheerful fire blazing away and supper cooked.

The faintest of streaks showed that dawn might be breaking soon when Hektor and a cheerful Rabbit's song rousted Billi out of his furs.

He set off still eating breakfast. The Hunters chivvied Billi on by pointing out that he needed to toughen up for the wake since the bear had a lot of very lively maids to catch. If he kept one he'd need even more strength. That kept Billi's mind occupied and also kept him embarrassed. Hektor in particular seemed to find the chasing and catching jokes very funny.

The sky had turned black with a hint of red and the sun barely showed on the horizon as the group left the trees and Billi had just made the fastest trip ever, for him. His leg and the shoulder using the crutch were feeling it despite carrying little in his pack but Billi found a bit more energy at the sight of the smoke from his hut, twin lines.

"Here, apparently Rubyn will be disappointed if you forget." Mikkel and Cynel laughed when Hektor handed over a selection of blooms and feathers. "I have to bring some back now, or get my ears frayed." The three Hunters bid Billi goodnight, claimed they had to report in to avoid a scolding, and set off down the lane laughing. Spots barked, Rabbit replied and when the door opened there stood Ellibeth, with pie and bread as promised according to the lovely smells.

She helped him off with his coat and jacket, then as he turned from hanging them she said "Welcome home Billi," and hugged him. Billi hugged back because he really was pleased to be home and Ellibeth gave a little yelp, and looked up with a smile. "Oh no, I've been caught." Before Billi could reply there were soft lips on his and he tightened his arms and bussed her very firmly.

Definitely for a bit longer than might be proper. Then Ellibeth stepped back with two spots of colour in her cheeks and a smile, and tapped Billi on the chest. "Naughty bear. Playing on a maid's sympathy to catch her for a bussing. Naughty, crafty bear." She turned and headed for the fire. "Now sit down before I bring your cider or I might not dare come near." But Billi could hear the laughter in her voice.

So Billi sat and as he did the door burst open and Rubyn flew in from the bedroom. "I've put them all away Ma. Now can I talk to Billi?"

Between listening to a blow by blow of Rubyn's life Billi ate a big portion of pie and a slice of warm bread and butter with some cheese. 'Twas the first of Rubyn's cheese but not with his special cloth. He was making a proper one with that, bigger because the cloth was bigger and it would take time. When it was done the cheese would be firm and delicious, his Ma said so.

Ma watched with mischief in her eyes since she had to have given him exactly that description, and Billi tried hard not to laugh. Then Rubyn pounced on the flowers and feathers, and for the first time Billi realised Ellibeth steered him a little when choosing what blooms would stay here in the hut and which would go to Viktor's. Full darkness had fallen by the time he walked them to Viktor's door and bid them goodnight. Going back home Billi felt much more at peace than at any time since losing that arrow. Though now he felt bit of a mess really since he had two homes and they both pulled hard. Billi still worried about the reaction of the villagers, but would deal with it tomorrow.

* * *

The Eldest had her talk with Billi the following morning and the elders made much of it happening between the lakes and the Village. Kina shrugged. "That means the whole affair might be your problem to deal with anyway. We assumed you didn't want those six out there?"

Billi didn't hesitate. "No I do not. I did wonder about trying to take the whole group that way to keep everyone safe. I debated if we might get there quicker than back here, but I don't want them six to even see the valley."

Kina spread her hands. "That's it then. Banished from the lakes and banished from Trail's End means the Wild or a caravan. They've no Hound so they'd best take the first caravan out."

Guthra smirked. "Some have suggested the Wild without an option, and they can take those two dogs to keep them safe." Billi stared and Guthra shrugged. "Those suggesting it were mostly kin of Arikk."

Kina spoke up again. "Though you've a decision to make about Edan, Billi."

"Edan? How?" After all, Billi had killed him which seemed final enough.

"You might want to put this in your Laws of the Farm as well. Since Edan committed a banishing crime, 'tis up to you if Edan's skull is allowed on Skull Rock." Kina sighed. "Banishment can be applied after death, and then the skull is smashed and scattered in the Forest instead of going with the rest."

Billi thought of Canitre's face out at the valley, and couldn't do that to the distraught Hunter. "No, I'd not ask for that. Because of Canitre, not Edan."

"That's it done then. Now you'd best get that valley sorted out, and a name would be handy. Big Black Beast? Bearr's Den?" Billi left before the elders really started.

Billi spent two days in the Village, and there were no black looks, though some were definitely curious. There were also shrieks and several times someone warned a maid the bearr was on the prowl. The youths and maids had certainly made their decision, and they were backing the bearr. Though despite the warnings about Billi getting back in time for the wake, Arikk still wouldn't decide on a date. He knew Kelli had gone on, but his family and friends agreed to him having more time before admitting that in the hall.

Billi had enough time for another valley trip, so he took Syman out to the valley to look the place over. The stonecutter spent a lot of time looking at the rock wall at the back, and where they'd marked everything out, then he sat over supper with Billi to give his verdict. "There's plenty of good rock of course, with that cliff at the back." Syman pointed with his skewer full of cooked meat.

"Will it all come from there?"

"Enough to build the corners at least because that is granite, strong tough stone, tougher than the slopes at the sides. I would like to sink my place at least halfway into that cliff face, deeper if I can find a flaw, a fault to work with, which will give a lot of cut stone for the cottages." Syman pointed with his now less loaded skewer. "The stone either side of the valley is fractured here and there which will be handy. If we move the second and third cottages a little, still on their claims, I can take full advantage."

"Do it, because we haven't people for those huts so the new spot will be what's on offer." Billi looked at his own hut. "What about this place?"

"They will be cottages, not huts, though that is definitely a hut." Syman laughed. "As a stonecutter I should be weeping at the waste of good big boulders, since some of them will split several times. Adalmar the carpenter will definitely weep when he sees whole trees used like that." He looked at the structure for a few moments, assessing. "Ye can make it bigger using half the materials, though the idea is to build at least two more like this, I understand?"

"Three more for speed, to get people here. Then when the first proper cottages are built, these can be used to help build the rest." Billi pointed to the rest of the dead trees, still upright. "There's plenty of good timber right here."

"Aye. The boughs from the tree making the dam are good timbers and some of the small boulders and timbers the beavers used should be rescued. Get a few youths in that pond while the weather is good." Syman chuckled. "They'll end up competing to show off their muscles, especially if ye get a couple of maids out here that day."

"I doubt maids will take the trip, not unless they've got a bonding in mind." Billi smiled. "Then they'll not be much encouragement for the youths."

"A few will want to look, especially if you get an unbonded youth moving out here, or a Hunter." Syman wore a little smile and Billi laughed.

"Mikkel?"

"Oh yes. I can tell ye two names who wouldn't run if he made any sort of move. Not only that but the best applicant to be my apprentice is a maid. She'll stay with a family instead of me, of course." Syman chuckled. "That will make building my hut easier."

"You could build two small places side by side? Like my hut back in the Village with the bedroom on the end, but with both halves the same size and no connecting door. Then if she ends up with the whole thing?" Billi shrugged. "As your apprentice, putting in a doorway won't be hard."

"True. I'll think on that. I'll spend the rest of the summer cutting blocks and getting the first plots cleared, then I'll make some deep cuts where I want rock to split." Syman smirked. "That way the frost does a good bit of the work, and saves me some sweat. In the spring there'll be lots of blocks and loose rock so the first proper cottages won't take long, especially with folk out here full-time. You'll need the carpenter then." Syman looked over at the dead trees. "We can manage building the first three rough huts this summer, using some of those without needing a carpenter as long as ye bring a few planks for doors." Billi explained his wedges and hammers, and they talked long into the night working out which huts went up first and where.

* * *

Kelli's Da still looked hollow-eyed but finally started coming to proper terms with it all. He'd asked if anyone wanted the horse because he couldn't stand the sight of it now, and a Farmer from the other end of the Farm took it and the other three and the colt. He had a lot of big rocks deep in the soil there and would use the horses to plough deep and lift them. Once the rocks were out the horses would be sold to a caravan unless, with all the grazing out in the nearby Forest, they were bought for the valley. Either way the silver would go to the Village. The Farmer said he hadn't paid for the horses and he'd not take a profit from two deaths.

Gerant came for a talk with Billi about Edan's livestock. "I'd like to take those two big dogs and the pups, for out at the new village. But you'll have to agree." He smiled. "When will we have a name?"

"Soon now." Billi thought about the dogs. "None of this can be blamed the dogs, Gerant, they just did what they were trained for. In a way it will be right, another three legged dog to join me, Rabbit and One-shut." Billi frowned. "They'll be big dogs to feed."

"Not really because there's small prey can be trapped while watching sheep up on the moors. With the grazing out front and on the moors, I'm thinking of maybe taking a couple of those horses as well for dragging travois back here, to Trail's End. The pups might already be enough to guard sheep on the moors from all but large hunters. Once grown they'll stand off most things long enough for the Hunter and Hound to get there." Gerant shook his head. "I've seen them close up now and if they were both whole, the pair of adults could stand off a small hunting cat, I reckon. Though they've got some respect now and won't bother the Hounds."

"Aye. On their own they'll see off a fox, and maybe the three legged one can help guard down in the valley and watch over the geese and ducks." Billi liked the solution, since it would have been more pointless deaths if they'd been put down as useless. The pups would be brought up properly, with Hounds about and a proper job to do.

* * *

Most villagers didn't mention Edan unless as 'that lot' or a quick word to tell Billi they had no problem with the death. Several made a point of telling Billi they were pleased all the trouble was finally settled, even at the cost of a life. Hektor let Billi know that Canitre had taken Edan into the Forest for his pyre, and scattered the ashes there though the family hadn't had placed his skull yet. Canitre had sent his thanks that Edan's skull could go on Skull Rock, which made Billi uneasy. A man shouldn't have to be grateful for that.

A Trader caravan came and went, and there were six extra people when it left. The six sullen youths and young men were escorted to the wagons just before the Traders left and the Traders were paid to take them to the next settlement. Though as the wagons started to move Aescon had to have the last word. "You've not heard the last of this, cripple. You're a murderer and you'll pay!" Three clods of mud flew towards him and the Trader cuffed Aescon into silence, probably annoyed about the mud on his wagon.

Billi hadn't wanted to come, but this came under an Elder's duties because he'd refused to take them into the valley. "He might find someone to bring him back from the next settlement."

Kina laughed. "I doubt it. The Traders will pass the story on, and 'tis unlikely those six will be allowed to stay there after being banished." Satisfaction sounded in her voice. "That means they'll have to work their passage onwards." She pointed. "Those three Hunters and Hounds will follow the Traders until dark, to stop any foolishness." Even as the wagons went out of sight, laughter rang out as some maid teased a youth about missing the mark with his mud. The crowd broke up joking and laughing, relieved the whole thing could finally be put to rest and the whole mood in the Village lightened.

There were still a few speculative looks, but those were to do with the wake and some were from maids. Billi needed a plan! He felt certain that a few would be caught 'again' and expect beguiling practice. How he managed that without moving past bearr dancing into chasing a maid who might only be flirting worried Billi. So did somehow making sure not to move past flirting with a maid who really might be chasing. Though Billi did accept that this worry had to be much, much better than his previous ones.

Dealing with whatever Ellibeth had in mind taxed Billi more than anything since she seemed to be determined to keep a lead over the rest. Billi once again wondered if perhaps she really might be chasing? Then Billi reminded himself that Ellibeth said the night by the lake would be enough for her, strong arms now and then not a peg leg all the time. Billi had time to think, because Arikk still grieved too much for a wake. With no need for a pyre, nobody would push the man. So Billi turned to another problem, a name for his valley. No, a name for a new Village, a worry all on its own.

Endings and Suitable Gifts

The late summer raced by and Billi began to find signs that someone occasionally came looking around his hut, though not when his hut guards were there, or with him in the hut. The scratches around the lock and splinters on the edge happened while Billi visited the Village or the elders. Worse, whoever did it must have taken note of what Edan's friends had done and all tracks led to the stockyards or manure heaps. Since whoever did it seemed unable to open the door, and Billi didn't keep stones or sparkuls there anyway, he didn't make a fuss. Billi made his trips to the Blacksmith and others shorter in the hope of catching someone still on his plot, but without any luck.

Billi spent most of summer at the lakes either alone when he would search for stones, or with the potential settlers including Ellibeth and Rubyn. Billi slept outside but with so many visiting the valley stayed too crowded for lonely bears and wandering maids. Billi maintained the ponds and helped to plant more bramble hedges since they all liked that idea, and helped with building the three rough huts. Billi also helped with setting the flat rocks to let everyone reach the outflow for fresh water in winter or flood without getting wet feet crossing the gravel.

The three extra huts were a little better than Billi's but not much and weren't really fit to live in yet. That would come with spring when the ironwork for ovens and the pot-bellied stoves would come out with the furniture and the villagers. Nobody could come to live here until then because the stock wouldn't be ready. Nor would the furniture or ironwork but the stock would make this a village not an overnight camp. Billi talked to others and names began to go on the landclaims, for later next year when the cottages were built.

As Billi had been told, sibs and parents pitched in to help the new villagers. Hunters came along to guard the travellers and workers without asking for pay, just to see the valley and the area. Willing hands cut hay from the Forest in front of the valley, and brought it up to the slope to build stacks above the pastures. The scattered trees out the front did look sparse and lonely without the long grass but were still too many for that part to be Farm. Some of the hay would spoil by spring, though Billi thought the stacks would pay for the time by attracting game after the snow came. All that food would tempt grazers right in front of Billi's bow, and Mikkel's since he could use the huts to stay overnight.

While alone Billi sampled the gravel bar and found a strip at one end near his hut that produced all the larger stones, and smaller ones than any of the rest. One warm day Billi built a large fire, stripped down and looked on the bottom of the back lake where the spring outfall came in. As he'd expected Billi found five stones, all larger than usual. He'd become more interested now, because of the sheer expense of setting up a village. Just his own landclaim would be expensive, and Ellibeth's would need a plough and other farm implements so she could earn her keep. Billi spent some time trying to work out how to buy the equipment for her, or Rubyn, without Ellibeth saying 'too much.'

Billi assumed all the stones came from that vent, so the larger ones would only come during floods and settle soonest. More diving over the next two days showed a deeper channel cut by the current, from the outflow to the richer section of gravel. A channel made while the water flowed fastest, and the larger stones were concentrated in the silt in the bottom. So were a good few smaller ones.

The sediment wasn't very deep there since the flood no doubt cleared it. Further out into the lake there were some stones but fewer and all small, and in deeper silt. Billi mentally marked in an arc of lake as belonging to his landclaim, to draw on the map when he went back to his Billi-hut. On a future visit he'd drive in stakes and put in the fence for his water fowl along the far side of the richer, deeper arc. That would keep Billi's nest egg or farm equipment buying stones safe until he needed them.

Billi could swim well because the family farm had been near enough to the river for him to learn before he'd lost his leg. Afterwards swimming had been a blessing to a boy with one leg, and later Rabbit loved swimming with him when they could do so without spectators. Billi had spent many happy summer hours in the river when a Hound was guarding stock nearby, which meant that he swam better than he walked. This year his diving and swimming also meant he'd have a good haul for the Tinkerers after Harvestfest.

The Carpenter came out, and marked several of the dead trees to be cut down for him. They would be enough for eight main roof beams and a lot of planks and frames for doors. Adalmar shook his head at the sight of the trees and timbers in the rough huts, and agreed there'd be plenty to finish all eight cottages. He split rough planks for the doors, and would re-split those later to make furniture. Fellip promised to come out and help with thatching the first rough huts once the reed had been cut. This year Billi would take his share of the big reed bed as reed for the cottages next year.

Billi had seen more pug marks but the Great Hunter hadn't taken offence at Edan's invasion or the dogs, and still lived nearby. He had taken the remains of kills made in the valley and left by the trees on several occasions since that incident. Billi gradually moved the tithe spot, and now left the offering out of sight of the valley on the other side of some trees and thick bushes. Billi didn't want someone seeing the beast, and maybe sparking a confrontation in sheer panic. Nor did he want ravens and crows too near the lambs, now there would be flocks here. The beast didn't seem to mind and still took the tithe, though he still fished in that one pool.

Syman's apprentice, Abbe, came as a shock for some since she looked a bit small for splitting stone. With a big smile the Stonemason claimed that she'd soon persuade some youth to use a big hammer if needed. What gave her the job was her pottery, and her wood carving which Syman claimed showed great promise. Two maids did come out to the valley for a trip. That gave Billi a little revenge, as he could tease Mikkel instead of suffering the bearr jokes. Both maids were well behaved but both made it very clear they would start chasing, or stop running, if Mikkel gave them a hint of being interested.

As a bonus the maids, and Abbe, ensured that four youths did come out to the valley to work hard, supposedly for their own Bro or Sis who might get a claim. They also set into the beaver lodge with enthusiasm, a lot of splashing, and a lot of flexing of muscles. The three maids encouraged them, and Abbe did get two of them pounding on wedges with big hammers. Syman teased her a bit afterwards, but she smirked and pointed at all the split rock.

Seeing the first three places for permanent cottages stripped of grass and soil was sobering, because the valley would never look the same once they went up. So far, if the rough huts had come down, the valley could have slipped back into the Forest. That changed when Abbe and Syman started cutting holes into the hillside. When the holes were finished and the dressed stone blocks put in place, that would be permanent. In Billi's head, that would be the final step from Forest to Farm.

* * *

Arikk finally, over two moons later, agreed the time had come to say fare thee well to his Kelli. He'd realised the Wild took her when he saw the Great Hunter because Arikk accepted, deep inside, that she couldn't have survived in the Forest with that living among the trees. The time since then he'd been putting himself back together enough to face everyone else. Part at least was shame that he'd allowed himself to be used by Edan and his cronies. That eased once the culprits left.

The mood at the wake started more sombre than usual because of Kelli's age, and because of the circumstances and the disaster afterwards. A wake should celebrate a life but this one had been cut terribly short, a mere fifteen summers. Her Da thanked everyone for coming, and sat back. A few others spoke about Kelli, what a bonnie maid she'd been and 'twas a shame the Wild took her. The elders spoke up, about how the Wild always lurked, and would sometimes take an innocent who hadn't broken any Law.

None of the speeches mentioned Edan, nor his gang. The villagers noted Canitre's family's absence of course but didn't mention it. The Hunter had told Arikk's family that he grieved for the maid and meant no disrespect but couldn't face the village just now. Those who needed it would hold a private wake for Edan tonight, and his Da would put the skull on the Rock.

As the evening wore on people relaxed a bit, the conversation and dancing became livelier, and sure enough the call went up for ssrrong bearr. Billi, among others, glanced over at Arikk since that didn't seem quite right. Arikk stood up again and looked straight at Billi. "My Kelli loved hearing about the dances. She came to the last one, though still just too young for bearr dancing so this would be her first. She'd even chosen a scarf Billi, to wave at ye. So I'd be obliged if ye all dance properly, and make this a really good one for her." Then he sat again and the musicians struck up.

This time every maid old enough wore a scarf and a smile, some with real intent. Most were there purely for fun, and perhaps some had to be bravado. Even the maids at their first proper dance wore their scarf and a determined look. Bearr dancing had become a rite of passage now, the first step to flirting and chasing. What Billi had been told turned out true enough, bearr dancing would stay even if ssrrong bearr stopped.

Some of the youths were already growling and threatening, so the dancing after the bear tired and sat down would be lively. A youth put the chair out to a cheer, Billi put the gloves on and the first maids stepped out to a lively tune. These were the younger maids who weren't too sure, especially those at their first dance. Most made sure the bear didn't catch them though a couple insisted on having their scarves or shawls caught and ransoming them with a quick, shy buss and a blush.

The next shawl ransoms were less shy and then a few were decidedly firm, and Ellibeth ransomed her shawl with a smile and a twinkle in her eye. The stakes rose as some were 'caught' when their shawls didn't come free and they had to sit on the bear's knee for a Tinkerer bussing. Then the first of those caught last time appealed for help, for rescue, since she'd been caught twice. She sat on the bear's knee and carried out a bit of beguiling by stroking his hair and cuddling up a little bit before the Tinkerer bussing.

More followed and Billi found out he could tell the difference when a maid went on to seriously tempting and maybe a bit of chasing. Eweyna had undone an extra button on her blouse again and she told Billi very quietly he could check for tattoos if he wished. Her version of a Tinkerer bussing left Billi a bit breathless. Eweyna stood with a shriek. "The bear looked, he looked for tattoos."

"I wonder why?"

"I would check as well."

"Did he see any?"

She glanced down and shrieked again. "Sneaky bear! I never even noticed." Eweyna did up the button with a shocked expression while most of the hall laughed at her act. Some laughed again when soon afterwards she joined the dancing with it undone again.

Billi wondered if he'd need bussing practice for all the different sorts from shy pecks to Eweyna's version. Then he realised he'd done more bussing tonight than any training programme was ever likely to supply. None of it went as far as Tinkerer bussing of course. The maid version stayed gentler, more innocent, and always in the knowledge that the villagers watched them including the maid's Da.

The noise actually dropped when Ellibeth danced by again, and nobody seemed surprised when the bear caught her. Billi held her good and tight which made her smile, and there were some whistles and comments. Billi leaned closer and whispered. "So what terrible fate is in store for you tonight?"

He saw the flash of laughter in her eyes. "Wait and see, naughty bear." As expected now Ellibeth appealed to her Da, her Bros and her Sis. They all told her, through their laughter, that she'd been caught dancing with a bear so 'twas her problem. Viktor even bemoaned the fact that he'd tried to bring her up proper, but Ellibeth just couldn't stay away from bears.

"Oh no, cheeky bear. He says I've had time to practice my beguiling, and he wants to see what I've learned! Bear wanted his Tinkerer bussing first." Ellibeth put her ear near to Billi as if listening.

So he whispered, "Bear likes that idea."

Ellibeth giggled then raised her voice again. "But then I have to sit on his knee and beguile him. If I can't convince bear to accept another bussing, he's keeping me after dark!" The place roared with laughter. There were a lot of comments about how keen bear probably was to get the second bussing, and some thought bear should definitely keep Ellibeth this time. Some laughed at Billi needing to be beguiled into accepting a Tinkerer bussing from Ellibeth. Even Arikk raised a little smile.

Billi did his part. "With all the beguiling tonight I'm getting more resistant, so this will take some time. I'd better sit at the side with this maid and give the young bears a chance at the rest of the them." Billi gave them all a big smile. "Then if I hold out until dark that won't stop the others dancing."

"Oh no, not until dark!" The firm hold Ellibeth had on Billi's hand didn't quite fit with her shocked tones, and neither did the laugh that followed.

The first youth stood wobbling on one leg and clutching at scarves and shawls before Billi sat down. The first bussing from Ellibeth felt definitely firm. The whispering and stroking Billi's hair, and the cuddling in a bit that followed, were very nice. A lot of the whispering told him the gossip about the maids and youths and commented on the dancing and the bears tottering about. That meant Billi wore an absolutely genuine smile even if the reasons weren't clear. Before long a few looks and comments were speculating if Billi might actually keep Ellibeth this time. Ellibeth encouraged them by periodically exclaiming, in a loud voice, "Not yet, bear? Oh no."

Mikkel took a turn at being the bear, and he caught three. All three were, according to Ellibeth, serious about their bussing but the young Hunter didn't give any hint about a preference. Ellibeth giggled and said they'd try harder next time. The two maids who had been to the valley had been talking to the rest, and one of them had just been bear bussing. Abbe didn't get caught by a bear, even though a couple of apprentice bears chased her while waiting their turn.

Then Ellibeth gave Billi a bussing that left him breathless and stood up. "Ooh, I nearly didn't get away that time!" She turned to the other maids in the hall, still dancing. "You'd better watch out at Harvestfest. If bear catches someone next time, he might keep them after dark!" Eweyna definitely looked interested in that idea. Billi was, but not with Eweyna, and only if he could persuade himself a certain bonnie maid might actually agree.

It was already dark outside of course. After dark meant the end of the dancing when everyone left to walk home through the night. If a maid and youth walked off together into that dark, publicly, that meant bonding sooner rather than later. There would be a good bit of trying to get a maid into the dark very privately of course and sometimes that succeeded, but if it did that might not be completely the youth's idea. He might find out he wasn't the one chasing, or so Ellibeth had told Billi about one couple.

Billi walked back with Ellibeth, but also with hers and several other families, and she 'hid' behind her Da. Billi enjoyed that part, the walk and the teasing from Ellibeth and two other maids, but not as much as he might have. Canitre would be out there tonight putting his Edan on Skull Rock and that came down to Billi. When he finally arrived back at his hut,

Billi sat for a bit before sleeping. None of the three bright eyes watching and listening could tell Billi if Ellibeth might be chasing now. Maybe she had just reminded Billi she'd like a strong pair of arms sometime? Either way the memory of her bussing helped Billi to sleep despite thoughts of Canitre.

The following morning Billi didn't feel so rested, not when daylight showed what he'd missed last night. He thought everyone had been guarding stock or at the wakes, for either Kelli or Edan, so who had been at his door? This time they'd brought a hammer and chisel and tried to cut out the lock, but Billi had a good solid door and the lock had stayed put. Once again the trail led to a manure heap. Billi took a quick trip to see Kravitt and the Blacksmith made him two big plates he could bolt on around the lock. They weren't expensive, but needing them really did start to annoy Billi again.

* * *

After the wake the Village settled down to stock up for winter. Billi took his swirling dish when hunting this year and made forays along the cliffs and steep hillsides either side of the valley entrance. He found more, smaller valleys, but the others were all choked by heavy growth. Each valley had some sort of a stream issuing from it, and in one of the streams Billi found a few small nuggets. Billi tried the dish and found dust in the sand and fine gravel where the current slackened, as promised. By autumn four little pouches heavy with dust joined the one holding small nuggets. A welcome bonus as Billi didn't range as far and wide this year because of his time at The Lakes. The Lakes, or Two Lakes, he could feel that settling into his head because the stream had brought him but the lakes kept him here.

Early in the autumn several flocks of sturdy mountain goats came through the moorland above the valley. Their meat tasted gamy and needed boiling but the Hounds and dogs loved it. Better yet the long fleeces were luxurious once the tangles were removed and the long hair cleaned. There were discussions about eventually catching some to tame and breed for the fleece but for the first few years the goats would be a harvest. That meant taking just a few rather than hunting them heavily.

Billi finally made it up the hillside, helped by Syman, when Mikkel reported another herd or flock on the way. The Hunter wanted a second

Hunter, but also claimed he wanted to keep the Elder happy by letting him get a couple of fleeces. The Hounds laid in wait and then drove the animals close to the Hunters and their bows hiding in the rocks around a sinkhole. Because of the lack of cover the Hunters had already settled on that as the best strategy. Hunting from ambush came in handy when others arrived for a share of the spoils.

These goats were being followed by a small pride of lions, but they stayed well clear of the Hounds and Hunters. Later flocks were followed by large wolf-like predators that weren't wolves or used to men. As big as a Hound and heavily built with very powerful jaws, they could be either predator or scavenger. All the prospective settlers were pleased these Wild hunters travelled as loners or in pairs. Three times a Hunter took one of the beasts, and their thick soft pelts would make wonderful winter bed furs once Viktor was done with them.

The remains of any hunting were brought down off the hills to the same spot by the edge of the trees, tithe for the Wild. That went into the Law of the Farm, to try and keep larger scavengers away from the flocks up above. The sheep and goats would be kept off the moors as the hill goats and their predators came through each year, and so would Rubyn.

Rubyn ended up terribly torn. He wanted to look after the chickens and trap rabbits and whatever else he could in the fields near the Village, but that wonderful moor called to him. Ellibeth had been right and Rubyn loved the valley, the fish, the moors, everything there. He would talk any Hunter there into guarding him while the littlun set his traps and emptied them. Rubyn now had a dozen long tail feathers, a good selection of smaller ones from the moor, and great plans for trap lines to collect more. The hares and a fox that had been seen up there were too strong for his wood and twine snares, so Hektor taught Rubyn how to use a sling. Rubyn hadn't hit a hare yet but became decidedly dangerous for a few weeks until he got the hang of it.

The littlun saw Stoats, and a larger type that Rubyn named a Ferrit since 'twas always ferreting around the piles of rocks near sinkholes. He wanted to set Billi's metal traps up there, but that had to wait until the big move next year. Then the bits of meat in the traps should bring Rubyn a thickly furred harvest in the snow. Billi expected a similar harvest in the valley even when everyone moved in because the little hunters would risk the side with only two cottages to get at the fish.

As the days began to shorten Billi finally came to terms with Edan's death, and accept there was little else he could have done. The man forced him into a place with only two ways out, and one meant Rabbit and possibly Billi dying. The occasional attempts to get into his hut were down to scratches around the metal now because Billi never left the place empty for long. Another sort of apprehension replaced his worrying and self-searching and even his concerns about this new village, but a very pleasant sort of apprehension. The leaves turned, the fields were shorn, and Harvestfest approached.

* * *

Fifteen days before the Harvestfest, the comments started about how early the dark arrived at Harvestfest dances. Eweyna wasn't the only one wondering what happened if the bear caught more than one maid for the third time. How many maids could sit on a bear's knee? Billi made a trip out to the valley to collect his stones, for the Tinkerers who would arrive just afterwards. He spent the time alone thinking of the Harvestfest and bear dancing. The catching was going to be a delicate operation this time especially with that careless button!

Billi wondered what Ellibeth would come up with this time and reached a decision. He didn't want to let Ellibeth go, and he didn't want to catch the other maids. That was a big decision, but Ellibeth kept saying his leg didn't matter. She'd been saying that for a long time, but Billi finally let himself believe it. Ellibeth said she enjoyed their night and hinted she might do it again. "Maybe Ellibeth would like strong arms every night?" Rabbit's song lifted when Billi said that, so did the Hound agree?

When he went to the Two Lakes to collect his stones for the Tinkerers, Billi thought hard about that. Billi needed to work out what to give Ellibeth that would tell her straight, the bear was chasing her and only her. A gift that, if she took it, meant the bear would only dance with one maid. It might have been the thought that Ellibeth would be living here, in the valley, at the other end of the gravel night after night that sparked the idea. Because now he allowed himself to consider the idea, Billi admitted he wanted Ellibeth this end of the gravel, in his hut, and not for the dusting or bread. Billi sat a long time thinking of a gift.

Then he sat even longer with all the bright stones twinkling in the firelight, and in the end he chose to take the two oval sparkuls set as eyes. Ellibeth could wear them side by side, or as earrings if she felt daring. He carefully wrapped them in the kidskin and folded that in a bit of fur before tucking it in his pocket. He would give them to Ellibeth when he took her home. Billi firmly refused to think about what might happen if she said too much, though he'd offer them in private just in case.

Sorting the rough stones became a lot more fun as he wondered how those two would look on Ellibeth. He also thought his resistance to beguiling would improve with her in his head and his hut if Ellibeth accepted. That distracted him, thinking of Ellibeth in his hut, and Billi took a lot longer cleaning and sorting stones than expected. Then he went to bed determined to get home, the other home, straight away the following morning. Otherwise worrying about Ellibeth's reaction might stop him going through with it.

Billi tried to get home in two days as he'd managed it once, and had a real urge to get there now. He set off at the first hint of light and it went well enough until the wind got up during the afternoon and thick snow started falling. Not a huge amount of snow but the wind blew it into drifts. As he pushed on Billi remembered that his fast trip had been with other Hunters helping, including carrying everything and making camp. He pushed on late into the night, taking a risk for once. While a drift made a good shelter for his fire overnight, the rest of them were soft, clinging and right across their path.

Normally Billi would have been admiring their beauty, but this time the drifts were between him and something more important. Billi and Rabbit struggled because there had been no frost to give a crust, so both sank deep into every drift. Eventually Billi had to give up, because he had already slipped twice. Even if he only sprained an ankle. 'Twas his only ankle so he'd never get home and Rabbit would stay with him. After all, a day wouldn't alter whether Ellibeth said yes or no. He made another shelter against a snowdrift and slept restlessly, with Ellibeth and those two sparkuls burning away in his mind.

At one stage during the following day Billi started to wonder if he'd make it even in three days, because the Forest seemed determined to slow him up. Once past the old Wood Hunt place the drifts all lay right across his path, but now Billi had the bit between his teeth. Luckily, as they came nearer to the Village, Billi saw signs that Hunters and Hounds had been out. They would have been following the fresh tracks to find game and had broken through some drifts. Heartened, Billi pushed on despite the lengthening shadows.

That helped but full dark had fallen long before Billi came clear of the Forest. 'Twas too dark to see smoke from the chimney but as he came across the fields Billi saw firelight in his tiny window. He'd arrived home late before, but this time too late to be rousing a maid. He'd be rousing her since that glow came from a damped fire, not a candle, so Ellibeth and Rubyn would be asleep. Billi would peek through the door into his room just to be sure, and if they weren't up the chickens had a lodger. Him and Rabbit would sleep in there with One-shut and supposedly arrive in the morning. Spots might not bark as he had accepted that Billi belonged in his pack, or maybe that he belonged to Rabbit's.

Billi took care with his crutch and hushed Rabbit as they came near and Spots stayed silent. He swung off his pack and carefully eased the door open, then peered round it. Ellibeth was still up! In fact, she had her coat on, so had she been waiting to go home? "Hush, Spots roused but Rubyn's still asleep. Come in, quick." Ellibeth beckoned.

"No." Billi whispered as well. "If he's asleep you can stay. I'll sleep with the chickens."

Ellibeth stifled a giggle. "You will not. You'll sleep in your own bed and I'll put the bar up so a bear don't break the door in. Now get in here because the draught's cold." Billi grabbed his pack and put it inside by the door before shutting it, then he pulled off his big coat and jacket.

When he turned back from putting them on the pegs Ellibeth had come across and she shrugged her coat off as she stepped in and hugged him. "That's warmer. I worried with the snow and you late back."

She only whispered but Billi only half heard anyway, because Ellibeth only wore a night shift and now it wasn't under the coat! Billi looked down and a pair of soft lips came up, and his arm tightened a bit. When Ellibeth pulled her head back, he could see her eyes sparkling in the firelight. "Naughty, crafty bear. Now I'm really caught. I hope my beguiling is enough to get free." Billi opened his mouth to reply but she

wrapped the two not-so-little sparks that were such a big problem, and picked up the meat. Her Da would want that for the pot at least. He stumped into the Village with Rabbit bouncing alongside and the song had a curious note. What's the problem? "Nothing you can help with this time, Rabbit. I wish it was that easy. Now if she'll just speak to me." Billi sighed and kept going as fast as possible.

Ellibeth wouldn't talk, couldn't talk, and Billi didn't get past the front door because her Da blocked it. Viktor looked angry, but tried to stay polite. "She's gone to her Sis to cry her eyes out, and ye'd best not follow."

Billi tried to explain. "But I only gave her a gift."

He saw Viktor pull the surge of anger back under control. "She told me why. My maid isn't some Tinkerer beguiler."

Billi wanted to stamp or kick something, but he couldn't. "No! They were supposed to be a chasing gift!"

"Ha, you just happened to have some Tinkerer sparkuls handy more like, no doubt intending to do a bit of beguiling? Not likely, now go." Viktor pointed to his gate.

"No! I brought them from the valley, to ask. I don't keep sparkuls here since Edan or the Trader tried my door and someone else still does. Anyway, Tinkerer maids don't get sparkuls, they get roughs." Billi shook his head, because that wasn't the right thing to say! He ploughed on. "I looked through them all, all my sparkuls, before I came back. I thought those would please her." Billi looked Viktor in the eyes, willing the man to believe him. "So I didn't have to let Ellibeth go if I caught her again. So I didn't have to dance with the other maids." He proffered the little parcel. "So everyone would know," he finished miserably.

At least he'd made Viktor curious about just what had upset his maid. He tipped the sparkuls into his hand and when the fire flashed in the sun, Viktor made a strangled noise. When he looked up he still looked upset, maybe angry, but the heat had gone. "You sat in the valley and sorted these out? For my Ellibeth? Before she came home and, well, before?"

"Yes, I had them in my pocket when I came in and well. Er." How do you say dragged your maid into bed to her Da? Even if it wasn't dragging?

"She's been married, and well, it's not like a young maid, and you made her happy." Viktor knew! "Of course, I didn't know that until this morning, young man." Oh damn.

"She said sometimes was enough, but I wanted more. I wanted always." Billi willed the man to understand, to let him talk to her. "She said my leg didn't matter. Maybe she really did only mean sometimes. I'm sorry."

Viktor looked at the flashing stones. "I've never seen these on anyone but a Tinkerer maid, and not many have sparkuls like these. How many more have you got? No, not how many but why, for Tinkerer beguiling?"

"I've got nine now and a dozen little ones and a good few tiny ones. But not all in gold settings and one is green and another two are red, and not worth as much. For my old age and now for building the village, for stoves and farm gear and the Carpenter. For all the things Two Lakes will need." He sighed. "Tinkerer maids beguile for the roughs." Then Billi gave a short laugh. "I spent ages choosing and got it wrong."

"Did you explain any of this?" Viktor didn't seem angry now, he seemed bemused.

"I just said I'd brought something special for her. I thought she'd understand; why else would I give her those?" Billi gestured at the two sparkuls.

Viktor snorted. "To buy a farm? There's probably enough for a tidy landclaim. What's wrong with a claw necklace? It's enough for most."

"I've got a box full of claws and teeth. They mean nothing and I've given plenty to Rubyn just because he likes them." Viktor nodded, so he'd no doubt seen those. "I wanted something special. I did think of the two spotted pelts?"

"I've heard about those." Viktor seemed perplexed now instead of angry. "Where did you get your ideas on gifts, Billi?"

"Well they all say something special." Billi gestured to the sparkuls and shrugged. "I've tried, but I can't get my head round all these unwritten rules."

"A pair of spotted pelts, or proper Tinkerer sparkuls? By special they mean a prize fang or a trophy horn. A pretty pebble on a silver chain, maybe on a gold chain for the rich." Viktor waved his free hand at the stones.

"I haven't got any pebbles or silver chains, and I've pouches full of gold. It's just found goods."

Viktor laughed suddenly, and he sounded relieved. "Billi, nobody but you has two spotted pelts waiting for the right maid, or Tinkerer sparkuls, enough so you have a problem choosing." He sobered. "By Forest and Farm you must never tell anyone you have. One loose mouth and there'll be those who'll come for them, probably not from this Village but there are Hunters elsewhere who'll be bought."

Viktor closed his hand over the two sparkuls. "I'll talk to Ellibeth, and explain the why, what you just said. She may still say no, but it'll not be because ye don't know what to give a maid or when. I'll not mention the rest so if she says yes, it won't be for pelts and gold and stones." Viktor sighed. "You need to know that if Ellibeth says yes she's not been bought. There's plenty of maids who will say yes for those if you end up stuck."

"I only want Ellibeth. It's a bit picky when I should be glad to get a maid, but that's how it is. If she says no, tell her I'll stay away from the valley as much as possible and in my hut when I'm home. She's to keep the landclaim for Rubyn." Billi felt that spark of hope again, but daren't let it grow.

Viktor chuckled at that. "Oh, Rubyn will make sure she takes that. The littlun's blossomed and can't wait to try out all his new skills up on the moors." Viktor glanced up at Billi. "He'll not let you be."

"I don't mind that but I'll stay clear of Ellibeth. Those are a gift and I'll not take them back. She can sell them in her old age or to the next Trader but I don't want them, not now." Billi realised he'd still got the parcel under his arm. "Here, it's her meat, she earned it. Er, cleaning and cooking."

Viktor took the meat, smiling now. "Not the two spotted pelts? That's a relief. Now if I talk to Ellibeth, and she wants to talk to you, I don't expect to hear she's had to trek out to the lakes."

"Ah, um, well." Billi wished he had two feet to shuffle, because he'd been going there. To wait a bit and let Ellibeth think about it all.

"Yes, you go there if there's trouble. I know and so does half the Farm

I wouldn't wonder. This time ye stay put, Billi. If you really want to know." Billi couldn't hear any give in Viktor's voice.

He took a deep breath. "I'll wait. But the day before Harvestfest, if Ellibeth's not come, I'm leaving. There'll be no dancing bear this time, Viktor. I couldn't." Not ever again if Ellibeth said no.

"Someone else will play the bear because the youths and maids won't let that stop now. I'll tell Ellibeth, and she'll make up her own mind. If she says no there's no bad feeling, Billi." Viktor sighed. "You've been a good friend to my family, right back to the Wood Hunt and Bliss's share of the boar." A note of humour leaked into the Tanner's voice now. "I know Bliss and Hektor are grateful. Now go home, and I'll find Ellibeth." Billi got out of there. No bad feeling was better than nothing, but not much better.

* * *

When he came home Billi looked at the marks where someone had tried his door again and simply didn't care. Whoever it was could steal sparkuls and furs if they liked, because they couldn't take what he really wanted. On the way home Billi had realised how bleak his life would seem without Ellibeth there after a hunt with warm bread and a warm smile. How did that happen? When? Billi beat it around and couldn't decide. Ellibeth made his hut tidy again and then baked bread and then one day she became more important than the bread or the tidy hut. He couldn't even work out when one started to be the other.

That kept Billi's brain going around while he sorted out the hearth because it was full of ash where he'd just chucked logs on top of embers. Billi checked over and oiled his bow and exchanged the bowstring for a new one. The old one would be good enough for practice until it broke. A new one went into the spares in the pack, and Billi put a bit of an edge on his spear and nicked his finger. He'd been listening for the gate and not paying proper attention. Billi decided against sharpening knives or cutting up meat or he'd lose fingers.

There were plenty of chores such as new bedding for the goats, but that turned out to be done already. Billi went to tend the chickens and Rabbit ate the two rats One-shut had laid outside. The big tom must already be full so the cold spell had brought them in from the fields. The chickens already had plenty of straw and still enough feed and water. Billi wasn't really necessary here and couldn't leave. He could lay some traps, but that would also cost fingers. Billi fussed and fidgeted, and moved things that he moved back again.

When the gate went and Rabbit whined and wagged, Billi knew a friend had arrived and carefully didn't assume Spots with Ellibeth. After all, it was dusk, so too late for being out without a Hound. Sure enough Hektor called out and Billi told him to come in. Dapple said hello to Rabbit, then Spots bounced in to do the same and Bliss, Ellibeth and Rubyn followed; Billi stood there a bit nonplussed.

They all looked at each other a moment and Ellibeth waved at the door. "Rubyn, please show Unk Hektor the chickens. You too Sis, and take Spots since it's dark out there." Bliss opened her mouth, no doubt to point out she'd seen chickens, and shut it again as Ellibeth continued. "I've got something to discuss with Billi. Just between us."

She made shooing motions, face serene and voice level but a spot of red showed on her cheek and Billi couldn't see her eyes. Discuss? Was that good or bad? They all left and Ellibeth stood there, in her coat just as she'd left except she'd turned a bit so Billi still couldn't see her eyes. They waited long moments as the excited chatter went down the path. "When did you wrap up the sparkuls for me, Billi?"

"Before I left Two Lakes, you see…" Billi stopped at the raised hand.

"Why?"

"To give you a gift, a proper one." Ellibeth stayed silent. "A chasing gift." Ellibeth sighed and turned towards him. The coat slipped off her shoulders again and two points of fire blazed just below her throat.

Her smile broke and her eyes were dancing. "I'm not running, you silly man." Billi might have made one clumsy step. Ellibeth made the rest and then the crutch hit the floor as he needed both arms and neither could speak.

Not even when footsteps pattered, the door opened and a voice said, "Ma, One-shut got a rat and Spots is eating... oh." Billi started to draw back but Ellibeth's hand tightened on the back of his head and he didn't actually want to stop. Bliss's quiet voice explained, with some amusement, that Ma and Billi were discussing something.

The door closed on a littlun's voice explaining "but he's bussing her" in the right tone of voice for discussing gargling with pond scum. Rubyn wasn't a fan of maids and all that nonsense, not yet. Billi quite liked Ellibeth trying to giggle and buss so he kept right on doing it.

When they did stop, both decidedly breathless, Ellibeth giggled again. "He thinks bussing is disgusting."

Billi grinned. "Well I like it."

"I think I could be persuaded to try again." So they did.

Billi chuckled at the next pause for breath. "Well you can't say no. You're caught now because after all there are witnesses."

"Ha, I can keep those pair quiet, or I can deal with Bliss and she'll deal with Hektor." Ellibeth's arms were round Billi so she tapped him on the back. "You can't though so you, Ssrrong Bearr, are the one who's caught."

"But I'm not running." Billi laughed. "My crutch is on the floor so I'm even slower than normal. I might make the gate by morning?"

"I'll hunt you down."

"Rabbit would help."

"What?" Ellibeth glanced at Rabbit, startled.

"He is very, very happy. It's in his song." Billi felt well beyond pleased about that. He didn't know what happened if the Hound disliked the maid, or objected to the bonding, or if they ever did. The surge of pure joy in Rabbit's song had been a relief and a blessing.

"The mystery of Hounds. Will you tell me all about it? Not now, on a cold winter night." Ellibeth hugged a bit tighter.

"Tucked up warm." Billi hugged a bit harder as well.

"With strong arms."

"And soft ones." The silence left them both breathless again and Ellibeth pointed out they'd better let that lot in, they'd be imagining all sorts. Then she looked at the bed and wiggled her eyebrows. They were both still giggling when the dogs and folk were back inside. Billi sat in his chair and Ellibeth sat on his knee with an arm round his neck, while Bliss tried to look scandalised and then looked closer.

"What are they?" She looked again and gasped. "Those are Tinkerer sparkuls!" She looked at Billi and then back to her Sis. "You said a Tinkerer maid's beguiling gift. I thought you meant stones, you know, from a stream!"

Ellibeth wore a huge smile. "It's his idea of a chasing present."

Hektor choked briefly and got his breath back. "I don't know which is funniest. His idea of a chasing gift or the idea that Billi thought he was chasing." Billi looked at the three adults, all grinning now.

"You mean?"

Ellibeth leaned in to whisper in his ear. "For a long time, but very, very slowly so I knew you'd been caught on purpose, that you'd let me catch you. Then I thought you'd got it all wrong."

Billi wasn't whispering, though he kept his answer quiet. "Do you know how many hours I spent wondering if I dare try to chase you, if you really liked me?"

Ellibeth giggled. "I just said. Very, very slowly."

Bliss and Hektor had collapsed into each other's arms and Hektor got out, in a bad imitation of Ellibeth. "That's safe with my Da here, but don't be taking any more liberties."

"Since then?" Hektor nodded since he couldn't talk and Billi remembered how often the young man had done the same, collapsed laughing for no apparent reason. He started to smile because it didn't matter, in fact that meant Ellibeth liked him before fancy hats and bear dancing and the stones. Ellibeth really didn't care about his leg! "So I suppose you'll be running through the Village telling everyone?"

"Oh no he won't." Hektor had been nodding but now he stopped. Ellibeth glared at him, then looked at her Sis. "Sis, if you breathe a word before Harvestfest, I'll sew your mouth shut. Hektor, if you don't keep your mouth shut, I know where Billi's good knives are." Hektor winced, most of the Hunter's knew about Billi's good blades by now as when he was butchering near them the wavy pattern in the shining metal was distinctive.

Then four sets of eyes went to Rubyn who had started to grin at whatever he'd made of the situation. He immediately looked defensive.

"What? I didn't say anything."

"Rubyn, would you like to live in Billi's hut at the lakes, and help him mend the traps and suchlike?" The littlun's eyes widened to match his grin and he nodded rapidly, temporarily speechless. "Well you say nothing about these," Ellibeth touched the stones. "Or bussing or hugging, or sitting on knees. Not until after Harvestfest."

"Then can I tell Eddwyn? He will be so sick." Three pairs of eyes looked baffled, but Bliss sniggered.

"His Sis is Eweyna, the maid with careless buttons." Bliss touched the one the maid left open for the bear to look for tattoos. "That sounds as if she thinks she's in with a chance of catching the bear."

"She never was." Well! That brought Billi's first proper public bussing. It was a good job he wasn't running! "Thank ye kindly, fair maid. Now why do they all need to wait until Harvestfest? Because I wanted to do some hopping about and shouting."

"Because these," Ellibeth touched the stones gently, "need the right setting before they are shown. Otherwise everyone will think Tinkerer beguiling. So the bear needs to dance one more time." Billi stirred; he didn't want to. "With one maid. Then he'll retire since he's caught one that he's not giving back."

"Never." This bussing didn't last as long but tasted just as sweet.

"See, he says the nicest things." Billi would be thinking of more if he could. "My Sis is going to help me because these need something special."

"They've already got the best setting." Hektor rolled his eyes and Bliss grinned.

"You get thanked for that later." Billi thought that sounded wonderful. "Rubyn, would you like to stay with Unk Hektor tonight. You can help with the babe?" Rubyn looked torn until Hektor whispered something. Ellibeth nodded towards Spots. "Take Spots, he's a good guard dog." Not as good as Dapple but nobody mentioned that.

"There is one problem. We'll be going back by Da's house, since the babe's with her Ganda." Ellibeth looked stricken and hugged Billi's neck tighter, but Bliss laughed.

"He told me that if you two need more time to discuss things I should bring Rubyn home. Da said you had a lot to sort out." Bliss had trouble getting the last bit out and Hektor was off again, laughing. Ellibeth didn't care and neither did Billi. A long time sorting things out sounded wonderful. The three of them got their coats and left, because "You'll want as much time as possible to get it all sorted out." Which meant the adults were still sniggering as they went down the path. Everyone knew the bribe by then. Rubyn had asked if he could actually hold the tusk so he'd be seeing the Great-Boar trophy.

Then there they were. All alone and Ellibeth still on Billi's knee and not trying to get off. They practised creating heavy breathing, then did talk for a while about chasing and the choice of chasing presents. Then how this present was to be presented, and how they only needed one hut in Two Lakes now but it would need a room for Rubyn. Ellibeth liked the name which settled it.

Their eyes went to the bed more and more often. Until Ellibeth extinguished the lamp and Billi wasn't worried about his stump at all, and this time the little bird didn't wake Ellibeth and she was still there at dawn. Their late, slow breakfast came with a lot of smiling, and Billi finally took her home.

Viktor brought Billi in and privately admitted the whole affair had baffled the Tanner. Viktor had thought Ellibeth was chasing and Billi might be, right up to when she stormed into the house. After that he'd been angry at Billi for taking advantage. Then he'd heard Billi's attempt at an explanation and realised that wasn't the Hunter's intention. Now it seemed to have worked out well but he'd been asked to keep quiet about it. Once again Viktor admitted to being baffled, but this seemed important to Ellibeth so he'd do it. Viktor did point out that his maids had both baffled him many times as they grew up, so it wasn't really that unusual.

Perry knew, though sworn to silence on pain of being banned from hut-minding and reed- cutting. He'd started sort of chasing a maid and she'd dropped by the hut a couple of times in the daytime, according to some, so he really, really, wanted to keep the job. Billi stopped for the evening meal since he'd supplied it, Viktor pointed out. They all had to sample Rubyn's cream cheese which really was very tasty. Not the firm and delicious yet, though that was ready to come out of the Dancer's cloth.

* * *

For the next three days Billi and Rabbit spent a lot of time with just Rubyn. They put out or emptied traps, saw to the goats and chickens and threw sticks for Spots. Billi gave Bliss the whole box of fangs and claws when she asked for a few. He told her to use as many as they wanted since he wouldn't be needing any for a chasing bracelet. At least with Billi and Rubyn there nobody tried his hut, important now because there were rough stones in his hidey-hole. Though the hut wouldn't be left empty again because Viktor had picked up on Billi's comment about someone still trying his door. He had suggested a solution and now Spots stayed in the hut while Billi sent to see his Sis.

Billi went round to see his Sis to talk about what to do with the hut, while Rubyn played with her littluns. The reason he gave had to do with moving to the valley, with no mention of catching. Billi offered put someone in it until one of Sis's littluns grew big enough and then it would be theirs. Her glance at Rubyn showed that Sis assumed Ellibeth would get the hut, but Billi meant Perry. He'd get it on the condition that if Billi, Ellibeth or Rubyn needed a bed for the night when visiting the Village, the extra room was theirs.

Back in Billi's hut he spent more time drawing a new house in the dust with Rubyn, and eventually on a piece of parchment. This version included an extra room for Rubyn, just for him. Ellibeth and the stonecutter would explain what was wrong with their notions but this kept Billi and Rubyn busy and out of the way. The planning and drawing occupied Billi's mind but not as well as Rabbit's joyful song.

He didn't have to plan what he'd take to Harvestfest because Ellibeth had been planning anyway, even if 'twas only for winter. Billi had stuffed his store with salted, dried and cooked meat, and fish. He had plenty of meat as he'd spent a lot of time out at the lakes this summer and Billi always hunted on the way back unless he'd filled his pack before leaving. Better yet, anyone who came along carried extra back for a share. He'd also pillaged the bramble hedge and the Forest trees for extra fruit this year after Ellibeth mentioned how popular the wild fruit seemed to be in the Village.

Ellibeth had converted a surprising amount of what he'd brought into sausage, pots of berry preserves and meat spreads, and pies and pasties. Billi never really noticed since often Rubyn, Perry or Timath carried his catch down the steps. Now he realised that behind the usual lumps of this and that Ellibeth had been hoarding bits away all year, all carefully sealed and stowed in the deepest, coldest parts. Billi wouldn't go hungry regardless of the winter. Ellibeth came from a house without a Hunter and wasted nothing which sometimes puzzled One-shut.

Billi would be taking a big pie to Harvestfest, venison this time, and a smaller pork pie that Ellibeth said would only feed two families. Though just now the stores were far from his thoughts.

Eventually Harvestfest arrived, and Billi dropped Rubyn off at the party for the littluns. Spots stayed in the hut all on his own, after dark for the first time. Spots already thought he should guard the hut, and would bark, and that should be enough to alert the Hounds if anyone tried the door. Rabbit's song seemed to agree, that he'd hear Spots and come running and the eagerness meant he'd come very fast. Viktor had agreed to keep quiet about the reasons rather than spoil Ellibeth's night or start up a lot of rumours.

By rights Timath should miss this Harvestfest, his first, while babysitting his two younger Bros, Rubyn, Bliss's babe and two neighbour's littluns. But Timath would babysit next year instead since Viktor arranged for a neighbour's youth, Currin, to stand in so the youth could see the bearr dancing. Currin would no doubt know all about the gift and Ellibeth and Billi before long, as Rubyn's silence would only last until he left the littluns party for home. The littlun had already mentioned calling round to see his friend Eddwyn on the way with some excuse, any excuse. Rubyn wanted to make him so sick before Eweyna came back from the dance with the news.

Ellibeth turned up at the hall with her Da, and Perry looking as if he'd swallowed the finch and the cat as well. Hektor failed to keep a straight face but that looked normal, as did Bliss's happy smile, though Timath looked baffled. After Perry whispered in his ear a huge grin spread over the youth's face and he kept glancing at Ellibeth. Billi kept looking at Ellibeth as well, then pulling his eyes away before everyone realised. She took off her coat to show a big shawl around her shoulders, one with fringing. The rest thought that must be for bear dancing, but Billi couldn't help wondering what Ellibeth wore under the shawl.

Although Billi knew the setting for the sparkuls would be a cat and the stones were its eyes, he had no idea of anything else. He only guessed cat from Ellibeth and Bliss wanting claws and fangs, so he had to sit impatiently through the build-up to the dancing. The Eldest said her bit including about the valley and that next year some of those present would miss the Harvestfest; they'd be watching their own flocks and herds out on the far side of the Forest. Kelli was missed, as were two Hunters and their Hounds, a farmer's lass, a babe and an elder. The babes who had survived their first year were named and welcomed to the Village, though Bliss's babe was too young and would be named next year. Edan and the banished were carefully ignored, especially because Canitre and his family were here.

The dancing struck up and Billi sat with the older men as usual and watched with mounting anticipation. He had trouble keeping his mind on the talk of crops and even the valley. There were a lot of scarves and plenty of anticipation tonight, and Eweyna had already started playing with her careless button. Eventually someone placed the bear chair, the call came for the ssrong bearr and his gloves, and Billi went out and braced himself against the post. The music struck up and this time there were at least three maids who were looking determined. Billi now had a large and proved landclaim, and some of the Village maids had been to the valley and confirmed it.

As before, the younger maids were allowed to dance first. Except that even as they were plucking up courage Ellibeth joined them, with her shawl still almost covering her top except for her arms. Ellibeth danced out first, which made it clear the first catch would be hers. The other maids held back and everyone watched as Ellibeth danced a bit closer and Billi grinned. He caught and pulled the shawl and as he'd known he would, the bear caught the maid.

There were gasps since this was a bit early to catch Ellibeth and last time she'd had to give two bussings and the beguiling. What would it be this time and would it be blatant enough to be classed as definite chasing? Maybe even catching, since a lot of them thought the chasing had been going on for a while. Ellibeth shrieked, beat his chest and then sat on Billi's knee as she'd been caught before so it was required.

While Billi allegedly demanded a prize she appealed for rescue, for help. Da, Bros and Sis were unmoved. When Billi asked her very quietly when he was to see the real prize she smiled happily, and Ellibeth turned to the room. "The bear is mad! He wants to keep me! He going to carry me off to the new village, Two Lakes!"

A cheer went up as Ellibeth announced the name of the new settlement but quickly died away. Everyone wanted to hear what else the bear had to say. Billi whispered in her ear. "No need to wander about outside next time."

Ellibeth tried to look horrified, but spoiled it by laughing. "He says he won't catch any more maids but there are conditions. I have to be tattooed and wear Tinkerer sparkuls so I can practice proper beguiling."

Once again Ellibeth appealed to Viktor but he shook his head. "I've given up. Ye keep going back to be caught by this bear and I'm starting to wonder if you want him to keep ye." That brought a gale of laughter. Ellibeth went tragic, which failed due to her big smile and the laughter from the crowd. Perry almost wept with mirth and only the wall kept him on his feet and this time Timath joined him. "In that case, what can a maid do, tattoos and sparkuls it must be." Ellibeth whipped off the shawl and turned to face the room.

Everyone went dead silent, and then a storm of laughter, whistles and cheering broke out and Billi wanted to join in even if he'd only seen a bit of it. She had a striped hunter on her blouse, right across the front! Billi could see the buttons down the back so the needlework wasn't even marred by the fastenings. There had to be strips and patches of eight or nine different pelts at least to get the striping and shading, probably from scraps as Viktor cleaned and cured them.

The claws and fangs were realistic because they actually were real and there was a chasing necklace's worth of claws ruined because only the tips had been cut off. But the real shocker were the eyes, blazing out in the lanterns and lamps. As the maids rushed in to look the exclamations began while Ellibeth sat there proudly. She'd certainly found a way to stop any Tinkerer jibes. She'd told them the sparkuls were to make her Billi's personal Tinkerer beguiler and the stripes were her 'tattoos' of course.

What nobody had expected was real sparkuls, the genuine big flamboyant type flaunted by Tinkerer maids. As Viktor had pointed out earlier nobody had ever seen them on a Village maid, which made them even more shocking and exotic here in the hall. Now they all wanted to see the sparkuls up close and a good few maids were also wanting detail about how the cat was made.

Billi moved to a chair at the side of the hall and announced that as this bear had retired the youths must compete to find another. The winner, judged by how many maids he caught and what sort of bussing he attracted, would get the gloves and start the bear dancing at the next dance. After he'd danced with all the maids, the youths must all compete again to find a bear for the next time. That idea, the competition, came from Hektor and Bliss so none were too jealous of the new bear.

The youths were soon vying for the chance, and Ellibeth whispered that Eddwyn's Sis had found a new target. A strapping youth soon had to sit on the chair to get a look at the careless blouse button, so Eweyna really did like strong arms. It hadn't taken her long to shift targets but she'd get second prize, Ellibeth told Billi with a smug smile. Billi had to rely on the other comments or Ellibeth since his view remained blocked by her, other maids, lasses and some men. They all wanted either instructions about how she'd made the striped hunter or a good look at the sparkuls.

The older men each side moved away and his Bros and Sis took the chairs! They smiled happily and congratulated him, though his Sis pretended to be annoyed. Only pretended since she laughed while berating Billi for fooling her about why he'd not need the hut. Billi didn't think he could be happier, but now something else eased in him. They really had forgiven him any extra work on the farm, and any trouble he'd caused them since. All three promised to come out when the new settlers moved to Two Lakes, to look over the valley.

Then Billi had to answer a few questions from a lot of people. Billi told them the truth about why he had the sparkuls. They cost a huge number of tiny roughs and he'd bought them for his old age. His leg took more use than any two so Ellibeth needed a better nest-egg than most, to keep them both when the time came. A couple of people reckoned that a Great-Swan, if there was such a thing, wouldn't lay a nest egg like that. Viktor had a clump of older men round him asking questions. He did a lot of shrugging, don't know, and told Billi later everyone wanted a value and he didn't have one.

Billi had a good idea because the Trader had bid hard for that one sparkul, and a Tinkerer had bid for the pair Ellibeth had. The value wasn't for public knowledge as it would be a temptation, since Viktor had been a bit wide of the mark. One stone in a setting like that would buy a landclaim on its own, as a matched pair they would more than double in value so a good farm and the stock. That came as a shock for Billi especially since they were all found goods, even the gold for the setting.

At the end of their dancing the bears were judged and a winner announced. The strapping young man was congratulated by his erstwhile captures and allowed a last dance with the gloves to prove their worth. He ended up with a second look at the careless button and some beguiling and two bussings so the gloves were working. Some general dancing and a bit of growling and chasing followed for a while and then the dance ended. Ellibeth got off Billi's knee after a very thorough bussing.

"That's not a forfeit. 'Tis because I'm entitled now, and so is the bear." Ellibeth laughed at the whistles and comments even if she went a bit pink. So did Billi and he thought his head might fall in half since his smile was so wide. Even a glimpse of Edan's Ma glaring at him couldn't affect his mood tonight. At least part of Billi's smile came from the sheer joy in Rabbit's song when Ellibeth sat on his knee and made her disclosure. Was the song because Billi felt so happy? Billi didn't care; the song soared gloriously and fitted his mood perfectly.

Billi held onto her hand just a moment longer. "You won't have to hide on the way home." Ellibeth squeezed his hand, then went to join her family.

Ellibeth put her hood and coat on but came to Billi as he put his own coat on. "Since my Da can't protect me in the lamplight, there's no point him trying in the dark."

Those who heard laughed, especially when Viktor shook his head sadly. "That's true. You'll be safer with a Hunter, a Hound and a Bear to look after ye." That caused more laughter, followed by some scandalised tutting when Ellibeth left the dance all alone except for Billi and Rabbit.

When they reached Viktor's house, the long way round, Ellibeth snuggled up close. She pointed out that everyone thought the bear had dragged her off to inspect her tattoos and behave badly. What a pity not to take advantage when everyone thought they might have anyway? Not only that but this blouse fastened up the back. That made it hard to get off on her own and where could she find help at this time of night? After all that bussing Billi had no intention of even trying to talk her out of that idea!

* * *

When they arrived back in his hut Billi helped a very giggly Ellibeth off with her coat, then took off his own. As he turned back to the room Ellibeth came into his arm and he tossed the crutch to the side to use both arms. This time he bussed her like he'd wanted to for a very long time, and Ellibeth didn't struggle at all. Her eyes twinkled a little as she looked over at the door to her bedroom. "Do I have to go in there and wait for a bear to break down the door?"

"Maybe for a pillow?" They both looked at the single pillow on Billi's bed.

"But if we squeeze up? If strong arms hold very tight?"

Billi had trouble keeping talking, and not just because of the maid in his arms. His head seemed to be alive with the song, the sheer joy and triumph made him want to dance and sing. Since Billi was short of a leg and a singing voice, not a good idea. "We could manage with one?" Billi could barely speak. Ellibeth was here and she was his and this would be her home.

Even as that worked into his mind it blazed with glory and Ellibeth's eyes went wide. "Rabbit?" she whispered. "Just then, just for a moment?"

Billi couldn't answer. He'd been stunned and even now had trouble thinking straight. The Hound's song rang out cleaner, clearer and brighter than ever before, encouraging him, just a little. Rabbit really wanted Ellibeth in his pack! Billi had to get to the bed before he fell over because he felt drunk on the sheer happiness, his and Rabbit's, and the wonder that shone from Ellibeth's eyes. He concentrated because since he'd thrown his crutch away this would be awkward on one leg and then a shoulder slipped under his arm.

He didn't have to manage, he wasn't alone now and never would be, and getting to the bed turned out to be no trouble at all.

THE END

The People of the Farm

Abbe - Syman's carver apprentice

Adalmar - Carpenter

Aescon - Edan's most rabid supporter

Anise - Prostitute at the Village alehouse

Arikk - An old Farmer. Has a daughter, Kelli, late in life

Autumn - Canitre's Hound

Barimar - Hektor's Da, a Hunter

Bettram - Stockman

Billi - Aka Stumpy - Hunter with no left leg, childhood accident

Bliss - Maid on the Wood Hunt

Canitre - Edan's Da, a Hunter

Cynel - Hunter on Winter Hunt

Dapple - Hektor's Hound

Devved - Elder Farmer - one of the elders

Edan - Impetuous youth hoping for a Hound

Eddmune - Experienced Hunter

Eddwyn - Littlun of nine summers. Friend and rival of Rubyn's

Ellibeth - Oldest of Viktor's, back home with littlun. Widowed and the landshare isn't available yet.

Eweyna - Eddwyn's older sis, careless button

Ewward - Youth on first winter hunt, Hunter on second

Farimer - Hunter

Fellip - The Thatcher

Fleet - Raban's Tan Hound

Gerant - Bettram's second born,

Gordi - Thatcher's nephew - youth

Grantel - Youth on the Winter Hunt

Guthra - Musician who plays on six shoes from carthorse down to small pony. Also an elder

Hektor - Youth waiting and hoping for a Hound

Hurwald - Farmer. Friend of Arikk

Kina - Eldest - old woman - eldest surviving villager

Kravitt - The Blacksmith

Lilith - Gerant's bonded, waiting for her brideshare

Kelli - Young maid - Arikk is her Da

Mandy - Mother of three who tends to take charge of firewood collections

Midnight - Farimer's Hound named because he turned up at midnight and roused the house.

Mikkel - Young Hunter

Nortan - Hunter injured on Winter Hunt

One-shut - One-eyed cat that guards Billi's the chickens and grain, never has two eyes open.

Patches - Hound

Patre - Farmer. Tempert's Da

Perry - Slightly older Bro of Bliss

Raban - Hunter on winter hunt,

Rabbit - The three-legged Hound that chose Billi

Robbin - Hunter - Seifort's Da

Rubyn - Ellibeth's littlun of eight summers, his Da died when he was five summers

Seifort - Youth - Da is Robbin

Starr - Elder woman

Steban - Mandy's bonded

Streak - Eddmune's Hound

Syman - Stonecutter, wood carver, basic potter, widower.

Sythyl - Seamstress

Tempert - Youth - Winter Hunt

Timath - Slightly younger Bro of Bliss

Treese - Raban's lass

Viktor - The Tanner, widower, Bliss's Da

Werne - Fiddler with a real fiddle - an heirloom. Also an elder

Wynn - Billi's eldest Bro

Terms Used on the Farm

Babe - Baby

Beguiler - Tinkerer maid with few clothes and many sparkuls and tattoos. Will sell kisses or perhaps more

Blackstone - Coal

Bonded - Married

Brideshare - Portion of the family business or land inherited by a daughter

Buss, Bussed - Kiss, Kissed

Elders - Group of the oldest villagers who advise the Village and enforce a few Laws

Eldest - Oldest surviving villager

Full-weight - About a hundredweight, eight stones or fifty kilos

Gobbler - Turkey

Greenstone - Copper ore

Landclaim - New land or business registered with the Eldest

Landshare - Portion of the family business or land inherited by a son

Lass - Wife

Littles - Toddlers

Littluns - Children

Maid - Unbonded Female teenager

Skull Rock - Huge boulder covered in niches containing the skulls of dead villagers and Hounds

Sparkul - A stone that shines with an inner fire, diamond

Stones - Pebbles exceptional enough for the Traders or Tinkerers to want them

Tithe - Portion of a kill left for the Wild, usually guts and bones

Travois - Triangle of timbers that allows people or ponies to drag large weights

Village - The small settlement of Trail's End, the only one on this area of Farm

Wake - Dance and feast to celebrate the life of a Villager who has gone on

Youth - Unbonded Teenage male

The Forest and the Farm

The Farm - Land which is cropped and kept clear of weeds. This land comes under the Law of the Farm. Every effort is taken to ensure that any land in the Farm never returns to the Forest, and every inch is claimed by someone. The Village and all the farmhouses are on the Farm, since no man can live in the Forest.

The Forest - The great woodland stretching across the world's edge, all the land not settled and farmed by Man. It is guarded by the Wild and cannot be cut, and any farmland not maintained is taken back to the Forest. Only fields, and trees in tended orchards, hedgerows or occasional lone trees permitted to grow by man on farmland do not belong to the Forest.

The Wild - All who live in the Forest and they protect it fiercely. They will raid the Farm but are fair game then. In the Forest Wild hunters will take or attack anything but Hunters with bows and Hounds, and occasionally them as well. There is more sentience and purpose about the Wild than the tame beasts of the Farm and there is a recognition of a balance, a bargain.

Laws of the Wild and the Farm - The rules agreed between the Forest and the Farm. Their origin is lost in time.

Great-Beast - Animal of extraordinary size and strength, Great-Bulls, Great-Stags, Great-Boars, Great-Cats and Great-Wolves have been seen. There is on-going controversy over if they are oversized beasts or a different species. Rare but pelts are highly prized and very dangerous to get. They are never intentionally hunted because they are so dangerous, though occasionally killed while raiding farms in hard winters. Great-Hunters are the largest and nobody has seen one of their striped pelts, and only a few have even seen their paw prints.

Hound - Possibly the dog equivalent of a Great-Beast. Large, powerful and have some sort of a mental connection to 'their' person. Each Hound comes out of the Forest and bonds to a young man, making him a Hunter, one of the select few entitled under the Law to hunt in the Forest with bow and spear. Hounds will not outlive their Hunter but can reach ages of more than three-score summers, allegedly, if their Hunter does.

Hunter - Man who has a Hound and a bow, and is therefore allowed into the Forest to take prey according to the Law of the Wild. It can happen to any youth and most practice the bow just in case, though only about one in four is chosen. The song of 'his' Hound is always present in a Hunter's mind. If the Hound dies the Hunter will grieve deeply, and usually go out into the Forest with just a spear to meet the Wild and never returns.

Landclaim - When there is a chance to take more land from the Forest it must be described and the location given. This is so that the land will not be lost to the Village if the claimant dies. All land is precious. The heir or heirs to a new landclaim must be revealed to the Elders at that time, to avoid any dispute. If they are too young to work the land when they inherit the Elders will rent it out until the heir is sixteen summers. This keeps the land clear and cropped so that the Wild does not reclaim it for the Forest.

Landshare or Brideshare - The inherited portion of a parent's holdings. This inheritance cannot be claimed until after the last parent has gone on and their skull is on Skull Rock. Until then, a bonded couple will live with the family of the man. This can cause overcrowding and is why the family home is so large. It is impossible for the couple to move out before then as there is no unclaimed land on the Farm.

Tinkerers - Itinerants living in gaily painted and carved wooden carts who set up small fairs. Their leatherwork, metalwork and jewellery are expensive but high quality, and they love to bargain but only for the better quality products of Forest and Farm. They do not steal or cheat, but bargain very hard. Their women assist in bargaining by 'beguiling' the victim, flaunting sparkling stones and delicate gold jewellery as well as their tattoos. Tinkerers tell fortunes, play tunes, sing and organise dancing. Their women are exotically tattooed and dance for silver, often removing items of clothing if the bids are high enough. Reputedly loose with their favours for silver or stones, and notorious for parting a man from his goods without paying though few complain. Tinkerers will pay good prices for the right rough stones and have the secret of making them shine as the stars do.

Traders - Trader caravans with a score or more wagons bring goods that cannot be produced in Villages and take the pelts and meat of the Forest back to the great cities to sunwards, allegedly beyond the Forest edge. They sell anything and everything and will take most things in trade, but the quality they supply can vary so beware. Usual source for blackstone, iron, charcoal, salt, rough cloth and most plain goods. Reputedly steal if they can't buy. The purple wagons carry dancing girls who do most things for silver or even for copper in hard times. Traders offer huge rewards for the secret of the glittering stones or for a Hound.

Sparkul - A found stone that has been enhanced. Only the Tinkerers have this skill and nobody else even knows the process. The Tinkerers can make a rough stone of the right type burn with an inner fire, which makes the sparkuls very expensive. Tinkers will only trade for the right type of stone, the Traders will take any pretty stone but won't give the same value even for potential sparkuls. Pretty stones and occasional nuggets are usually found in streams by Hunters.

Vance Huxley

Vance Huxley lives out in the countryside in Lincolnshire, England. He has spent a busy life working in many different fields – including the building and rail industries, as a workshop manager, trouble-shooter for an engineering firm, accountancy, cafe proprietor, and graphic artist. He also spent time in other jobs, and is proud of never being dismissed, and only once made redundant.

Eventually he found his Noeline, but unfortunately she died much too young. To help with the aftermath, Vance tried writing though without any real structure. As an editor and beta readers explained the difference between words and books, he tried again.

Now he tries to type as often as possible in spite of the assistance of his cats, since his legs no longer work well enough to allow anything more strenuous. An avid reader of sci-fi, fantasy and adventure novels, his writing tends towards those genres.